Iraqi Icicle

Iraqi Icicle

Third Edition

Third Edition published in Australia by Bent Banana Books January, 2017.

First edition published in Australia in 2007 by Bent Banana Books. 24 Lorraine Court Lawnton, Australia, 4501.

bentbananabooks@gmail.com. www.bentbananabooks.com

All characters are fictitious and any resemblance to actual persons living or dead is purely coincidental.

A CiP catalogue record for this book is available from the Australian National Library

ISBN 978-0-9925934-8-3 **third edition** paperback

Cover design: Dhrupod

Iraqi Icicle

a novel

Bernie Dowling

Introduction to the third edition

THE Australian library supplier with the delightful business name Peter Pal asked me to sell them a hardback copy of *Iraqi Icicle*. My publishing hut Bent Banana Books had not produced a hardback edition. But the customer being always right until they are proven otherwise, it was high time for such a format. The new format meant it was also timely for a new edition in paperback and eBook. Yoo-hoo!

A new format might induce other changes.

One was the cover. I absolutely love the photography taken by professional shooter Russell Brown in provincial Dayboro on a winter morning. It has foreboding and evocative images suited to a neo-noir novel like *Iraqi Icicle*. Unfortunately it has no ambience of humor. So I shared my ideas with cover designer Dhrupod and he came up with a cover which is humorously sinister or sinisterly humorous.

Next I considered whether I should render the text in American spellings. Many of my book sales have been in the United States and so again the customer is always right until proven overbearingly parochial. I concede my spelling might prove challenging/ difficult/ annoying for an American reader. My novel also is replete with Australian slang, the meaning of which is rarely explained. One of the novel's reviewers wrote: "Seriously, at one time I had dreams of going to Australia. Thinking they spoke English . . ." Glenda navigated my slanguage enough to give Iraqi Icicle five stars. In the end, I decided I would trust the generosity of most American readers in understanding why I used Austral English to complement the colloquialisms. I did change US to U.S. and LA to L.A. along the lines of the principle 'when in Rome . . .'

As a compromise, for readers who are not so understanding of Australiana, the third addition has a glossary of the Australian slang scattered through the book.

I do like the concept of a novel with a glossary at the end, far more impressive than a map at the beginning. And slang is fun.

It is still fun after the academics took hold of it and called it argot or, worse, cant, supposedly a secret language to include/exclude strangers. British Professor of English Julie Coleman put it succinctly: 'Using slang can operate as a kind of password.' That definition works for academics as it implies passing between two universes which is what the professional slangologists do.

Another way of seeing slang is to look at the context of three institutions in which it is present: the army, the prison and the high school. These three can be considered total institutions, as defined by Canadian sociologist Erving Goffman. A total institution is a closed social system in which a minority group (officers, guards, teachers) tries to direct the behaviour and thought processes of the majority (enlisted personnel, convicts, students) In these contexts, slang is best seen as the language of the Resistance. Check out one of the vids for the Ramones' *Rock 'n Roll High School* to see what teenage slang is about.

Finally slang is fun fun fun. In *Iraqi Icicle* the reader meets an array of shady characters who might on occasion have call for coded lingo but for the most part the novel's slang is what has been dubbed 'the poetry of the streets'.

It is no real surprise how slang enters the common language when we understand how culture drifts upwards. The underclasses with little to lose are more adventuresome in most cultural pursuits including lingual play.

As much as I like a glossary at the tail of a tale, and I remember being most impressed by Anthony Burgess' invention of a language for *A Clockwork Orange*, I am not sure how a reader is supposed to use the thing. If they come across an unfamiliar word or phrase, do they head to the glossary to seek explanation? Or like me, do they take a stab at the meaning, press on and read the glossary from start to finish at novel's end.

Smaller changes to the third edition came from my being impressed by colloquialisms which really should have been in the second edition. One example is how Australians by and large do not say okay but quite a few do say akay.

The Australian expression with all the versatility of okay is 'all right' though it is pronounced as one word, awlright, and I have rendered it as such.

Similarly, I have rendered yer or yeah as yair which I have a notion was how it was written in dime westerns. You can call this my homage to American style.

Enjoy *Iraqi Icicle, third edition*. It is not quite a text from the neo-noir crime school. There are no exams.

– Bernie Dowling Pine Rivers district of Australia,

January, 2017.

For *Trish, Kevin and Daniel*
and

In memory of the Go-Betweens' lyricist/ bassist

Grant McLennan

Born summer, 1958

Died autumn, 2006

Iraqi Icicle

Watch the butcher shine his knives
And this town is full of battered wives
....
They shut it down
They pulled it down
They shut it down
They pulled it down

Round and round, up and down
Through the streets of your town
Everyday I make my way
Through the streets of your town
Brisbane rock band the Go-Betweens

Where I grew up there is an annual picnic race meeting where the people from the surrounding cattle stations come and race their horses and relax. Whenever I'm there I get asked to play some songs but I find it really difficult because I don't know any of the songs they like. If I play my own, especially the early ones, they say "do you know any with a tune?" (much laughter)
Grant McLennan in conversation with Nick Cave, 1993.

Even as I approach the gambling hall
as soon as I hear
two three rooms away
the jingle of money
I almost go into convulsions.
Fyodor Dostoevsky, *The Gambler*

Book One

At play

1

Brisbane, late spring in November, 1986

'YOU WOULDN'T KNOW anything about this Brisbane Handicap fiasco, would you Hill?'

Would I ever? Kidnapping, deprivation of liberty, extortion, supplying illicit drugs . . . I was looking down the barrel of a minimum of fifteen large at the tender age of twenty-one. I would be lucky to be outside the nick for New Year's Eve 1999.

'No, Boss, I don't know anything about it,' I said meekly, staring into the face of the chief steward of racing, with a bloody great copper standing by. On the few occasions any of us got to meet the chief steward, we always called him 'Boss'. I'm sure another name is on his birth certificate, but, for our purposes here, he is Mr Joe Boss.

Mr Boss waved the copper out of the tiny office, saying he would call him when he was needed. As the copper shut the door, Boss stood up and leaned forward, spreading his fingers like two fans onto the table. He made a great effort to give me a look of utmost sincerity. 'I'm sorry about what happened to your mate, Clarence. Is it true he rang up the Canterbury stewards and abused them for ten minutes for moving the barrier stalls five metres after a sudden downpour?'

It didn't seem important any more, but I wanted to give Mick Clarence due credit.

'It's true, Boss. Mick stood to win ten grand on a horse beaten by a nose at the Canterbury midweeks,' I said. 'He'd worked out that his horse was a certainty, even though it was paying twenty-to-one. He told me he had calculated it would win by a head or so.'

'How old was Clarence when this happened?' Boss asked.

'I guess he was about seventeen at the time.'

'What, was he crazy or something? How could moving the barriers five metres have changed the result of a six-furlong race?'

'Mick wasn't crazy,' I said evenly. The chief steward let me go on. 'Well, maybe he was just a bit crazy, but he was a mathematical genius. After he gave the stewards a prolonged blast, he redid his sums with the barrier moved five metres, and it came out that his horse would get done by a nose rather than winning by a head.'

Boss looked at me in disbelief across his desk. 'You're only a baby, Hill. What the fuck are you mixing with these lunatics for? What do you think's going to happen to you?'

'I haven't done anything, Boss. Is this about that mad Russian?'

_____ooo_____

Brisbane, two weeks earlier

MORNING PEAK-HOUR traffic in Brisbane plays as a slow and noisy industrial carnival band: engines on vocals, the bass of tyres on bitumen and wind on bonnet. The horn section cuts in without notice. The whole show is a cacophony of nose-to-tail metal, lit by strobing brake lights. I ponder this musical analogy to dull the torture of the inane pop song on the car radio.

I'm sitting in my Holden EH ute, an elbow out the window,

the other hand on the leather steering wheel cover. This baby's a vintage beauty, lovingly cared for over the years by a fastidious copper, who would tear around all day in his police car and then come home to polish and oil his pride and joy, ready for a leisurely Sunday drive up and down, round and round Mt Mee.

That was the beloved routine. Until around midnight, a month ago, at an illegal card game, the red ute changed hands, due to the copper being a few beers worse for wear and my steadfast loyalty to three eights in the face of a probable ace-high straight.

Now the crimson beauty is mine, all mine. The ute's already not quite what she was; there's a little rattle coming from the back that I'm sure wasn't there before, but there's plenty of leg room, enough even for my long angular frame. With the driver's window down and the breeze scattering my longish straight blond locks, on the rare occasions when the roads are free of congestion, I am commander of the streets of your town. But not today.

I insert my pirated tape of the Go-Betweens 1982 single *Hammer the Hammer*. That's all there is on the fifteen-minute cassette, *Hammer the Hammer*. I foolishly tilt my neck to the left to see what is causing the delay. There is no cause. If there were no delay in the morning peak-hour traffic, there would be a cause. I am crawling along Sandgate Road in the metal parade of stiffs, fantasising murder, suicide and all shades in between. That's the stiffs pondering all that morbid stuff. Me, I'm a placid sorta bloke.

I notice a teenager sprawled across the footpath ahead. He is wearing black jeans, an unbuttoned denim coat and, under it, a black T-shirt with a graphic below a band name I cannot read. Sitting on a brick fence behind the prone body are three other teenagers, two boys and a girl. All wear black jeans; one has on a black T-shirt and the others flannelette shirts, in the middle of a boiling hot Brisbane late spring – it would pass for high summer in most countries, but not in Australia.

The trio on the brick fence aren't looking at their prone companion. They keep glancing down the road. My bet is they are not seeking a cop car. Drug overdose, smack or speed, I reckon. Take your pick, as I'd say the young bloke, flat on the footpath, did. I hope his mates are watching out for an ambulance they have called.

A bag of fruit is walking down the street with his nose inside a plastic folder. He glances over its top edge, takes in the prone body, and pretends to be lost, backtracking down the concrete path and turning into a side street. That is what you call going out of your way for the unfortunate.

I duck down the one-way Frodsham Street at Albion to save a second on my journey. I would save a few seconds this way, but savvy stiffs are following me or leading me down Frodsham Street to save their own precious second. For stiffs, every second counts. By stiffs, I mean the clock-watching, bored and boring sods who do what they do because that's what they did yesterday. Experts of all persuasions are lining up to convince them they are time-poor, and in need of greater efficiency. Me, I have plenty of time up my sleeve, but I am not letting the stiffs better me by my going the long way round. My life is extended by a second.

A few hundred metres on, I get stuck in a traffic snarl beside Bogan Street. Ever since I left the orphanage, I have met teenagers and young adults who dream of escaping Brisbane to Sydney, Melbourne or London. For them Brisbane is

Boganville, full of unsophisticated young Bogans living squalid lives, unenriched by the gifts of youth culture.

Me, I like Brisbane. I am on my way to its inner-city suburb of Spring Hill – the Go-Betweens wrote a song about it – to see Mick Clarence, the bloke who taped *Hammer the Hammer* for me.

I had fruitlessly scoured Brisbane underground record shops for a copy of the single. Promises of imports never came through. Then I thought of Mick. He was using American military spy computer programs to pick the winners of horse races, so I figured he could track down a copy of the single, and he came good.

The tape was still rewinding when I heard a siren in the background. I hoped it was an ambulance for the ill lad. I can never tell the difference between a police siren and an ambulance wail. I don't want either coming for me.

Mick had asked what else I wanted on the fifteen-minute tape. He smirked. 'What about an album by the Ramones?'

I replied, 'nothing.'

Mick, true to his word, left me with the one short song, alone in a world of static, which no one could quite figure out the meaning of.

2

Brisbane, summer in early December, 1989

IN MY BOOK, theatre is a foreign country. The only Greek tragedy I know is Australian television's alleged comedy *Acropolis Now*. Which is why I pretended to be mesmerised by the form of the horses for the Dalby races when Natalie spoke.

'You'll have to go to Bub's opening night, Steele.' Nat often speaks in absolutes. There are facts and there are instructions. I kept my head down, searching desperately for a dead cert for Dalby and a way out for me. The last thing in the world I wanted was to go to some play. Especially if Bub was in it. Nat's little sister and I had pretty much exchanged only frosts since I refused to help Jane – Bub's formal name – paint her room. Black.

Now, you will say that anyone born Jane is entitled to adolesce into art, gothic-rock music, theatre and a black bedroom. I would be the first to agree with you, but I reserve the right of refusal to be an accomplice. A hard-nosed handicapper of horses like me is entitled to a tiny travelling satchel of the gambler's basic baggage: superstition.

Natalie repeated her order for me to attend the theatre. I had that dull ache in the pit of my stomach that attacks me when I lose a photo finish, or when a domestic looms from a corner of the lounge. Strange how fighting words erupt when a blue is the last thing you want. 'I heard you,' I growled, though

I knew there were extremely long odds of me winning this blue.

'There's no need for that tone,' Nat admonished, in a beautifully modulated tone of her own now that she had me on the defensive. 'I can't go to Jane's opening night because I've got a three-day managerial course at Noosa. I don't want to do the course, but I have to. You know how the juniors are breathing down my neck at work.'

Yair, I know. Life in 1989 is tough for a 21-year-old assistant manager, fruit and veg, in a large supermarket chain. Sometimes – quite a lot actually – I'm grateful that I haven't had a regular job since I was warned off all racetracks for life, over what everyone, including punters who don't know what the word means, call the Brisbane Handicap 'fiasco'. Good to know your partner is always there for you when you are short on vocational stress.

I grabbed at a long shot. 'I'll fall asleep. How embarrassed will you and Jane be then?'

'I don't care,' Natalie said. 'This is Jane's big chance. La Boite is almost a professional theatre, you know. Who knows where she will go from here?'

'Yair, right, an 18-year-old first-year student at Kelvin Grove campus of the Brisbane College of Advanced Education in a play nobody ever heard of. Be very afraid, Nicole Kidman.

I could see it though. Bub had that erratic, volatile quality that you could imagine splashed across the front page of some tabloid rag one day. **CRAZED STARLET THROWN OUT OF NIGHT SPOT** could be a good fit for Bub.

At least her college might become a star as there was talk it would be taken over by recently evolved Queensland University of Technology which added to Brisbane other universities, Queensland and Griffith. I had been to all three as each put on free rock concerts from time to time.

'You're joking,' Natalie said. '*Waiting for Godot*; nobody's ever heard of *Waiting for Godot*? Everybody knows *Waiting for Godot*.'

'Is that what the play's called? I couldn't remember. Come on, Natalie, three months ago you'd never heard of *Waiting for Godot* either. Admit it.'

'Well, I've read about it since. He got a Nobel Prize, you know.'

'Who did – Godot?'

'Don't be silly. The man who wrote it, he won the Nobel Prize.'

'What's his name, then?'

Natalie changed tack in the face of forgetting the playwright's name. 'You know you can use my ticket, so it won't cost you anything. And because it's opening night, they give you free food and wine after the show.'

Why did Natalie always do this: leave the significant details till last?

'I'm there,' I said, and returned to prognostications of the races at Dalby, a rural town I suspect most of Australia has never heard of.

I had almost been to a play once. I'd been planning to buy tickets for Natalie and me. It was about Sid Vicious, former bass player of seventies British punk band the Sex Pistols. Nat didn't want to go.

'A play where someone dies of a heroin overdose in the last act? Boring,' she declared.

I had to protest. 'But that's what happened.'

Vicious died in February, 1979, but it was not until two years later, when I left the orphanage, that I caught up with this news. At the time of his death, Vicious was awaiting his day in court, facing a charge that he had knifed his girlfriend Nancy Spungen to death. Some people, including his former Sex Pistols' bandmate, Johnny Rotten, thought him innocent. Vicious, being heavily under the hammer when Spungen died, was not sure whether he had done the dark deed. All this was fodder for a pretty good play, I thought, but Natalie was not having any of that.

'It's not art; it's just a cliché.'

The condescension returned. 'The artist's job is to ignore the sordid banalities and find the extraordinary in the mundane; to give us something fresh and different.' Ah, Nat, with your hands on your hips, cheeks slightly flushed, a wisp of that dark hair slightly out of place, setting the world's moral compass straight. Is it some schoolteacher fetish of mine that places me under your spell?

'Buddha, I thought a writer's job was to tell us what's really going on outside our own front door. Or is that another cliché? I don't know why I'm even arguing about this. I'd probably be bored to death at having to watch a play anyway. It just sounded interesting, that's all.'

Natalie put her arms over my shoulders. 'And I love you for trying to broaden your horizons, Steele. Don't worry, we'll find a play we both want to see.'

SO NOW there I was, on my way to see *Waiting for Godot*, a play Natalie wanted me to go to because she could not. I am not really a play person. There is some evidence I am John Lennon's lovechild, conceived during the Beatles 1964

Brisbane concert. Well, not during but after. Or maybe before. Whatever, I did not inherit my Dad's theatrical bent.

I fronted up to the ticket booth at La Boite, on the border of the inner city suburbs of Petrie Terrace and Milton. I grabbed a program, thinking it was free. It wasn't. The first-year drama students of the Kelvin Grove campus of the Brisbane College of Advanced Education took me down for a dollar.

The form guide in the program told me La Boite was French for The Box, and that the venue presented theatre in the round. Round theatre in a cubic box sounded more like a geometric challenge than an artistic one.

I looked through the cast list for Jane Applebee. There she was, playing a character called Lucky. Three other actors made up the main cast. They all appeared to be women: Caitlyn Meares, Suzanne Lu and, of course, you all know Alison Kahn. I had never heard of Kahn, but they rarely put the arts pages beside the racing guide.

Alison Kahn was a professional actor, about twenty-five by the look of her photo. She was a graduate of Kelvin Grove campus and had done the college proud by appearing in plays, a television cop show and even a feature film. Well done, Alison. The director's notes said it was a coup to have Kelvin Grove old-girl Kahn return to assist the new chums of the drama school.

Director Sandra Blaine was a drama lecturer at Kelvin Grove. Blaine wrote to us, in the program that, as far as she knew, women making up the entire cast and crew of Samuel Beckett's Nobel-Prize-winning play was an Australian first. Even the cameo part of Boy was played by a Girl, Blaine herself.

The director also wrote the first Australian production of Godot had a woman of sorts in one of the leads. The play had a two-week run at the Arrow Theatre, Melbourne, in September 1957, and Barry Humphries, 23, played Estragon. Humphries went on to stardom as the comic Dame Edna Everage, a character he had created two years before doing Beckett. Ah, don't say any of us would not wear lilac hair, silly glasses and a sparkly dress for a crack at fame.

GIRL, YOU KNOW IT'S TRUE. Or at least that's what Europop duo Milli Vanilli was telling us during their glory year of 1989, before proof of onstage lip-syncing to pre-recorded vocals sank their career like the Titanic Two. In 1990, during a live performance by Rob and Fab at a Connecticut theme park, the track *Girl You Know It's True* jammed in a groove, repeating the line *Girl You Know It's True* over and over.

Smart management might have said the glitch was a remix, but one thing led to another and out came the admission the lads had not sung any of the songs on their hit album.

This career-ending confession served as a lesson to all of us: life is not always as it seems. A night at the Box would not end as uneventfully for me as Natalie would have hoped.

I RAISED my glass of cheap red to an Australian first for the sisterhood, translating this Beckett stuff into the language of belles. Bells rang.

And they're off. Trumpets, bugles or bells, I know when an event is about to start. I was caught up in the crowd surge, and swept up a circular staircase into the theatre, with raked seating in four blocks forming a rectangle outside the curtainless stage. It looked like someone had pinched this theatre-in-the-round from the boxing ring. I took a seat near ringside, the prized spot for Hollywood royalty, from what I have glimpsed on television.

It was not half bad, this play, once you realised what it was about. Nothing. Nothing was something I could appreciate. The first scenes were like alt-comedians HG Nelson and Roy Slaven doing their routines about bugger all. The only difference was that Suzanne Lu and Caitlyn Meares were spruiking their nonsense as clowns with bowler hats, like those worn by the ancient comic duo Laurel and Hardy.

Lu was a Stan-Laurel simpleton called Estragon, who came out with some childish wisdom when you least expected it. Meares was an Oliver-Hardy clown called Vladimir.

They were waiting for someone called Godot, though most of the audience were waiting for Alison Kahn to appear, as a character called Pozzo. I was waiting for Lucky Jane.

Bub came on as Lucky, shackled by ropes and weighed down with travel bags. Kahn followed, cracking a whip and firing a pistol. It could have made a lasting impression on all of us in the audience, had Suzanne Lu not dropped down dead. Quite an exit.

3

Brisbane, spring in late September, 1986

BUB WAS IN YEAR 10 or something when Natalie said I had to see her sister's principal.

'I don't think I want to do that,' I replied honestly.

'She is being bullied unmercifully at school,' My Cucumber told me.

Nat and I were living in our respective Hendra flats in the same building. It was a humble wooden block of flats, but we did have a row of roses growing along the front fence. The roses produced luxuriant clusters of white flowers. Iraqi Icicle, that was the breed of the roses, I think. Neither Natalie nor I was responsible for the roses but we were delighted when we were invited to pick some.

Nat's sister Jane was living with her early-retired parents, up the North Coast. I could not see why I should feel any obligation to visit the school in place of her loco parents. I told Nat as much.

'You know Dad won't do it. He says a bit of bullying is good for Jane; that it's character building.'

'There's something to be said for that, Nat.'

My Cucumber rounded on me, planting her feet solidly on the linoleum floor two feet from where I was sitting. Hands on hips. I couldn't possibly win. Bound to lose. Game over.

Technically it was spring, a time for verbal ripostes with your loved one, but actually, it was far too hot to drag out an argument I was sure to lose. Everyone knows our designation of seasons is a joke. But Buddha forbid getting rid of the tradition of pretending Mummy Nature's Australian climate can be described in the same terms as Mother England's.

'Since when have you even remotely agreed with anything Dad says?'

'Well, he has to fluke it right some time. I mean, he's been lucky in the past, siring two lovely daughters.'

The flattery sounded lame to my ears and failed utterly.

ONE FINE MORNING, before the heat set in, I pointed the EH ute northward, buoyed by the walletful of cash Nat had provided as provisions for my trip. I just love to hear that engine roar, as Robert Forster and Grant McLennan of the Go-Betweens put it.

The North Coast is north of Brisbane, rather than being in North Queensland. Whoever made up the geographical concepts of Australia decided state capitals are the centres of their respective universes and all other places exist only in relation to them.

Another quirky thing about the North Coast is that it does not officially exist. There is a collection of addresses known as the Sunshine Coast, which is the area a lot of people, including me, known as the North Coast.

What a coy name, the Sunshine Coast. Sounds like a Disney movie setting, where the bad guys come to destroy the idyll. For bad guys, it can't compete with the Gold Coast, where a spiv or hustler lurks on every street corner. Don't get me wrong: I love the Gold Coast, or the Goldie, the coy name the stiffs give it, but its thoroughfares are an acquired taste if you plan to consume them regularly. The North Coast seems friendlier, but I visit rarely and I don't see much of the scum floating on the ocean waves.

Coastal towns are funny places. Even when they contain enough people to be touted as a city, there is invariably a small-town mentality that does not tolerate blow-in eccentrics like Bub. There is also the importance of being cool, way cooler than the tourists who are totally gross. American blues-rocker John Cougar Mellencamp could have been singing about any Australian big small-town when he sang his syrupy tribute to rural life, which had enough subtle unease about it for cynical city-dwellers to make it a hit single in 1986.

We had no doubt that John learned the fear of Jesus in a small town, but we would need more evidence to believe that same small town tamed his L.A. girlfriend.

Bub's high school was a State institution, like most in Queensland. Having been educated by nuns in an orphanage, I believe I was setting a record – my first day at high school, at age twenty-one. I found the office and asked to see the principal. He was down on the sports oval with most of the school, it being Sports Day.

There was something strangely lacking from the scene outside. All of these sports going on and not a single bookie to keep the punters interested. Hundreds of students sat around on the grass outside the oval, with lime-marked running tracks up and down and round and round it. Flags indicated the winning post, or the finishing line as the betting-deprived know it.

I looked around but I couldn't make out Bub. This pleased me as I did not want to see her, anyway. Just make a quick lame effort at heroism before hitting the nearest totalisator with Nat's cash: that was my A-plan.

Exchanges with a couple of teachers led me to a tallish, black-haired man in his late forties, bare-headed and thick-necked, yelling in an American accent through a megaphone. I reached Principal Carter just as he screamed at a field of runners to get ready.

The boys aged about fourteen, reacted to a sharp bang of the starter's gun by racing down the oval over a distance that looked to be about a hundred metres or half a furlong if your mind operates that way. By the time the bunched field of nine had gone forty metres, they had left a tenth runner twenty metres behind. He was a long, ungainly lad, his feet splayed out from either side of bandy legs. I had to look away.

I introduced myself to Principal Carter, who brushed me aside with a downward motion of his left hand. He looked towards the cheer squads on either side of the running track. Some students were laughing at the bandy-legged straggler, who had only covered thirty metres when the others were at eighty. This abject loser was crying profusely and noisily.

I looked over at Principal Carter and saw that the bastard had a smirk on his face. I yanked at the cord on his megaphone, introduced myself again and asked Carter why he allowed the inept athlete to run.

'If it's any of your business, it is compulsory for all students without a severe disability to compete in sports. And I have never heard of you, Mr Hill. Have you an appointment?' That Yankee twang made my shoulders shudder.

The sobbing teenager finally limped across the finishing line and the laughter died down. One or two students began to clap his ineffectual effort and some of the laughers joined in, either out of shame or thinking it added more spice to the fun.

Carter grabbed back the megaphone cord. 'Congratulations, Tom West, on winning your heat. And Joshua Banks, though you came last, your effort to finish was brave. Let's give the two of them and all the runners a big hand.'

Half-hearted applause emerged from the students. I eyed the hypocrite with the megaphone and shook my head. He turned slightly towards me, keeping his gaze on the runners for the next event. 'Are you still here?' He chopped the air with his free hand to emphasise each word of a command. 'Make an appointment with my secretary.'

I took a business card from my wallet. It was not my business card; just one I had picked up somewhere. I wrote two sentences on the blank back of the card and handed it to Carter. He glanced at it, and then re-read it at least twice, maybe three times. He put the card in his shirt pocket and gave me an assessing look. I responded with my best dead-eyes. I've practised, watching old film noir, starring Robert Mitchum. Ah, everybody loves film noir and monochrome slapstick flicks. They are the only true peacemakers in the world.

Carter went over to a teacher, said a few words to her and handed over the megaphone. As I followed him to the shade of a tree 200 metres away from the action, I heard a woman's voice call up the runners for the first heat of the under-fourteen girls' one-hundred metres.

'What is it you want that can't wait?' Carter asked, retrieving the note and handing it back to me.

'You keep it,' I said and watched his face redden. 'You've got a girl at school here, her name's Jane Applebee.'

He nodded; the name was familiar. I explained to Carter that Bub was being bullied and I was assigning him the task of putting a stop to it. 'What's an American doing teaching over here, anyway, unless you're Canadian?' I asked him.

'I was born in Chicago,' he replied proudly.

'Yair, I knew you were American. I'm pretty good with accents. Just wondered if you might claim to be Canadian.'

'Why would I want to do that? I'm proud of my heritage and I'm a graduate of the University of Queensland. I have as much right to teach here as anybody else.'

More than some, I thought, recalling a punter I knew – thirty-two year-old Bob Somers, who had bestowed a couple of education degrees on himself, after a few disappointing years in his previous chosen profession of pro gambling. At the start of term, I waved him away as the *Sunlander* train took him to a North Queensland teaching post.

Buddha knew what he had put himself down for instructing in. I did not ask. Bobby was never the brightest light on the Ferris wheel of life. He had stumbled into his previous job of professional punting because it took more guts than brains. He had never quite got on top of probability theory and had few connections with those in-the-know in the racing game, so he had survived longer as a pro gambler than most expected.

All of us who knew him decided that inventing teaching qualifications was the cleverest move he had ever made by a street. While the odds were always in favour of him being exposed, a few North Queensland bookies and casino operators would celebrate Somers' late and temporary entry into the academic ranks.

Having justified his own teaching credentials, Carter was becoming more comfortable, slipping back into principal-in-control mode. 'We do not tolerate bullying at this school, Mr Hill. I'll look into it. You could have written me a letter and saved yourself all this trouble. What relationship do you have with this student, for the record? I need to know before I can divulge any further information.'

Yair, right, I thought. *You have given me nothing, mate, and you're coming on all smug again.* A whole plate-load of insinuation was piled into Carter's remark about my relationship with Jane, legally a minor at the time. I pointed to my note on the business card in his shirt pocket. 'I'm not the one who is in trouble, pal. I'm a friend of the Applebee family, but none of them, including Jane, needs to know I'm here. They also don't need to find out about this.' I tapped his shirt pocket with the card inside. 'Unless you want to tell them.' I paused. 'I don't think you do.'

Carter put his hand over his pocket. 'Okay, Mr Hill, we will resolve this matter to our mutual satisfaction. I will look into the bullying, and you can give me one of your real business cards. I will be in touch very soon. Fair enough?'

No, this wasn't enough. I didn't budge. Did this vague concession pass for negotiation in the stiff world? Fob a person off and they just take it, saving up the indignation until they get their turn to give the brush-off to someone else. Very different from the robust philosophical and intellectual discussion I was used to on the streets. I summoned up all of my not-inconsiderable height, a great advantage in situations like these. I drilled into him with my eyes. 'If you want to play it that way, Carter, it's up to you. But remember, your days of screaming down a megaphone, or yelling at a slack student, or taking home that hefty pay packet, are numbered. You'll be a zero sooner than you can say maths equation.'

I let him think about that before I continued. 'I know Bub's being bullied by some other girls, mainly verbally but sometimes physically. When I leave this schoolyard, you will never see me again. But you will see some other people if I don't hear, within a month, that the bullying has stopped. I am giving you thirty days, and I can't be any fairer than that. You got me?' The last three words I hissed at him, just as I had seen the real toughs do during street altercations. A friend once told me that you focus your gaze behind your adversary's eyes, to the middle of their head. Just as a karate kick is aimed, not at the knee to be broken, but six inches behind it.

Carter rubbed his hair back with a sweaty palm, and I took this as an acceptable gesture of fear or submission. I rode my luck. 'And if I find that gangly kid is made to take part in any more sports against his will . . .' I reached into his shirt pocket, retrieved the business card and pushed it towards his face before putting it back into my wallet.

I had one more under-educated jibe for the road. 'By the way, wear a hat or a cap out in the sun next time, you prick. What sort of a bloody role model are you?' I stalked away, leaving the principal to review the lessons of the day that I had set him.

Bub told Natalie that the bullying pretty much stopped after that. Two girls were suspended, and another six students, girls and boys, were threatened with expulsion.

Months later, Jane cornered me in Nat's flat. 'I saw you at school on that sports day, Steele. You know everyone thinks I'm a total geek now, getting my big brother to settle scores for me. I keep telling them we're not related, but they don't believe me. I even said you were my lover to try to get back cred, but they didn't believe that either.'

She started to wind herself up, as she regularly does. I wonder is it acting practice, or maybe acting for her is life practice. 'Did I ask you to put in your two cents' worth? I could have handled it. The bullying only started because I made fun of the cool kids, and they hate that. I could have stopped it at any time.' Her lovely almond eyes were narrowing, her shoulders rising.

I don't know whether she could have stopped the bullying, but I believed it when she said she had a hand in starting it, with her sarcasm and refusal to acknowledge her place in the social pecking order.

'Well, why didn't you stop it, Bub?'

'To tell you the truth, I suppose it was getting a little out of hand.' And off she bounced.

I took that as a thank-you.

A FEW WEEKS after Bub's sixteenth birthday, I was tonguing for a feed of veal in pyjamas. Nat makes me order parmigiana properly now, though waiters in the past always brought a top serve of veal in pyjamas when I selected it without even a glance at the menu. My order sometimes brought a smile to the waiter's face, and sometimes a scowl. I never counted whether a smile or a scowl was winning. Nat said my jest was stale and embarrassed her, so I stopped.

I raced past the Iraqi Icicle roses along the front fence, bounded up the steps to My Cucumber's flat and tested the doorknob, to find it unlocked. Full of joy I burst in. Bub was on the couch, reading a book of the play *Romeo and Juliet*. Deflated, I said, 'Oh.'

Jane lowered the book slightly and said, 'Glad tidings to you, too, Steele.' She continued reading and I asked where Nat was. 'Natalie had to go to an important meeting. Her big supermarket chain has swallowed a small string of grocers, and the meeting is to decide how they will digest their new acquisitions.'

'Nicely put, Jane. Shakespeare must be rubbing off. Are you studying that at school?'

'No, but if my acting career takes off earlier than I have planned, I may be called upon to play Juliet.'

I feigned interest to muffle a laugh. 'How's the reading coming along?'

She put down the book to think about it. 'Quite a few dirty jokes should maintain the audience interest. But he tells them like Uncle Harry.' I had never met Uncle Harry, but everyone has a relative who tells jokes that way – except for poor orphans like me.

I sat on the couch beside Bub. 'You and Nat are two peas in a pod. You think too much. I caressed her temples, a remedy which works on Nat. It was a mistake, but I could not stop. It was like that black-and-white horror movie in which doctors graft new hands on a bloke who cannot control them. Jane kissed each of my palms and moved on to my lips. I was shocked to find her lips soft and malleable. My girlfriend's younger sister was far too adept at foreplay for my liking.

Bub pushed me flat onto the couch and pinned my shoulders. Romeo and Juliet were glued to the back of my shirt. Standing up, she removed her dress to reveal matching black bra and panties. 'I know where Natalie keeps her condoms,' she said.

She went to Nat's bedroom and I followed, thinking I would talk her and me out of this misadventure. The drawback to the plan was my erection, which felt the size of a lobster. I hunched over, stupidly thinking that that might hide the desire in my jeans. Jane was already scrutinising opened packets of condoms in a drawer. She triumphantly raised a pack. 'Ooh, Steele, *Rib Ticklers*, I didn't know you had it in you.' She looked down at the bulge in my jeans. 'Obviously you have.'

'Put those back,' I said. I was nervous, flooded with visions of Natalie catching us. The whole episode might have ended there, had not my mouth followed the lead of my hands and acted independently of my brain. 'Use a plain one,' I said. I was trapped. 'Only one?' Bub quipped, as she undid her bra and dropped it on the floor. She had firm, round breasts, eager for action. I remember thinking they looked bigger than her older sister's, and that did not seem right. Jane leaped on Nat's bed and rolled onto her back, waving the condom in the air.

I was aghast. 'On Nat's bed? We can't do it on Nat's bed!'

Jane frowned. 'I guess not.' She put the condom in her panties and slid slowly from the bed. She approached and kissed me wildly, undoing the buttons of my shirt at the same time. Satisfied, she took my hand and led me like a horny lamb to the couch.

Regaining a little control, I insisted Bub would be on the bottom this time, and I gallantly removed Romeo and Juliet for her. I need not have bothered. By the time we had taken off all our clothes, amid frantic preliminary screwing, we had fallen to the floor.

Perhaps Bub was destined for the part of Juliet after all, as the book found its way under various parts of her tanned, taut and thrashing body, the upper side of which I explored with my fingers and tongue.

You know the next bit. I put my DH Lawrence into Jane's DH Lawrence, and we both made satisfied incoherent noises. I rolled off and we looked at each other sheepishly. I gave her a peck on the cheek to suggest everything was above board.

What she said next was a pleasant surprise: 'Promise me, you won't 'fess up to Natalie.' She slipped on her panties, giving me a parting glance at her abundant alluring pubic hair.

I guess it was down to loyalty to Jane that I never did tell Nat, despite the provocations of love, intimacy, sex or alcohol. I was sure that Bub's personality would not allow her to keep the secret. Yet Nat never did bring it up. The incident was just another brick of guilt in my knapsack on my journey through life.

I never had sex with Bub again except for two other times and neither was my fault.

BY THE WAY, you are probably wondering what I wrote on the back of the business card I gave to Principal Carter. I didn't know what it was going to be myself, even when I was fishing the card from my wallet. I had a scantily formed notion that I might say a couple of heavies would break the principal's legs, or kneecap him, or something else gross along those lines.

As I took out a pen, I thought of how heavies reshaping limbs could be an occupational risk for someone like me. It was not worth tempting karma by making such a threat.

Instead, I wrote: 'The most embarrassing thing in your life. I have the witness.'

If you run near the edge, as I do, your brain would be spinning, trying to recall which of half a dozen escapades the note might mean. But I figure stiffs zip themselves inside a straitjacket most of their social lives, until the booze or drugs or just plain randiness turns them into Houdini one night.

If I do say myself, writing I had **the** witness instead of a witness was the clincher. Not only was Carter replaying the most embarrassing moment in his life, he was imagining who the one witness was and how I had run into that person. It had to be the stuff of nightmares for weeks. He probably did not get a decent sleep until he or his good luck stopped the bullying.

4

WHEN BUB'S FELLOW FIRST-YEAR acting student Suzanne Lu dropped dead in a La Boite production of *Waiting for Godot*, I thought it was in the script. Even when Jane screamed, it seemed to fit. More astute theatrical punters near me in the first row of raked seating picked up on the discordant vibes and a Mexican scream started, washing out behind us.

Godot star Alison Kahn pitched a plea to the assembled crowd above the cacophony. It's funny how in crisis we seek comfort in clichés.

Without a hint of irony, Kahn raised her arms like Atlas and asked, 'Is there a doctor in the house?'

A bag of fruit swept passed me, as I eased out of my seat to see if Jane was all right.

As I passed Kahn, she touched my shoulder and asked, 'You're a doctor, too?'

She turned to the suit. 'Maybe he should handle this, Efram.'

I shook my head and Efram agreed with me.

'I see no problem with my assisting, dear,' he said.

I didn't either, what with such an ingratiating dead-side manner, calling Kahn 'dear' and all.

I relinquished any pretence to medical qualifications. 'I'm not a doctor. I'm a friend of Jane's.'

Bub made the introductions. 'Alison Kahn, this is Steele

Hill. Steele, this is Efram Kahn, Alison's husband. Efram's a doctor.' How nice, a fresh corpse giving the Kahns an opportunity to work together.

Only a tiny grimace at the corner of her mouth gave any hint that Suzanne Lu was disappointed at her passing. Overall, her unlined face looked serene.

There was living panic on the faces of sundry staff of La Boite, roughly ushering the audience outside. Caitlin Meares, a living actor from the play, was in a state. I moved towards her, holding out my arms into which she reeled.

'It could have been me,' she kept repeating, trying for just the right delivery, as the room emptied.

Our turn will come soon enough, I thought.

I looked across to a face from the program. It belonged to the director, Sandra Blaine, deep in conversation with Efram Kahn.

'Was Suzanne on medication, Sandra?'

'Not that I know of, Efram, except for some herbal concoction she was into.'

'I'll have to have a look into that,' Kahn said with grave professionalism. 'What about water?' he added. 'Did she drink a lot of water?'

'I guess so. Why?'

Efram frowned the concerned doctor's frown. 'Could she have been on that new drug the papers are talking about: ecstasy?'

'Before a performance, I wouldn't think so. Kelvin Grove is a professional training ground, as you well know.'

Efram Kahn ignored the advertisement for the college. 'What do the rest of you think? Jane? Caitlin? Alison?'

The young women shrugged. I shrugged. I was no expert on

eccie, having only had the new party drug a few times. Eccie was for jumping around to a relentless dance beat, hugging people you don't like and processing muddled thoughts about living in a wonderful world. I've never had the urge to drop a tab or two before a hard afternoon's work, punting on the ponies in the TAB.

I only had to start thinking about the nags to conjure up those cranky brumbies, Detective Sergeant Frank Mooney and Constable Bill Schmidt. The last time I was within worm's length of a dead body, these coppers tried to fit me up for murder.

Mooney was a 197cm – six-foot-five in the old lingo – son of an Irish family. The Irish are generally known for their wit, their fists, their commitment to causes and their carrot tops. Black-haired Mooney was known for his fists. I once told Mooney that he was as cunning as a water rat and as thick as a wharf plank. You would never have thought a fifty-something pudgy cop could hit, not to mention kick, so hard. When I got out of hospital, the magistrate was kind enough to suspend my sentence for assaulting Mooney. I never did like Detective Sergeant 'Bull' Mooney after that, or before that, really.

Bill Schmidt was an over-achiever in his late twenties. Drunk one night at a card table, Schmidt told me what he would do if he was Police Commissioner. He might just be Police Commissioner one day. If he was, he would do what he was told to do, and then get drunk and tell anyone who would listen what he would do if he was elected Police Minister. Schmidt was only a fraction shorter than Mooney. He was better looking, if you didn't mind those crazy-as-a-headless-chook eyes, with sandy-blond hair cut in military style, and pale skin stretched across a square jaw and jutting cheekbones.

Schmidt was the bad cop. Mooney was the even worse cop, and a smirk broke out on his big red face as soon as he saw me.

'I should have known, Hill,' he snarled. Mooney was as out of place at La Boite as Oedipus on Father's Day, as Nat likes to say about me during some of our cultural outings, funnily enough the ones she chooses. I got the joke once she explained it to me.

Mooney was not here for the culture 'Another day, another corpse,' he said to me. `What did you do to this one?'

Efram Kahn answered for me. 'Heart failure, I suspect.'

'Drugs,' Constable Schmidt declared, as if a post-mortem was but a formality.

Schmidt was a uni graduate. He enjoyed barking monosyllables as rehearsals for his destiny as a no-frills police commissioner, the boss job in the Queensland police force. As unlikely a partnership as they were, Mooney and Schmidt were the best of mates at work and at play.

Schmidt's drug proposition sounded reasonable to Sergeant Mooney, but, of course, I had to be in the frame. 'What did you sell her, Hill, that new craze, ecstasy?' As he always does he berated me for being a clown.

We played cops and killer for half an hour. It took Mooney only a couple of minutes to realise I had not known Suzanne Lu from a bar of soap. The cops used the other twenty-eight minutes to remind me again and again that, one day soon, they were going to put me in jail for life, and a bit more.

I did not have the chance to talk to Jane. The cops asked me to leave after our chat.

Mooney whispered in my ear, 'Get lost, Clown.'

I did.

It was a week before I saw the cops again. They tried to kick down the door of my flat, which is on the floor below My Cucumber Natalie and not 800 metres from my beloved Brisbane racetracks. I was listening to the latest Go-Betweens album, *16 Lover's Lane*, and letting the sound vibrate through me as I sat in my armchair. The album was more than a year old, no album from the band in 1989. A bad sign? Distracted from the rock/pop magic, I had to get up, or risk the two detectives breaking my door down and claiming I had assaulted their feet.

I invited the dees in and offered them cups of rat poison. Mooney and Schmidt exchanged meaningful glances. They didn't worry me. Meaningful glances come as easily as breathing to coppers; they mean nothing.

I did open my eyes a little wider when Constable Schmidt barked, 'Cyanide.'

Mooney supported his junior. 'But you already know that, Hill.'

Cyanide had killed Suzanne Lu.

Mooney and Schmidt knew I had not murdered a complete stranger with a poison I would not know from Vegemite. I decided to stop this nonsense. I looked straight at Mooney, into those hateful eyes.

'It's a fair cop, Senior Sergeant.'

Mooney would love to be a senior sergeant, come pension day, so I could always get a bite with that one. I saw the blood rise in his eyes and I pressed on. 'After you have proved that one, you can start on the Theory of Relativity.'

The Sergeant growled back at me. 'You're a smart-arse clown, Hill, too smart for your own good. But you're in this up to that long hair at the back of your neck. Seven-thirty, tomorrow night, La Boite. The others already know about it. Be there, or we will kick down whatever door you're hiding behind and then start on your face.'

'I'm there,' I said.

You have to admit the invite sounded compelling.

The next track playing on the sixth Go-Bees album was *The Streets of Your Town*. They had released the single twice – once the previous year when the album came out, and more successfully in June of that year of 1989.

The band, which had started in Brisbane in the late seventies, was signed to the major U.S. label Capitol, and fans were saying that the guitar-based pop rockers were going to grab the world recognition they deserved. Clouds inevitably darkened any rock band's horizon and now, by December, rumours had erupted that the Go-Betweens had broken up. If the rumour of a bust-up was true, it was an inopportune time, when even a deeply unhip copper like Mooney could recognise the chorus of the band's disturbing but radio-friendly single.

Round and round, up and down
Through the streets of your town.
Every day I make my way
Through the streets of your town.

'That's that slag's song,' Mooney screamed at the record player, his fleshy lips quivering. 'That drummer, what's her name, Morrison. Fucking bitch stole my watch.' Mooney's great sausagey fist feigned to slam down onto my record player, then recoiled. 'I'm not listening to that crap any more. When you're done, Schmidt, I'll see you in the car.' He stormed out the cracked door.

Schmidt looked all around the room, like a Teutonic landlord determined to retain a rental bond, before he approached the record player. 'Congratulations, Hill. You play the only song not recorded by Dean Martin or Kenny Rogers that Mooney knows. And now I have to hear about her stealing his watch for the rest of the day.'

'What's that about? If Mooney's been to a Go-Betweens concert, I'll have to throw out my entire record collection.'

Schmidt moved away from the stereo and began to rummage through kitchen cupboards and drawers.

'It was way back in 1978, before Lindy Morrison was even in the band, as far as I know. You remember, the Premier at the time, Joh Bjelke-Petersen, banned street marches as a form of civil protest.'

'Vaguely, I was only thirteen or fourteen at the time. The nuns in the orphanage weren't big on breakfast-table discussions of the political news of the day.'

'I wasn't much older myself and cannot remember taking much interest, but the old coppers tell me the uni students and their crackpot mates would call a demonstration at the drop of a hat. After a scuffle at one demo, Mooney charged Morrison with stealing his watch.'

'And did she?'

'From what I gather, his watch came off in a melee and Morrison held the watch in the air as if to say, "Who owns this?" And Mooney pinched her. Anyway, she got off at the pre-trial committal stage. But Mooney swears black and blue she got away with trying to nick his watch. If you ask me, he probably only charged her because he did not want to be grateful to a twenty-something girl for returning it.'

I nodded. After a few more minutes of watching the

unenthusiastic searching, I asked Schmidt, 'Are you awlright; need any help?'

'I'm supposed to give you an early Christmas present,' Schmidt said.

A 'present' meant planting something like dope or a firearm. Schmidt threw me a plastic bag, which I instinctively caught. It contained about thirty grams of marijuana.

'I can't be bothered. You will be in jail soon enough. By the way, I would plan not to be here around dawn on the 19th, when some unwelcome visitors from the Drug Squad are likely to arrive.'

I smoked all the dope that night. It was crappy stuff, full of leaf dust and twigs which I discarded. I guess I wasn't worth much of a present.

The next day was Thursday, and it was back-to-school day for Steele Hill. Kelvin Grove campus of the Brisbane College of Advanced Education is in the inner-city suburb known as; yes you've guessed it, Kelvin Grove. It was summer holidays so the place was pretty desolate and I was one of its few students.

My own educational background is nothing flash. The nuns at the orphanage were happy to show me the front gate after I had sort of done grade ten. A few female penguins, marginally better at teaching than the other nuns, were my barely adequate mentors. Since that time, I picked up a little learning on the streets, in nightclubs and coffee shops, so I was not daunted by all the numbered building blocks of higher education. I tracked down some lecturers in the drama department and gave them a good grilling.

I found the bookshop and bought two copies of Samuel Beckett's *Waiting for Godot*. The chatty shop assistant told me there had been a rush on the play since that terrible tragedy where the girl died. I replied there was nothing like death to add a little spice to life. She smiled and said I had made a witty paradox. Was I a writer?

I told her I was a gambler by profession and the only reason I looked broken down and miserable like a writer was I had not had a good win on the ponies for a while.

She smiled again, and said I was funny. I had to be a writer. I gave up trying to convince the woman that my interest in Beckett and Suzanne Lu was strictly personal – staying out of jail – and not professional.

It took me about half an hour to decipher the microfilm index system in the college library. After that, I was able to use a microfilm reader to look up the author section – B for Beckett. I looked up the subject section too – P for poison.

As long as you look remotely literate, and you do not want to take books home, you pretty much have a free run of the Kelvin Grove campus library. I studied for five hours, quite a feat when you consider that, some Fridays, I do not spend that long on the racing guide. An article in a Brisbane cultural mag made me laugh. Robert Forster was in a band called the Godots before he formed the Go-Betweens with Grant McLennan. By five o'clock that afternoon, I was ready to consult the biggest brain I know, Con 'Gooroo' Vitalis.

The Gooroo could handicap any event in the universe, and had contacts from Mars to Melbourne. I gave him the moniker Gooroo, after the local Aboriginal word Gooroolbah, meaning deep place, or something like that.

Local for the Gooroo is the Gold Coast and northern New South Wales. He is something of a distant father figure for me, keeping me calm when I need it. He's a great man for perspective on things. For thirty-five years, he has been plying his more or less honourable, though more than less illegal, profession of SP bookmaking. SP stands for Starting Price, which is the final price a horse finishes at before the gallopers leap from the barriers. Illegal bookies gave you SP when you were lucky enough to back a winner.

Only licensed bookmakers on racetracks were allowed to take bets. SP bookmakers resented this restraint of trade and from at least the early 1900s, set themselves up in pubs and shops and other places where the punting public gathered. Alexander Bell's invention of the telephone was a boon for the illegal industry, just as the mobile blower was for drug traders in the 1980s.

I wanted to see the Gooroo in person, but I had to make do with an expensive long-distance phone call. I had an idea that the Gooroo might be in a little trouble himself, so I sussed that out before he explored my woes.

'You and Cheerful aren't going to be had up before that Fitzgerald Inquiry are you?'

A newspaper reporter named Phil Dickie and a television bloke called Chris Masters had been nuzzling their news' noses into tales of police corruption for a couple of years, and it had ended up costing Queensland's longest-serving premier, Joh Bjelke-Petersen, his job. The premier's replacement in the conservative National Party bore the great moniker of Bill Gunn, and he had reluctantly set up an inquiry fronted by lawyer Tony Fitzgerald.

I always wondered whether Gunn had given himself his name, like I had. He headed a rural-based party, and guns are icons in the Aussie bush.

Anyway, one illegality the inquiry was looking into was payoffs to the coppers from illegal gambling. The Gooroo was always reluctant to talk about unwritten contractual arrangements he and his boss Cheerful Charlie Evatt had with the police. He was pretty dismissive this time, too.

'We have the word we're right,' he said. 'I mean, how far can they seriously pursue victimless crimes?'

'I'm not sure about that victimless stuff, Gooroo. We both know blokes who, after a disastrous run of outs on the punt, have taken long walks off short piers.'

'You're playing Devil's advocate, Steele. You've been down to the bones of your bare arse plenty of times. The last time I looked you hadn't topped yourself. One thing I know, people have an illegal bet or take drugs because it's fun. How it gets out of control and turns out to be no fun anymore is too complicated for me to sort out. And I doubt if Mr Fitzgerald will have much luck working that one out either. Just serve up a few sacrificial lambs, the designated villains of the piece, and all will be well. Thankfully Cheerful and I don't look like being cast in the villains' roles.'

This was my cue to tell the Gooroo that Mooney was trying to stitch me up for Suzanne Lu's death. Vitalis immediately handicapped the event. He had had his own run-ins with that big Irish bastard. 'Mooney would not know his arse from Aratula,' the Gooroo declared. 'I could sell him a racing saddle personally autographed by Bernborough.'

Bernborough was a champion racehorse of the 1940s, much more admired by the 1989 gambling community than most two-legged animals walking around forty years later.

'What's the name of the play Lu literally died in?'

When I told him, the bookie was impressed. 'Great play.'

'Is there a curse on this play, Gooroo?' I asked. 'You know, like in Macbeth. All that spraying salt and garlic around the stage?'

'Not that I've heard, Steele. The only curse I know is it's not exactly *My Fair Lady*. I can't imagine theatrical punters breaking their necks to see it. What has you talking about a curse?'

I related how Caitlin Meares went all goofy on me, and kept repeating how it could have been her instead of Suzanne Lu. I gave the Gooroo the outline of the rest of the cast in this real-life murder drama.

'Ah, the theatrical goss,' Vitalis admired, 'the only product more durable than Shakespeare.'

'These thesps like a yak,' I agreed.

Vitalis was most interested in the Kahns – Alison and Efram. I asked why.

'Coincidences, Steele. Always look to the coincidences. An actor is murdered. The doctor on the scene is married to another actor in the play. Perfectly understandable, perhaps, but a coincidence, all the same. I'd like to know more about the husband.'

'Not much info there,' I said. 'A med student from the University of Queensland, just one of a swag of blokes who were magnetised to Alison Stuart. Comes from a filthy rich family does our Efram, and actually financed the first production Alison Kahn starred in after she graduated.'

I heard a biro click at the other end of the line. The Gooroo was making notes.

'Doting husband,' he spoke down the line as he wrote, 'who quickly suggests prescription drugs or ecstasy as the cause of death. Efram Kahn's history includes overcoming a large field of contenders for the glittering prize of a potential bride, Alison. Would hate to see his trophy humiliated by a younger actor, Suzanne Lu. Suzanne was playing Estragon, wasn't she? Quite a plum role.'

The Gooroo was putting together a pretty parcel of suspicion, but I was not buying it. 'The way you tell it, Gooroo, no one's much interested in the play.'

'That's right,' the Gooroo agreed. 'Your average working stiff does not want to see a play that tells them, while they were asleep, someone killed God, cut down all the trees, and took away meaningful work. That's the last thing they need reminding of. But maybe the play's not the thing. After all, she could have died performing *Snow White.*'

'I wish I could picture the murder without the play muddling it up,' I said. 'This switching from drama to real life and back is hard to get your head around. I mean, murder is so straightforward – greed, hatred, envy, rage; they're worth killing for. Not because you're cast in a weird play.'

The Gooroo summed up. 'You would like to believe the play is not the centre of this, Steele. But we both have doubts on that score. Anyway, let's continue the run-down on the bit players in this murder mystery. What about Natalie's sister, Jane?'

The Gooroo knew Natalie well from our visits to his Tweed Heads unit, but I was unsure if he had met Jane.

'From what the director Sandra Blaine says, it seems Bub – that's Jane – and Lu did not get on well. Suzanne Lu was apparently even-tempered and focused on the play. Jane is moody and wilful. She wanted to play her character Lucky right over the top. Everyone else wanted the role low-key, a quiet slave.' I did not see this dispute as a motive for murder and I told the Gooroo as much. 'Jane wouldn't kill anyone in a blue over how to play a role. It's not her style. She loves the drama of arguments, but she doesn't take them seriously.'

Vitalis was not convinced. 'It's like I always say, Steele, straights can be more bent on the inside than the Hunchback of Notre Dame. What you've told me has Jane in there with a chance. So, what about Meares, the one playing Vladimir? What do you know about her?'

'Only what Blaine told me. Caitlin Meares is very co-operative, but she can be anxious. Her father has worked a little two-person gold mine out the back of Kilkivan for the past twenty years. Fancy that, Gooroo – mugs still fossicking in the dirt for specks of gold. The family barely scratched together a living in any of those twenty years.

'When she was nine-years old, Meares decided to find gold on the stage. Hasn't wavered from the dream since. As I said, Meares got on with everyone, even if they did not think much of her idea of cast members swapping roles every few nights.'

The Gooroo was also surprised by the novelty of Caitlin Meares's idea. 'That's a new one, the cast swapping roles. Sounds like a lot of work and more than a bit risky. But who knows what passes for avant-garde in the theatre these days? It would seem Meares had a stake in seeing the play run its season – if she wanted her changes made, I mean. If she killed Kahn, it would be a turn-up for the books.'

I heard his pen scratching across paper, which I imagined was a page of the racing form guide *Best Bets*.

'That's most of the known form, Steele. Who else is in the market?'

I did not need a market. I knew who the killer was. Knew it with absolute certainty, without a clue as to why. I was in a hurry to get off the phone to grab one of my copies of the play. 'Gooroo, you're a genius,' I yelled down the line. 'Even your subconscious is a genius. You bet the killer is a turn-up for the books. The answer's a turnip. Tell me quickly, Gooroo: what is the significance of the carrot in the play?

'The clown Vladimir gives the clown Estragon a carrot. Lots of talk about it. Went over my head, if it meant anything.'

'Yair, it means something,' the Gooroo said, with the confidence of someone who sees no difference between handicapping a play, a horse race or a game of marbles. He ran it down for me. 'The carrot is what keeps the two clowns turning up at the same spot every day to wait for Godot. The carrot is the metaphor for what makes the stiffs catch the 8:01 to work each morning. Without the carrot, the social world would collapse.'

I was beginning to catch on to the play, or at least the Gooroo's angle on it. But I needed more.

'But what is the carrot?' I asked.

'That's the beauty of it, Steele.' I sensed the Gooroo beaming at the other end of the phone. 'The attraction of the carrot is that it's not a turnip. No one wants turnips.'

That Beckett bloke might think the Gooroo's carrot and turnip analysis a load of horse manure, but the bookie warmed to his theme. 'The carrot is not a reward. It's the threat of something worse, that the stiffs could be landed with turnips. So they catch the 8:01, the *Carrot Express*, each morning.'

I knew the Gooroo's mind was flying fast and high, well above and ahead of the 8:01. I knew he would make the connection. 'The carrot was poisoned, wasn't it Steele?'

As chubby American comedian Oliver Hardy used to say in those grainy old black-and-white comedy movies, it most certainly was. Lu actually ate the carrot instead of pretending to. And someone who had been at rehearsals knew she would. Realism killed Suzanne Lu.

5

DOCTOR EFRAM KAHN PACED up and down, round and round, the foyer of La Boite theatre like a novice actor on opening night. It was 7:50 p.m. and the coppers had not showed. I could have told Kahn that Mooney and Schmidt would be having a beer somewhere, letting the suspects stew and loosen lips. I could have told him that, but it suited me to let his annoyance boil.

Like a colleague, or a fellow Marx Brother, I paced beside Kahn to talk poisons. 'How long would it have been between her taking the poison and her heart packing it in?' I asked.

'So you know about the cyanide. Did the police tell you?' He answered my question with another. Annoying that, isn't it? I nodded. He decided to grace my earlier question with an answer. 'Well, despite the amount of cyanide in her system, she was young and healthy. I could only guess, but I would say between two and twelve minutes.'

Kahn noted my surprise, and smirked. 'It's not like in the movies, you know, where they keel over instantly.'

'Would the form of the cyanide affect the speed of death?' I asked. 'If it took twelve minutes, you'd think she would have realised she was dying. So maybe it was in a quick-acting form. What was the compound the cyanide was in, Dr Kahn? What was it the police said again?'

Efram Kahn gave me a half-wary, half-disdainful look. 'Only the killer knows in what form the cyanide was administered. Post-mortem tests are made for individual substances such as cyanide, not for compounds containing cyanide. I think you may be a little out of your depth, Mr Hill.'

Maybe I was, though my study of poisons had given me much the same information as Kahn supplied. My study had told me only the killer knew what exactly he or she had given Suzanne Lu. I had been fishing, and it was a successful trip.

'So, you are experienced in pathology?' I asked Kahn, reeling him in.

Suspicious, he admitted he had worked in pathology. Watching his unease, I pressed my advantage. 'But I still don't see how you knew how much cyanide was in Lu's body?'

Kahn replied indignantly. 'I perused the post-mortem report. It was my right, naturally.'

Acid dripped from his tongue as he said 'naturally'. His tone spoke of the insolence of my questions. It was obvious I was a yob, so I might as well get offensive at a personal level. 'Were you and Suzanne Lu close friends?'

But my three-minute consultation was up. 'Excuse me,' Kahn said. 'I have to see my wife.'

I thought of following him, just to really piss him off, but I broke sharply to the left when I saw Jane's hand beckoning me. Beside Bub was Caitlin Meares, dressed not in Vladimir's clown costume, but in ankle-length green velvet, despite the heat.

'What did he say?' Jane asked excitedly.

'He said the all-ordinaries will rise thirty points on the stock market but that I will never find true happiness until I improve my backswing.'

'Very funny, Steele. Is it true Suzanne was poisoned? What an exit!'

'Shush, Jane,' Meares advised. 'We shouldn't talk about it till the police arrive.'

I knew better and leaned towards Meares to share the wisdom born of experience. 'That could be right, but I reckon the time we definitely don't want to talk about it is when the police get here. There's a lot to be said for the right to silence.'

'Steele's a petty crim,' Jane explained to the other woman, making it sound like a compliment.

I pretended offence at the description and even managed a snooty voice. 'I'm rarely petty and I have never been to jail.'

Jane stood on her digs. 'You're just lucky.'

'No,' I contradicted. 'You're Lucky.'

I turned a palm towards Caitlin Meares. 'And you're Estragon? That's right, isn't it?'

Meares shook her head. 'Vladimir. I was Vladimir. Suzanne was Estragon.'

'Oh yair, that's right,' I conceded. 'I loved that bit about the carrot and the turnips. I like carrots. And aren't they cheap at the moment? Where did you get your carrots from?'

Both Caitlin Meares and Jane looked at me as if I was a couple of root vegetables short of a bunch.

'I don't know,' Meares said. 'Sandra brought them in.'

'I will have to ask our director, then,' I replied and walked towards Sandra Blaine.

Jane followed to whisper in my ear. But first she turned back to Meares to reassure her friend. 'Don't worry, Caitlin, it's not about you.'

I hate people whispering in my ear, no matter how much juice is in the goss. What Jane had to say was pretty juicy.

'You know Suzanne was having sex with Kahn.'

'Is that right?' I said with indifference, though I was hoping that this was as unreliable as most 'good oil'. It threatened to throw my certainties about the killer out the window.

'So you think Alison Kahn may have killed Lu?' I asked Bub.

'Why would she do that?' Jane asked, suggesting she and I had our wires crossed.

I was getting cross with Bub and might have spoken a little too loudly. 'Because Suzanne was having sex with Alison's husband.'

Jane laughed softly. 'Who'd go to bed with that creep, unless you had to? Suzanne and Alison were lovers. And I bet Efram found out.'

With Jane around, it was a good bet everyone found out. The only question was whether it was true.

Sandra Blaine was talking to the Kahns when I butted in to ask to see the director privately.

When we were alone, I said I was sorry the production had been cancelled. Blaine replied there would always be another opening night. Though it was a shame the cast had given up nights and weekends for rehearsals during already stressful exam times. That was the deal struck with the college to obtain some meagre funding for the play: rehearsals outside class hours and performance off-campus during the holidays.

"I see you had a bit part,' I said. 'Do you act much yourself?'

'A little at college,' she answered. 'But these days I am content to be a teacher. I am better at it.'

'So you've been a teacher ever since you graduated from Kelvin Grove. While classmates like Alison Kahn lit up the stage. The same as Suzanne Lu was likely to do.'

If she considered my statements pointed, Blaine pretended not to get the point. 'Suzanne had a lot of talent. More even than Alison, if I am any judge. And much more talent than I could ever have mustered. I'm certain of that.'

'And what did you think of Suzanne Lu personally?'

'Well, I hardly knew her socially. She was certainly ambitious; anyone could tell that. Ambition is hardly a crime.'

Ambition of a long-term nature is not in my line, but I know more than I would like to about crime. 'Sometimes, I think crime, like beauty, is in the eye of the beholder,' I said.

'How poetic of you, Steele. But it is extreme artistic licence to suggest that I murdered Suzanne Lu out of some warped jealousy of performers. In theatre circles, quite a lot of kudos falls to directors, you know. Sometimes, even to teachers.'

'Don't mind me, Sandra, I was just being, um, theatrical. What I am really interested in are root vegetables. For the play, where did you keep the carrots and the turnips?'

'In the fridge,' she replied without hesitation.

'So almost anyone had access to the vegies?'

'Yes,' agreed Blaine. The penny dropped. 'Then it's true! Suzanne was poisoned. I bought those vegetables from the local fruit shop. It was just an accident, chemical poisoning. I should have bought organically grown produce. Horticultural chemical companies have a lot to answer for.'

In the scheme of things, it probably is true that horticultural chemical companies have a lot to answer for. But not for Suzanne Lu's death.

'Maybe the play is cursed,' I suggested.

Blaine was not having any of that. '*Waiting for Godot* cursed, what rubbish,' she insisted. 'I'll put this play on again next year without a hitch. It is our century that is cursed. A play like Godot helps lift the curse, not reinforce it.'

Powerful words. I thought it was just a play, with Beckett hoping to keep himself in Parisian rough red for a few months from the proceeds. 'Will you cast Alison Kahn again?' I asked.

'Alison may not want to do it again next year,' Sandra Blaine replied. 'She is a busy professional and, this time around, it was only a favour for her old school.'

'But if she does volunteer, will you cast her again?'

Blaine looked at me with peeved rather than angry eyes. I thought she might lie to me, but in the end she could not be bothered. 'No, I won't,' she snapped.

Flourish, that is what allows Alison Kahn to stand out. She is only a little over average height. Nothing spectacular strikes you about her brownish hair and greenish eyes. Yet she flourishes when she snakes her lithe body and directs attention to herself with her arms. You can see why men and women desire her. Some of the more impressionable might love her. Me, I am just an unbiased observer with my mind on murder, not love.

After we exchanged intros, I began, as people often do, by talking about the woman's spouse. 'Your husband seems annoyed with me. Is he a jealous man?' I was hoping to catch Alison Kahn off-guard, so she might not ease into her routine of having a man jump through hoops for her.

'You probably rubbed Efram the wrong way, Steele,' Alison Kahn said, in a manner that suggested she herself was beyond being offended.

Though she was not beyond handing out the odd gratuitous jibe. 'The way you work the room, like Hill, Amateur Detective, I can imagine you putting Efram off.'

I half-lied. 'That's the price I have to pay. You see, the police think I murdered Suzanne Lu.'

Alison Kahn nodded her head in sympathy and asked sweetly, 'And did you?'

I smiled. 'No, not so's you'd notice. Did you?'

'Let me see." She placed a finger on the middle of her chin. "I remember murdering in *Macbeth* and in *King Lear,* and then there was *Medea,* but you wouldn't know that one. But Godot, I don't think so. No, I definitely did not murder in Godot.'

'And what about in real life?' I persisted.

'The only real life I know is the theatre.' She continued her theme. 'Before I'm through, I will have lived perhaps a hundred lives, every single one of them more intense and exciting than Steele Hill's or even Alison Kahn's.'

'Or Suzanne Lu's?' I asked, reverting the conversation to more worldly murderous affairs.

Alison Kahn replied in an even voice. 'I loved Suzanne. But even if I hated her, I am not going to throw away my career for the fleeting pleasure of revenge. If I feel a lust for blood, I will audition for the part of one of the great murderers. I will not participate in a squalid and mundane variation on a theme.'

'That's the trouble with acting,' I suggested. 'At least, I would imagine that's the trouble – the pressure to be great. It's not enough to be good; you have to be the best.'

'I would not know about that,' Alison Kahn replied, with distaste at my ignorance. 'I am the best.'

It was time to put my little plan into action. I went out to the car and retrieved my two copies of the play. I had already marked some lines in each copy with a highlighter pen. I asked Caitlin Meares for a favour; I needed to remember a certain scene in the play – would she read some lines with me? Sandra Blaine obligingly gave me the keys to the theatre room. I asked Alison Kahn if she would read for me a little later. Dr Kahn overheard us. I was glad of that.

Caitlin Meares and I went into the darkened theatre space. On cue, Sandra Blaine activated the overhead lights. The director went out. I motioned Meares to the centre of the round, empty stage surrounded by rectangular rows of empty seats. The movable rows of seating had not been moved since opening night. Dust slowly circled in the stark, white light. Ours was a stage without a world to be the centre of. I dragged two cheap plastic chairs from a corner of the room and placed them centre stage.

'Could you read your part of Vladimir from where I have underlined on page twenty?' I asked Meares in a polite manner. 'I'll read Estragon. The others will come in later to read their parts.'

Caitlin was happy to comply, to act, even if it was with a rank amateur director/performer like me. 'Is this it? "Do you want a carrot?" We start there?' she asked.

I looked at my copy and confirmed that was our first line.

Meares paused for one moment. Then, 'Do you want a carrot?' in a totally new voice, the voice of Vladimir.

'Is that all there is?' I asked as a disappointed Estragon.

Vladimir replied that she might have some turnips, but I prefer a carrot, only to bite on the vegetable and discover it is a turnip.

'Oh, pardon!' Caitlin apologised. 'I could have sworn it was a carrot.'

Meares rummaged through the pockets of her dress to find me an imaginary carrot.

'There, dear fellow,' she said affectionately.

'Fancy that,' I said.

Caitlin objected. 'Hang on; you've left out a whole stack of lines.'

'I know. Just humour me.'

'You can't do that. This is Godot; you can't just leave out a bunch of lines.'

I ignored her objections.

'Fancy that,' I repeated, holding up the end of the imaginary carrot by the stubble of a leaf. 'Funny that the more you eat the worse it gets.'

Meares spat out her line, angry with me for playing about with the script. 'With me it's just the opposite.'

'In other words?' I asked.

'I get used to the muck as I go along,' Caitlin said.

Omitting more lines, I said, 'Nothing to be done.'

I dangled our conjured carrot in front of Meares. 'Like to finish it, Caitlin?'

'No thanks.'

I put down my copy of the play, and spoke evenly. 'I saw you palm what was left of the carrot after Estragon died.'

Meares put her book on top of mine and replied just as calmly. 'No you didn't.'

'Are you saying you didn't palm the carrot?'

'I'm saying you didn't see me do it.'

'You're right. I didn't see you palm the carrot.'

'Of course you didn't.'

'Then you admit you did it. You injected the poison into the carrot.

'I admit nothing.'

Meares' shoulders sagged suddenly, as if expelling a great mental weight of tiredness. 'How did you know?'

'You said something to me on opening night. In fact you repeated it. You said it could have been you. It stuck in my head, the funny words you used. The distraught way you said them.

'I asked everyone around if the play was cursed like *Macbeth*. That could have explained it. No one knew anything about a curse. Your unexplained phrase kept lurking in my head.'

Caitlin Meares spoke with disdain, 'Your generation always looks for explanations.' She said it with loathing and I felt the need to apologise for every one of my twenty-four years on Earth. Though we were only a few years apart in age, she summed up 'my generation' in one damning phrase: 'You're so pathetic.'

That was me done, a wasted life, just waiting to eke out the dregs, including tidying up a small murder. 'I couldn't work out the why, so I wasn't sure. But I found out about your father and his small gold mine. They use potassium cyanide in processing, don't they? It poisons the wildlife something shocking, so they tell me. You know all this, Caitlin.'

'Congratulations,' Meares said flatly. She stood up and slow-clapped. 'Steele Hill turns out to be the unlikely hero of the piece. You give me over to the police, and the audience retires to their sanctuaries in suburbia.'

I shook my head. 'No, I'm not going to give you up. It's not my style. Just tell me why, and my part is done.'

Caitlin Meares looked up to where the ceiling met the wall. 'I should have played Estragon. I told them.

'Vladimir,' she scoffed, 'one of your kind, a too clever moralist. But Estragon, Estragon. He's a poet, a poet of the void. I told them.'

The why was drowning in a sea of theatrical criticism. I gave it one last shot. 'You're not telling me you committed a murder because they gave the part you wanted to someone else?'

I did not expect answers and I got none. Meares continued to stare at the spot on the wall. Out damned spot, though that's the wrong play. 'You know what they said to me? They said Vladimir had more lines. As if it's about who has more lines.'

Sensing that there was nothing more for me here, I walked towards the door.

'You won't tell the police,' Meares called after me.

I did not even shake my head, just turned the doorknob, trudged down the staircase, and walked through the foyer of La Boite theatre, out into the hot night of the real world.

SINKING INTO one of the Gooroo's leather armchairs, I took a mouthful of red wine.

'She gave herself up then?' the Gooroo asked.

'Yes,' I replied. 'I doubt it was from guilt. I guess she figured if I worked it out, anybody could.'

'I think you underestimate yourself, Steele.' The Gooroo starred into the depths of his mug of strong black tea. 'You know he totally disapproved of women playing Vladimir and Estragon.'

I wasn't sure if he was talking to me or to stray tea leaves at the bottom of his ceramic container. In those days, people still made tea in a pot. Fancy that.

'Who did?'

'Beckett.'

'Oh,' I said, expecting the Gooroo to elaborate but he stared silently into the black liquid.

Finally he raised his head. 'He died today.'

'Who did, not Beckett?'

'Yes.'

'Who killed him?' I asked.

'He was 83-years old.'

'Oh,' I said. 'Alas poor Beckett, I knew him well.'

'You haven't quite got the Shakespearean quote right, Steele, but, in a way, I think you did.'

I said I was saddened by the playwright's death but I was glad my part in his comedy-drama was almost over. 'You know what you said, Gooroo, about the straights being more bent than the crooked. I could not see the sickness on Caitlin Meares. I mean, normally you can see the sickness, in the eyes, or around the mouth, even among the straights. Maybe especially among the straights. I know it had to be there, but on Caitlin Meares, I could not see it at all.'

The Gooroo reassured me that, after an appearance or three in court, I could forget the whole thing. 'That'll be the end of it,' he said.

'Not quite,' I contradicted. The Gooroo raised an eyebrow. 'This writer woman came around to see me. Seems she's going to write a book on it.'

The Gooroo shook his head sadly. 'Now, that is sick.'

We sat in silence for a few seconds. The Gooroo leaned towards me. 'How much is she going to pay you, this writer?'

'She said she would try to squeeze two grand out of the publisher for me.'

'That's not too bad,' the Gooroo figured.

'Not too bad at all,' I agreed.

Book Two

At lessons

6

Brisbane, summer in December, 1991

BAD LUCK, they say, comes in threes.

I copped the treble that hot Thursday arvo and warmish Friday morning in early December, when any working stiff with a smidgen of sense was slowly clocking off for the year. For once, I wished I was one of them.

It seemed pretty much plain sailing as I glared at the clock on the wall of what was then called the Commonwealth Employment Service. Still waiting at 2:20 for a 2 o'clock appointment, I could live with that. A public servant letting you know who's boss is a small price to pay for another six months of hassle-free dole, or unemployment benefit or social welfare if you want to go all ideological about it.

'Steele Hill.'

It was a soft voice, pretending to be hard. I looked up. She was young, too young, not more than twenty. I like my dole public servants at least ten years older, well into their world-weary routine: 'Steele, we both know there are no jobs out there, but we gotta do this bureaucratic bullshit. So let's get it over and done with. Then it's on your bike, Steele. You don't mind me calling you Steele, do you, Steele?'

That routine I like.

But with the youngies, you never know. Holy Buddha, some

of them can be ambitious – dreams of being first secretary, or whatever the chief head kicker is called.

I was at a dangerous age myself. When you are approaching twenty-seven, some stiffs out there think you can still be rehabilitated into a useful member of society, whatever that is. This young woman might be one of the rehabilitators.

Let's not forget that rockers Jim Morrison, Janis Joplin and Jimi Hendrix, who will probably all live forever, died at age twenty-seven. It's a spooky age, one you need to brace yourself against and get over. If I have a child, I will tell them to beware the age of twenty-seven: it is the modern Ides of March. Must remember to ask my mate the Gooroo what Ides are.

I did notice the young public servant had a useful pair of sleek legs under the Business Orthodox grey skirt, topped by a white blouse and a lilac jacket. With shoulder pads. For packing down in the Man's maul.

I walked towards the little gate they have in dole offices, there to assure you that you are up for a stroll along the garden path to grandma's house. She opened gran's gate for me.

'I'm Kathy Billings, Mr Steele. I'm your review officer.' A little smile appeared on her perfectly groomed face, for about a half-second.

My review officer. **My** review officer. You can't go through life without collecting personal property, even when you don't want it.

I looked into her eyes. No sign of recent drug or alcohol abuse. The absence of drug taking might not be as bad as you first think. Sure, druggies may not give a shit; maybe even fancy themselves as rebels with blue pens. But they can turn on you in a flash, too. 'Pleased to meet you, Kathy,' I said, sticking out my right hand.

I was born left-handed, but the nuns at the orphanage decided that it was one of the marks of Satan. Satan left so many marks around the orphanage you had to wonder if he was any good at all at his chosen career of soul-stealing. The nuns performed a prolonged exorcism on my left-handedness. I won't go into the details, but it worked.

'Come into my office,' Kathy Billings said, with a generous sweep of her left hand.

My office tinkled a little warning. There was that possessive again.

She had barely settled behind her huge desk and pointed me to a chair before she plunged into the heart of the matter. 'Four years and four months, Mr Steele.'

I pretended to rack my brain to place the anniversary, but I knew what the time span meant, right enough. 'That long,' I said after a bit. Kathy Billings gave me her blankest look. I followed up. 'It's Hill; Steele is my first name.' Now humour to throw her well-laid strategy into a spin. 'Don't believe those people who say "Steal" is my middle name.'

Kathy Billings was not deterred from her plan by my tactics. 'I won't lie to you, Mr Hill. A few of our clients have been receiving unemployment benefit for longer. But, for someone as young as you, four years and four months without gainful employment suggests that something is wrong.'

Well, it depends on your point of view. Things had gone wrong and things had gone right during those four years and four months. Things could start to go really bad if she had an idea that a stretch without the dole might rehabilitate me. It's not just the meagre dollars; life gets complicated when you have to start explaining what it is that you do. The taxman starts looking up your number, and you feel the need to justify your existence. "Unemployed" is simple, self-explanatory.

When Kathy hit me with the empathy card, I began to sweat just a drop or two. 'I'm not here to judge you; I'm here to help you,' she said.

The help this tidy little office woman had in mind was not the painless continuation of my unemployment benefit. No, she was devising a much more convoluted strategy to achieve what straights would consider a desirable outcome. 'Looking through your file,' she said. Nothing more, as if the phrase said it all. She let me stew for a few seconds.

I blame the eighties for the strategic thinking of youth of the nineties. Blame the eighties for every bad thing of the nineties and you can't go far wrong.

In the eighties, Melbourne rocker Jo Jo Zep sang about his baby getting him in the shape he was in. Jo Jo – not Joe Camilleri's real name, how'd you guess? – unknowingly predicted how that greedy, grasping, guzzling decade would have the young adults of the nineties all bent out of shape, trying to squeeze through the keyhole into the room of treasures. The kids of the nineties wanted it all, but were not sure why.

In 1991, Michael Stipe of American indie rock band R.E.M. – Random Equivocal Meanderings – no, I just made that up – sang a song with meaningless lyrics about losing religion, which most of us took to mean that the pursuit of fame and fortune had no meaning. Being in the spotlight he had lost faith. If we fans weren't so stoned and up ourselves, we would have realised that we had never been in the spotlight, and whether or not we gave up Godbothering wasn't a big deal to anyone else.

In Mick Stipe's industry, losing religion was a minority

position. Other aspiring pop stars sang it out loud that they were born again, to endear themselves to the legions of young, record-buying Christians. In my book, losing, finding or maintaining religion is best done in the privacy of your own church or home. It is just plain ugly as a spectator sport.

REM's lead singer mused on whether he had said too much, but Mick had said just enough to shove the band into the mainstream of the emerging nineties, where angst held hands with the ambition born in the eighties.

From 1987, a monstrous heap of documentation had evidently been assembling itself on the subject of yours truly. I should have been flattered but I was the ungrateful type. Ms Billings produced my unemployment bio triumphantly from a filing cabinet behind her desk. She pretended to thumb through the dozens of pages.

'One of the problems you have, Mr Hill, is one of identity. There is no birth certificate on file; no record of your parents' details. In the circumstances . . .'

This was low, trying to bust me on a technicality. But, as the Chinese say, my crisis of identity may have an opportunity enfolded within it. 'I'm an orphan,' I said, and was pleased to see the public servant lower her eyes in an appropriate display of mild discomfort. 'You'll see my bank accounts and my licence, and where I changed my name by deed poll when I left the orphanage.'

'Why did you change your name?' she asked.

'Unpleasant memories,' I said glumly. There was not much truth in that, but it was a good angle in this situation. One of the first things I saw on release from the orphanage was a billboard down the street. In large print on that board, a company fancied itself as The Big Australian, and below were the words Broken Hill Steel. I couldn't take my eyes off it, and it came to me that a name like Steele Hill would give me an edge on the street. I reckon it has too – some of the time.

You don't want to know what name the nuns gave the foundling who became Steele Hill. Even if you do, I don't want to tell you.

Being John Lennon's lovechild, I could have given myself the old man's name. But it rhymes with lemon, and my old man John met a decidedly sour end. Imagine there's no creeps with guns. It's not easy, even if you try.

The public servant lowered her head closer to the documents, scanning for evidence of who I was. 'You have never married, Mr Hill?'

Innocent as charged. I raised my ringless fingers towards Kathy Billings to indicate my singular marital status. The love of my life – Natalie, My Cucumber, – lives in the same block of flats as I do, but we could never be an official couple without my losing my public subsidy. Marriage vows could not be accommodated in my social compact with the government of the day, whose protocols would not allow the payment of my unemployment benefit if I could be construed as Natalie's spouse.

Besides, if I married Natalie, I might gain a dangerous in-law in the shape of Nat's younger sister Jane. Bub collected trouble as easily as another hobbyist might gather model cars.

'Even if we accept the bona fides of your identity, we have the problem that you cannot get work in your field,' Ms Billings said. 'Your occupation is listed as bookmaker's clerk.'

I agreed being a bookie's clerk was my vocation.

'That's the gambling industry, isn't it, not someone who publishes books? The gambling industry is booming at the moment.'

I sighed. 'It must be on my file. I've been warned off every racetrack in Australia. I can't work in my profession. I couldn't get the dole for twelve weeks because of it.'

'Warned off?' Kathy Billings asked for clarification, as she rummaged through my bulky file. Before I could answer, she found another notation. 'It says something here about "failure to comply with a stewards' inquiry". Can you explain this, Mr Hill?'

'It's all a little bit complicated, Kathy. It still upsets me. I sometimes wake up in the middle of the night reliving it.'

She nodded – kept nodding, in fact. The nods said, 'Go on, and tell me a few lies. I've got all the time in the world.'

I opened with self-righteousness. 'I've got no time for crooks on a racetrack. My job is to take bets, so where's my percentage if the baddies are hustling me. Being warned off racecourses means not being able to enter any Australian track from Hobart to Home Hill.'

Kathy had trouble finding a note of sympathy. 'Must make work as a bookmaker's clerk hard to come by,' she said. Sarcastically.

'No, look, Kathy. Every year I appeal. I know I'm this close to winning. My instincts tell me January next year is it.'

'But what about this inquiry business? This all happened in 1986, more than five years ago, and your licence has not been reinstated since.'

'I gave all the information I could. A horse was found to have been given a "go-fast", and a couple of us innocents got caught in the net.'

Her nods were getting faster, more impatient. But I was enjoying the story, as I do every time I tell one of my many versions of it. I pretended Kathy's nods were keeping time to the rhythm of my gripping yarn. 'I was doing what I was supposed to do, placing bets for people,' I continued.

She waited for me to go on, but I had finished. Kathy was exasperated. 'Then, why did they warn you off?'

This was not an opportune moment for the whole truth. The racing stewards could not understand my betting patterns, placing so much money on a seemingly hopeless horse. If professionals in the racing industry could not understand it, how could I possibly explain it to an outsider like Kathy Billings?

'People lied about me,' I said.

True, because someone always tells lies about you, even if it's out of ignorance rather than malice.

'If what you say is true, and I do not doubt it, Steele . . .' She paused, to silently tell me she didn't believe a word. Which was fine by me, as she might be warming to an engaging liar. A lousy $150 a week dole is a small price to keep a good liar out there, engaging people.

' . . But why haven't you considered retraining?'

'I've done a couple of computer courses. I can use those skills inside or outside my trade.'

I had done the courses, but the rest of it was 300 percent pure bullshit. Everyone on the dole with an IQ above sixty-five is sent on either computer or hospitality courses. Be on the dole long enough and you will do both. Would you like Microsoft Office with those fries? But there is no way I'm working with rotten computers. We just don't get along, which is why I'll probably never be a bookie's clerk again. By the time they give me back my licence, every clerk will be recording bets on a computer instead of using a hand ledger as I was trained to do.

My S.P. bookie mate, the Gooroo, despite his advanced years, loves those computers, the only fault I can find with him.

Kathy Billings surely couldn't deny that my computer courses were retraining. Retraining, in the eyes of the dole office, is the next best thing to employment. Maybe they pinched the model from Chairman Mao's re-education programme. It seems more about presenting statistics to central office than finding your pesky dole bludgers employment. In the eyes of the seriously unemployed, such as me, retraining is a necessary evil to keep you on the dole.

I would not like my flippancy to suggest I am a dole bludger. I have always supported the work ethic. The ethic has always been a basic part of me. However, my career has invariably involved alternative work, work that does not necessarily receive the social recognition it deserves.

'Well, Steele, it boils down to this,' Billings said and paused.

At last, show us that card you have up your sleeve.

'We are not entirely convinced that you are a willing work-seeker.'

Go on, Kathy.

'You are obviously reasonably intelligent, whatever your background. And you are still relatively young.'

Relatively young, that's rich from someone twenty going on fifty-five.

'As you know, you have signed a contract with us, and it has penalties for non-compliance.'

Come on, give us the sentence; I can't plead mitigation until I receive your sentence.

'Which is why, if I were you, I would seriously consider how I approached the job interview we're sending you to.'

Job interview! I almost burst out laughing. This was why I

sounded so earnest. 'You know, you have only sent me to four interviews the whole time I have been on the dole.'

Which was true, and what horrific jobs they were. If I didn't have a finely polished interview technique, I might have copped a bad report to the dole office from one of my prospective employers. Or worse, landed one of the jobs.

I like a good job interview. It's fun talking to jumped-up stiffs who pretend you are their equal, while deciding which loser gets to lick salt off the walls of their mine. All you have to do is show that you too regard them as equals, or, at least, not much inferior to you, and you have no show of landing the job.

Later, you ask the stiffs for a written assessment of your interview. The least they can do is say nice things about you, considering how glad they are you will not be working for them. A copy of that assessment to the dole office secures your payment for twelve months or so, until another serious review comes your way. Sweet!

That's why they call it social security. The stiffs are secure in their offices and I jingle a few public coins in my pocket, secure on the Brissie and Gold Coast streets that I call home.

I was sentenced to another job interview. Where was the pain?

Ms Billings was about to tell me where the pain was. 'We would be very surprised if you were not the most suitable candidate for this job, Mr Hill.'

How flattering, but then flattery can be cover for sinister intent.

'In fact, Mr Hill, we intend not to put this job vacancy on our noticeboards until after your interview.'

This did not sound good. We both knew the odds: more than a million unemployed in a workforce of under ten million.

Why give me the inside running when the equal employment racing rules say no runner will be hit with a go-fast needle at the expense of other competitors?

Australia had been in recession for the best part of two years. This concerned me little, as I had been in and out of recession since the aftermath of the '86 'fiasco' when they warned me off. I was used to it.

But stiffs perform badly under prolonged adversity. The treasurer of the good ship *Australian Economy* when she hit the recession reef was Paul Keating. While everyone was partying in the late 1980s, Keating told all the stiffs he was the World's Best Treasurer, and the prime minister of the day, Bob Hawke, seconded the motion.

I could be wrong, but my understanding is that, in economics, you try to slow down the party when the economy becomes oversexed, or overheated, as the Puritans prefer to say. The World's Best Treasurer upped the ante in 1989, slapping an 18 percent interest rate on the love-in. This might have played some part in hundreds of thousands of Aussies losing their jobs. As I say, I could be wrong about the economics of it all, but the record shows stiffs losing their jobs in droves in 1990 and 1991.

I thought I was immune to the worst effects of the recession, but Kathy Billings seemed intent on kicking me off the dole. She probably figured that a stiff would be less creative in surviving without dole money than I. You could not fault that reasoning, but I was always a bench warmer in the game of economics, so why should I have to play, just because the team was copping a flogging. I felt for the stiffs, but if they did not get the shitty end of the financial digestive system, they wouldn't be stiffs.

With a clear and morally defensible objective of staying on the dole, I was keen to know the form of this job, this new obstacle between my goal and me. Kathy Billings handed me what appeared to be an oversized betting slip.

It read, 'Turfologist, Mr Caulfield Jones, Suite 4/116 Montague Rd, West End. Friday, 7:45 a.m.' Kathy Billings giving me less than a day's notice for the job interview was sus but better to get it done and dusted quickly as far as I was concerned.

It sounded straight up enough, because only a hustler connected with horse racing would have the hide to set up a job interview before eight in the morning.

The lovely Kathy (I have to admit, I do like them stern) let me puzzle over the cryptic slip of paper, which I laid on the desk. It wasn't invited into my wallet until more information might let it lie comfortably inside the leather.

The public servant took a larger card from her drawer. Ms Billings had the advantage when it came to props. She read from the card: 'Turfologist requires a person to develop legitimate racehorse betting systems. Must be familiar with both horse racing and computers. Suit former bookmaker's clerk. Wage: $300 plus commission. Start ASAP.'

Of course, as soon as I heard the bodgie term 'turfologist', I was a furlong ahead of Ms Billings. (Some of you younger punters may not know a furlong is an old distance measure of about 200 metres. Forgive my anachronistic lapse and just put it down to an amateur horse-racing historian saluting the gambling bloodline. I know little about punching time clocks, but I can tell you Archer won the first Melbourne Cup in 1861.) If you look up 'turfologist' in a dictionary, it'll probably say something about lawn care.

'So you concede you might get the job?' Ms Billings asked.

I was conceding zilch. 'If I get it, what if he doesn't pay me?'

'I've spoken to Mr Jones. He sounds an honest businessman.' She played it straight and so did I; neither of us smiled at 'honest businessman'. 'In fact, he sent me a copy of a bank passbook entitled "employee's wages". There's thirty-thousand dollars in that account, Mr Hill.'

I bet her eyes lit up at the sight of the thirty with a dollar sign in front and lots of noughts after. How much was in her joint account? She and her boyfriend, who sold insurance, were saving for a house deposit, and visiting lovely three-bedroom display homes beside artificial lakes on Brisbane's outskirts.

Bank accounts were totally secure documents in our age of manic security. You needed 100 points to open up a bank account: a birth certificate, a driver's licence, school results, membership of a trade association – this, that and the other, ticked off down the stiff's checklist.

Some stiffs had trouble getting those 100 points. The Caulfield Joneses of this world could put together 1000 points over a cup of coffee. That was why they owned a dozen bank accounts, some from actual banks. I could show Kathy my six bits of plastic from the Bank of Earnest Endeavour and Dedicated Printing Reproduction. But I was small potatoes. As for the thirty grand? In one day and out the next, or a friendly computer printer offering you noughts to infinity.

Still, I did not mind going to this interview. Might be an angle in it for me. Who's the easiest person to sell to? A salesperson. Who's the easiest person to hustle? A hustler.

'This looks promising,' I said.

I meant I could not see much danger in it. That was bad luck number one, and I would soon find the dead body to prove it.

7

AS SOON AS A STIFF BUYS an alarm clock, The Man's got them. To ruin my Christmas holidays, Ms Kathy Billings from the dole office was sending me to see turfologist Caulfield Jones for an early Friday morning job interview. Ms Scrooge might have ruined my Christmas, delivering the first of an inevitable three parcels of bad luck, but I wasn't going to let her wreck my Thursday night's rest with the eruption of a devilish noise.

I have not owned an alarm clock for almost ten years. I used one for a few months after I left the orphanage. I never liked that relentless shrillness frightening me awake, and the continual waking even before that in fear the alarm wasn't working. I read once that we all have a pleasant little alarm in our heads. It works if we trust it. Mine works pretty well, but then I don't scold it if it misbehaves. And I hardly ever anticipate it and wake early.

It worked pretty well that Thursday night and woke me at 11 p.m. A quick shower; grilled chicken, tomatoes with basil, toast with coffee for a midnight breakfast, and off to work.

I turned my old grumbling EH ute into an inner-city service station. You wouldn't want to know where, and if you did, I wouldn't want to tell you. I parked the car beside six taxis, flying the flags of three companies, and hopped out to greet the midnight below the sign A & A Fiorini managers.

Anita was serving some suit, chasing cigarettes and coffee

after a night of business, booze, drugs, tom-catting, whatever. When she saw me, Anita flashed that big smile of hers, and nodded towards the wall behind her. She was indicating what was behind the wall.

Anita and Antonio Fiorini managed the servo on behalf of an international oil company. In the seventies the newlyweds bought their own little garage in the burbs. The eighties shake up in the industry saw that go, along with a lot of other independents. Then they landed this job, running what was basically a twenty-four-hour convenience store that sold petrol, as well as newspapers and magazines illegally. Since the business-is-beaut eighties and the following recession, everyone wanted to get into everyone else's business. As proud Italians, the Fiorinis did not like working long hours for someone else, but they persevered and managed to keep smiling too.

When the suit had taken his coffee and cigarettes outside, Anita came from behind the counter to punch me lightly on the shoulder.

'Steele, you look so handsome tonight. You should be taking that Natalie out on the town.'

'Some of us have to work, Anita. The back door open?'

'Of course, Steele. Feeling lucky tonight?'

'I don't know. Lucky might object. There's just a slight technical hitch, Anita.'

'Oh, Steele, you don't tell Tony, eh?'

She reached behind cases of soft drinks stacked eight high, to fetch a leather handbag. From its contents, which I couldn't see, came a hundred, a fifty, a twenty, a ten and four fives.

Handing me the stake, she asked, 'You got the fifties?'

I showed Anita three plastic coin holders crammed with

50c pieces.

'You always got the fifties, Steele.'

'Tools of the trade, Anita. Ta for the loan.'

'That's fine. Just don't tell Tony.'

I wouldn't. After all, I never told Anita when Antonio lent me money.

I went through the narrow archway bearing the warning 'Staff only'. Behind the table cluttered with magazines was a door, which opened into the garage. I nodded happily at the magnificent sight, cut off from outside view by the small door on one side and a huge aluminium roller door to the right. A third entry was an inconspicuous metal door. Three keys to that door were kept under a rock in a garden bed.

The round hydraulic platform for working on cars had been raised to table height. The green felt from a billiard table was draped over the platform. Eight men sat around the table. Six were cabbies. The others were Antonio Fiorini and his mate, Luigi 'Lucky' Leggo.

The game was Manila poker, sevens up. The cards 2 to 6 of the four suits were not required. Not that I had to look to know the game was Manila. The game was always Manila. I pulled up a chair and placed it to the right of the dealer, a wiry cabbie called Phil. A couple of the players said hello. The rest just nodded, refusing to break concentration on the hand in progress. Antonio flicked his finger in the direction of the refrigerator in the corner.

I opened the fridge, ignoring the dozens of cans of beer stored there. I took a glass and poured from the carafe of Chianti, placed squarely in the centre of the fridge. I also ignored the open jar with its pile of gold coins and a few notes. This was Antonio's pocket money, earned from the grog he sold to the poker players and other select customers, and he used it to buy his wine for the week. It was not quite legal. To be fair, if you pushed the point, it was downright illegal, but authorities had failed to push it yet. The money also covered expenses such as coffee and sandwiches for the game and a cab home for anyone who got too pissed, so no one cried foul if it also bought Tony a few glasses of wine.

I rarely needed a cab. A few glasses of Antonio's chilled Chianti saw me through the night and in shape for the drive home. I made the mistake once of putting money in the beer kitty for the wine. If you have ever seen the carry-on of an Italian who feels his hospitality has been insulted, you know why I didn't make that mistake again.

By the time I sat down, Herb Willmott, fifty, fat and florid, was shuffling the deck. I asked to be dealt in, and exchanged a proper how-you-going with each player.

Forget your five-card stud. That is regarded as a uniquely American game, and the Red, White and Bluers haven't yet realised that no other nationality has a high enough boredom threshold to play it. By the Holy Law of Averages, a high pair will win most hands of five-card stud. So much for those American movies where a straight flush wins the cattle ranch, the fair maiden, and the honour of beating Nick the Greek who holds a lousy four aces. To get that straight flush in a two-person showdown, a filmmaker would need 32,000 takes, unless the deck was doctored.

No, forget your five-card stud; Manila is the only game of poker. The cards come round with two dealt face-down to each player. Everybody antes, in our game it's 50c a head. This entitles you to bet on each of the next five cards, turned over one at a time. These five cards are communal. Using the two cards in your personal hand and any three out of the five communal cards, you make the best poker hand you can. Simple and sweet.

The best hand can win you lots of money. If you consider $150 or so a lot of money. That Friday morning I did. Most Friday mornings I did.

As always, I played the percentages. I never doubt the existence of the God Probability and his wife Lady Luck. The Lady is a fickle Goddess, while Probability is a harsh God who suffers fools endlessly as He takes them to the cleaners. Neither God is to be taken lightly.

By one o'clock I was $300 up. It was my deal.

'By the way, I have to finish at 4:30 on the dot. I've got a can't-miss appointment for 7:45 this morning.' I said this emphatically, as much for my own benefit as for the other players.

'Gotta see the duty solicitor before your court appearance,' said Laughing Laurie.

The last time anyone remembered seeing Laughing Laurie even smile was when U.S. President Kennedy was shot dead in '63.

'Yair,' I replied. 'I'm prepared to swear your wife thought the blond lad next door was over sixteen.'

Some players laughed and Laughing shut up.

I dealt out the two down cards each, deciding that whatever cards fell my way, I would go in hard, to pretend I would play the rest of the night on muscle rather than maths. I spread the five common cards face-down across the centre of the table. I looked at my 'hole' cards. Seven of diamonds, ace of spades, worst possible hole: ace and seven of different suits.

If you don't know ten and jack of the same suit are the best possible hole cards, you shouldn't play Manila. But you are welcome in my game anywhere, anytime.

A ten of diamonds was the first card I turned over from the communal five. A bet of 50c was doubled by a second player and doubled again by a third. By the time it got around to me the bet was $4. I doubled the bet on a hand that I had a principled politician's chance in Canberra of winning. I committed myself to the bluff.

Four of the nine players dropped out. No one raised me back. Next card up, nine of spades. Looking good. I badly wanted a small straight to win the hand, so the other players would remember my bluff. If a big hand such as a full house or flush won, my efforts in throwing away money would be ignored.

The first bet on the second communal card, the nine of spades, was, as always, to the dealer's left. Thankfully every player, up to me, checked, so they could all stay in the game, providing they matched a subsequent bet. I bet $8 again and another player dropped out, leaving four of us.

Card three was the Queen of hearts. Best possible hand around the table was a king-high straight, if someone had a Jack and a King in their hole. Everyone checked again, and I bet $16. They had to pick me for the king-high straight. I figured at least one of those three bastards really had the king-high and was foxing.

Fourth card was seven of clubs, and I smiled. There was no chance of a flush with four suits showing on table. With a lonely pair of sevens, I had no chance of winning the pot, but no one could be sitting on a full house or four of a kind. With one communal card left, the best possible hand so far was still the King High straight.

Laughing Laurie was the first to bet — $8 when he could have bet $32. Chances were he had the king-high and he was testing me out. I doubled to $16. Only Lucky stayed with me and Laughing. What Lucky was staying in on I couldn't guess, maybe three of a kind and a miracle.

Fifth card was a ten of spades. With two tens on the table, the best possible hand was four tens, but the odds were against it, with a full house based on three tens a more likely winner.

Laughing looked at me suspiciously before he bet $16. For all Laughing knew, I had four tens, or the full house tens over queens, after I had bet on the first ten. Lucky doubled the bet to $32. I doubled again to $64. Lucky looked. Laughing threw in his cards.

'A pair of sevens with the tens,' I said, as if my world had collapsed. My starting bank certainly had shrivelled after my outrageous bluffing.

'Queen-high straight,' said Lucky, showing an eight and a jack with one hand while raking in his winnings with the other.

'Shit,' Laughing said. 'I had a king-high straight. What the fuck were you doing, Steele?'

What I was doing was establishing my credentials as a bluffer, giving Lucky a false sense of security, ruining Laughing's concentration for the night and losing most of my winnings in one hand. I knew, from then on, I would have a good night.

At four o'clock I said, 'Half an hour and that's me.'

'What the fuck you talking about?' demanded Laughing, looking at the pile in front of me.

At a rough guess, I would have said I had at least $900. Lucky and Laughing had contributed about $300 each to the haul.

'I said that hours ago,' I insisted.

'He did.' Antonio, who was winning a couple of hundred himself, wouldn't mind seeing the back of the big winner.

'What the fuck,' Laughing said. 'The game finishes at 5:30. Everybody knows that.'

I began to fold up my money. For me the game was over. Laughing slammed his hand to my left wrist. It reminded me of when I was seven-years-old and a nun slammed her coffee cup on my left hand, breaking three bones. I half-rose from my chair, with extreme malice on my mind, as the door opened and in walked Detective Sergeant Frank Mooney and Detective Senior Constable Bill Schmidt. Bad luck number two for me.

Mooney looked at the scene with mild interest as he handed Schmidt two coins. Schmidt returned with two cans of beer. Laughing withdrew his hand from my wrist. Mooney leaned against a pile of tyres, while Schmidt rested against the wall beside his senior officer. No one in the room said anything.

I continued to rake in the dough, wondering why everybody had shut their traps just because a couple of dees had intruded. Uniformed coppers had been strolling in and out all night, buying beers, drinking them and going back to what they called work. They didn't worry any of the players. What difference did Mooney in a cheap leather jacket and Schmidt in a trendy sports coat make?

'Knocking off early, Hill?' Mooney eventually asked. He didn't expect an answer. He was probably pissed off he'd walked into agro when he just wanted a beer, but there was too much copper in him not to ask a sarcastic question.

'Steele's got an appointment in the morning,' Antonio explained. He waved the tension away. 'Let's play cards.'

I stuffed the money in my pockets and went out through the

door. Shutting it behind me, I smiled towards Anita and rapped two fingers towards the ceiling.

'You win?' Anita smiled back.

I dragged some money from a pocket and handed her $250.

'Two hundred, that's all, no more,' she said.

'Take the fifty,' I insisted. 'Buy yourself some flowers.'

'Why you don't buy me flowers?' mocked Anita.

'Because they spray flowers with deadly substances to keep them alive even after they are dead.'

'Do they? Oh, you only joke again.'

'Buy some flowers, awlright, Anita? From me.'

'Awlright, but you should laugh when you are joking. It's not so funny in a foreign country.'

Tell me about it, Anita, I thought.

Every day I make my way
Through the streets of your town.

Even in the bad interior light of the car, I counted more than $750. The 50c pieces were threatening to burst their three plastic pockets, and I poured some coins into the glove box.

I was exhilarated driving home, with just a niggling tiredness at the back of my head. Lady Luck was in the passenger seat. Her winning smile lit up Nudgee Road at four in the morning in a way a thousand streetlights could not. Under her glorious spell, I was convinced my short run of bad luck at the dole office and running into the dees had stopped at two.

8

UNDER THE SHOWER, I began to fantasise about making a packet from Mr Jones's touting job. I pictured myself letting Jones dud me for a few months, while I learned the nuts and bolts of the hustle. No harm in that if it meant I could start my own touting business. I could see the ad: Steele Hill International Tipping Service, Est. Ascot, England, 1922. I read somewhere a number with double digits such as 1922 impresses the mugs. I really have to stop remembering all this shit I read.

I walked down to the Feed Bin in Nudgee Road for breakfast. At 4:45 the café was crowded with trainers and jockeys, along with the odd owner.

All owners are odd. They pay thousands upon thousands of dollars to feed and house and exercise and otherwise maintain horses, just for the slim chance of one day getting to stick a photo on the lounge-room wall of their nag winning at Eagle Farm. Still, Buddha bless their photograph-loving souls which, no doubt, are very much under-exposed in their other business activities. Without these owners, all of us there in the Feed Bin would have been out of work and scrounging for a feed.

Veteran trainers Eric Kirwin and Roy Dawson chatted jauntily to their respective stable foremen. Chris Munce, then one of Queensland's top two jockeys, was telling a joke he had picked up at the wharfies' club. Talented apprentices Jim Byrne and Nathan Day were looking through form guides.

Apprentices in Brisbane and Melbourne rode their share of Saturday winners. Not like Sydney, where everything was old dogs for a hard road, with the hungriest senior jocks from New South Wales, interstate and New Zealand divvying up the spoils. The heart of many a young jockey, as well as many a fair maiden, has been broken in old Sydney town.

I nodded to the familiar faces, and wasn't hurt by the lack of warmth in their acknowledgment of my presence. I've been warned off every Australian racetrack for life, so I have the mark of Jonah on me. Put yourself in their places, especially the jocks. In this job you have to get up at four most mornings to ride track work. By yourself, you have to control half a tonne of one of the most highly strung animals on Earth. You risk broken bones or worse on the track, and the stewards can take your job away from you for a month or more when you least expect it. In this atmosphere, superstition runs rife, and jockeys do not need the company of a Jonah like me. My ban prohibited me associating with almost everyone in the room, but the café was still a public place. Not in the least slighted, I grabbed a table in the corner.

They won't let me onto a racetrack, but they can't take the racetrack out of me. There is just something about 500 kilos of steaming horse muscle with a temperament as fragile as a flower. You watch in awe as the tiny fearless jocks on top of these fractious giants try to transmit race strategy through the flimsy reins.

I can see the day when racing stables will have psychiatrists attached to them, as most other professional sports already have. Some of the psychiatrists will be for the jockeys. Others will demand full reports from the stud where a horse was foaled. What was its relationship with its mother? Did it show any recognition of its father when the sire came for another $5000 quickie with a strange mare? How did it react during its first thunderstorm? When this happens, all of the jockeys and most of the trainers will think the racing world has gone mad. But they will be silent. The jocks will continue to ride track work at four in the morning, go for a hated psych session at 6 and try to communicate strategy through the reins on race day.

At my favourite Feed Bin table, I read the form guide as I waited for my avocado on toast and coffee.

As my early breakfast arrived, a tiny voice spoke in my ear. 'Do you mind if I sit down, Mr Hill?'

I am only used to being called Mister by magistrates and dole officers, but Billy Scharfe's voice had respect, not sarcasm, in it.

'How you doing, Billy?' I replied. 'Pull up a pew; want some coffee?'

He declined. Billy Scharfe was an eighteen-year old apprentice jock. He wasn't the brightest lad about, and was not over-endowed with ability, but, Buddha, he was keen. I had gained Scharfe's gratitude at this same table six months earlier. When he had walked past my lucky table, I called out to him, 'You're Billy Scharfe, aren't you?'

The country lad was embarrassed at being recognised, but sat down. I had done my money on one of his mounts, a horse called Rasta, at its previous two starts, when it had run fifth and sixth. Scharfe had jumped the horse out well both times, but things did not happen the way either of us would have liked in the straight. Rasta was running the next day, and Scharfe was up again. The price in the paper was fourteen to one.

We started to talk about Rasta. We agreed the horse settled well in his races, which was a comfort to both jockey and punter. The big problem for Rasta was the changeover into top gear in the straight. From what I'd seen on the racing channel, it wasn't smooth enough; the horse became unsettled and couldn't concentrate for fifty metres or so. A lot of punters put it down to the inexperienced jockey, but I had more faith in humanity.

'Ever thought of leading on it?' I asked.

'Mr Harris don't want that,' Scharfe replied. 'He says blokes up front cut each other's throats in sprint races.'

Fred Harris was the horse's trainer and the apprentice's mentor, or boss, as the jockeys often called their master.

'Yair,' I said, 'but they might give you a bit of peace, because Rasta hasn't led before.'

'I don't think Mr Harris would like that.' But I could see Scharfe was thinking.

I softly nurtured those thoughts. 'You could say nothing else wanted to lead.'

'I don't think Mr Harris would believe that.'

I was betting Mr Harris would believe a cheque for the winning trainer's percentage.

'Worth thinking about it,' I said, and left it at that. Scharfe went away thinking.

When you look at it impartially, I did wrong by the lad. Trainers go all mental when senior jockeys, let alone apprentices, disobey riding instructions. If Rasta led and folded up badly in the straight, word might get around that Scharfe was a cowboy. Even the horse's winning was no guarantee against a backlash. Scharfe should not have been even talking to me. He was probably too dumb to know that and I was too smart to tell him.

Rasta won the next day, leading all the way at sixteen to one.

I won more than a thousand dollars. The kid retained the ride next start, and it led all the way again. After that, Scharfe was replaced by a senior jockey with a smooth gear change. Rasta came from midfield to win his third race in a row. Three jockeys had gone berserk in a mad speed contest in the early part of the race. The three jocks were all surprised that Rasta was not up there, joining in the chaos. Mr Harris received a trainer-of-the-month award, which included a seafood dinner for two.

Billy Scharfe still struggled for good mounts, but, for a while, trainers remembered him as the kid who won two races in a row on Rasta. Scharfe told me he was always careful not to disobey Mr Harris's instructions again. He did not tell me, but the grapevine did, that Mr Harris was always warning him about sitting at or near my table in the Feed Bin.

Sitting beside me six months down the track, Billy Scharfe was going against instructions again. The lad looked up, and my eyes followed his to watch a suit enter.

You do not see many suits in the Feed Bin. Even rich owners who brave the early morn go casual. The suit who had attracted Billy's attention was familiar to me. Marcus Georgio was a tall, lean, pro punter, noted for wearing thousand-dollar suits and million-dollar chicks. That morning, no female was latched on to the sleeve of his suit. Maybe they only came out on horse-racing afternoons and racy nights.

Neither Scharfe nor I knew Georgio well enough to even nod in his direction. We returned to our form guides, as he went for his coffee. Billy did not fancy either of his mounts for the next day, and I had no inspiration for him. A few minutes of chit chat, and Billy headed off to work.

I drank too much coffee and studied lots of form, for about

two hours. Most punters have given up studying the form closely, with so many race meetings to choose from. Big mistake. A punter should study the form of every horse in every race they are likely to bet on. If I followed my own golden rule, I might have been rich. Knowing what's good for you is a lot easier than doing what's good for you.

At 7:10, I walked into the morning light and home, to pick up the EH for the drive to West End and my interview. She doesn't like to start so early in the morning, but a few words of encouragement eventually did the trick.

I parked the ute outside the block of units. There was no sign of life as I walked down the front footpath. Units one and two were on the left, three and four were on the right. A curtain behind the glass panels blocked the view into Unit four. A glow of electric light framed the edges of the curtain.

I knocked on the glass-and-aluminium door of Unit four but got no answer for my trouble. I half-turned to go back to the car, but found the aluminium door handle slid across easily in my hand. And so I found myself standing in the office of Caulfield Jones, turfologist.

It was a little untidy. A glass was upturned near a wet spot in the carpet. A cigarette had burned a hole in the same carpet. White ash encircled the cigarette stub. And a man who I took to be Caulfield Jones was stretched out on the floor.

Except that I knew him as Marcus Georgio. If Georgio was Jones, why hadn't he said anything to me at the Feed Bin? We knew each other by sight and had exchanged a few words over time. Maybe he wanted to surprise me. He did surprise me. Marcus Georgio surprised me by being dead. Recent bad luck number three for me; worse for Georgio. At least his bad luck was over.

I am not real keen on looking at dead people, but I have to admit to a certain fascination. Georgio had a lot of holes in the shirt around his chest, from which blood was seeping and drying fast in the heat. He had holes in his imported silk tie and a couple in his $1000 suit. His relatives would have to patch up that suit coat before they donated it to a charity shop. His killer had been pretty liberal with bullets. None in the head suggested an amateur killer, maybe someone like me.

I pressed my face close to the edge of the curtain to see that there was no one outside. Still early for office stiffs. Pulling my shirt out from my trousers, I wiped the door's outside handle. I wiped the inside handle in the same way, with the shirt covering my hand. Without enthusiasm, I picked up Georgio's wrist with my shirt-covered hand to confirm he was brown bread. No pulse.

Adrenalin pumped through my body. Too many thoughts were coming at once, but I knew rushing out of the office would be a mistake. What do they do in the movies? They investigate. I looked around. Apart from an upturned glass and the dead body, which I had seen enough of, only a mahogany desk and swivel chair intruded into the musty air of the office.

The desk calendar told me that the thought for the day came from Salvador de Madariaga:

First, the sweetheart of the nation, then her aunt, woman governs America because America is a land where boys refuse to grow up.

I might have pondered this metaphysical message, but I was stopped in my tracks by the script in red ink above the de Madariaga wit. It read: Steele Hill 7:45 a.m. I carefully ripped out the entry, as well as the next five. That would give the cops something to think about, other than looking me up.

Checking out the rest of the sparse room, I could not find the ashtray that should have gone with the errant cigarette ash near the body. I left the light on, as it logically suggested Georgio's demise at a time before my appearance. I again used my covered hand to try a doorknob at the back of the room. It turned.

Hot and cold water taps perched above a sink. A coffee percolator bubbled happily on a bench covering a cupboard. I used a wash cloth to open a door to the cupboard. Inside were some detergent and bleach, nothing else. Turning around, I saw a tall, freestanding wardrobe with three framed photographs above it.

I opened the robe. Two French labelled shirts, a silk tie and two paisley ties were draped over hangers. A container of deodorant, socks and underwear lay on the floor. The spirit of Marcus Georgio as displayed in this robe was a lot more stylish than his representation in the other room.

I looked at the photos. They were prints of newspaper social-page pics, framed in black and silver. Kinda tacky and kinda upbeat, the framed newspaper cut-outs told the Georgio story precisely. Marcus Georgio and Dianne Usher are at a Gold Coast theme park. Marcus Georgio and Simone Freer watch a Gold Coast car race. Marcus Georgio and Crystal Speares sip champagne at Eagle Farm horseracing track during the Winter Carnival. All three women are beautiful in that plastic, social-page sort of way.

You might be wondering, just now, why a law-abiding citizen such as me, with no jail time, was so cautious about fingerprints. In theory, the authorities destroyed copies of my prints when I had my sentences suspended and was a good boy for the requisite period. But I am not one for theory when it comes to dealing with police. Besides, if the coppers got chatting with Ms Billings of the Employment Service, I knew they would quickly arrange a meeting between an inkpad and me.

I retrieved the de Madariaga wit from my shirt pocket and wrote the names of the three women above mine. Three more suspects took the edge off my red-lettered guilt.

The siren made me jump. I settled a little and thanked Buddha most coppers wanted to be Mel Gibson. If they had played it subtle, they could have been sticking a Ruger up my nose by now.

I clutched at the back door with my covered hand. No luck this time; it was locked. But the window above the sink was open. My exit would not have scored many points for elegance, but it was up with the best for speed. It would have been a graceful landing, had my heel not caught the gun.

If I told you I know next to nothing about guns, it would be the truth. This make of gun was the next to nothing I knew. It was a .38, a police .38. The first time one of these bang bangs was pointed at me, I almost laughed. They look like toys. The coppers had been replacing their .38s with Rugers and .357 Magnums over the years. Although of smaller calibre than the .38, the .357 looks much more menacing.

No doubt, some of the redundant .38s found their way into the nostalgic hands of those on the other side of the law.

On instinct, I slipped the thoughtlessly discarded gun into the pocket of my sports coat. I was clearing up after a messy killer, because I had a hunch this killer might be humble as well as untidy. Humble enough to give me the credit for their work.

My senses jangled, but I was confident the siren was still half a kilometre away, on the street parallel to Montague Road. I turned the EH into the next side street and waited. Sure enough, the cop car blasted past my street on its way to the scene of the crime. I waited and it seemed only the one police car was called to the scene.

I joined the stiffs' metal parade to work as I drove north towards my flat. I kept on driving to Toombul Shoppingtown, which has a car park bordering an artificial creek with the exotic name of Schulz Canal. The canal became the new owner of a police .38, carelessly left at a West End murder scene.

Strolling through the centre, I waited for various shops to open. I bought compact discs, food, clothing, and all sorts of stuff I did not need nor want. Buddha, how could I have killed anyone kilometres away at West End? At the time, I was in the savage grip of shopping mania at Toombul.

One thing I did want was a phone book. I looked up S. Freer. I jotted down an address and phone number, then flipped onto Speares. Bingo, C Speares at Ascot, an upper-middle-class suburb near Eagle Farm race track. As I have said, I lived near Eagle Farm too, at Hendra. But Ascot and working-class Hendra are light-years and billions of dollars apart. I dialled the number. Bingo indeed. 'Crystal Speares,' said a husky voice, soft but with an annoyed edge. I hung up.

To get to Unit five or to any unit in that block, you press a button beside a high gate, and give the intercom your excuse for bothering one of the good people of Ascot.

'Yes,' was all I got from Crystal Speares when I pressed the button.

I explained I had a message from Marcus Georgio. The gate swung open and I walked through, to climb a flight of brick stairs to Unit five.

Tiredness showed in her eyes, surrounded by cascades of blonde hair. She held the door open, but didn't seem inclined to let me in. The uninviting way she held the door only went to emphasise her firm breasts and rounded hips, barely concealed by a Country Road T-shirt. The leggy blonde was in her late twenties, and you could tell she could sprint with the best of them in the fast lane.

'What about Marcus?' Speares asked, with little interest.

'He's dead,' I said, untactfully.

At least she bothered to raise her eyebrows at that, making those green and black centred sockets even wider.

She turned, leaving the door open, and took a cigarette from a packet on a coffee table.

'Did you phone earlier?' she called from the lounge.

She was not taking the news badly enough for my liking. To give her something more to worry about, I lied. I had not rung. Closing the door, I joined her in the lounge room.

'Georgio had a car accident,' I lied again. You get on a roll once you start.

'Really,' was her only comment as she sat down on the sofa, revealing black panties as the T-shirt crawled up her thighs.

'No,' I corrected. 'That's right, he was shot.'

The eyebrows elevated again. 'Did you kill him?' she asked, as though inquiring how my morning had been so far.

'I came here to ask you the same question.'

She smirked at that, her most expansive reaction yet. 'I prefer my men alive, at least from the wallet up.'

'Did Georgio keep his wallet in his trousers pocket or his inside shirt pocket, near his heart, as far as you were concerned?'

It took a few seconds for Crystal Speares to get my smart-arse inference. When she did, she laughed. More responsive all the time. In twenty years, she might shed a tear.

At least the phone made her jump. She was in no hurry to answer it. It rang three more times before I asked, 'Is that the phone?'

Crystal Speares glared at me and grabbed the receiver, but was relieved to find the caller had hung up. She turned sharply in my direction. 'What do you want from me?'

As she did, I saw a hint of a bitter, fifty-year-old woman, whose effective hustling days were long gone. You can do it – see the face of a child in an old person, or see a young woman's face twenty-five years on. You can't look for it, only be aware when it's showing. I didn't want a thing from Crystal Speares. I just wanted to get out of there. I said I was only a messenger, hurried out the door and skipped down the stairs.

I was about to persuade the EH into gear when I saw a boyish figure walking past the units I had just left. Only, he did not walk past. He spoke into the intercom and was admitted. Apprentice jockey Billy Scharfe was paying someone a visit.

9

Summer, December, 1989

BUB'S ABANDONED PLAY *Waiting for Godot* had been due to finish on December 20, when Nat and I were supposed to go to the cast party. The cast and crew were looking forward to it. They had had to promise to work feverishly through their summer holidays in order to get semi-famous former student Alison Kahn on board, before the university would come up with the meagre budget for the production. They figured they deserved a party.

But murder and a one-night run had destroyed all enthusiasm for the scheduled knees-up. So Nat decided the three of us, in need of cheering up, should take in some of the entrants in the annual radio station Christmas Lights display contest. My Cucumber invited Bub to ease the pain of having the tyres slashed on her vehicle to Hollywood stardom. I figure a sadistic streak in Nat made her invite me.

Bub politely declined, saying she would rather drink a bottle of bat's piss while watching grass grow. I envied Jane Applebee her ability to openly express her feelings to her sister. I would have to go the long way around in verbalising my apathy for the event – a few dozen citizens putting up fancy party lights for the rest of us to gawk at. I was pencilled in for the evening's activities. I could have mounted a concerted campaign against the idea, and come across as more tactful than Bub, but I was conceding this point to Nat, planning to bring it up when next our ideas for a night out were deadlocked. The truth is, Nat must be obeyed sometimes, well actually a lot of the time. She has an unbending quality about her that I find mysteriously alluring. I am far more likely to cross My Cucumber by not consulting her before I do something which she later insists falls along the scale from unwise to fucking insane.

Still, I had a premonition that Christmas-lights watching would cause me pain. To ward off danger, I wrote down the addresses of eight promising entrants, having read somewhere that eight is a lucky number among Asian numerologists of various spiritual persuasions. My only selection criterion was each street being between our Hendra flat and Fortitude Valley. I was planning to amaze Nat with how close to the bright lights of rock music we had, by sheer chance, ended up. Under each street name, I wrote a brief description of how to get there, and I circled the addresses in my street directory.

What I had not bargained for was the difficulty of reading Brisbane street signs at night. It was stressful. Whenever I took my chances and averted my eyes from the street ahead to look at displays Natalie kept pointing out to me, I missed turns, wobbled across the roadway, and narrowly avoided hitting vehicles driven by other electric-light voyeurs. This annual hunt for Christmas lights must cause more than a few prangs.

By the time we found the third of our eight displays, I was sincerely wishing I could just go back to my flat, crawl into bed and berate myself for lacking Bub's courage in standing up to her sister. Apart from the navigational hiccups, it was a hot night and at each display, increasingly bizarre and elaborate with countless lights, Santas, reindeer and Baby Jesuses, I had escalating feelings of weirdness.

The snowball dropped at the fourth house, as I climbed

from the hot car into the hot atmosphere. Snow covered the sub-tropical windows and garage of a suburban house in mid-summer Brisbane. Crazed white-bearded men in thick red overcoats stood all over the garden. Deer were grazing and bearded elves, rugged up against the freezing cold, were making presents.

Ah, London's calling, I thought, *and we're out like mad dogs under the midnight moon, leaping at the phone.*

I couldn't wait to finish our tour of festive duty and take in some live hard rock in a crowded, dark and sweaty room at the Orient Hotel. Last Christmas the pub even put on snacks of olives, gherkins and small wedges of boutique cheese. I love the baby chesses at Christmas time.

THAT SAME DAY, of December 20 1989, 27,000 American troops invaded Panama in *Operation Just Cause,* to arrest that country's President Manuel Noriega for drug and arms smuggling. British Prime Minister Margaret Thatcher applauded the American invasion, for upholding 'the rule of democracy'. Only the cynics wondered if Mrs Thatcher was confusing ballistics with ballot boxes.

What sparked my interest in an otherwise routine U.S. invasion of a country they could wup purdy easy, was the use of rock music as psychological warfare. I suspect I was not the only shallow hedonist who forsook the music reviews for the world news pages at this time. I had to take a peek when I heard that Uncle Sam was shaking his booty.

I studied the form of the Noriega arrest with the Gooroo, who dubbed the invasion *Operation Just Cause We Can.* A lot of speculation about American motives for the stunt sprang up, as always happens with these adventures. The cynical money was on the treaty that said that the politically and financially strategic Panama Canal had to be handed over to a Panamanian girl or boy to play with by January 1, 1990. The landlord of the canal could charge a ship more than $100,000 for passage and the Americans had built most of it.

Most of the world never found out what was correct weight on the deal, as the Washington nobs reading from the full script were not giving the plot away. The stated reason for arresting Noriega – for drug trafficking – seemed a little thin, as the Americans had refused to take the naughty president from rebel members of the Panamanian Defence Forces when they had captured him in October. The Gooroo speculated that the planning of the invasion must have been well under way by then. The joint chiefs of staff were not going to have their big Christmas party upstaged by a few disgruntled nobodies in the Panamanian military. As for Manny's cocaine smuggling, human rights abuses and election rigging? His form suggested it was no better nor worse than when he was a friend of the US, purportedly on their payroll to the tune of a hundred grand a year to spy on the bad guys in the area, such as the reds in Cuba, Nicaragua and El Salvador.

As I say, my interest in such matters grew from international media stories about the hip ploy of rocking with the war machine. Armed Forces Radio playing rock music was nothing new – the practice was top of the charts in the Vietnam War. The aim then, though, was to raise the morale of the good guys, not to lower the spirits of the bad guys, or in this case The Bad Guy, Manny Noriega.

It seems that U.S. troops on the ground in Panama shared

our infatuation with the reports of rock weaponry. When the good news reported in the U.S. media rebounded to Central America, the soldiers on duty inundated military DJs with musical requests, thus reinforcing a budding myth.

International journos decided that rock music warfare was a better Sunday read than stories of thousands of Central American civilians being killed. They knew their readership tastes better than their history. Before the world press found Manny in the Vatican Embassy, they dutifully repeated military PR speculation that Noriega had probably fled to the Cuban or Nicaraguan embassies. But Manuel, for fun and profit, had been spying on those two socialist countries for the Americans.

Still, it made good sense to all the suburban hawks, stretched across their couches in the lands of the free, that the Cuban or Nicaraguan lefties had given shelter to the Antichrist. To make sure Noriega was demonised by all political persuasions, the military PR machine planted a photograph of Adolf Hitler in the President's unoccupied abode.

As it turned out, Manuel had taken refuge in the Vatican Embassy in Panama. The story of U.S. military blasting the embassy with rock music was embellished for the entertainment of all us citizens of the global village. As far as eyewitnesses could piece it together, the GIs had started to send in requests to their radio station for songs that they felt had anti-Noriega titles or lyrics. These requests were being played, but the music was not physically directed at Noriega until late in the piece.

One group of soldiers decided to direct their loudspeakers at the Vatican Embassy, perhaps as late as Boxing Day and certainly after the rock-music war was exaggerated in the world's newspapers. Once the quirky newspaper reports rebounded about the tactic of using rock music as a weapon, other groups of troops followed the leader and directed their speakers towards the hallowed ground.

It seems the Vatican complained to U.S. President George Bush about the racket, if not the tactic, and the practice stopped before Noriega surrendered on January 3. That part of the story rarely filtered out, and we were savouring the image of the Antichrist leaving the protection of the Vatican embassy and falling to his knees in tears.

'No more top forty, no more Twisted Sister's *We're Not Gonna Take It*,' we pictured Noriega begging of the troops besieging the Holy Ground.

Compared to the myth, the truth of the rock weaponry never lived up to its potential for drama and humour. Luckily for the spiritual nourishment of us global villagers, our educators in the international media printed the legend and not the truth. The juicy image of the Devil's music being strategically trained on an Embassy of the Holy City to smoke out the drug-peddling Antichrist became the reality.

The Gooroo had more contacts in Australia and overseas than the entire Australian secret service, so he was able to feed my obsession with the Panamanian proceedings with as much of the real news as possibly anyone here was receiving.

A lot of the requests to blast out Noriega were for rock classics by the Beatles, the Stones and the Hendrix Experience. Of course, Steppenwolf's *The Pusher* was a fave. Some historical selections bordered on the satirical. Outstandingly humorous examples included Paul Simon's *50 Ways to Leave Your Lover*, Springsteen's anti-authoritarian *Born to Run* and Funkadelic's weird *Electric Spanking of War Babies*.

Metal and hard rock dominated the requests for contemporary 1989 material. Metalheads White Lion earned their stripes with *Little Fighter*, while Danger Danger got *Naughty Naughty* on the playlist. As you might expect from the band's title, Guns 'n' Roses were in demand with *Patience* and *Paradise City* going for a few spins. Much of the American material really spoke to and about the invaders more than the besieged Noriega.

Paradise City was particularly unflattering, with its declaration that someone had done in Captain America.

If the ideals of the invaders had lost their way, the youthful soldiers imposing those ideals often had no way to lose. At least, that was the message Skid Row was screaming at Noriega through their 1989 hit *Youth Gone Wild*, a tough, anti-authoritarian anthem.

Some of the contemporary hits seemed to have a perverse undercurrent of sympathy for The Bad Guy, as with Megadeth's resurrection of the Alice Cooper hit *No More Mr Nice Guy*.

On Christmas Day, the DJs declared a break from playing the anti-Noriega requests, and they only spun Chrissy tunes. Hey, they might have played Bruce Springsteen's version of *Santa Claus is Coming to Town*, released on a single in 1985. New York hip hoppers Run–D.M.C. might have got a run with their infectious 1987 ditty *Christmas in Hollis,* the neighbourhood where the trio of rappers grew up.

In that year of 1989, the Bob Geldof and Midge Ure 1984 charity tune *Do They Know it's Christmas* was re-recorded. Both recordings raised money for relief of African famine. Maybe it was played when Santa Just Clause came to Panama.

The DJs probably gave Prince's 1984 epic ballad *Another Lonely Christmas* a miss as it recalled the death of a lover on Christmas Day.

They probably didn't play my Dad's 1971 release *Happy Xmas (War is Over)* either.

_____ooo_____

NAT WANTED TO GO to a midnight religious service on Christmas Eve rather than see in the festive day at a live music venue. I agreed when I found it was not going to be a staid Catholic service, but an all-singing, all-clapping affair at one of the more flamboyant churches. I am not bigoted against the Micks, despite the harsh road to Heaven the orphanage nuns dragged me along. But I had celebrated Christmas Eve for so long in secular merriment that song and dance were parts of my Yule ritual as much as tinsel and ornaments were to others. If we were to go to church, at the very least, it had to groove.

I was indulging in my third glass of red wine at 10 p.m. We had one of Nat's Madonna albums on, which is as close as we usually come to religious observance. All was very pleasant until My Cucumber tapped me on the shoulder and asked me not to drink any more.

'I'll make us a fruit punch,' she said.

'That will be nice,' I said.

'Without alcohol in it,' she said.

'That won't be so nice,' I said.

You make an effort to please the one you love and they tend to stretch the advantage they have over your joint historical course. Christmas in church sounded like a small sacrifice, and a new experience, but Nat could have forewarned me of the virtual teetotality expected to accompany it. If Natalie could have Madonna, I should be able to indulge in red wine – it was, after all, one of the Christmas colours. My limited Biblical scholarship told me that Christ, at the wedding feast, turned the water into wine, not into non-alcoholic fruit punch.

This line of argument did not go down well with Nat, unused as she is to compromise.

'You do what you bloody well like, Steele,' she said. 'You do every other day, anyway, so why should our attempt at a quiet, contemplative Christmas Eve be any different?'

I was spending our quiet contemplative Christmas Eve getting sloshed. What a pathetic yobbo. In contrition, I made an elaborate fruit punch without a drop of alcohol in it. I banished Natalie from the kitchen as I prepared it, ever so lovingly and slowly that I was able to consume two more glasses of red before contemplative sobriety overwhelmed me as Nat and I sipped punch amid Madonna's stereophonic assault. At 11:45, Nat drove us to church, though I said we should have walked with Frank's incense and mirth.

It was a nifty service with the highlight, for me, the singing of the hymn *Onward Christian Soldiers*. Thoughtfully, the Christian mob running the do had provided hymn books – if you can call four A4 pages, folded and stapled, a book. After my fave religious song's title, it even had the names of the Pommy geezers what done it: 'Words by Sabine Baring-Gould (1865) and music by Arthur Seymour Sullivan (1871),' it read.

One of my embedded myths was destroyed by that attribution. I always fancied American soldiers of the civil war had made that song up around the campfire after a hard day at the front lines, killing and being killed. This harsh history lesson did not, however, prevent my relishing a song that expressed the true bloody spirit of Christmas and bugger the herald angels singing.

As I joined in the rousing verses and chorus, I thought, this was what they should be using to smoke out Noriega:

Satan's host doth flee;
On then, Christian soldiers, on to victory!
Hell's foundations quiver at the shout of praise;
Brothers, lift your voices, loud your anthems raise.
Onward, Christian soldiers, marching as to war,
With the cross of Jesus going on before.

I kept the hymn sheets as a souvenir for the Gooroo, for when we went down the Coast to see him on Boxing Day. I expressed my admiration for the prescient lyrics about Satan's host Noriega. The Gooroo was quite taken with his present. He said he had heard that one half of the Gilbert and Sullivan operetta team wrote the music to *Onward Christian Soldiers*, and now it appeared confirmed.

The Gooroo said that some American versions of the song deleted my favourite stanza about Satan's host. Most Americans profess to belief in God, but quite a few take exception to the notion of there being an immortal Satan in opposition. When America imported the song, its citizens decided to exorcise the Devil from the lyrics. Their spirituality allows only for lesser demons such as the Antichrist Noriega to be disarmed by the forces of the Good with Guns.

<u>10</u>

Autumn, May 1990, in Brisbane

SIPPING CLARET AT THE BAR of the Beat nightclub, I was wondering whether the dancer enjoyed his job.

He was covered from toe to tip in oil and not much else – one leather-and-feather anklet, a G-string and a cowboy hat.

The Beat's moniker pretty much tells the story: a gay nightclub in Brisbane's Fortitude Valley.

My Cucumber Natalie believes that gays bear sole responsibility for the evolution of Madonna, Japanese restaurants in Australia, and twentieth-century drama, all of which she holds very dear. Nat feels obliged to participate in the gay social scene on an irregular basis. I could not get Nat to any my cultural shrines, the major metropolitan racetracks on Australia's east coast, before I was barred from them all. But, somehow, I have to tag along with her for the occasional evening of disco music accompanied by the smell of amyl nitrate. I tried to spot her in the thick, heaving Friday night crowd. Nat likes talking with strangers. I noticed a bloke watching me.

I turned my attention back to the television above my head. Queensland Treasurer Keith De Lacey was announcing that the social-democratic Labor Party would honour some of the financial promises of defeated conservative National Party Treasurer Mike Ahern. Labor was elected in December, mainly as a result of the police corruption uncovered by the Fitzgerald

Inquiry. Tax relief for religious organisations and religious education were two of Ahern's budgetary measures that Labor would keep. I was kind of getting the gist of his concession through the din, with Treasurer De Lacey chanting some mantra about education being sacred, as Queensland was becoming the Smart State.

A voice, belonging to the bloke who had been eyeing me off, spoke close to my ear.

'Hello,' he said.

He was about fifty, grey suit, greying hair, thin furrowed greying face, medium build. What Americans might call distinguished. As far as I know, distinguished people are like eccentrics; we don't have any in Australia.

'Gooday,' I said, nodding.

'I'm not looking to pick you up,' he said. 'My name is Joseph Lavinsky.'

I gave my name as Steele Hill, as I do most of the time.

'I'm a professor at the university,' Lavinsky said. He also said which university, but to protect the innocent, I won't repeat it. The guilty don't need protecting, as they usually have a mob of lawyers on retainer.

Oh, all right then. It was the University of Queensland, which I believe is the State's oldest. You might have guessed, anyway, as there are not many unis in Brisbane. The way the professor was referring to it as **the** university, it looks like its academics think of it as the only fair-dinkum one. I suppose if you can't have snobbery in places of higher learning, where does it belong?

Lavinsky asked what I was drinking, and I tapped the last pickings of my red grape. It looked like his tale was to unfold leisurely.

'I'm worried about my students,' the prof began.

'Who isn't? They tell me the three Rs are up to ess.'

Lavinsky either didn't know or didn't care I was taking the piss. 'They are so sheltered these days, my students,' he continued.

He turned away from me when a barman approached, and he ordered a bottle of the club's best red. The barman said they sold wine by the glass.

'Fine,' replied the professor. 'I'll have five and a one fifth glasses of wine. In the bottle. Thank you.'

The barman went to consult with another bloke, and Lavinsky began to sing in a harsh Irish accent while he awaited the decision.

Now that my ladder's gone,
I must lie down where all the ladders start,
In the foul rag-and-bone shop of the human heart.

The barman returned with a bottle of red, from which Lavinsky poured a glass for me and a thimbleful for himself.

'Driving,' he muttered.

I asked him if the song he had sung was from the Irish folk-rock band The Pogues, because he sang it in the rough and ragged style of the band's lead singer Shane MacGowan.

'William Butler Yeats,' Lavinsky said. 'Great poet. As far as I know, he was never in a popular musical group.'

The professor changed the subject. 'I'm looking for someone like you, somewhat representative of the underclass. I hope you are not offended by that term. I find "underclass" less patronising than "lower working class".' He opened his eyes wide and nodded three times at me. 'Do you agree?'

'Very much so,' I answered. Always agree with whackos: first rule of life on the streets.

'From looking at you, I feel you fit to a tee,' he decided. 'Sharp, inquisitive, but wary, looking out for the next obstacle in your path.'

I took a swig of my wine and thought the well could dry up with my next comment. 'Look, Mr Lavinsky, I don't know what two-legged lab mouse you want for your students, or what that mouse is supposed to do, but you're knocking on the wrong maze here.'

On cue to my maze metaphor, the Beat's speaker system pumped out the chorus of the Go-Betweens' *Your Town*.

Round and round, up and down
Through the streets of your town.
Every day I make my way
Through the streets of your town.

The rumours of the previous summer proved right. The Go-Betweens did announce their break-up in the first half of 1990. Everyone said it was a shame. By everyone, I mean the small fraction of the Australian population who had heard of them.

'Sorry,' said Lavinsky. I had clearly declined his offer and he moved his chair back, as you would when you're leaving.

Only, he was just making himself more comfortable. 'I did not even tell you what I teach. It's Cultural Studies.'

'Yogurt?' I asked, which puzzled him till the penny dropped. Then he laughed more heartily than the quip deserved.

I continued. 'I don't know what Cultural Studies is; I don't know what an underclass is, and it's odds-on I won't know whatever else it is you have to tell me.'

I guess you need persistence to end up as a professor. 'That's just it, Steele. You speak a different language to my students. All I want you to do is to talk them through your lifestyle.'

'You don't even know me, Joseph. I might be an accountant in a bank.' I stood up and started to walk away, to find My Cucumber.

'As a guest speaker, you could earn probably $500, maybe a thousand.'

Now he had sparked my intellectual curiosity. 'Can you write down all the details, and tell me if I need to wear a silly cap?'

It turned out that Joseph Lavinsky wasn't a bad style of bloke. All he wanted was for some youngish, street-smart person, with a few run-ins with the coppers, to lay it on thick for his students. He told me this in a lot of big words, but I figured, if the truth were known, he was boring his students shitless with his enriched brain fodder. All he wanted from me was a few half-lies to keep them awake for an hour or two. I could do that.

To show I was giving value for money, I told him about the subsequently defrocked nun from the orphanage where I was raised. She insisted I was John Lennon's lovechild. I added I did not believe it myself but shrugged my shoulders to suggest it could be true. It was an old routine of mine and it worked best out on the street when I could raise my granny sunglasses to reveal my honest eyes as I also raised my shoulders to indicate impartial scepticism. The bit had a reasonable indoor strike rate as well.

Lavinsky looked closely into my face. 'Your disbelief is wise,' he said. 'You look nothing like John Lennon.'

I quickly changed the subject, or, more precisely, I allowed

Lavinsky to leap from topic to topic. Then I made a mistake. During one of his raves, I said he was wasting all his philosophical musings on me; that he should talk to my SP bookie mate, the Gooroo. The professor perked up.

He wanted to know whether the Gooroo was a convert to Hinduism. I told him I had given Gooroo the moniker, derived from an Aboriginal word for 'deep place' or something like that. Lavinsky wanted Gooroo's phone number. I thought I had just talked myself out of the gig, but Lavinsky assured me that I was still the pea for the job.

When I told Nat about my uni gig, she was keen on the notion of my placing myself in a room full of students. I think she hoped some of that erudition might rub off on me. She said she would take the day off work to sneak into the lecture but I made her promise not to do that.

<u>11</u>

THE NOTE WAS STUCK TO THE DOOR of Lavinsky's unit in the middle-class suburb. It told me the keys to the professor's unit and four-wheel-drive wagon were in the letterbox. What a trusting fellow. The professor had ridden his pushbike to uni and I could take the 4WD, if I liked. I liked, and slid into the driver's seat of the green Toyota Landcruiser V8, leaving the ancient EH ute to fend for itself in this rich people's street.

I wonder what the poor greenies are doing this evening, I thought. Evening it was, 6:30 on a Tuesday. The greenies would be tucking into their lentil soup, as I gunned the 4WD to meet my date.

With murder.

'He's got a killer smile,' said Clarissa Dunne, as we stood outside the lecture theatre at ten to seven.

No one else was around to hear the teenager's appreciation of Professor Lavinsky's mouth. My guest appearance was scheduled for seven and I had checked with Dunne, a pale-skinned attractive redhead, that I was at the right place.

I pondered how a woman some eight years my junior had come to notice the fatal smile of a professor some thirty years my senior. I prompted Clarissa to expand on her appreciation of the professor.

'Do you really understand what he's on about?' I asked.

'Sort of. It's only my first year at uni. I'm still learning the ropes.'

I persisted, displaying all the commercial savvy half a working life on the dole imparts to you. 'But what good is this Cultural Studies stuff going to do you?'

'I'm studying arts-law.'

I volleyed. 'I've never met any lawyers with 'arts.''

'Aven't you?' she replied. It's great to talk to educated folks who can appreciate a bad pun.

Joseph Lavinsky hurtled around the corner of the corridor and lent us his killer smile. 'Clarissa. And you have met Mr Steele Hill, our guest lecturer for tonight.'

I raised my eyebrows at being made a lecturer without so much as having to cut out an application form for a dodgy correspondence school.

'I have, Joe,' she replied. 'And I'm sure he is going to be witty, incisive and thought-provoking.'

'Or your money back,' I added. 'But then you don't pay fees, do you?'

Dunne and Lavinsky looked at each other to see if I was making a cryptic joke. It was plain I had said something stupid.

'I thought tertiary education was free in Australia,' I defended myself.

'It was,' Lavinsky replied, embarrassed by my stupidity. 'For a little while, but we are now in the era of "user pays".'

His student steered the subject away from my ignorance. 'What's your lecture about, Mr Hill?' asked Clarissa Dunne.

'I'm glad you asked,' I said, and I was. It was about time for me to think about that. 'I've given it a lot of thought.'

Totally untrue, but I couldn't tell the young woman that the lecture was about five hundred to a thousand dollars. I got in some practice for winging it. 'Part of it is about the question, if we citizens are supposed to intuitively understand our rights and obligations under law, then why do we pay lawyers hundreds of thousands a year to interpret laws for us?'

Lavinsky was pleased. 'I told you last week, Clarissa, we were in for a treat tonight.'

I was pretty pleased myself. I didn't understand what I had said, but it sounded good. Excusing us both to Clarissa, Joseph Lavinsky tugged my arm towards a corner. 'I feel bad about this,' he said.

I all but groaned. That had to be the straight man's opening to my punchline: 'not half as bad as I'm going to feel'. Sure enough, I was about to be stiffed.

'Not even $500,' I moaned.

Lavinsky shook his head.

'$250?'

Shake of the head. The cultural studies department of the university with a multi-million dollar budget was giving me an expenses allowance of fifty dollars.

I had to vent a protest, though I knew it would be useless. 'But you said . . . I mean, that can't be right . . . look, you're the professor of this whole show, you should be able to fix it.'

Lavinsky joined in the bluster, defending himself. 'But I'm not head of department; it rotates, and Jan Russo's got it at the moment. I'm not even sure that Jan could have got you anywhere near the payment we talked about. Still, it's my fault. I was complaining about my kids being naive. I don't even know how the university works anymore, let alone how to get around those workings to make it morally accountable.'

I was deflated and beyond further protest. 'Let's just do it, professor. Every rock band in the world has been stiffed on more than one occasion. I'll put it down to entertainment that won't cost me anything.'

'That's the spirit,' he said.

Yair, I thought, *the spirit is willing, but the wallet is weak.*

About 100 bodies trundled into the lecture theatre. How many minds and spirits were attached to those bodies, I couldn't guess. I knew one of the bodies at least had an active mind, as I saw Jane 'Bub' Applebee settling into a corner of the last row of seats. I knew that Bub had transferred from Kelvin Grove campus of the Brisbane College of Advanced Education to the University of Queensland after the unfortunate death of Suzanne Lu at La Boite Theatre. It hadn't occurred to me that she might be doing a Cultural Studies unit as well as drama.

Or that she might have given me up to Lavinsky as the kind of underclass representative he wanted. The Professor probably thought his young student was currying favour, but this was another of Bub's sick jokes. She knew Nat and I were going to the Beat that night; she probably suggested the professor would profit from being there as well. In the distance, Jane's right hand protruded above the bench in front of her seat and she waved her fingers up and down. I did my best to ignore her, but couldn't stop myself from shaking my head in her direction.

The professor introduced me as a hybrid of the Kellys – bushranger Ned and folk-rock singer Paul – grafted on to the mean streets of Brisbane. Without a word of a lie, he used the words 'mean streets'.

I opened with the line that, as I hung about Chinatown, they would have to be 'chow mean' streets. I dredged for sympathy by mentioning my upbringing in an orphanage. Most stared up at me like cattle. I didn't know if I was doing well or slowly dying. So I pictured the Gooroo sitting there in the middle of it all, with a mug of tea in his hand, in his comfortable armchair.

That made the bullshit flow more easily.

I was about to tell them how I had changed my name by deed poll to Steele Hill after the billboard I saw when I left the orphanage. But I wondered if these hip teenagers would think I had done a daggy deed. For similar reasons, I did not say my best mate was a sixty-year-old illegal bookmaker, called Gooroo, after an Aboriginal word for deep place or something like that.

Leaving out my being told I was John Lennon's lovechild was the hardest. I figured the odds were, only a fraction of the class would believe me even when I added the ambiguous clincher I did not quite believe it myself. Quickly weighing up the odds, I decided to ditch the Lennon bit, but it was a photo-finish decision. If a few students sought me out for a post-gig discussion, I would bring Lennon out then.

I told the students of my love for horse racing, and how I was unjustly barred from all Australian racetracks for life. For simply doing my job, placing a few bets – well okay, a lot of bets – on a rank outsider.

I'm a good spieler, even if I do say so myself, once I get warmed up, and forty minutes flew by. When Lavinsky called for a break, sighs of protest preceded much applause for my efforts. I was quite surprised at that, because I had told only as much of the truth as I felt you should give a bunch of stiffs without sacrificing your self-respect.

Lavinsky said the break would be fifteen minutes, and we would play the second part by ear, as a question-and-answer session, letting it run until all concerned had had enough or wished to retire to the nearby Royal Exchange Hotel for port, cigars and more bullshit. Well, okay, Lavinsky did not say the pub part, but I figured enough kindred spirits in the audience would join me in the hotel and some city haunts to while away the night. My lousy $50 fee would cover a few wines and the taxi fares after I handed Lavinsky the keys to his Landcruiser

The professor indicated for me to follow him up a flight of stairs, and down a corridor. He stuck his head in after opening a door. The nameplate read *Postgraduate English Students*.

'I hope you're looking after those computers,' Lavinsky said to no one in particular of the four students hunched over keyboards.

His head popped back out the door as quickly as it had invaded the room.

As we walked on down the corridor, I asked him what that was about. The English students were getting new 486 computers, he told me, and Cultural Studies would inherit the hand-me-downs from that room. Just on spec, I looked back to take in the room number.

We came to an office bearing Lavinsky's name and designation, but scurried past it and into a staff room. Four people sat about, three of them drinking alcohol: two glasses of red wine and one scotch. The fourth was a cola.

One of the red wines I had already met – the vibrant Clarissa Dunne, who had beaten us there from the lecture. Then again, I suspected her as a fast mover. The other red wine was a woman in her early forties, thin, glasses, wrinkles, and a face that hinted at a history of beauty savaged by late nights doing whatever. The scotch was her male alter ego – also thin, mid-forties, ravaged.

The cola was a drop-dead-gorgeous teenage girl, obviously too young to be a uni student. She was the first to speak, as we entered the room. 'ProJoe,' she said to Lavinsky. 'You made it.'

I noticed the female forty-something red wine wince.

'Of course, Cassandra. But shouldn't you be studying Greek mythology, if that is still your latest fancy?' Lavinsky teased.

Cassandra did not get a chance to answer, as the professor wheeled on the older woman to introduce me. 'Jan, this is Steele Hill, our lecture guest. Steele, this is Jan Russo, our head of department. Precocious Cassandra here is Jan's daughter.'

We exchanged nods and mutters, and Lavinsky turned to the scotch – Steven Dupont, senior lecturer, though Lavinsky said senior lecher, a pretty lame joke, even by liberal academic standards.

Lavinsky's weak jibe offended Dupont. 'At least I don't cavort in a 4WD,' he retorted, 'the fuck truck of the middle-aged Aussie male.'

Was I detecting a bucketful of hostility here? You bet.

I took the glass of red I was offered, as it seemed a useful prop. But I really needed to do a deal before I went back for the second half of the lecture. I downed the wine and excused myself.

I tried a few of the keys Lavinsky had left for me and opened the door to his office. No surprises: wall-to-wall books lined two shelves of the cramped cubicle; papers were strewn over the desk, and a telephone sat on top of a book called *Eros Revisited*. I leafed through the thick pages, containing scholarly text above and below obscene drawings, etchings and paintings. *Porno for Pundits* would have been a suitable subtitle. I put the book back under the phone and dialled.

The Gooroo answered the phone from his unit. I told him the computers were not hot; they were payment for a job I was doing. I said he could have the lot for a grand. He should enter the twentieth century, when we were so close to the twenty-first. The Gooroo still wasn't quite sold. He wanted to know for whom I did the job. I was mildly offended at the inference that I might be trying to pass off dodgy goods, but I gave Lavinsky's name, thinking it couldn't do any harm.

Not such a good idea.

'Joseph? Why didn't you say so? We had quite a yak the other night. Three hours yarning. We talked about everything from semiotics to sex.'

'You're slipping, Gooroo. I thought you would say "everything from aardvark to zoon". But what's this about Lavinsky and sex? Do you reckon he could be a pants man, Gooroo?'

'I'd say so, Steele. Didn't you get that impression?'

'Kinda,' I admitted. 'But he struck me more of an eleven-letter word man than a four-letter one.'

Silence at the other end suggested the bookie was doing some calculations.

'Like fornication,' countered the Gooroo.

I laughed and conceded the point. I asked Gooroo if Clarissa Dunne, Jan and Cassandra Russo or Steven Dupont had cropped up in his conversation with Lavinsky. Dupont, Gooroo remembered.

'Lot of bad blood there,' he said, obviously meaning between the two academics.

When I asked for more info, all the bookie would say was I should ask Lavinsky.

I did on the way back to the lecture hall, after the Gooroo had promised he would spring for the grand for the computers. The professor, as you would expect, came up with a parable that I would have to sift through for an answer.

'You know how a commercial painter's houses is always in need of a paint job, and the pipes always groan in a plumber's place?' Lavinsky said. 'Well, Dupont is the chair of our Ethics Committee. Our equivalent of the unkempt painter's walls is making the morally bankrupt the head of an Ethics Committee.'

'Cream may rise, but curdled cream is sure to surface,' I said.

'What he does,' Lavinsky said, 'is trade passing grades for sex with his students.'

'I see,' I replied, 'and you don't think that's much chop.'

He swung it back on me. 'Do you, Steele?'

I was unimpressed with the display of professorial indignation. I made a pretty good guess about Lavinsky's own behaviour. 'But what if a lecturer uses his image as the refined intellectual to help himself to the odd bit of extracurricular indoor sport? Wouldn't that be pretty much the same?'

Lavinsky wouldn't wear this. 'You make the same logical mistake as so many of my callow students. To be truthful, Steele, that same sort of mistake is made by too many of my colleagues. You have not recognised degrees of behaviour. You can't excuse a deplorable act by saying it is only taking another act to the nth degree.'

That sort of made sense. Kinda.

The second set of my gig was uneventful, except when Clarissa Dunne asked a question. Did I agree with Goffman that prisons should be seen as total institutions? I answered truthfully that I didn't read the papers much and asked what Goffman was in for. Guffaws of laughter from some of the students woke those who had dozed off. I gave the laughers the benefit of the doubt that the mirth was with me and not at me.

Dunne explained Goffman was some Canadian bloke from the 1960s who wrote that prisons, and places like them, were total institutions. When the stiffs put you into these institutions, the screws went on with a little number Goffman called 'mortification of the self'. The way Dunne told it, this Goffman must have taken his inspiration from that 50s sci-fi movie *Invasion of the Body Snatchers*. With this mortification number, the boss stiffs took away your personality or soul or self-concept or whatever, and replaced it with their own understanding of the world. There was more blah to Dunne's explanation than that, but, to tell you the truth, I only half-listened.

If these kids were dredging the 1960s for inspiration, why didn't they go to half-forgotten rock bands like the Kinks or the Who. It worked for me.

I didn't even try to answer Dunne's question. I told my audience it had been my so-far successful ambition to stay out of jail. I advised them to do the same. Crims were not glamorous, I said. The coinage of prison was violence, I said. And you don't get much worthwhile change from that, I said. It got a few stray claps. But I swear some of them looked at me as if I was a goody-two-shoes who'd sneaked in with a false passport.

I left the argument with a horticultural analogy. The way I understood it, thirty years ago you went to jail because you didn't have enough cabbage. Today, you went to jail because you had too many derivatives of the opium poppy. Clarissa Dunne smiled at that and left the room. I saw Professor Joseph Lavinsky follow her out after he had a quick conversation with a woman in her thirties. I found out afterwards Lavinsky had told her to wrap up the lecture.

Ten minutes later, questions over, I took my bows and found my way back to the postgraduate English students' room. I was glad to see four youngsters still playing with their digitals. I introduced myself as Mark Caine from First Degree Computers. I'd come to replace four computers and a printer with new 486s. No one said anything, except for one young woman who asked if they could give me a hand. I said sure.

I was grateful that they let me carry the lightweight printer. The four able bodies and sound minds wound electrical tentacles around the computer screens, placed each screen on its rectangular box and awkwardly and slowly followed me down to the car park.

The plan hit an almighty snag when I went to open the driver's door of the four-wheel drive to release the back door of the wagon. I quickly made some lame excuse about having to rearrange the boot, and asked the students to put the gear on the asphalt. Thank Buddha for unsuspicious minds. They did what I asked.

It shouldn't have taken me what seemed half the night to put the computers in the wagon. But I kept jerking my head around in every direction, responding to imagined footsteps. With the task done and me in the driver's seat, I felt better. Still not good.

And worse when the beautiful teenager Cassandra Russo rapped on the passenger-side window. I resisted the urge to drive off, groaned, threw the printer from the front seat to the back and opened the window.

'How about a lift, seeing you're obviously ProJoe's favourite at the moment and he's lent you his car?' she asked brightly.

I stalled, making no movement towards the lock on the door. 'Where's your mother?'

She shrugged, saying she was not her mother's keeper. Not wanting to stick around debating the issue, I unlocked the catch on the door. Cassandra's handbag flew onto the floor of the cab and she jumped onto the seat beside me. I carefully reversed the four-wheel drive.

I only turned on the lights as we left the car park. The car park where lay the body of Professor Joseph Lavinsky. That body had at least four bullet holes where flesh and bone should have been. A hole in the head and a trio or more around the heart.

This dead professor was the same one who ripped me off to the tune of a promised grand. A fact department head and Cassandra's Mum Jan Russo knew full well.

I was driving away in the dead professor's top -of-the-range $70,000 car, loaded with stolen computer gear and Jan Russo's teenage daughter.

12

I ONCE HEARD AN OLD DIGGER say there are no atheists in a fox hole, and I certainly called out the Lord's name under my breath as I pondered how to get out of this hole that someone had dug for me.

Captured Panamanian president Manuel Noriega had only been a trifling few months of early 1990 in a Florida nick when he found the Lord. Manny wanted to be born again, immersed in the waters, baptised, call it what you like. The screws were considering the idea, but Manny's own lawyers put the kybosh on the deal. They said their client's new identity as the Redeemed was too much for a suspicious American audience to grasp only months after his headlining role as the Antichrist.

If the coppers caught me late at night in a murdered man's car with an under-aged girl by my side, I would have nothing to look forward to but a judge's vilification as one of the Antichrist's low-life trainees. A judge's self-righteous sermon I could stomach, but a fifteen-year sentence on top would be hard to swallow.

'Where to?' I said, asking myself as much as the teenager tearaway.

At a time when I should have become immune to surprises, her answer surprised me. 'The Go Kat Klub, it's in . . .'

I told her I knew where the club was. I drove straight towards Fortitude Valley, reckoning I'd ditch the girl fast. If she wished to go to a notorious dance club at 10:30 at night, as far as I was concerned, it was as appropriate as her having supper at her grandmother's. I did ask her age though. She was fifteen.

As we turned into Wickham Street, I asked if she was still going to school. Of course she was. She was coming fifth in her class. She could be coming first, but it wasn't worth being hassled as a braniac, so she put down some wrong answers. This was fun because she could tease her teachers, who couldn't understand how she could be so dumb at times. As she opened the door to get out near the Go Kat Klub, I had to ask. I pointed towards the two Goliaths, standing on bouncer duty to illustrate the ambience of the place.

I looked at the teenager, too smart for her own good. 'You remind me of a lad I saw years ago, forced to race at school against his will,' I said. 'He was a mile behind the rest of the field. Only you're a mile ahead of the field.'

She didn't appreciate my conversational drift and let fly with sarcasm. 'And you're the working class hero of the masses with nothing but a borrowed car and a pocketful of self-righteousness. It's been fun, Steele, but I gotta go.'

She got out of the Landcruiser and walked towards the entrance of the Kit Kat Klub.

'So what are you doing here, Cassandra?'

Cassandra Russo turned and replied casually. 'I work here.'

'You know the difference between the running lad and you?'

'No, and I don't care.'

'He allowed himself to cry.'

Cassandra half-opened her mouth but said nothing. She turned her head and tottered off on her heels into the club.

I toyed with the idea of driving the Landcruiser to Sydney, selling it and splitting the country. I was picturing the passport in my bedside drawer. I've never used it, but they've never taken it from me.

Still, I'm a Brisbane boy. Two thirds of my life spent in an orphanage in this city could not take Brissie out of my soul. Nothing could.

Outside the professor's unit, I swapped the computers over to my Holden ute. I still had the key to Lavinsky's unit in my pocket, and I decided to have a quick poke around. How much deeper could I get into this hole? There were lot of photos inside – Lavinsky with a boy and a girl growing into woman and man, taken over a period of twenty or so years. None of a woman around the professor's own age. Smells like divorce.

The first message on the answering machine simply said, 'Get off my case, you bastard.'

I had heard that voice earlier that day, and it did not take me long to give it a name: Steven Dupont.

Message two was a reminder about a symposium Lavinsky was supposed to speak at. Unless the topic was spiritualism, the professor would not be contributing.

Message three was from Clarissa Dunne, apologising for her part in an argument they had had. She would see the professor, also sometimes known as darling, tomorrow. That was a longshot and if she did see him, unless she had killed him, she wouldn't much like the shape he was in.

The next message started, 'Hey, ProJoe, have you been avoiding me?'

We all know who that one was from.

'Well, let me warn you . . .,' continued Cassandra Russo. She hung up, without finishing the warning.

I wiped the answering machine, the front doorknob and the 4WD clean, posted all the corpse's keys into his letterbox and pointed the EH towards the coast.

The Gooroo poured me a coffee, a port and ten hundred-dollar bills for the computers before I told him Lavinsky was dead. He didn't flinch.

'Murder seeks you out again, Steele Hill. Or am I wrong?'

I nodded grimly, and gave Gooroo a run-down of my evening.

The Gooroo considered for a moment and decided, 'This Dupont, he's the villain what done this dastardly deed.' He continued, 'Lavinsky and Dupont may have been competing lovers of the same woman. Or maybe Lavinsky was going to expose Dupont for his sexual blackmail of students.'

I was buying this. 'So, Gooroo, I've got to nail Dupont.'

There wasn't much percentage in my going back to the uni in the hope that the guilty party had been uncovered and I could strut the walk of a free and innocent man. But there was one place I could go. Where there was a smart girl who could have been top of her class, only she was too clever for that. I knew a girl who knew a lot, inside and outside of university. I apologised to Con Vitalis for leaving him to go back to the place I had just left. He understood and we unloaded the computer gear into his garage.

The Go Kat Klub is the sort of place where you go if you are eighteen to thirty, wear expensive clothes and have access to lots of spending money, either your own or someone else's. It is open till 5 a.m. so I was fashionably lateish at two in the morning. Once inside, you danced a bit, socialised a lot and drank caffeine-saturated soft drinks and litres of water. If you can't work out what else you took, you probably think clubbers are those nasty people who kill baby seals.

Ignoring the mirrors, flashing lights and pulsating noise, I checked out the inhabitants, about 300 of them. A good racket for somebody but no sign of Cassandra Russo.

'Nice jacket, sweetie,' said a voice in my ear.

He was a tall, thin, redheaded man in his early twenties.

'Yair, I know,' I said dryly. 'And one of these years it's going to come back into fashion, right?'

The snappily dressed redhead was hurt. 'No, I meant it; I really like it,' he said.

I apologised, as he picked up a glass from a plastic-and-steel table welded into a pillar. He had some stamp of authority, so I asked him if Cassandra Russo was in.

'Who?' he asked, in a voice that told me he knew the girl, but he was not the sort to meet and tell. 'Excuse me, I have to serve some customers,' he said and went over to a group of four young people, two of them men.

It wasn't bar service, because the two blokes followed him to the male toilet. The transaction was brisk. By the time I had a glass of red in my hand, the blokes returned. The redhead went to chat with a monster in a white shirt and bow tie. They both looked in my direction, and I smiled back at them.

The redhead disappeared behind the bar, and the monster came over to me.

'Mr Malone will see you now,' he said softly, as if he was a diminutive office secretary.

'He's already seen me. Wasn't much of an interview.'

'That was Mr Franks you saw. Mr Malone will see you now.'

The penny dropped. 'Oh, you mean that Mr Malone.'

That Mr Malone. Frank Malone was the one Irish name that cropped up among the mostly Italian monikers of Fortitude Valley's night-life businessmen, men who the local press would call 'colourful'. This was code for 'crooked', not a reference to their ties or silver jewellery, though there was plenty of that too. I had never met Malone, but I had seen his short, fat and fortyish body stalking the half-dozen or so Valley streets that were his playground.

I followed my huge guide behind the bar, through an empty kitchen and to a room with 'no admittance' on the door. I was admitted.

Four bar stools, covered in black vinyl, sat on one wall of the surprisingly large office. A big rectangular table was across one corner with enough room on either side for someone to get in and out. Behind the desk, a massive leather armchair bulged, and inside it sat the squat frame of Francis Malone.

He looked at me and I looked at the thick green carpet attached to all the walls, giving the place the appearance of a soundproofed recording studio.

'Do I know you?' asked Malone without rising from his chair.

'You may have seen me around. I'm Steele Hill.'

Malone's eyes were red and darting every which way in his head. He looked like he was having a stockbroker's Christmas party all by himself. He was coked up to the max.

'So what the fuck are you doing, coming into my club, asking questions?'

'You mean questions about an under-aged girl who claims to work here.'

'You say I'm running hookers from here. Listen, pal, I charge eight bucks to get in; I charge five dollars for a short nip of watered-down bourbon: what the fuck do I need with hookers?'

'Strangely enough, though,' I said, 'not too many of your customers seem to fancy that bourbon.'

Malone sniffed and played with his nose as he got up from

his armchair. 'You stay right there. Don't you fucking move!'

I was pleased to see him dart through a back door rather than out the front way, where the monster was on guard duty. He came back in a few minutes, but he had not fetched anything from the next room. I guessed he had gone for a snort, his version of a coffee break. He was a little calmer.

'This is a dance club. All our customers are young. Some of the young bucks get lonely. So we have young girls they can talk to. They buy the girls drinks, only we don't give the ones under eighteen any alcohol. And we tell them not to turn tricks, not even outside the club. I don't know if you are a relative or a friend of this young girl you're after. But there's nothing in it, you see. So why don't you just piss off?'

I answered him casually. 'Well I might have, but Franks said you wanted to see me. He likes my jacket, apparently. Maybe he thought you would, too.'

Malone's face went a shade deeper than its usual red. 'Paul always tells me what's going on. And now I've seen you. So get lost.'

Standing my ground, I asked, 'Paul's told you all about the deals he's struck tonight? Or did he forget them in his rush to tell you about me?'

Malone jumped up from his chair, and this time he did go through the front door. I heard him bellow he wanted Paul Franks.

The redhead Franks shut the door behind him and flashed a big smile at Malone, who settled again behind his desk. I sat down on a bar stool against a side wall.

The redhead stopped in his tracks when he saw the expression on Malone's face.

'We were going to start selling later,' the club owner yelled.

A hurt look creased the young man's face, and he reached a hand into the inside pocket of his jacket. I smirked, looking around. There was a soft sound of a drawer opening, before four bullets ripped into the redhead's body.

I sat there stunned, thinking the fat man could not have done that. But there was Malone, blubbering and bouncing his fat up and down, with a gun falling through his fingers to the table.

Tears were streaming down his face and he sniffled. 'I loved him. Why did he rob me? Why?' He stopped crying to snap at me. 'You, see what he had in his pocket.'

I looked at the gun on the table and did what he asked. Only a folded manila envelope that had collected some of Franks' blood came out of the pocket. I looked inside to see maybe $1500, neatly folded. A piece of paper with initials and amounts between $50 and $300 was behind the notes. Nothing more. Franks had been preparing a fully audited surprise for the boss. I showed Malone the contents of the dead man's pocket and he started to cry again.

'But I loved him,' he squealed.

'You know what Wilde said,' I reminded him. 'Wilde said, "You'll never be so wrong". I know it's not much of a comfort, but what can you expect from Kim Wilde?'

It was not a comfort, because he turned on me. 'You did this. I'm going to kill you.'

'You're not going to kill me,' I said casually, though there was a fair chance he would.

But he didn't. Malone told me to go, and take the bloody money with me. Some industries seem to consider a bullet and a bribe to be bills of exchange of equal value. I put the dough in my pocket. Malone opened the door for me, told me one last time that he loved Franks, and watched to make sure I had free passage out of the Go Kat Klub.

Cassandra Russo was hopping out of a taxi, just as I reached the bottom step.

'You don't want to go back in there,' I said. 'There's a dead body inside.'

She said, 'You killed someone.'

I shook my head and grabbed her elbow, urging her down the street.

An Aboriginal man asked me for a dollar. As I fished into my pocket, he upped the request to two dollars. I gave him all the money from the envelope.

'It's got blood all over it,' he said.

'Sorry,' I said.

The EH found the car park of the nearest suburban hotel that had late-night music. I turned the engine off, and asked Cassandra what was the connection between her, Lavinsky and the Go Kat Klub. She said there was none. Lavinsky wouldn't be caught dead in a place like the Kat.

'Was someone really dead in the club?' she asked.

'No,' I lied. 'I just wanted to find out what you knew about Lavinsky's murder.'

Her lips quivered and her eyes reddened, but she overcame her momentary grief. 'ProJoe's dead? You killed him, Steele.'

'I never killed anyone,' I said, wondering if I had just played a part in Paul Franks' death, when all I had wanted to do was create tension to loosen lips.

I looked hard at the girl. 'I reckon Steven Dupont killed Lavinsky, and I reckon you know all about it.'

'Me?' said Cassandra Russo, soft and wide-eyed.

She turned her knees towards me, across the one-piece

front seat of my car. She lowered her head and tilted it to one side to look up at me. Then she twisted some strands of her hair around an index finger. Cassandra was having some fun, trying to bury her grief over a dead man who had been close to her when closeness was something she feared.

It was time to catch her off-guard. 'What were you warning Lavinsky about on his answering machine?'

My aim was poor. She shook her head from side to side and smiled, as if I was an amusing little boy. At least she stopped twirling her hair. 'It was a joke, Steele. Cassandra, get it? I am named after a character from Greek mythology. She was cursed with always having to tell the truth and no one would believe her.'

I didn't believe her.

'ProJoe and I used to share jokes like that,' she continued.

'Were you and Lavinsky lovers?'

'Of course not,' she said, like I was that little boy again. 'We just had sex a few times.'

That one, I had to think about.

'And you and Steven Dupont?'

'Yuk,' was her only answer.

'And your mother?'

'I've never slept with my mother. Though I shouldn't say that categorically, should I, till I've had regression therapy.'

'Come on, Cassandra, you don't have to prove you are cleverer than me. I went to grade ten at an orphanage. My life's ambition is to back the program one day at Eagle Farm racetrack. And I'm being hunted for murder because I accepted a $50 job that I was supposed to get a grand for. Buddha, I'm dumber than Harpo Marx – don't ask who that is. Just help me nail Lavinsky's killer and you can go on pursuing your future, which I'm sure will sparkle with wit and wealth.

Cassandra sat up straight in the car seat. 'You know what really scares me. What really really scares me. I'm afraid the dumb kids will pick on me all my life. That I'll be working for the dumb kids all my life.'

'You mean they won't all go into pop music. Answer my question and I'll protect you from the dumb kids. Did your mother have a relationship with either Lavinsky or Dupont?'

You could see her conquer the urge to say something smart. 'I don't know,' she said instead.

'Did Clarissa Dunne have a relationship with either of them? And it's not your mother I'm talking about.'

'I don't know.'

'That's helpful,' I said. 'That Greek Cassandra might have saved herself a lot of grief with a few don't-knows, but they're not doing much for me.'

'Why don't we ask Dupont?' Cassandra said cheerily.

'Yair, right, later on today, I'll ask the coppers swarming all over the uni whether I might have a chat with Dupont.'

'We can go to his unit.'

'You know where he lives?'

'Yes. My mother took me to a cocktail party to watch the Academy Awards on television. You wouldn't believe it; they were all dressed up in formal gear, and arguing over who was the best actor of all time. I stole a bottle of Chivas Regal and split. But I can find the place again. For sure.'

13

CHAPTER 13 MIGHT bring bad luck. There is no Chapter 13.

14

ON LIFE'S JOURNEY the only person who will piss you off more than the directionless is someone who is certain of where they are going.

Cassandra's 'for sure' navigation took us an hour, though it was only twelve kilometres from the pub. After dozens of misturns, we parked down the road from what turned out to be a townhouse, not a unit. Townhouses are more welcoming than units. Many, even in middle-class suburbs such as Dupont's, do not have the elaborate security of the modern block of units.

I hid in the bushes and let Cassandra ring the bell. After about a minute, a light went on and Dupont came to the door in cotton pyjamas which had various pictures of Scottish singer Annie Lennox printed across them. I had never seen PJs on a performer's merchandise table so I wondered what they were about. Before I could ask, Cassandra yelled, 'Surprise!'

This made the lecturer open the door wider, even as a startled frown crossed his face. The girl skipped over to me, grabbed me by the arm, and dragged me inside. Dupont, bewildered and still clutching the doorknob, swivelled his body to stare at us. Admitting his bafflement, he threw his hands in the air, and quietly shut the door.

Cassandra turned on Dupont, as he wiped the tiredness out of his eyes. 'Why'd you kill ProJoe?' she accused.

Dupont could only begin, 'I . . .'

Cassandra continued the attack. 'Don't lie to us. Steele's got a gun.'

I put myself between the girl and Dupont, and put my arm on her shoulder to tell her to back off.

'I haven't got a gun,' I said calmly to Dupont. 'I don't like guns. Guns kill people.'

Cassandra challenged my last words. 'Guns don't kill people; people kill people.'

'Fine,' I answered, 'the next time I want a personalised T-shirt printed, I'll remember that.'

I looked at Dupont and waited for his contribution. He shook his head. 'As if I'd kill Lavinsky. I would not give him that satisfaction.'

A novel denial, but I wanted more. 'Though he was going to expose you for sexual blackmail of students. It would have finished your academic career.'

I thought he would lie, but he was the sort of bloke who liked to verbally surprise. 'That hypocrite Lavinsky would never put me in.'

'Are you saying you had something on him, too? You never mentioned it when you told him to get off your back.'

Dupont answered casually. 'I may have taken some advantage of my office. Nothing worse than any employee using the resources of his employer for a little outside activity.'

'I doubt if you could sneak that argument past your Ethics Committee,' I said. 'You might have killed Lavinsky for less than what we know about you.'

'He would never put me in. I knew it; he knew it. Lavinsky was a lecher at heart. He traded his brains for sex, and I know which party got the better of that deal. So did he. He was guilty about his own indiscretions. On and on he would go about the beauty of fresh young minds. He was after something, but if it were minds, he didn't know much about anatomy.'

'But he told you to stop, Dupont.'

'Repeatedly, ad nauseam, continually. And I have stopped.'

'Because of Lavinsky?'

'Because I'm living with AIDS.'

Cassandra or I must have given a funny look. 'Oh yes, I am, or was, bisexual. I'm now asexual, though I don't think that's the right word, because that would make me an amoeba or some such thing.'

Even if it all were true, he could still be sexually active, with a continuing reason to kill Lavinsky.

'Couldn't you practice safe sex?'

'I did for a while, but it became a bother. I discovered that abstinence has pleasures not unlike promiscuity. Abstinence is its own reward. As time passes, hypocrites like Lavinsky won't have examples with any currency with which to persecute me.'

I was dealing with a very sick man here, with a chronic illness that predated his AIDS. But illness is no crime, and I had to call it one way or another. My call was that Dupont was not a killer. I told him we were going, and asked him not to call the police.

When we got out the door, Cassandra spoke sarcastically. 'Well, that went well. Good interviewing technique, Steele. He was lying through his teeth. That crap about AIDS. God, he only had to mention that and you went all soft and blubbery. What a sook.'

'You finished?' I asked.

'No,' she replied. 'Why didn't you hit him? Or at least make him think you had a gun? Like I said.'

I was about to ask her to shut up, when I heard someone

calling my name across the dark. Turning, I saw Dupont standing in the doorway, spot-lit against the night. He screamed at me, 'The cowardly lecher does it with a compliment, Hill.'

I yelled back. 'Didn't Kim Wilde say that?'

He shut the door on the darkness.

Cassandra was still in my ear about my slack efforts, but what Dupont said twigged my memory of one of Lavinsky's raves. The professor was disappointed in how students, and even academics, compared two things without considering the degrees that made them different. Like two killings with guns.

Malone had killed his lover with a fast draw from a drawer, but the spray of bullets could have gone anywhere. Dumb bad luck killed Paul Franks. There were a few bullet holes around Lavinsky's heart too. But also one in the head. That was the difference. The killer left her signature, and I figured I had a match for it.

Cassandra protested against my driving her home, but she looked tired and appeared glad to see me pull up to her mother's house, in another middle-class suburb. No lights on here.

Hoping to be caught by an outraged parent, Cassandra invited me in for coffee. I accepted. I had a couple of sips before the parental radar kicked in. Jan Russo, in nightgown, appeared in a corner of the lounge. I had not heard her footsteps and she announced her presence with three short coughs and a shake of her head. She ordered her daughter to bed. Cassandra refused. I asked Mum if I could have a few parting words alone with Cassandra. Jan Russo begrudgingly withdrew.

'Cassandra, could you wag school tomorrow arvo. Meet me

in your mother's office at 3:15, awlright?'

I said I had to talk with her mother, but that she wasn't to know Cassandra was coming the next day. The intrigue was enough for her to agree to go to bed. I continued to sip my coffee as I watched the teenager enter her bedroom, out of hearing range of adult conversation. Her mother reappeared in the lounge as soon as Cassandra shut her bedroom door.

'Well, aren't we the persuasive one?' said Jan Russo, settling into an armchair.

'Do you know where your daughter goes gallivanting around at night?'

She was affronted. 'Of course I do.'

I took that as a no.

'What I didn't know, Steve, is that she's been hanging around with a murderer the police are looking for.'

So the cops had found Lavinsky's body. Homicide was probably still at Queensland Uni, trying to fit me for the deed.

'The police are always looking for a murderer,' I said. 'Sometimes they find the right one. Who's dead this time?'

She smiled thinly. 'You won't be on your own, protesting your innocence from a prison cell.'

I let that pass, putting on a braver front than I had a right to. 'Dupont has already put his hand up for killing Lavinsky. Tomorrow, he'll make it official before the coppers.'

Jan Russo didn't blink. 'That's it, then. It's all over. Goodnight.'

She did not move from her armchair.

'Why do you think he did it?' I asked.

'I don't think he did it. I don't think he confessed. I think you want some sort of reaction from me.'

'Yair, you're right, Jan. By the way it's Steele, not Steve. And

I do know who killed Lavinsky.'

She countered well. 'I should think you would.' She was obviously sticking to the story, popular with almost everyone, that I did it. But I was getting somewhere, because she could not hide a look of worry.

'Cassandra doesn't think I did it,' I said.

'Leave Cassie out of this. You seem to think, quite ignorantly, that I am a neglectful mother, because I allow my daughter her freedom. You may know she is only fifteen, but do you know what her IQ is? What was your IQ when you were fifteen, Steve, Steele?'

'We were a deprived lot in the orphanage. The nuns would never let us have an IQ.'

She ignored that remark. 'Cassandra has an IQ of 155. That's approaching genius territory. So I owe it to her, I owe it to Australia, to let her mind roam free. Apart from that, I would do anything to nurture and protect my daughter.'

'Including covering up murder,' I said.

'Don't be stupid,' she said.

'That's a good tip. I'll try to remember that in future. Only, first, I need to know if Clarissa Dunne has classes tomorrow.'

'I think so. In fact I'm sure she has. At least one at 2 o'clock I know of, Introduction to Australian Society, in Lecture Theatre three. I've given a couple of those classes.'

'And what about you, Jan, have you got any class around three tomorrow?'

'I don't think so. Two to three is the last one, I think.'

'So what do you do between classes?'

'I don't know why you're asking all these questions. I'm usually in my office. It really is getting late. I'd offer you more coffee, but . . .'

I could take a hint. I was in the dark night again, but spoke before she could close the door on me.

'Why did you kill Joseph Lavinsky?'

Jan Russo shut the door in my face.

I WAS HANGING around Lecture Theatre three at ten to three. I soon spotted the red wavy hair of Clarissa Dunne, one of a group of students happily withdrawing from their Introduction to Australian Society. Dunne spotted me and excused herself from her companions.

She smiled. 'How are you, Steele? We could have used you in that lecture. Boring. Got time for a coffee?'

I had time. Clarissa Dunne certainly was not letting a little murder interfere with our contribution to café society.

Over our cups, I asked, 'Clarissa, what was the relationship between you and Lavinsky?'

Her face clouded. 'I don't think I did anything wrong. He'd buy me things, but I only accepted them because it upset him when I didn't. You don't know what it's like at uni, Steele. A lot of us students are totally broke, living on government assistance. I work two part-time jobs, which really makes it hard to find study time. And all Joe did was shout me dinner and some clothes. Only once did I have to ask for some money towards the rent. And . . .'

I was starting to see where Clarissa Dunne was coming from.

'I know bugger all about uni, Clarissa. I always thought you were kids from rich families, just doing the apprenticeship to carry on the tradition of privilege. I guess I was wrong.'

'You are wrong, Steele. My father works for the railways, and Mum is only part-time.'

I mustered as much sympathy as I could. 'I guess you really shouldn't worry about what you and Lavinsky had going. You only have to answer to yourself.'

That cheered her up. 'I probably overreact. I just want to get ahead on my own ability. This university is like a game of snakes and ladders. Personality, politics, physical appearance, family background, can all hold you down or push you up. For a lot of students, their entire future is at stake. Has anybody told you about Steven Dupont?'

I nodded to let her know I was aware of Dupont's activities, and she continued. 'His kind is the worst, but there's all sorts of pressure on students to get the best results, any way they can. I just don't want to play that game, whether I'm sliding on a snake or climbing a ladder. Fortunately, I've been surviving with medium grades so far.'

'On more mundane matters, Clarissa, how good a shot are you?'

'You mean with a gun? I've never had a real gun in my hand in my life, Steele.'

'Yair, that's what I reckoned. You know, you could probably end up a professor like Lavinsky. You seem smart enough.'

'Maybe in twenty years' time. For the next five years, I'll be living in poverty and finishing my arts-law. Then I'm going to live like a queen, keeping rich corporate criminals out of jail.'

'Someone's got to do it,' I said. I glanced at the clock. 'Better go, Clarissa. Keep up those medium grades.'

After I left, I realised Clarissa probably did not know Lavinsky was dead. I had not mentioned it and the coppers would have told uni staff who did know to keep it to themselves. I wondered how she would react, but only for a moment. I was more concerned to track down someone who did know Lavinsky was dead, his killer.

Hiding around a corner, I watched Jan Russo enter her office at ten past three. Steven Dupont was with her. No coppers in sight. I hung around for another five minutes for Cassandra Russo, but she was a no-show. I went down the corridor and tested Russo's door, to find it open. The department head and Dupont stopped talking as soon as I entered. From the shifty looks on their faces, it was a fair bet they had been talking about me.

'Good afternoon,' I said cheerily. 'So this is where the heavy-duty thinking goes down.'

'You can knock, you know,' Jan Russo said.

'It's a surprise. I bet Joseph Lavinsky was surprised when someone put a bullet through his brain.'

Before Jan Russo could answer, her daughter Cassandra entered the room. 'Surprise!' she said. I reminded her that she forgot to knock, while her mother asked if she had been suspended from school again.

Dupont told me he was calling the police this time.

'Why?' I asked. 'So they can arrest Cassandra for truancy, or Jan for murder?'

'No,' said Dupont. 'So they can take you down for murder, and for stealing thousands of dollars' worth of computer equipment. Which, by the way, no one has mentioned to the police. Yet.'

'I did it,' Cassandra said. We all turned to look at the girl.

I thought she was going to try to cover for me about the computers, but she went on. 'I killed ProJoe.'

'Cassie, don't say any more,' her mother warned.

Dupont threw in his two cents' worth. 'Yes, that's enough, Cassandra.'

She ignored them both. 'What will happen to me, Steele?' she said in a frightened sad voice.

Jan Russo interrupted. 'You are a minor, Cassie. Nothing serious is going to happen.'

I had a suggestion. 'You could say Lavinsky sexually assaulted you, Cassandra.'

'He raped her, that's what he did,' Jan Russo said enthusiastically.

'He didn't rape me. He didn't sexually assault me.'

'Then why did you do it?' I asked.

Cassandra looked glum. All she could say was, 'Just because.'

'That'll go down well as an excuse,' I said. 'And where did you get the gun?'

I thought she wasn't going to answer me, but after a few seconds she said, 'At the club, the Go Kat Klub.'

'You got it from a stranger in a club,' I repeated. 'That's an old favourite for the police. They always believe that one.'

'It was a woman. I got it from a woman at the club,' Cassandra said, defying me to call her a liar.

She was lying, all right.

'Why didn't you just use one of your mother's guns?' I asked.

Cassandra appeared bewildered. She looked at her mother and pleaded desperately. 'I didn't tell him, Mum. Honestly, I didn't.'

'But you did, Cassandra,' I contradicted. 'When you said "guns don't kill people; people kill people". That was so different from the way you speak, and what you have to say.

You know, it's funny, no matter how cool teenagers are, they still repeat what their parents say, just like when they were little children. Or maybe you saw it on the wall of your mother's gun club. How long has your mother been in a club, Cassandra?'

Jan Russo answered for herself. 'Since before Cassie was born. A lot of women I knew were learning martial arts for self-defence, but that was too much of a hassle. So I joined a gun club, though I only told my closest friends. But how did you know?'

'Lavinsky told me before he died.'

'That's not possible,' Russo said.

'I don't mean straight before he died. You made sure he wasn't doing any talking at all. But he told me earlier, that two things that look the same can be different by degrees. And two killings by bullets in the last thirty-six hours were different in one respect.'

'Two killings?' asked Cassandra. 'You said no one was killed at the club.'

'I lied. But, as a matter of historical record, I doubt we will find any mention in the papers of the death of Paul Franks at the Go Kat Klub. He was killed by a spray of bullets. Unluckily for him, they landed in the wrong places. But Lavinsky had one neat bullet hole through the middle of his forehead. Lavinsky's killer had expertise with a gun. She probably killed the professor with the first shot to the head, and just pumped the other bullets into him, like I might have done, as the police were meant to think.'

Jan Russo took in a long breath and I thought, *here we go, here comes the justification.*

'I would never have let Cassandra go to prison, even a prison for minors. But as far as I'm concerned, Lavinsky did rape her. Cassie is still a child. Her intelligence works against her. She won't admit how inexperienced she is. Joseph took advantage of that. He did damage that could be with my daughter for the rest of her life. He could have side-tracked Cassie from the great tasks she's destined for.'

I did not state the obvious: that knowing your mother had murdered someone you admired might give the teenager a few sleepless nights.

Jan Russo lamented the aftermath, if not the murder. 'She wasn't supposed to find out,' she said hoarsely.

The chairman of the departmental Ethics Committee cleared his throat to intervene with wisdom. 'The simple solution of unsolved robbery will satisfy the police. You'll get out of this lightly, Hill. I'll corroborate your story. And you can keep the computers. However, if you try to advance a different scenario, those computers will bring you undone, as will my revised memory of your whereabouts. Nothing will bring poor Joseph back, so I think it is in everyone's best interests if we tidy our own nest.'

I had heard enough. I left the room.

THE COPPERS GRILLED me for three hours, but they let me go at the end of that, and only called me back twice. Both times, they appeared to be going through the motions.

THE GOOROO INSISTED we get rid of the computers, though I told him we didn't have to. He kept saying I had cost him a grand, but, to this day, he has never asked me to give back the money. We loaded the gear into the tray of my EH ute, and at midnight, under a full moon, drove to a relatively isolated reach of the Tweed River. We threw two video monitors in, before we realised that an old Aboriginal man was watching us. He waved; put down a net he was holding and came over.

'Could I have that thing?' he said, pointing to the laser printer in my hand.

'What are you going to do with it?' I asked.

'Put it in my crab pot,' he said.

'You still catch crabs around here?'

In way of reply, he went back to his camp and retrieved a large mud crab from a hessian bag.

'Do you like muddies?' he asked, offering the crab to me.

'Sure, but you can have this printer for nothing. I don't think it'll be much use to you, anyway.'

'It'll be good,' he insisted. 'Tie some old bones to it. Once the smell gets through it, I'll be able to catch muddies, even when I run out of bones.'

Sounded reasonable to me. I gave him the printer, and two computer boxes for other pots. The rest of the electronic gear we threw in the river.

Despite our protests, he insisted we take the muddie.

We ate the crab the next night. It was delicious.

Book Three

At large

15

Summer in Brisbane, December, 1991

IF YOU CAN'T STAND THE HEAT, it was damned thoughtless of your parents to let you be born in the northern half of Australia.

It was an unmercifully hot summer and someone was trying to frame me for the murder of racecourse hustler and playboy Marcus Georgio, also known, shortly before his demise, by the professional name of Caulfield Jones, of the little-known profession of turfologist.

I had tracked down one of Georgio's women friends, a hard-bitten sleek blonde by the name of Crystal Speares, who could not give two flying ducks about his mortality. She had an icy temperament and her indifference to Georgio's death, about the only sincere reaction I received from her, might have been because she now had to trouble herself to cross him from her social diary. Maybe she killed him herself, but had no need for remorse because I could not prove it.

I didn't have much info to go on. I did not know how struggling jockey Billy Scharfe got to swim in the intoxicating but dangerous waters dominated by a shark like Speares.

Back in my flat, after I left the leggy blonde giving the lacklustre jockey a leg-up into her unit, I was in no great hurry to play smart and get out of Dodge. Natalie was on holidays and up the Sunshine Coast with her parents and her younger sister, Jane. I settled down to a cup of coffee and a phone call to the

Gooroo in Tweed Heads.

A stone's throw from the Queensland border is the town of Tweed Heads, officially in the State of New South Wales. Queensland-owned illegal bookmakers and brothels flourished in this sunny venal paradise in the eighties. Queensland coppers could not touch you here, and Sydney heavies and police had to come 800 kilometres if they wanted to discuss a silent partnership with you.

The Gooroo loved Tweed Heads, even though extended betting hours and live race coverage in pubs and clubs was quickly killing the SP bookie profession. That was about the only subject Gooroo never talked about. A softly spoken, silver-haired sixty-one-year-old, he could quote you the odds on a royal divorce, an invasion in the Middle East, or on contracting an STD when you did not use a condom. The Gooroo managed twelve phones, but I knew which one I could get him on.

'I'd like $100 each way on the winner of the first,' I said when he answered.

Gooroo had told me about a former Queensland Police Commissioner who took his cut from the then-flourishing SP bookmaking trade. At the time, registered legal bookies also controlled most of the illegal off-course SP. Differentiating between legal and illegal ventures back then was like distinguishing dollars from their equivalent in gold bullion. Anyway, the Police Commissioner always managed to have fifty pounds each way or win and place on the last winner in Brisbane. After the last race, the legal/illegal bookie would record a winning bet of fifty pounds each way in his ledger at the racetrack. The highest-ranking copper in Queensland would wake up each Saturday morning knowing he was going to back the last winner of the day.

'Sure, you're set, no worries, mate,' the Gooroo lied. 'How's it going Steele?'

'If you turn off that cassette recorder, I'll tell you how it's not going real good.'

A click down the line told me the Gooroo had turned off his protective taping machine.

'Well, what do you make of it?' I asked after I laid out the whole story, from seeing Georgio in the Feed Bin café, to finding him dead in a West End unit, to my little chat with Crystal Speares and seeing apprentice Billy Scharfe outside the blonde's place.

'Looks like someone has you the favourite for a murder charge. You didn't do it by any chance, Steele?'

'For Buddha's sake, Gooroo, what do you think?'

'No, I can't see it myself. I'd say you'd be a hundred-to-one. What about one of those three sheilas in the photos? Sounds like Georgio was a pants man. That can be a dangerous hobby.'

'I think Crystal Speares is in the clear,' I surmised. 'She's a cannibal, without a doubt. But I think she prefers to roast her men real slow.'

'And the other two women?'

'I don't know anything about them,' I admitted. 'Why would they want to set me up? At least Crystal was running with the racing crowd, so there might have been something in that.'

'Well, there's always that public servant who sent you to the interview, what's her name?'

'The lovely Kathy Billings. But she's a stiff; stiffs don't kill people. Do they?'

The Gooroo refused to eliminate the possibility. 'Who knows what stiffs do? Look at it this way: Kathy Billings falls for hustler Georgio. All his other chicks don't mind about one another – they're hustling Georgio as much as he is hustling them, so no one has time to keep score. Except for this employment service sheila. She finds out about Georgio's full book of rides, and decides she's being dudded.'

'Sounds farfetched to me,' I said.

'Maybe, maybe not. So, this Billings woman decides to lodge a protest with a .38. But she needs a bunny, because her protest might stop her going places in the world of stiffs. She checks out her files for the form of a humble starter called Steele Hill, and decides he is perfect for the daily double. She gets rid of mug lair Georgio and at the same time shafts you, a veteran performer in her unemployment stable who she is sick of feeding. Motive, opportunity and whatever else those dees on TV say. Correct weight and placings stand.'

I would never be rash enough to dismiss out of hand anything the Gooroo surmised. But doubt was gnawing at my belly. Talk about a new frightening possibility in a world of scary possibilities! That's all the world needs now – stiffs taking Kathy Bates and Robert De Niro classes.

'What about the .38?' I protested.

'Could have been Georgio's. What do you know about the bloke?'

'Not much. You picked him in one – mug lair. Flashy gambler, who never hits the surface without a splash of bugs bunny. Did he bet with you at all?'

'The name's familiar. I'll look him up.'

I heard Gooroo turning the pages of a book.

'Yair, he was into us for a grand. That's peanuts. Not even monkeys kill for peanuts.'

'Maybe he was into some heavies for more.'

'Not that I've heard. There's not much you can do, Steele.

Worrying will only make it worse. They tell me New Zealand's nice at this time of year. I might be able to lend you a few quid.'

I told him I did not want to leave Natalie behind. We talked about her, and about Gooroo's wife June. We talked about his kids and his grandkids. We talked about the next day's race programs, and the odds on the Sheffield Shield cricket competition. For a beautiful half-hour, Marcus Georgio, dead or alive, didn't exist.

When I hung up, the funk came rushing back and nausea caught in my throat and my stomach. Okay, first thing is to get Kathy Billings off the suspect list. I dialled the Nundah employment service.

I was Kathy's cousin from Adelaide. Was she at work? No, she had the day off. What a shame, I was really keen to catch up with her. And I don't know her address, just where she works. Sorry, but we cannot give out the home addresses of staff. What a shame.

But she would be at the smoko in the city that afternoon. Smoko, what's that? Oh sorry, figured you might be a public servant too. Smoko is an interoffice get-together. Would you know the address? Sure, here it is. It starts at five. Thanks very much. I do hope I can catch up with Kathy. I'm only here for a few days.

Five o'clock was six hours away, so I sat and tried to study the form guide. What a versatile word study is. Kids at university study to become upmarket stiffs – doctors and lawyers and engineers; Rastafarians study their religion; people like me study form guides. The objects of the three studies are like chalk, cheese and marshmallow. But there is enormous fervour in all three.

Only, I could not concentrate on my studies. I switched on

the TV, to find an American talkfest hostess introducing Friday's parade of geeks to me and the rest of housebound AustralAmerica. Okay, I thought, that should slow my brain down a bit.

The front door slammed inward against the wall, rattling the windows and distracting me from the telly. A police boot hung in the air, before lurching forward, propelling the recently promoted Detective Senior Constable Bill Schmidt with it. Schmidt was unable to stop himself from crashing to the floor. The silly bastard had just smashed down an unlocked door with his size-eleven boot.

Sergeant Frank Mooney smirked at the antics of Keystone Kop Schmidt. Then the senior cop's face grew fierce as he looked down at the gun in his hand and remembered he meant serious business. He pointed the gun at me.

'Buddha,' I said. 'I know playing cards for money is illegal, but I didn't know you blokes took it so seriously.'

'Let's go, Hill,' Mooney scowled.

'Are you charging me with something, Sergeant Mooney?' I asked, wide-eyed and innocent. 'Do I need a lawyer?'

'Don't give us that bullshit, Hill. I'm from the old school of copper. You're from the old school of grub. You start talking legal rights and I start shooting you in the thigh.'

The Fitzgerald Inquiry of 1989 was meant to change police culture. The sergeant must have been washing his hair during the months the inquiry was on. I nodded towards Mooney's gun. 'That warrant in your hand looks in order. Only, next time, tell Schmidt that he has lousy style in picking up a date.'

The junior officer regained his balance and smiled. 'Lucky it was your door and not your face I kicked in.'

I know when I am beaten by superior wit, so I turned to

Mooney. 'Mind if I keep my hands down, and you keep that gun out of sight? What on Earth will the neighbours think?'

Mooney put the gun back in its holster. We went outside with the Sergeant and Schmidt on either side of me. I pulled the fractured door closed and managed to lock it.

'Don't want to encourage crime,' I said to my captors.

I nodded at Mrs Barnes, tending her roses. She looked at my escort.

'It's criminal what they get up to these days,' Mrs Barnes said. 'It's the heat. This heat plays havoc with them.'

Cue quizzical expressions all round.

'Aphids, I mean. Aphids on the roses.'

I nodded sympathetically.

AMELIA BARNES had invited me in for tea, one morning years earlier, after I admired her roses in bloom. I was in no hurry to get to the tote that day, so I accepted. She was 84-years old then. This I knew from the recent birthday cards she showed me. A slight woman she shuffled when she walked but still maintained a more-or-less straight back.

Mrs Barnes edged across the room and reached into her pantry for a handful of long flat green leaves with sharp edges. With scissors, she cut the leaves into a teapot; then added hot water, replaced the lid, wrapped a cosy around the pot, and spun it round three times. She looked a member of Housewives' Freemasonry. After a minute, I was looking warily at the dull-green liquid in my cup.

'Lemongrass,' Mrs Barnes said. 'Try it.'

It was not half bad, somewhat lemony and refreshing, a

little tame for someone with a caffeine dependency like mine.

'You like my roses, Steele?' the old woman asked when she saw me looking out the window in their direction. 'So, what's your favourite?'

I hadn't been looking at her roses at all, and I had no favourite, as they all appeared to be the same white variety. I was only staring blankly into the mid distance, which I often do when enjoying a cuppa. Not wishing to offend, I focused on one rosebush, a little taller than the others, and with plenty of branches radiating from a fork in the trunk. Masses of smallish white blooms burst from among the green leaves. I nominated it as my fave.

'It's called Iraqi Icicle,' Mrs Barnes said. They're all Iraqi Icicles but I think that one's the best, too.

'A lot of what we think of as European roses came originally from the valley of the Tigris and Euphrates Rivers. That's around Iraq and Persia, you know, what we call Iran now.'

I complimented Mrs Barnes for running rings around me in roseology.

She went on. 'You know, for some reason, many Australians think roses are English natives. They tell me many Americans think they originated in the southern United States. But they didn't. I don't think it's right that the rose is the national flower of the United States. What do you think, Mr Hill?'

She sipped her lemongrass tea. I took a hearty swig of mine, feeling a little bored and uncomfortable, as you do when you are with someone who has a passion you do not share. 'I never really thought about it, Mrs Barnes. I suppose they have had it as their national flower for a while.'

'I don't think it's right, and there should be some international law against it. They must have plenty of plants, native to the United States that had been there for centuries before they brought in roses. Why didn't they choose one of those? That would be right.'

Amelia Barnes had lived in one of the ground-floor flats since long before I moved in. Neighbours for years, we were polite without really knowing each other. It was not until our rosy morning tea that I discovered she was widowed.

'Clarrie planted the roses. He was tending them when he passed on,' Mrs Barnes told me. 'I took over because, when he died, they were still young, just babies really. I suppose you could say I'm completing my husband's unfinished business.'

She sipped. I sipped. I looked around at the family pictures on walls and on little tables in the small room. Clarrie was not smiling in many of the photos; perhaps he was camera shy. Still, in death, he was one of the lucky ones. His memory lived among the Iraqi Icicles as well as in his uncomfortable family photos.

The old woman put her cup down and her face grew stern. 'But the aphids always come for them.'

I had heard the name aphids before, but they certainly weren't something I'd given much thought to.

Mrs Barnes knew a fair bit about the creatures, pests that attacked plants, including roses, especially relishing the new shoots and buds. 'Aphids are very tiny; many don't have wings, so they can't climb rosebushes very well to get at the new shoots and petals. Ants give them a ride up the roses.'

Now this was interesting: a couple of Nature's creatures striking a deal for their mutual benefit. You would think such a contract would require human intelligence, but obviously not.

'The ants farm the tiny aphids,' Mrs Barnes said softly, warming to her subject, 'and protect them from predators such as lady beetles. Ants are like us humans, Steele. They don't mind making war, even against their own kind. Raising an army, that's unusual in nature, Steele, but ants do it. We do too.'

I took Mrs Barnes's word for it, but I had a question. 'Sounds great for the aphids, Mrs Barnes, but what's in it for the ants?'

'Oil.'

'Oil?'

'Oil. After feeding on the rosebuds, aphids secrete a sweet, oily substance sometimes called honeydew. The ants love this sweet oil, and for some species it is a basic part of their diet.'

'Everybody wins,' I said.

'Everybody except the roses,' Mrs Barnes said. 'The arrangement does not do much for the Iraqi Icicles.'

I WAVED WEAKLY to Mrs Barnes as she sprinkled a powder on the roses in her relentless war against the aphids. I would have liked Mooney and Schmidt to let me walk rather than push me to the unmarked police car. I have a certain standing, however wobbly, in my community, and Mrs Barnes might misinterpret my helping the detectives with their inquiries. She looked up at me, wedged between the two detectives.

'It's criminal,' she said. 'Bloody aphids.'

16

FROM THE MOUNTAINTOP we could see over the whole of Brisbane, up and down the Brisbane River, round and round the bends, all the way out to Moreton Bay. Senior Constable Schmidt had driven Sergeant Mooney and me past the city's botanical gardens to Mount Coot-tha. The mountain, modest in height, is home to three of Brisbane's television stations. It is also known as a lovers' lane. Mooney and Schmidt knew it as a place to show someone a hundred-metre sheer drop.

They parked the piggy bank on a side clearing. We only had to move ten metres to be on the edge of the rock-encrusted cliff. You'd be a thousand-to-one to survive a fall from the top of that cliff.

Mooney did the talking. 'It's like this, Hill. You're a clown and a pest.' He arced his arm proprietorially over the city. 'We've got people out there who are murdering and maiming, robbing and pillaging.'

'Maybe you should tighten up your police recruitment procedures.' Sometimes I have no control over my mouth.

'That sort of smart-arse comment is what I'm on about,' said Mooney. 'You're too lazy to work and too gutless to break and enter like an honest grub crim.'

Eloquent man that Mooney, he must have kissed the Blarney Stone.

'Then you go stuffing up our day of grub-catching by killing Marcus Georgio.'

Mooney stopped talking and looked hard at me. I returned a blank look. He grabbed a handful of my shirt, twisted it and thumped me in the chest.

'Hey!' he shouted, while he pushed me back and forth.

I know he meant nothing by it; it was just a copper's way of emphasising a point. He thumped me in the chest again. 'Hey!' the sergeant repeated.

Me, I still looked blankly at him. Schmidt intervened, grabbing hold of Mooney's wrist. 'Hang on, Frank.'

Oh Buddha, I thought, not this good cop, bad cop shit. Yes it was.

'Hang on nothing; I'm gunna throw this shithead right off this mountain.'

Mooney pulled me by the shirt towards him, spun me around, grabbed my shirt again and pushed me away from him, into the empty air beside the cliff. The colour deserted my face, leaving me white. Buddha, we were talking mass-produced polyester cotton shirt here. That cloth could have ripped apart in the copper's hands and sent me to the gambler's dreamtime.

My fear seemed to restore a semblance of sanity to Mooney. He turned me around again, released his grip and lit up a cigarette. Schmidt moved towards me.

'What the fuck, Steele,' the Senior Constable sympathised, shaking his head. 'So Georgio was a Mr Hollywood wanker, it's still gunna cost you twelve years. Christ, you'll end up doing at least eight.'

By this time, my heartbeat had steadied from a gallop to a canter. I started to smell fish and it wasn't coming from Moreton Bay which I could see in the distance. What were we doing having this conversation on Mount Coot-tha, rather than in police headquarters in Roma Street? I decided indignation, despite my fear, was the way to go. 'I haven't a clue what you're on about. Mooney just scared the shitter out of me. He's still scaring the shitter out of me. And all I know I've done is win at cards last night.'

Mooney perked up at the mention of his name. He brushed Schmidt aside and pulled a metal object from his pocket. 'Seen this before, Fuckface Clown?'

I could not help but stare dumbly down at that police .38, just like the one I had thrown in Schulz Canal.

'Where do you think we found this?' Mooney asked.

I was glad he did. There is nothing like a question from a copper to get your mind back on track.

'It's one of yours, isn't it? I suppose you found it wherever you keep daddy's little helper.'

Mooney grabbed and twisted my shirt again. It had worked last time, hadn't it? 'We found it in your garbage bin.'

Well Buddha, that was it. These coppers had set me up for a murder. Watched me take the gun away; watched me throw it in the creek. They'd fetched it out and shoved it in my garbage bin. This was a top fit-up, and I needed to find out what trading cards we were playing with.

'Awlright,' I said, 'I'll tell you what happened.'

'Shut up,' said Mooney.

He threw the gun high into the air and it skidded down the cliff. No living person would ever see that gun again.

'Here's what's happening,' Mooney said. 'I'm counting to twenty. You're going away and not coming back unless you know 150 percent that I'll let you. I mean, if you come back before you know I'll let you back, I'm gunna drag you by the balls all the way up this cliff and throw you off. You got that?'

I didn't get anything. I didn't know what was going on. I looked to Schmidt to see if he could interpret. He shrugged his shoulders. He didn't know what was going on either. Mooney held all the cards and he was hiding most of them.

'I'm counting to twenty, and you'd better be gone when I'm finished.' Mooney grabbed the palm of my hand, turned it over and started counting. Imagine terror by numbers '. . . five, six, seven, and eight . . .' I wanted to leave, but Mooney would not let go of my hand.

On top of Mount Coot-tha, I was the most frightened I have ever been in my life. '. . . nineteen, twenty.' Sergeant Frank Mooney had just deposited two thousand dollars in my hand and walked away.

It was a fair hike from the summit of Mount Coot-tha to Hendra. I never wear a watch, but it must have taken nearly four hours and that's with grabbing a bus for a couple of kays.

I could have caught a cab when I hit the bottom of the mountain, but I needed to walk more, and think. Apart from Gooroo, Marcus Georgio was the person I had the most sense from that day. And he was dead. Everybody wanted to tell me it was odds on I did him in.

All I needed to top that off was sixteen kilometres of some cabbie telling me it was the feminists or Asians or politicians or Aboriginals or public servants or a combination of the aforesaid who set me up.

Maybe it was the public servants, or one public servant: Ms Kathy Billings.

On my walk, I was thinking how odd it was Ms Billings gave me about 16-hours' notice of my appointment with Caulfield Jones. In my experience of the public services, the gears grind slowly and there appear to be a heap of review staff.

Surely one of Ms Billings' supervisors would have said, 'Hang on you have to give Hill more notice than that.' It is quite possible they stuffed around with my file for so long they had given me plenty of time but that time had run out. One way to find out what happened . . .

MOST PUBLIC SERVICE BUILDINGS have a security guard at a desk in the foyer. It has been like that since some psycho blew away a mob of office workers in Melbourne. I was hovering over a retired army officer supplementing his service pension by sitting behind a desk trying to vet the harmless loons from the harmful ones.

I gestured with my open palms that I was no trouble at all. It was 5:30 p.m. so he had to be near the end of his shift. He would be itching to catch the 7 p.m. news on the ABC, to see how many charred bodies had been sacrificed in the northern Victorian bushfires.

I was polite and deferential. 'My cousin Kathy Billings has invited me to the inter-office smoko. Is that awlright?'

'They're on the roof,' he yawned, and didn't even bother to cover his mouth.

I yawned, too. Hours into a bad dream, I was dead tired. 'What floor is that? I'm from Victoria,' I apologised.

He nodded. He knew all about directionless Victorians trying to take over Queensland after they had stuffed their own state senseless. You had to feel sympathy when one of them could not work out that the roof would be the top floor of a building.

'Twenty-eight,' he yawned again.

'Thanks,' I yawned in reply.

The lift opened to show me Kathy Billings' back retreating towards a concrete platform seat in the middle of the roof, enclosed on four sides by concrete walls. Buddha, twenty-eight floors! If we don't stop these developers, they'll build a skyscraper so tall we can all stand in line for our turn to shake hands with God.

Billings put her vodka-and-orange on the concrete beneath her seat. She sat down between two bucks whom she was probably playing off against each other. The bucks were drinking spring water, and trying to make an impression. Time for some orphan bastard to shake up the studs.

'Kathy, you're looking great,' I said, picking up her vodka and handing it to her.

I could see by her eyes it wasn't her first.

She waved her finger, trying to place me. I put my hand over that finger and reminded Kathy it was rude to point. The studs looked across at each other to agree I was not welcome. Forty other public servants stood around in groups, complaining about work and talking extra-curricular bullshit. A surprised facial expression, slowly fading, showed that Ms Billings recognised me. I did not want the studs to do their macho shit and give me the boot, so I threw in a wrong 'un.

'Come over here, Kathy, and I will tell you what happened to Jenny.'

I grabbed her vodka and used it as a carrot to entice her to a corner of the building, where we were higher than smog.

'Who's Jenny?' she asked, as she obligingly eased into a corner of the concrete rectangle.

'Don't know,' I admitted. 'Remember me?'

'Yair, I saw you yesterday. You're Steele Hill, a beno.'

'Beno?' I asked.

'Beno, as in unemployment beneficiary. Only we can't call you that any more. Now you're a client.'

'Thanks for the promotion.'

I got down to business. 'Have the police seen you?'

'The police, why?' she asked, convincingly enough.

'You know that job you sent me to.'

'Don't tell me,' she said in mock sympathy. 'You didn't get it.'

'No, I didn't, but my prospective employer did. Someone shot him full of mortal holes.'

I wasn't sure whether she was surprised or excited by this choice gossip. Whichever, she did not say a word, just waited for more information. She would have to wait, because that was exactly what I wanted from her.

'When he rang up about the job, did that Jones bloke mention me by name?'

'Would you like a drink?' she replied, ignoring my question.

Apparently, years ago, when you joined the public service, you swore an oath to the Queen of the Commonwealth. Now, in the early nineties, it seems that you swear an oath to always ask the questions.

I played question for question.

'Have you got any wine?'

Billings brushed me aside, moving towards the makeshift bar, and I followed. She turned her head.

'Are you following me?'

You bet. In some ways, the modern woman can be surprisingly old-fashioned, like screaming for the coppers, only using a mobile phone to do it.

'Red or white?' she asked.

The wine came from that young vineyard, chateau de cardboard, so I just tapped the nearest cask.

When we retired to our corner again, it was my turn to ask a question.

'So, how long have you known Marcus Georgio?'

'Who?' she slurred, as though genuinely trying to follow my erratic conversation.

So much for the Gooroo theory of a deranged stiff out there, knocking off a cheating hustler.

'Look, I shouldn't have crashed your party. Ever since I ran into that defrocked nun who told me I was John Lennon's lovechild, I sometimes tend to indulge in inappropriate behaviour.'

I could see her face perk up at the Lennon angle, so I followed up with my usual disclaimer: 'I don't really believe I'm Lennon's lovechild, myself, but . . .' The graceful shrug of my shoulders suggested it was a real possibility.

I suppose there was some chance chronologically, given the timing of the Beatles' visit to Brisbane. But I would not put five cents on it myself. Still, it was one of my proudest creative fictions, and had the desired result of gaining Ms Billings' full attention. I wanted a brief yet truthful account of her place in my life.

'Tell me a bit about this job you lined up for me and I'll go.'

Kathy tried to concentrate, which was her mistake and mine, as introspection seemed to remind her of who was who in this relationship. She turned on me.

'You seem like a nice guy, Steele, but if you think I worry a shit about your problems, you've got me confused with someone who gives a fuck. So I gave you a hard time about this job referral. I wasn't going to follow it up. What do you think?

I'm going to be stuck in that shitbox suburban office all my life? Do you know how many women have been the head of the department in Queensland? Come on, Steele, have a guess. How many women have been the head of the Department of Employment in Queensland? Just have a guess.'

Well, I knew the correct answer had to be none or close to it, and that I was a thoughtless bastard as well. Worrying about doing a lousy ten-to-fifteen years for someone else's murder, when this woman was about to change the course of Queensland history.

'Let me guess,' I said, like the selfish sarcastic bastard I was. 'It's either 146,234 or you are going to be the first.'

'That's right,' she nodded.

They must pass out these tickets to dream at high school. Twenty million nobodies make Australia go round, and eighteen million of them are told to be somebody. Oh well, Kathy Billings probably had a better chance at that lonely big time than most.

'I hope you get there,' I said.

It was the least I could do. One day, she might wish me well in my quest to back the entire card at Eagle Farm racetrack.

'But, you see, you set me up for a tremendously opportune meeting with this Mr Jones, who turns out to be Marcus Georgio, who turns out to be dead.'

'Oh,' she said, resurfacing on Planet Real. 'Mr Jones? Well, he just rang up, said he wanted someone who knew about horse racing, maybe someone who had been a bookmaker's clerk. Also someone who could work computers. But no, he never mentioned your name.'

'I see, so he wanted a bookie's clerk who knew computers. And how many people like me do you have on your books?'

'Only you; it was our best chance to get rid of you.'

Only me. My lucky day.

I finished my wine. She finished her vodka, looked at the last slither of ice and scrunched up her face. Deliverance was not in the bottom of the glass, after all. She would have to look elsewhere.

'You owe me a drink,' she said.

I took the empty plastic cups to the bar. None for me, just a vodka and orange for Kathy. I took the drink to our corner. Leaning close to her, I lifted her hair above her ear. 'And you know what? The world owes me a living.'

As I kissed her, I was surprised at the way her lips melted against mine. I heard the silence as forty public servants took in the floor show of the future head of the department and the beno. When we were done, she ran a finger across her lips.

'Give me a ring at the office next week.'

I shook my head. 'It depresses me, Kathy, to see the modern woman slumming it with the likes of me.'

THE EH UTE and I headed down to the Gold Coast. With Mooney's two grand and the nine hundred I had won at poker, I should have been on top of the world. But all I had was three-grand of running-away money.

I drove through Southport and Surfers and Miami and Burleigh and Palm Beach and Currumbin and Coolangatta, and all the beach villages in between, to finish up at Gooroo's unit in Tweed Heads.

June answered the door. June liked me. We didn't see enough of each other for her not to. She pretended gambling was not my life. For five years, June had been pretending that Gooroo did not work for Cheerful Charlie, the SP bookie. For thirty years before that she had been pretending that Gooroo was not keeping book, whether on someone else's behalf or, more rarely, for himself.

One of the things I liked about June was that she accepted the Gooroo as an honest man in a dishonest job. June was just worried that there could be something intrinsically wrong about our gambling business. That I didn't understand. Perhaps that's why we were such good friends – we didn't understand each other.

Gooroo told me I looked like shit. June asked if I had eaten, which reminded me that it had been almost twenty-four hours since I had tasted food. I told her I couldn't eat a bite. She sat beside Gooroo as I tucked into reef fish, chips and fresh salad.

I felt the need to speak as I ate. 'You were wrong about the public-servant woman, Con,' I said between mouthfuls.

June was concerned. 'You and Natalie haven't split up, have you, Steele?'

'No, it was just that Gooroo, er Con, thought I might be able to score a job down here for a bit.'

Mrs Vitalis was relieved. 'How long you down for?'

'Quite a while, I think. Nat's on holidays, staying with her parents, the ones who don't like me.' I had put that badly – as though Natalie had another set of parents who did like me.

The Gooroo could see my getting into trouble explaining why Nat was up the coast and I was down the coast for what I anticipated could be a while. He stepped in to help. 'Listen, Steele, I think I can get you a job with Cheerful Charlie, just answering phones.'

Buddha, I was tempted. Honest work was what I needed.

June wasn't having any of it. 'Come on, Con, you know enough people. Can't you get Steele a real job?'

'Course I can, Sweetie, but we're all tired right now. Can you set up the spare bed for Steele?'

June went to the linen cupboard, and then to the spare bedroom. Her husband watched her go out of hearing.

'What?' demanded the Gooroo, softly but forcefully.

He whistled when I took out my wallet to show him the three grand.

'A couple of coppers gave me most of this and told me to piss off out of Brisbane. But this whole state is so hot, I'm thinking of going to Tassie for the cooler climate. Maybe Natalie could extend her holidays and join me.'

The Gooroo considered that. 'Tasmania, that's not a bad idea. I can probably come up with another grand or so, if you have to be away for a while. But why would the coppers want to stake you?'

'I was hoping you might be able to figure those odds, Gooroo.'

'Steele, I have been hustling one way or another for nearly fifty years. In that time, the cops have never done me one single favour I did not pay for. You're quite right to be looking this gift horse in the mouth, because it probably bites.'

June returned and settled into an armchair.

'Should we get out a video?' she asked.

Her husband nodded. 'Let's get out *The Grifters* again. Have you seen that one, Steele?'

I saw it at the cinema earlier that year. It's a fun movie, but you have to be in the right mood to watch Angelica Huston as the aging but still leggy hustler who accidentally slits her son's throat. I begged off.

'Don't think me an unsociable bastard, but I go all funny if I'm not out and about on Friday night. What's on around the traps tonight, do you know?'

'Well the basketball's on at Southport. That usually drags in a big crowd,' the Gooroo said.

Yo, not my go. I don't mind testosterone-enriched white Aussies pretending they're Afro-Americans. But the truth is I hate the taste of American popcorn and I cannot convince myself that a hotdog is more than a red sausage in a bread roll.

June offered a musical alternative. 'There's usually live music in the lounge bar of the Kirra Beach Hotel. That's just down the road.'

The suggestion jogged Vitalis's memory. 'That reminds me. I'm supposed to ring Cheerful Charlie at the Kirra Beach to give him the latest betting markets from Darwin.'

He disappeared into his study. I gave June's idea the thumbs-up. 'That sounds awlright. I'll have a couple at the pub and then head down to Coolangatta airport to get flight info.'

'Why don't you and Natalie stay with us for a couple of weeks, Steele?' June said.

'We might just take you up on that.'

The Gooroo returned and walked me out.

'I didn't mean what I told June,' he said. 'I'd never land you with a stiff's job. Come down to the shop tomorrow. Cheerful will put you on for the day.'

The shop he was talking about was literally that. The bookie operation was conducted from the back of a butcher's shop. You got your lamb at the front and you were fleeced out the back.

I said I would think it over, but I was still keen to check out flights to Tassie.

17

THE SOLOIST IN THE PUB was what I call a street-fighting singer. When she couldn't hit the notes, she screamed noise at them. Still, she wore the obligatory black cocktail dress, cut low at the front, to attract those who preferred to look rather than listen.

I climbed a bar stool beside a short thick-set man, deep in thought. It was such a hot night that I fancied a beer rather than my usual glass of wine. I wanted to be alone with my worries, so I was annoyed when the stranger turned to speak to me. Oh well, at least he drowned out the singer, losing a wrestling match with a difficult number.

It was the standard strangers-in-a-pub conversation. Yair, I was new here. From Brisbane. Yair, he was a local. Yair, I was a bookmaker's clerk. Yair, he was a professional fisherman. But he wanted to get out. Enough of the pleasantries, we talked about him from then on.

'My brother was two grades below me at school. I was the smart one in the family. He'd kill me if he heard me telling you this, but they even kept him down one year. We both ended up as fishermen. But he got out; he set up that floating casino on the Tweed River.'

Now I was interested, as I usually am when the topic turns to gambling. '*The African Queen*. Your brother's Angelo Sebastion?'

'You know him,' the man said, almost in disgust. 'Anyway,

I'm Luigi Sebastion. People call me Lui.'

I introduced myself and admitted I only knew of Angelo Sebastion.

'All us other fishermen said they'd never allow him to set up a gambling boat,' Luigi moaned into his beer. 'We said that Jupiter's Casino would have too much pull; that they would stop him, by saying that drunken gamblers would fall off the boat and drown. But Jupiter's is in Queensland, and the Tweed River is in New South Wales. Governments love money. And now he's making a squillion of it for the government, and four squillion for himself.'

Luigi shut up and looked at me in earnest, for half a minute. 'You seem like a bright young bloke. Professional fishing is fucked. Between us pros and all those bloody amateur anglers, we have just about fished out every bay below Cairns. But I've still got dough. I can get my hands on nearly a million. You come up with an idea for turning that into two or three mill and I'll look after you.'

I believed the man. I can read a bullshitter nine times out of ten, and he was not bullshitting. If one little murder hadn't been occupying all my thoughts, I would have planted a big kiss on Lady Luck's rich red lips. Sure, I would have helped Luigi spend his, I mean our, million. More basic survival concerns held back my excitement.

'I would have to think about it,' was my noncommittal answer.

It was enough to send him off again. He leaned closer to me, and looked around. 'You know some of the other fishermen are bringing in drugs, but I won't come at that.'

This sounded like juicy gossip. 'How?'

'What happens is a ship passes the coast, but out at sea.

They don't even need to come within sight of a harbour. They drop the drugs overboard, tied to a buoy. The fishermen know what the buoy looks like and where it is. They collect the drugs in their nets and bring it all in. No customs, nothing.'

'What sort of drugs are we talking about?' I asked.

'Some cocaine; mainly heroin. But I won't come at that.'

Heroin, a white powder that might look like cigarette ash, if you don't look closely. I could see Marcus Georgio's office in my mind. The upturned glass of water, next to the burning cigarette and the white powder I took for ash. The thin corpse on the carpet. In the cupboard, the bleach, which you can use to clean fits. Even the ties in the cupboard, and the tall, thin, model-like figure of girlfriend Crystal Speares, also a cigarette smoker, as were many smackies, seemed to fit suddenly.

'Look, I gotta go,' I said to Luigi. 'But I might have a notion for you. Could I meet you tomorrow, say at eleven in the morning? We could discuss this business idea some more.'

Sounded all right to him. About eleven in the bar, or in the car park.

I didn't give a shit about formulating a business plan with Luigi Sebastion. But I wanted to find out more about the Gold Coast international heroin trade.

Georgio liked to get his picture taken at places on the Gold Coast where the glitterati congregate. He liked to be seen with women with slender bodies. If I told the Gooroo these and other details, I was sure he would set the market at even money that Marcus Georgio had been a drug dealer and a drug user.

As I walked out, the singer was strangling the Bette Midler song *The Rose*, which I read somewhere was a tribute of sorts to American rock singer Janis Joplin. She had died of a heroin overdose some twenty years earlier at the age of twenty-seven, the age I was approaching Smack could kill you without a doubt, and it could also get you killed.

COOLANGATTA AIRPORT WAS BUZZING, even at 10 p.m. Lots of Japanese tourists, but what took my eye were two nuns standing in line behind a slim 190cm army officer with savagely short grey hair. You would call the sixtyish military man distinguished if you were impressed by all that brass, glittering from his shoulders. He looked oddly compatible with the nuns, all serving a Higher Power that demanded strange costumes of Its disciples.

As I went up to check the flights to Tassie, via Sydney, I began to cool on the idea. It felt as if someone else was planning my holidays. I was not keen on other people arranging my life. Whoever killed Marcus Georgio was really starting to piss me off. And I felt even more pissed off when my name was called through the public address.

The Gooroo should know better than to page me, unless it was a matter of life or death. I listened to my name being called three more times to make sure I had not misheard. I went to reception as requested, if only to silence the transmission of a murder suspect's moniker through these echoing airport halls.

A redhead with a plastic smile, beginning to melt in the heat of overwork, grabbed the message from a pigeonhole. Could I go to the VIP lounge? Why not? I would have gone in the past, only no one was considerate enough to invite me.

I followed the pointing finger and sensed that someone was following me. When I reached the lounge, a hand from behind me opened the door. The hand belonged to a tall classy bloke, about thirty-five, designer shirt, designer tie, designer trousers, designer shoes.

'Thank you, Mr Hill,' said a designer voice, cultivated, deep and medium posh.

Designer man closed the door behind us and motioned towards my choice of chairs around an oval table. I moved towards the table, but did not sit down. He took this as a request for an introduction, and stuck out his hand. Jerome Bradshaw of the Australian Federal Police. He wanted to chat with me, but first, he wanted to put me at ease. 'Let me assure you from the outset, Mr Hill, you are not in any trouble.'

That was a relief. I was in trouble with the state coppers for murder. At least no one had assassinated a foreign diplomat on my behalf, to put me in the poo with the Feds. Bradshaw sat down. I sat down.

The Fed leisurely explained himself. 'You have incurred the displeasure of a Sergeant Mooney and a Senior Constable Schmidt.'

'Have I?' I asked.

'Yes, you have. They left a present for you, in the form of the corpse of one Marcus Georgio.'

I could see that Bradshaw was trying to shape up as my mate. As far as I was concerned, the only differences between this Federal cop and State coppers were better dress sense and rounder vowels. I pointed to the phone in the corner. 'Do you mind if I ring a solicitor? I don't know this area real well, but I should be able to find one or two playing the tables at Jupiter's Casino. It's not eleven, so they shouldn't have blown all the money from their clients' trust accounts yet.'

'You have a cynical attitude towards authority, Mr Hill. In the case of Mooney and Schmidt, it's quite justified. But, in my instance, you will come to realise that our interests coincide. Haven't you seen yet that Mooney killed Georgio?'

I scoffed. 'I don't know, you southerners, always bagging us Queenslanders. Now, why would Detective Sergeant Mooney kill Georgio?'

Jerome Bradshaw slowly poured himself a glass of water from the transparent jug set in the middle of the table. 'It was the termination of a business contract. Mooney and Schmidt are the absentee landlords of a large marijuana plantation in North Queensland. Georgio was in charge of Brisbane distribution. But you know a little of Georgio's lifestyle. He needed a lot of money, so he broke the unwritten financial clauses of the contract. Mooney decided to terminate that contract.'

I believed all this, as much as I believed anything a copper told me. But the story was still as loose as a failed entrepreneur's memory. 'And what's the Federal cops' interest in all this?' I asked.

'That cannabis is travelling all over Australia, across state borders, and some of the profits are travelling overseas in undeclared cash and gold. Our political employers were unhappy when they heard.'

He took a sip of water. 'It does not concern us that the Queensland police force cannot clean up its own backyard, but we don't like their rubbish blowing into ours.'

For the sake of politeness to my interstate visitor, I agreed to accept what Bradshaw was saying. 'Awlright, I can understand that, but why are you talking to me about this? I don't do casual police work.'

The Fed shook his head. 'You really do not have a choice, Mr Hill. You see, we know Mooney has been trying to fool you.

I spoke to your old widowed neighbour, the one who likes to potter about in her garden. Actually, I told her that a natural predator is the most effective pesticide for aphids. She was most grateful. In return, she told me that two police officers, whom she described as the spitting images of Mooney and Schmidt, took you away. I discreetly waited near your flat, though I honestly believed that would be the last anyone ever saw of you.'

More sympathy for my anticipated murder by Mooney and Schmidt might have varied the even tone of Bradshaw's voice.

'Did you follow me down here from Brisbane?' I asked.

'I am afraid so. I do apologise for that invasion of your privacy. But, as I have indicated, we have mutual interests.'

Buddha, why hadn't I sensed someone following my car, like in the American cop shows. Spun the EH snappily around the back streets of Southport and lost the turkey. Instead I reversed through a possible hole in Bradshaw's story to make sure he was leading me down a straight road.

'So I was set up for Georgio's murder, but then Mooney told me to disappear?'

'Is that what he did? Of course you realise, while you are away, they will be busily working to prove beyond the shred of a doubt that you killed Georgio.'

Even if he was right, I still copped two grand in the hand rather than a shove down Mount Coot-tha into the bush. If the Feds were moving in on the action, I stood to come out a surprise winner from this misadventure.

'That's it then,' I decided. 'I go on a holiday, and you catch the evil police officers who have defiled their uniforms. I come back. We live happily ever after, except for the bad bastards, of course.'

I started to rise, but Bradshaw put his hand on my left hand. For some reason I was reminded of the sadistic nun who broke it when I was seven to expel the demon causing my left handedness.

'It's not that simple, Mr Hill. I don't want you to take this as a threat, but you are going to help us arrest Mooney and Schmidt, Mr Hill.'

I laughed. I mean, that's what you do when someone tells a joke. 'No, you see, Officer Bradshaw or Detective Bradshaw or whatever they call you, I'm really not interested. You think I want revenge, because Mooney and Schmidt tried to set me up for murder. By your own admission, the fit-up hasn't stuck. After that, it's none of my affair.'

I took Bradshaw's hand from mine. 'I suspect that you Feds and State coppers don't get on. Again, that's none of my affair. As far as I'm concerned, I can concentrate on backing winners tomorrow.'

Bradshaw nodded in agreement and spoke sadly. 'Then, we will have to allow them to kill you when you go back to Brisbane.'

'What?'

'Once they have committed two murders, yours on top of Georgio's, it will be easier to make their superiors do something.'

'Run that by me again. Before, you said you weren't going to threaten me.'

'Inaction is hardly a threat. Besides, I presumed you would co-operate. If you do, you will be totally safe.'

Safe? I always thought, even though I was a bit of a bastard at times, that my basic principles were safe. You don't bet odds on. You don't chase women with violent partners. You don't trust anyone making more than $50,000 a year. You don't do deals with coppers. The problem with basic principles is that they can be in conflict. Bradshaw had found my weakness. He sensed that my first principle was, you don't get killed.

'Inaction is not a threat,' I repeated. 'That's some catch.'

'It's the best there is,' Bradshaw agreed.

'Tell me what you want me to do,' I said. 'I'll think about it.'

'We want you to ring Mooney.'

Bradshaw took a silver pen from his shirt pocket and a business card from his wallet. On the back of the card he wrote a telephone number. 'That is Mooney's silent number. Arrange to meet him tomorrow. Think of a good place. When you meet him, say you know about the plantation. Don't worry; we will be there. It will all be over tomorrow.'

All over, but for whom?

18

SOMEONE BUMPED OUR TABLE. I'm sorry to say I jumped. The silver-haired army officer I had stood in line behind was embarrassed.

'I'm sorry,' he said in an American accent with a voice even deeper than the Fed's. 'I'm looking for Jerome Bradshaw.'

The copper snapped to his feet.

'I'm Jerome Bradshaw. You must be Colonel Clark. Won't be a minute here, Colonel, if you don't mind waiting at another table.'

'Not at all,' Clark said and moved three tables distant.

Bradshaw spoke earnestly to me. 'Make sure Schmidt is with Mooney. Where do you think the meeting should be?'

I knew where the meeting should be, a place with lots of people. But there was one complication. Oh, yair, eleven o'clock with the fisherman Louis Sebastion. Well, that did not matter as much now.

'The artificial beach at South Bank,' I told Bradshaw. I'll meet there with Mooney and Schmidt at nine o'clock, in broad daylight. Do you know the place I'm talking about?'

'We'll find it.'

Yair, well, even if the Feds did not find the beach, hundreds of happy family members would make Mooney think twice about killing me there. Parental stiffs always tell their kiddie stiffs to look for a policeman when they're in trouble. The kids might not look for a policeman in future if they saw Detective

Sergeant Mooney shoot the shitter out of Steele Hill.

My new ally indicated he was satisfied, and I could go. I headed out, but turned to say goodbye. 'You know, we should set aside a whole country for all you coppers, military, and spies. Maybe throw in a few hardcore Melbourne crims and the odd business leader. Of course, we would have to repopulate the place every five years or so. But that might be a good idea in itself.'

Bradshaw was not perturbed by my suggestion. 'Thanks for your assistance, Mr Hill,' he said calmly.

On the way out I passed by the Colonel's table. 'Come to pay the rent on your Pine Gap spy base?' I asked.

Clark smiled thinly, as if he was struggling to understand my remark.

The veranda light of the Vitalis unit was shining, as June had promised it would be. I aimed to ease the EH beside the Gooroo's car, but the way was blocked. The silver BMW suggested a wealthy guest.

Before I could turn the key to the unit, the Gooroo opened the door for me. I looked through to the lounge to see the back of a head, sporting dyed jet-black hair. I knew the bottle brunette was Cheerful Charlie, SP bookmaker.

Cheerful Charlie Evatt was indeed a happy bloke, giving the lie to the common Australian practice of casting nicknames against type. In Australia, a redhead becomes Blue, a miserable bastard Happy, a fattie Slim. But Cheerful Charlie really was cheerful.

'How they hanging, you bastard? Long-time no see,' said Cheerful, leaping from the couch to pump my hand and slap my shoulder.

This hail-fellow, well-met number was a little embarrassing

when I only knew Charlie through the Gooroo. Cheerful continued his enthusiasm. 'The Gooroo tells me you're thinking of joining our team.'

I was non-committal. 'I'm just down here on a holiday, though you never know.'

I turned to the Gooroo. 'Has June gone to bed?'

'Yair. You know, even after thirty years, she's still got a thing about our business. You want a tinnie?'

I nodded and was presented with a can of beer. Cheerful was drinking scotch and ice. He excused himself to go to the toilet.

'How much does he know?' I asked the Gooroo.

'Nothing. I told him nothing. He came around to discuss tomorrow's book, that's all. Shit, Steele, you're getting pretty paranoid. No harm in telling Cheerful the whole bizo; it's just I don't tell stories out of school, that's all.'

'It's cool, Gooroo. I gotta be down in Brissie tomorrow morning, but I'll be back to sit in on the book in the arvo.'

'What's up?' the Gooroo asked just as the toilet flushed.

'I'll ring you at eight in the morning and explain. Awlright?'

Cheerful returned to the room.

'Look, Cheerful,' I said, 'I've gotta go. See you tomorrow afternoon, okay?'

A deadly earnest expression settled on Cheerful. That sort of earnestness makes you notice jolly short fat people when it possesses them. 'If you are ever in the shit, Steele, I'll look after you. No bullshit, I'll look after you.'

Buddha, what was I supposed to say? I mumbled thanks. I caught the car keys by reflex. Cheerful had thrown them.

'I mean it. You gotta go to Brisbane? Take the BMW. I'll knock off this half bottle of scotch and grab a cab home.'

I was tempted to accept the keys to the Beamer, but it was too much like the condemned man's last ride. And conspicuous, to boot.

I put the keys back into Cheerful's hand. 'Get pissed; catch a cab. Be a good citizen. I'm used to the EH. See you tomorrow, Gooroo. Bye, Charlie.'

He shrugged. 'At least take one of my mobiles. You never know when you might need to contact me or the Gooroo in a hurry.' Cheerful threw me the flash phone, which cost heaps in 1991. Catching the leather case, I slipped it into the left pocket of my pants, but refused the offer of a battery charger.

'You know how it is, Cheerful. If your time's run out, you can't do much about it. Thanks for the dog and bone.'

I walked towards the door, but stopped and turned around when I heard Charlie call my name.

'Steele, she would have killed him anyway,' Cheerful said. 'I'm a bookie, I hear what is going on.'

'And what is going on?'

'That model sheila, Crystal, she would have killed Georgio anyway.'

I looked at the Gooroo, who was supposed to have said nothing to his boss. He looked more surprised than I was.

I turned back to Cheerful with a questioning look.

'I'm telling you, Crystal would have killed him anyway.'

I did not like how he said it. It sounded as if the word was out on the streets that I'd killed Georgio. They were making excuses for my murderous nature already.

'I'm telling you. She would have done it,' Cheerful insisted. 'You see, Georgio gave Crystal Speares AIDS.'

<u>19</u>

A LOT OF DEAD PEOPLE were on the car radio. I switched
over from Triple J when the youth radio station had rapped me
into submission, and moved on to FM radio classic hits. They
played the dead Janis Joplin, the dead Jimi Hendrix, the dead
Jim Morrison and the dead Marc Bolan in succession. I was
laying bets with myself whether the dead Mama Cass or the
dead Ricky Nelson would be next. I lost when they played the
Rolling Stones, only one of whom was dead, though how they
kept Keith Richards animate was anyone's guess. I killed the
radio, and pulled into a twenty-four-hour service station.

A uni professor named Lavinsky had told me once that the
dead controlled the destiny of the living. The professor was
now among the dead himself, and it was the corpse of a flash
hustler named Georgio who had been calling the shots in my
life for the past two days. His decaying remains now forced me
to ring the copper who had given me a lot of money to leave
Brisbane, and who would be upset to hear of my planned
return.

Mooney's wife sounded pissed off at my calling at 11:30
p.m. She said he would not be home until after one. Unless it
was an emergency, she would prefer I did not ring at that hour.
I gave my name and left the message: Mooney and Schmidt
were to meet me at South Bank near the artificial beach at nine
the next morning. She hung up, almost before I finished and
without asking me to hang on while she found a pen.

I ordered three mugs of coffee in short succession. I had not slept for twenty-four hours. I felt as if I was inside one of those roadside billboards showing a mangled car wreck. But my adrenalin, or something, was still doing its job, because I was not tired. I decided to plough on to Brisbane and grab a motel room for a few hours' sleep.

I wanted to see apprentice jockey Billy Scharfe sometime the next day. I was yet to place Scharfe in the picture, but I figured, since he was at Crystal Speares' unit, he could be positioned somewhere in the foreground. Speares I still made for knowing an awful lot about the demise of Marcus Georgio.

With another phone call, I teed up a room at a motel in Ascot, so close to Eagle Farm racecourse that I should be able to dream the winner of the first. I did not want to go home in case Mooney had someone watching the place. The one good thing about the past two days was Natalie was not here to see the downside of my career in the racing industry.

Fumbling my fingers along the wall of the motel room, I found the light switch. I put my bag beside the double bed and fiddled with the alarm on the clock radio. I stopped halfway through setting the time. What was going on here? I was distrusting my in-built alarm, not a good sign. My confidence was shot to billy-o. With more on my plate than Elvis with the munchies, I had better put trust in the only person keen on my getting a good result: me. I showered, left my clothes on the bathroom floor and flopped down on top of the bed covers for a sweat-filled sleep in the summer heat.

I awoke to find my legs kicking out wildly and I wiped sweat from my face with both hands. If I had just booted home the winner of the first, it must have been a nightmare ride. The placings in fluorescent red on the radio clock were 3:45.

Another shower, a fresh T-shirt and jeans, a $50 note left on the table with the room key on top of it, and I was off to the Feed Bin.

Many race-day hopefuls were down at the café, Billy Scharfe among them. I nodded towards him, but was not surprised to see downcast eyes in return. I walked towards his table.

'Buy you a cup of coffee, Billy, seeing the stewards aren't watching?' I said.

Caffeine, of course, is a no-no drug for racehorses. Years earlier, an English trainer lost a big race and much bugs bunny when his horse tested positive for caffeine. The pony fancied chocolate bars, and its owner indulged his mate with a couple of them on race morning. The horse returned the favour by winning the big one. Caffeine was found in the horse's system and the only option for the stewards was to disqualify the champ, despite racehorse slang for winning a race being 'getting the chocolates'. It was kicks in the sweet tooth all round.

I grabbed the seat beside Scharfe and nestled among the crowd, maddening for race-day action. I reminded the jockey about a tip he gave me early in the week. 'That horse of Barret's you gave me in the first, Billy, what number is it?' I asked, avoiding a direr topic.

'Three, Mr Hill,' said a relieved Scharfe.

'Three-four-five could be the trifecta,' I said, recalling the time on the digital clock when I woke.

No matter what happens, a punter will always grasp that last straw of superstition. Hollywood Frank was walking to Doomben races when a car ran him down. The driver sped off. Hollywood grimaced from the pain. He asked his mate if he had copped a butcher's hook at the number plate. His friend said he had and asked Hollywood if he wanted him to call the police.

'Bugger the police,' Hollywood replied. 'Make sure the ambulance stops at the TAB on the way to hospital. I want to take those numbers on the rego plate in the treble.'

I picked Scharfe for the superstitious type. 'Do you believe in coincidences, Billy? Or do you think there are strange forces out there that we don't really understand, but that are controlling our destiny?'

Scharfe was starting to get nervous. 'I don't really think about them things, Mr Hill.'

His was not the reaction of your average horse player, who would sit bored or irritated rather than nervous when asked to contemplate philosophy on race day.

But I was only warming up.

'Let's put it like this, Billy: Person A goes to the unit of Person B to talk about a murder. Person B receives a phone call from Person C, while Person A is in the room.'

'I'm not following any of this, Mr Hill.'

I ignored that.

'Person A leaves Person B's unit, but Person A hangs around. Person X shows up. Was that a coincidence, or was Person X the Person C who rang Person B?'

Scharfe was starting to sweat, even beyond the call of the heat. I hoped the other customers were too busy with their own concerns to notice what might look like nasty banned-for-life Steele Hill intimidating a young jock with whom he is not even supposed to associate.

'I'll make it easier, Billy. I was A, Crystal Speares was B. You were X who turned up at B's unit as I was leaving. My money is on you also being C, phoning Crystal, who wanted me to know bugger all about what you wanted.'

Scharfe caved in. 'Akay, akay, Mr Hill. I rang Crystal, but I didn't know nothing about Georgio's murder till she told me what you told her.'

'You were trying to score from Georgio?' I asked.

His perspiration increased. 'How'd you know about that?'

'I know heaps. I've been studying the form.'

For whatever reason, the racing reference calmed him. 'Akay, but I don't use much, truly. Recreational, that's all. Georgio told me it would keep my weight down.'

'What about the other hoops? Did you or Georgio sell them any grass as well?'

'Grass?' Scharfe was surprised, but covered it quickly. 'Not that I know of. It was only between me and him.'

'Could Georgio have been dealing grass with other jockeys, or strappers or some trainers, or maybe even owners?'

'I don't know, Mr Hill. Truly, I only know about me and him.'

Scharfe was getting calmer all the time. If I was a copper, I would be kicking myself for having thrown away an advantage I didn't know I had. I was not a copper, but I was wishing I knew what advantage I'd surrendered.

'Did Georgio ever rip you off? Kathy Billings said he ripped her off.'

The name of the public servant didn't register with the jockey.

'He never ripped me off.'

'Grass must be expensive for a battling apprentice?'

'Georgio gave it to me. He said one day he would get a big return from me in spades.'

'Buddha, Billy, he was talking about a race fix.'

'You can talk about a fix, Mr Hill.'

'And where am I, Billy? You could be a bloody good jockey. But the way you're going, you'll be lucky to end up working some dead-end factory job, if they don't put you in jail first, or in the cemetery.'

I pushed my chair back, making to leave, but I leaned across for a parting shot. I whispered, 'Hammer will never make a horse run faster, or a jockey ride better.'

Scharfe's remark about keeping down the jockey's dreaded weight had finally sunk in. While Georgio dealt grass, probably to dozens of other customers, he wanted a stronger hold over Scharfe in anticipation of that wild and glorious race fix. What better temptress for Scharfe than heroin? After all, it worked on Georgio himself.

I had time to kill before my nine o'clock meeting with Mooney and Schmidt, so I drove down Nudgee Road from the Feed Bin. I parked the car on a side street near Doomben racetrack, and ambled down the footpath to watch the strappers and stable hands take the horses for a race-morning walk. Strolling beside the high fence around the track, I filled my nostrils with the bittersweet tang of horse sweat.

December can be a heartbreak month for owners and trainers. It is not only the heat. If there is no rain, the training and racing tracks can be as hard as a landlord's heart. Expensive babies, as the two-year-olds are called, can go down like summer flies. Shin soreness is the main ailment, with the babies' legs not fully developed to take all that weight at high speed on hard tracks.

Leaning against the side fence of Doomben racetrack, I watched the parade of horseflesh. Some of those animals cost more to keep than a factory worker's wage. This is why they call horse racing the sport of kings, rather than the sport of factory workers. The factory workers ultimately control it, though. If they went on a gambling strike, the industry would go belly up in a month.

It could have been instinct, or luck, or the sound of automatic transmission finding another gear. Whatever it was, I turned to see the late model Ford mounting the footpath. It looked like a sad mishap for a tired early-morning driver.

Until I spotted the near-black tinted windows and the gaping hole where the front number plate should have been. The big white Ford was wearing my number instead. The car was no more than three metres from me when I leaped skywards, grabbing for the fence around the racetrack. My left hand was lucky, gripping beneath the barbed wire. The right hand aimed a little high and the barbs bit into flesh. The pain was terrible, but I was not about to let go. I knew that being crushed by the white metal avenger would be worse. I kicked my feet up to rest on the wooden cross rail, a metre and a half from the ground.

The left side of the Ford crashed into the wooden cross bar and the wire just below my legs. The hardwood cracked and the wire above it caved in. The whole fence shook sickeningly, and threatened to collapse, but I held on for dear life.

I tried to concentrate on willing the driver to flip the car. The driver didn't lose it, but careered off towards a crash with two racehorses led by a terrified strapper. In desperation the young woman was forced to pull the horses onto the roadway. They clippety-clopped from side to side on the bitumen, but luckily didn't gallop off down the road. The Ford found the roadway in front of the animals and sped away down Nudgee Road.

I slowly disengaged myself from the fence and climbed down, trying to wring the pain from my right hand. I stumbled towards the frightened horses on Nudgee Road, where a motorist had the nous to turn her car sideways to block traffic.

Strangers began offering me waves of sympathy, barely concealing their excitement at viewing the top-notch drama. A young office stiff doing overtime Saturday morning volunteered to call an ambulance and the police. I said I would drive to hospital and call the police from there. The bloke told me not to be silly. I staggered off and when I looked back, I could see the bloke shaking his head. To him, I was just another bullshit macho bronzed Aussie tough.

I could only keep my right hand on the steering wheel for the seconds needed to change gear on the EH's stick drive. Even then it was murder. Luckily for me, this was only in the metaphorical sense. The bloke in the Ford would be pissed off that it had not been real proper murder. Luckily also, Royal Brisbane Hospital is only a few kilometres from Doomben.

If the casualty staff were pleased to be able to practice their miracle of healing on me, they hid it well. Some were coming to the end of the Friday night/Saturday morning graveyard shift, and all looked like they could use an aspirin and a good lie-down themselves. The great Australian Pagan piss-up still raged regularly on Friday nights in 1991. A minority of worshippers would go apeshit during or after the ceremony, and do savage damage to themselves, family and friends, as well as arbitrarily selected strangers. I must have looked, for all the world, like a late starter in the bloodfest.

I waited for five minutes, as my blood dripped all over the hospital floor. I demanded attention and was led towards the examination room, leaving the placid bloke beside me with the fishhook in his mouth to ponder his recreational choices.

They shot me up for tetanus, cleaned the wounds and doused the hand with antiseptic. It stung like all hell. The medicine woman told me I was lucky I had not punctured a vein. She decided against stitches, and bandaged me up. She offered me a hit of pethidine, but I had too much to do to be flirting with the Regent of the Land of Nod.

It was eight-fifty when I got to South Bank, after stopping off at a newsagent to ferret out racing forms from four different papers. South Bank is an entertainment area, built on the site beside the Brisbane River where the city hosted World Expo '88. If you asked your average stiff living in Brissie at the time, they would tell you that the international fair was the greatest progress since they set up the penal colony of Moreton Bay the previous century.

They promised us entrepreneurs fortunes from World Expo. Having been kicked off racetracks for life, I fell for it and racked my brains for months, trying to come up with the pot of gold marked Hill, S. It came to nothing. I joined the long queue of disappointed local business people, cab drivers and residents kicked out of their humble South Brisbane homes to build the Expo site. I did hear tales of gold and loot being smuggled out of Australia, so it was nice that someone made a dollar or two.

As a stiff's inner-city playground, South Bank is no left bank of the Seine, but it could be a lot worse. There are tree-lined walks, an artificial beach, waterways and DIY barbecues, alongside the Three-F eateries – feed 'em, fleece 'em and fork 'em off – that define the culture of your modern metropolis.

I pulled up a piece of grass beside the beach of the artificial lake, and began to study the latest race developments. The trial form of the Barret baby, number three in the first, was impressive. A top jock was up. My other digital clock dream numbers, four and five, were both twelve-to-one shots.

I marked the paper to remind myself to take a $20 trifecta on three-four-five, and a $10 trifecta on three-five-four. It speaks volumes about the allure of gambling that only then did I think to turn to page one for news of Georgio's murder.

Nothing. Not one line throughout the whole local daily. Someone had firmly closed the lid on the Georgio coffin. I was quite pleased about this result, though I felt a little sorry for the dead man. Fancy having your sure-fire chance of making page one nixed like that.

Poor Marcus. If he missed the cut for Saturday's paper, he would not be in the Sunday press. They file most of their stories on Thursday. Monday's newspaper would have no word on Georgio. With a skeleton staff of journos working the weekend, any media-friendly copper who heard about the hushing up of the murder would find no reporter to tip off. By Tuesday, a divorce action in the British royal family might eat up page one. In horse racing circles, they say there is no such thing as a dead cert. Robbed of page one, Marcus Georgio's corpse proved it again.

I had been at South Bank for the best part of an hour and thinking the ungallant coppers had stood ne up. A shapely pair of fake-tanned legs stood in front of my newspaper. I lowered the paper to see a flimsy white cotton dress covering the bottom half of a black bikini. Higher up was the upper half of the dress and the matching black bikini top. Under a broad-brimmed white hat was the cool face of Crystal Speares. She stood out like Lady Macbeth on Mother's Day among the ordinary citizens rolling up to play Happy Families. The consummate gentleman, I indicated a piece of turf beside me for Speares.

'You really know how to show a girl a good time, Steele,' she said, accepting my offer.

'I was expecting someone else, Crystal, someone you would not want to be having a chicken and champagne breakfast with. But you know about that. Are you sitting in for him?'

'I might be. Give it up, Steele. Go away. They are not making heroes in your size this summer.'

'There's no obituary in the paper on Georgio, your past hero, Crystal.'

She turned to look at the water and recited:

I want a hero: an uncommon want
When every year and month sends forth a new one,
Til, after cloying the gazettes with cast,
The Age discovers he is not the true one.

She turned her head back towards me and I frowned suspiciously.

'Byron,' she said. '*Don Juan.*'

My frown grew deeper.

She explained: 'When I was eighteen, I got a part in the mid-life crisis of a professor of literature. I came out of it with a $2000 watch and four lines of Byron. I pawned the watch.'

A beautiful woman's road to bitterness can be paved with surprising side-tracks. Maybe that was half the attraction for the poets. It was time for me to contribute a half-profound observation – any half-profound observation would do. 'And now you are trying to pawn Byron to me?'

She accepted the wisdom for more than it was worth and

nodded wistfully. 'Perhaps.'

I blew it with my next line. When you were raised down in the hard school of the streets, you could fly only so high with the Romantics. 'To buy some smack,' was my suggestion to bring us both down to earth.

She flashed fire and began to talk water. 'I'm not even going to ask what happened to your right hand. You're like a baby in the middle of that lake, Hill. You're out of your depth. And you forget you don't know how to swim.'

'Tell me a bit more about the water, Crystal. I'll start swimming soon enough, and in the right direction, too.'

She pointed towards a mob of kids, splashing and squealing happily in the lake and she spoke softly. 'A killer crocodile named Mooney is in the water. He sent me to tell you if you poke as much as one finger north of the border again, you are dead.'

I yawned. 'That's a stale threat. Tell me something new. Tell me what Mooney has on you.'

She laughed, a bitter sound, but still a laugh. 'Mooney and I don't mix in the same circles. He hasn't got anything on me. It is what I know about him. Whoever said information is power must have been talking about life in the clouds. In the real world, information is a death sentence. Unless you are a survivor, like me.'

'I plan to survive too, Crystal.'

'Good for you. I'll pay to have them put it on your gravestone. Let's get out of this damned heat. I think I'll go to Europe, where rich old men lust after snow-white bodies. Even if the old bastards live longer in the colder climate.'

'Talking of snow,' I said while helping her to her feet, 'they tell me that a few people are coming down with AIDS from sharing needles.'

'So what?' she shrugged, 'None of my business.'

She began to understand that the statement was quite personal. She shivered, despite the heat. 'You're talking about me? I would never share a needle.'

I believed her. The idea of sharing anything but her body repulsed Crystal Speares. I asked if I could drop her somewhere, but she pointed to the red Mercedes Sports parked down the street. I walked along with her towards the car, though I felt I was batting way above my place in the social order.

'Byron – he was a bit of a cripple, wasn't he?' I asked, as she slid behind the wheel and started the engine.

'He was a man, wasn't he?'

Crystal Speares drove off, stirring up the street dust around my feet.

<u>20</u>

I STOOD FOR A FEW SECONDS, staring through the dusty trail of the modern woman. Up ahead, the Mercedes turned left and out of sight.

I looked around in every direction for an educated Federal copper named Bradshaw. If he was following me at South Bank, he was as slick as an oil spill on wet clay. More likely, he had better choices than to stick around while Crystal Speares and I exchanged pleasantries. Mooney and Schmidt were the targets Bradshaw had in his sights. He probably figured Speares for a high-class scavenger, not worth the worry. If he looked closer, he would have found a shark who ate private-school boy-men like him for breakfast.

Another possibility. Bradshaw had tried to persuade Speares to do her duty for Queen and Country, as he had done with the reluctant patriot, me. I hoped he had. She would run rings around him. Dealing with a murderous drug runner like Mooney was child's play compared to dealing with a beautiful modern woman with street smarts.

Back in my humble vehicle, the car radio played me some more dead people. For variety, they were broadcasting living people singing dead people's songs. Did someone stop the rock world in 1985? Would we end up with tribute bands to tribute bands? Pete Townshend, formerly of Britrock band the Who, was right. Rock 'n' roll is dead. But he should have added that they're still looking for somewhere to dump the corpse.

By 11:15 a.m. when I hit the Kirra Beach Hotel, I needed a beer. As I pulled off the highway, I heard a sound that made me curse for being late. As much as I wanted the noise to be three quick backfires, I knew they were gunshots.

There was no one within cooee of the body, stretched out in the middle of the car park. The drinkers also must have figured car backfires. As the EH crawled past and halted at a discreet distance from the dying man, I could have sworn he looked up at me. When I reached his side, I saw a thick line of blood dribbling from the corner of his mouth. Disenchanted fisherman Luigi Sebastion's head fell to rest on the concrete as his boat crossed the bar for the last time.

Lui's eyes were wide open. He looked as if he was asking, 'Why?' For months, at the oddest moments, I relived the feeling that Lui was blaming me. Blaming me for being late. For not telling him why. I didn't know why. All the poor bastard wanted was a little help to get out of his brother's shadow.

I rose to split when a hand appeared on my shoulder. I looked back and upwards to see Senior Constable Schmidt towering above me. His cop car was parked across the road, with Mooney slumped in the passenger seat. Buddha, who was tailing whom? Who was killing whom?

'Don't worry about it,' Schmidt said softly. 'We'll take care of it.'

I stood up and wiped some thick liquid from my nose as I bowed my head. 'I didn't do it,' I said.

'We know. Look, the crowd's already coming out of the pub. You better go. It's just like Kuwait City, the innocents in the way get killed, too.'

I grabbed Schmidt by the arm as the pub regulars spilled out to take in the show. 'What are you talking about?'

'Kuwait City hospital,' Schmidt replied. 'Saddam's troops pulled out the life support tubes from the babies.'

I couldn't believe I was hearing this. 'For fuck's sake, Schmidt, you're giving me some fairy tale to explain this?' I pointed to Sebastion's corpse.

Schmidt was upset at my unwillingness to accept his poignant comparison. 'It's true, Hill. But a fuckhead clown like you always gotta have a different slant on the world.'

I was as mad as he was. 'Yair, you're all doing it to protect the babies. Everyone's doing it to save the babies. If I go over and have a sniff of Mooney's gun and it's been fired in the last five minutes, the bullets will be for the babies.'

'Fuck off, Hill, I've got a crime scene here.'

Schmidt began to push the crowd away as he dialled numbers on his mobile phone. I walked back to my car as Mooney hopped out of his. I called back to gathering bystanders, wanting to help out or to stare.

'It's okay, folks,' I said. 'We're all doing it for the babies.'

21

I EASED THE EH UTE onto the highway and drove towards Tweed Heads. There was nothing else I could think to do. I considered going home, but Nat wasn't there and I wanted to stay out of the way of Mooney and Schmidt while I figured out what these murders were all about. I desperately wanted to ring Nat, but what could I tell her? Certainly not the truth.

Back at the unit, I sipped a beer and June Vitalis ignored my silence. She excused herself while I made a call. The local Catholic priest knows the Sebastion family, but he has not seen Lui at mass for a while. Yair, he can go down to the pub and do the business. Last rites, yair, that's the one I was talking about. Only didn't you need to race down there quick or else the soul goes scampering off somewhere or other, doesn't it? The priest would take care of it. Good. My name? Oh, that doesn't matter. Could he just hurry?

I was halfway through the beer before June returned. She must have been dying to know what was going on. But thirty-five years with the tight-lipped Gooroo, miserly doling out information, made her used to not asking a single question when she considered the timing was wrong.

The Gooroo had told me about one time when the police put their steel mallets through the television and the plaster panels of the walls of the unit when June was home alone. The cops said they were looking for evidence of illegal gambling. When the Gooroo arrived, he saw silent June with a beetroot face. The cops were gone, having left a dozen infringement notices and the unit looking like a bomb had hit it.

June gave Con some looks with icicles hanging from them. But she asked not a single question. The Gooroo told me he wanted to crawl under the carpet when the local electrical retailer brought in the new TV and the builder came in to repair the walls. He said it was the day that he realised just how much he loved June. Because she never asked him what sort of a business he was in when the police smashed the TV and the walls under the pretext of looking for betting slips.

I rang the Gooroo's work number, listening as the phone diverter shifted the call from the widowed pensioner's home to the butcher's shop. I asked Gooroo for his TAB account number, and told him I was going to place $30 in bets, for which I would give June the money.

I had to persuade June to accept the $30 for my trifecta bets over the phone on Gooroo's account. I was able to convince her that the $2000 in my wallet would see me through a month or two, even if I went to Tassie for part of that time.

The clock dream worked out spot on. Number three, trainer Barret's baby, won easily, just as Billy Scharfe had told me it would. It ended up a short-priced favourite. But four and five, at good prices, ran second and third, in that order. The dividend for the trifecta was $62.20 for a $1 investment. I won more than $1,200 for my $20 bet. June asked if I had lost, because my expression did not change when the race broadcast finished.

The phone rang and the Gooroo gave me a tip for the next race. I put $200 on the horse through Gooroo's phone account, and won another $800. The horse was called National Designer.

Prepared to back another hunch, I went down to check out the butcher's shop, the front for Cheerful Charlie's illegal bookmaking. I parked the EH half a kilometre down the road and walked the rest of the way. The shop was shut, or at least the front door was. Around the back, I pressed my foot on a buzzer set in concrete among the bushes. I introduced myself through the microphone covered by the creepers, crawling up the side wall.

There were nine phones inside, the legacy of when the operation was more successful. A young bloke, a young woman and the Gooroo worked from desks, each supporting four wide ledgers, with one race to a page, drawn up in what would have looked like the work of crazed mathematicians to non-gamblers, and to most gamblers for that matter. One of the four desks, arranged in back-to-back pairs, was free and I got comfortable on a chair behind it. A lonesome phone with pre-programmed numbers hung from the wall.

The Gooroo was the general for the afternoon. He buzzed about, keeping an eye on each ledger and ringing through bets to other bookies when the book had more money on a horse than the operation wanted to cover. He gave us permission to go for a walk or to the toilet when the phones were running coldish. At one stage, when he was not too hyper, I told him about the two grand I had won on his account.

At another opportune time, I asked him when Cheerful Charlie Evatt would show. Gooroo said Cheerful never came to the shop before dark. That was a bit rich, I thought. Sure, Cheerful gave the Gooroo a job after the coppers smashed up the unit and made bookmaking life hot for Con. But the Gooroo was the best in the game. He didn't deserve to wear the lot if another raid came. Charlie should wear some.

All the Gooroo would say, when I persistently quizzed him on the point, was that the money was paid in all the right places, and that there was no risk. I had no doubt he knew the odds better than I did. I also had no doubt that there was always a risk, even when the money was paid up.

We ended up getting stung, not by the police, but by a group of professional punters. It was the last race in Sydney. The horse had not started for six months, when it had run a respectable eighth in the Derby of 2400 metres. By most reckoning, the 1200-metre race was way short of an appropriate distance for this nag. Except for the reckoning of a handful of cashed-up, infoed-up pro gamblers.

We had difficulty laying off. Other bookies were copping an earful of optimistic bets, just as we were. In desperation, the Gooroo rang through to back the horse with the three grand in his TAB account. Two grand of the money was my winnings, but I knew the Gooroo would cover it.

The punters took out $50,000 when the horse flew home to win by a head. We had managed to bet back to take $10,000 off the loss. Punters who lost on the race kicked in with another ten grand. We also picked up fifteen grand from the telephone bet. You might say we were lucky to drop only $15,000 on the race, but a bookie is not supposed to lose $15,000 when a five-to-one shot comes in. Such is horse racing.

The book broke about even on the day. The Gooroo ducked down to the TAB. The youngsters took the stragglers' bets on the last provincial races.

I brewed the coffee and watched the action wind down. I poured a cup for the young woman, who had time for chit chat.

'What's it like living in Brisbane, Steele?'

'I like it: not too big, not too small.' It was the truth, but as I had never met the girl before, her knowledge of me was a worry.

She saw my uneasiness. 'Gooroo talks about you all the time, all the mischief you get up to,' she explained.

On cue, a key turned in the door and the Gooroo came in. Con and Cheerful had the only keys, with everyone else using the buzzer-in-the-bush system. Gooroo held a cotton bag in his hand, from which he withdrew $200.

He gave the youngsters $100 each, and told them he and I could manage till seven o'clock closing. Although the book covered that night's dogs and trotting meetings, bets had to be rung through before seven. Reaching into his bag of bugs bunny, the Gooroo counted out twenty-five hundreds. I tried to stop him at twenty, but he made the good point that the book would have been another ten grand in the hole if it hadn't had access to the $2000 I had won. He handed me the money and three rubber bands.

My wallet was so full I stuffed two bundles of a thousand in one trouser pocket and put the other $500 behind my wallet in the other pocket. The Gooroo threw the money bag into the top drawer of his desk. He walked over to the coffee percolator and poured himself a cup. 'We were lucky to get out of that one as well as we did, Steele.'

'Yair, dumb luck, Gooroo. But my luck had to change.'

The Gooroo turned around before he went to pick up a ringing phone.

'Leave it,' I said, as Con reached down for the handset.

He looked at me as if I was asking him to commit a major crime. He moved his hand closer to the phone, but stopped when I spoke again. 'I said, leave it. Let's sit down and work this out. First, I go to the dole office to get trapped into an appointment for murder. Someone knew I was on the rock 'n' roll and was a good target. Then I go to meet with Mooney this morning, but someone knew I might look up Billy Scharfe at the Feed Bin beforehand. That someone was able to give a killer in a white Ford the drum. Enough good drum to be able to almost kill me.'

Gooroo moved to sit down, but I wasn't having any of that.

'Don't go near that desk,' I warned.

The Gooroo obeyed and began to dance about in small circles. His face silently said he did not like the direction of my thoughts.

'Even before all of this, I go to a card game where Mooney and Schmidt turn up. Someone knew I would be at that card game. Georgio's murder the next morning speaks for itself. Someone knew.'

He moved about nervously, as if pretending what he was hearing was different from the words I was stringing together.

'It's been a long afternoon,' Gooroo said. 'Steele, you're stressing out here.'

I was stressing out, but I was not done. 'And someone knew I had a meeting with a nice Italian fisherman, whose only problem was that his brother had made it big and he hadn't.

'That problem was solved when the nice fisherman got killed for a reason he could not understand. A reason that I cannot understand. Because he got killed before we could work it out together. All because someone knew.'

The Gooroo stopped his circling. He began to back away from me, even before I lunged.

'No Steele, no, you're wrong.'

I could see the tears in his eyes as my hands reached his throat.

'You set me up, you bastard,' I hissed, ignoring the click of the door lock.

The Gooroo began to splutter. 'No, Steele, no. No, Steele. No, Cheerful.'

I turned my head and released my grip on the Gooroo's throat. It was my turn to back off as I looked into the cheerless face of Cheerful Charlie Evatt. I looked at that face for a couple of seconds before I began to concentrate on the gun in his hand.

22

THE GOOROO GAVE ME a dirty look as he straightened his shirt. He turned towards Cheerful, who kicked the door shut behind him with his heel.

'Jesus, Cheerful,' Gooroo said. 'We've been mates for twenty years. You could have talked to me about this.'

Cheerful nodded four or five times, then shook his head. 'You've been in this game most of your life, Gooroo. It's all you know. You're the smartest man I ever met. How many times I tell you that? But how much did we make today?'

Gooroo conceded the loss. 'We got burned on the last race in Sydney. Apart from that . . .'

'Apart from that!' Cheerful screamed his interruption, his face reddening. 'Apart from that, we're fucking dinosaurs. The dinosaurs got frozen out thousands of years ago. And we are getting burned out in the last race or the first race or some race in between, every fucking week.'

I had to listen to a lecture on the plight of the small businessman, after being the bunny of a two-day murder and mayhem spree. I turned my anger on the bookie. 'So it was you, Cheerful. What'd I ever do to you, hey? Hey, what'd I ever do to you?' I was yelling now, too.

But Cheerful was still ranting at the Gooroo. 'There's TABs in every pub and club on every street corner. There's Sky Channel coverage of every race in those pubs and clubs. There are so fucking many races for the dumb shits to bet on, they're lining up like zombies and throwing their money across the TAB counters.

'But not the pros. No, not the pros. They work out a race to win on. Fuck about with the TAB odds, so the horse gets out in the betting. And then back the bastard with us. Cause we are fucking dinosaurs, and it's the pros' destiny to make us extinct.'

Gooroo looked at Cheerful and went red himself. 'You think I don't know all that? But I got it under control. Jesus, Charlie, you've got a BMW. I've got a unit. I've got last year's model car. Are we starving on the streets, Charlie?'

'We would be if I wasn't smart,' Cheerful persisted. 'It's called diversification, standard business practice. That's all. But I knew you would never understand.'

Gooroo leaned towards the other bookie. 'What wouldn't I understand, Cheerful?'

I had heard enough to understand. 'Drugs,' I told Gooroo. 'Grass, heroin, speed, coke, and maybe new drugs we haven't even heard of. And other diversification, too. Murder, blackmail, rigging horse races.'

Gooroo calculated. 'You're murdering people for weed, for powder. Is that it, Cheerful? We had a business where we sold some poor stiffs a dream for a few bucks. And you wanted to diversify into killing people for powder. For fucking powder.'

The way Cheerful moved his lips before he spoke, I knew the obligatory justification was coming. 'That's where you're wrong, Gooroo. We are getting some of the purest heroin ever seen in Australia. We are giving those junkies the best deal they ever had. I've been told.'

I had to buy in on the discussion. 'You've been told,' I repeated. 'You've been told, have you, Charlie? What do you know about smack? Have you ever even seen it?'

'I don't have to. I'm an investor, but I've been told.'

'Awlright, well, let me tell you.'

I began to move towards Evatt, but only made a few paces before the chubby man halted me by pointing the gun at my chest.

I stayed where I was, but continued to educate the man who had been told. 'You get smackies who have been shooting up low-grade hammer, full of chalk and Buddha knows what else sort of shit. And you think you are doing them a favour by giving them top-grade stuff? Leave me alone. It was probably your A-grade heroin which was banged up the arms of those two eighteen-year-olds who overdosed under that church hall in Brisbane last Wednesday.'

'For powder, Cheerful,' was all the Gooroo could say. 'You're killing people for powder.'

I followed the Gooroo's line. 'You going to kill us for powder, too, Cheerful?'

'I don't know,' admitted Evatt, wiping the sweat from his face. 'All I was supposed to do was put up the money. I gave you up to the coppers, Hill, because you mean bugger all to me. And I am sick of Gooroo talking about you all the time. But now, I don't know what I'm gunna do.'

For one of the leading SP bookmakers on the northern New South Wales coast, Cheerful Charlie Evatt didn't know much. He didn't know about kids dying of smack, about an innocent fisherman being murdered. Buddha, he didn't even know to listen for the sound of a key turning in a steel door.

He did know that only he and Gooroo had keys to that door. But he had that wrong, too.

It was his good luck that he knew nothing about the one bullet, clean through his back and the centre of his ignorant heart that killed him.

The Gooroo and I looked at each other as Cheerful's body slumped to the concrete floor. A second unnecessary bullet, just for luck, blew bits of his skull in our direction as he went down.

We turned towards another man, another gun in the doorway.

'Here's good fortune,' I said. 'The Federal cavalry has arrived in the nick of time.'

Jerome Bradshaw of the Federal Police moved forward to stand above the body on the floor. As they say on race days, it was all over bar the shouting. I went slowly towards the door, but Gooroo didn't move.

Bradshaw put the gun back inside a shoulder holster but he was in no hurry to speak or follow me out.

Gooroo nodded towards our guest. 'I am only guessing. I've been receiving all the info second hand,' he said. 'But this would have to be Bradshaw.'

I nodded to silently confirm his estimation. Con was playing it cool.

'You and Bradshaw should be able to wind it up between yourselves,' he said. 'You don't need me.'

Neither of us was getting off that lightly. I looked helplessly at Gooroo as I gave up the pretence that I was free to walk out the door. 'You know, don't you?' I said.

The Gooroo was not keen to declare. 'I'd only be guessing.'

The Fed walked around the room, checking out this and that.

I knew the Gooroo hated to guess. I guessed for him. 'All I've been hearing about from Federal Police Officer Bradshaw is this huge paddock of North Queensland grass which is supposed to be behind this.

'But all I keep running into is a mountain of smack. Georgio, a smackie. Billy Scharfe and Crystal Speares both users. An inoffensive bloke named Lui Sebastion starts talking smack to me in a pub and he ends up dead. Maybe you can help me out here, Bradshaw. You told me two state coppers were producing grass. I never doubted you for a moment.'

Bradshaw continued to search the room and seemed to ignore every word I said. I continued anyway. 'I never doubted you for a moment about the involvement of state coppers, because grass is a domestic industry. Whereas smack is an import business.'

The Gooroo helped me out. 'Balance of trade,' he said, 'a Federal responsibility.'

I had to give it to Bradshaw; he left his gun right in that pocket holster. He was confident he could kill Gooroo and me before we made it to the door. He stopped his survey to pay me a compliment.

'I underestimated you, Hill. Maybe it comes from dealing with such dunces as Evatt and Georgio. I considered you would be easy to manipulate. But between you and that Irish lunatic Mooney, you have stuffed it up good and proper.'

'Why did you kill Cheerful?' I asked. 'It's an extreme way to break up a business partnership.'

'I can't believe how stupid that man was,' Bradshaw confessed. 'We asked him for a Brisbane distributor and he comes up with a playboy junkie like Georgio. Well, Georgio had to go. At least Evatt had the brains to come up with you, Hill, as the ideal killer.'

The phone rang. The Gooroo moved to answer it, but Bradshaw shook his head and Gooroo stopped in his tracks.

The Fed continued his inspection.

'Then that madman Mooney got in the road. What is with these state police? I give them an easy kill, you for Georgio, and still they are not satisfied.'

I agreed with Bradshaw's assessment of Mooney. 'Yair, he's as mad as a cut snake, awlright. But was that true about him and Schmidt and the dope plantation?'

'Only true enough to get you discredited, Hill, if you spread the story. There is a plantation, but it is not in North Queensland. Neither Mooney nor Schmidt has been to North Queensland in their lives. I was just sweetening the pot for them to take you down. Nosey Steele Hill tells the coppers he knows about the plantation in North Queensland. They realise you have nothing solid, but they do have a plantation and they decide jail is the place for you, before you do get some more information.'

I needed to fit one more piece. 'And the nobody fisherman Luigi Sebastion? Why Sebastion?'

'That was indiscreet. I must admit you were beginning to annoy me, Hill. That's why I decided to run you down near Doomben racetrack. To be honest, I was even thinking about cutting our losses here and moving interstate. There are plenty of bays in Australia. Sebastion was my last card to see which way I'd go. With Sebastion dead, Mooney could have you for two kills and leave me alone.'

Relocation was a good idea for the Fed.

'So you're moving out, Bradshaw. Now you've killed Evatt, and there's no trace to you, you're pulling up stumps.'

'Maybe. I killed Evatt, mainly because he told you that stupid story about Crystal Speares having AIDS, trying to throw you off the track. That's when I realised just how dumb he really was. You always tell a story grounded in half-truths. Not a transparent lie like Evatt's. To top it all off, I find out Speares has some tie-in with Mooney.'

I inquired about how the sexy blonde racecourse hustler finished up. 'So what did you do with Crystal Speares?'

Bradshaw was surprised at my concern. 'She was just a distraction. She is probably distracting someone else right now. I have more important business than Crystal Speares.'

So she was right all along. Crystal Speares was a survivor, the only one guaranteed to live. I needed to find out what Bradshaw planned for the Gooroo and me. 'You've scored a respectable body count already, Bradshaw: Georgio, Sebastion, and Evatt here, not to mention at least two junkies. All in less than a week.'

Bradshaw's face hardened and he gave a scowl, an expression I had never seen him wear before. 'Junkies are vermin. Every one of them that dies proves the law of natural selection. Their deaths strengthen our society.'

Buddha, another speech of justification. What happened to the good old days when people stole, sold drugs and murdered for money?

I figured the Fed had already passed the death sentence on me, so little additional harm could come from adding sarcasm to my list of transgressions. 'Sure, I should have known. How could I possibly have suspected that greed was your motivation? We only have to look at you to see you are a noble man. I'm willing to bet right here and now, if you give yourself up, you won't be charged with any crime. You were only trying to decontaminate the gene pool. They'll probably give you a medal, Bradshaw. What say you, Gooroo?'

The Gooroo played along as he edged towards the

protection of a desk. 'Odds on, Steele. If we were to ring the Governor-General right now, I'm sure he would strike up an Order of Australia for Bradshaw overnight.'

That's the trouble with private school boys. They hate being ridiculed. Bradshaw backed towards a wall, snarling, and slowly reached for his gun. I went for a telephone. Not much, I know, but at least they have long cords. I dived towards a desk to my left as I threw the phone in Bradshaw's direction. Gooroo dived behind another desk. As I hit the deck, I wished I had not misjudged the distance to land behind Cheerful's bloodied corpse. I liked at the blood on my bandaged right hand and doubted if that would aid the healing process. I tried to make the best of a bleak situation by using the roly-poly frame as a shield.

23

'YOU AWLRIGHT, GOOROO?' I screamed, as I watched Bradshaw calmly flick the safety catch of his gun.

Gooroo found the strength to knock his desk over, so its top was between Bradshaw and him. Cheerful's corpse was the only protection I had. The desk I had dived towards was behind me.

My mentor's voice shook. 'Yair, I'm sweet. But Bradshaw's running a short-price favourite against the two of us.'

I screeched. 'Why don't you use your gun, Gooroo?'

He screamed back. 'What bloody gun?'

Our exchange made Bradshaw smile, and he removed his finger from the trigger of his weapon. He wanted to play.

I yelled back at Gooroo. 'No gun? You're supposed to be a big-time bookie. Next you'll be telling me you haven't got a buzzer on your desk to call your heavies.'

Bradshaw giggled.

I was growing hysterical, but it was time for a Gooroo speech. 'Listen to me, Steele. We're both gunna fucking die. We're both gunna die. You understand? We're both gunna fucking die, but no bedwetting private-schoolboy fucking stiff like Bradshaw is gunna kill us. You got me?'

Gooroo's bluster was meant to give me confidence. Its effect was the opposite. 'That speech probably means you have no heavies. Buddha, Gooroo, what sort of a crim are you?'

Bradshaw could not resist this. 'See what I mean about

natural selection, gentlemen? Some members of a species have no idea of self-preservation, let alone self-advancement.'

At least Gooroo had bars across the windows, for protection. The glass smashed into the room and a hand holding a long-bladed fishing knife poked between two bars and steadied itself. The hand lingered until Bradshaw turned towards the noise. I had to admire his professionalism. He got three shots away before the knife sank into his heart. Only an expert with a knife could have made that kill. The scream outside told me that at least one bullet hit its target. Bradshaw sank into a heap on the floor.

I got up and looked with distaste at my bloody hands. I wiped them on the pockets of my jeans, which were also covered in Cheerful's blood. I could not get the blood off my bandage. Gooroo stood up and whistled in relief. 'You know, Steele, maybe Kathy Billings and Natalie are right. You should get a real job. Anything has to be better than sitting at home bored all day.'

He moved towards the jug to fill the percolator as a fist pounded on the steel door. I knew the voice behind it only too well. 'Let us in, Steele,' Frank Mooney insisted.

I looked at the Gooroo, who asked, 'Is he planning to kill us too?'

I was at the stage where I was taking little for granted. 'Who knows? But I don't think so.' I pointed at Bradshaw. 'The fish he's after has already been caught. By a fisherman, I suspect.'

The Gooroo undid the lock. For some reason, Mooney was dressed in his sergeant's uniform instead of his usual tacky leather jacket and suit pants.

But the first man to step into the room was an American Army Colonel. He walked slowly and carefully around Evatt, inspecting the bookie's dead body while making sure he did not get a drop of blood on his highly polished shoes. Satisfied, he took a close look at Bradshaw.

Mooney was talking to me, but the words were not clear. I heard the Gooroo answering Mooney back, but couldn't pick up what either was saying. I was trying to remember the name of the Colonel who had interrupted Bradshaw and me at the VIP lounge of Coolangatta airport.

He knew me, right enough. When he'd finished his second tour of death, he turned to look in my direction. I will swear the bastard smiled. Colonel Clark, that's what Bradshaw had called him. Clark changed his mind about smiling, and looked severely at the scene. But I had seen it: Clark's appreciation of death in the back of a Tweed Heads butcher shop.

Watch the butcher shine his knives
And this town is full of battered wives.

Mooney started to poke at my shirt to get my attention.

'Stop that,' I said. 'I've had it with being pushed around.'

Mooney stopped as Senior Constable Bill Schmidt, wearing a suit, hurried into the room. 'I think the one outside is dead, too,' he said. 'I've called an ambulance.'

'Who is he?' Mooney asked the constable.

I answered for him, pointing towards Bradshaw's body. 'He's a fisherman, or was. I think you'll find he is Angelo Sebastion, late owner of the *African Queen*, licensed gambling boat. Bradshaw killed his brother.'

'You slimy Fed bastard!' Mooney, just to remind us that he was indeed a lunatic, yelled at Bradshaw's dead body,

Bradshaw had picked Georgio and Evatt badly, but he was

spot on about the crazed Mooney. And Mooney had Bradshaw pegged. The State and Federal coppers knew more about each other than they did about themselves.

Schmidt put on his thinking cap, demonstrating why he was worthy of future high office. 'This could work out sweet, Frank. Sebastion might have been legal, but he was still into gambling, right? Evatt and the Sebastion brothers, and Georgio too, they were running an Australia-wide SP bookie racket. Bradshaw was investigating, and here we have the gunfight of the century as the result.'

Mooney was buying. 'Yair, it fits. I just don't like Bradshaw getting off with a clean slate.' He kicked the body three times to express his distaste. 'But I guess his Fed mates will find out what went down. Teach those bastards not to shit in our nest.'

I was curious. 'Would that be a nest of grass, Mooney?'

'Piss off, Hill. You're lucky to get out of this alive; Bradshaw's been gunning for you from the start. We could still get you for whatever we want, even murder. So shut your trap.'

Colonel Clark cleared his throat. 'Well, gentlemen, I will be on my way, now that everything is settled.'

Mooney waved the American army officer on. But I put my hand on the Colonel's shoulder. The officer drew in a deep breath to hold his temper at seeing a bloodied hand stain his uniform. I wanted to know the score, and I addressed Mooney. 'Where did you meet Colonel Clark?'

The sergeant gave me a compliment. 'You know him too, Hill. If you weren't such a fucking clown, you would make a good cop. I saw Clark waiting in a hire car down the road.'

The Colonel began to move. I clutched a handful of his shirt in my fist. His eyes went wild and I realised this man probably knew ninety ways to kill someone with his bare hands. Still, I held firm to the fabric of his expensive shirt.

Mooney looked into Colonel Clark's fiery eyes, to see the hatred and aggression there. He held his hand up in a stop gesture. 'Take it easy, Colonel. We're all the good guys together, remember.'

Mooney spoke softly to me. 'Let him go, Hill.'

I protested. 'But this bastard is in the thick of this. You can't let him go.'

Gooroo moved up close to Clark. 'A Colonel, hey? That's pretty high up in anyone's army. Were you involved in the recent Gulf War fracas against Iraq, by any chance?'

The Colonel stiffened his body, dropped his fists and closed them beside his outer thighs. 'I am proud to say I served my country in that action.'

The Gooroo poured coffee into four mugs, not extending hospitality to the Colonel. 'Uh-huh,' he said. 'You'd better do what Mooney says, Steele, and let Colonel Clark go.'

'What am I missing here?' I yelled.

Sergeant Mooney agreed with the Gooroo. 'Let him go, Hill. You see that crap on his shoulder below your hand? You see the crap on my upper arm? His crap shits all over my crap. But I fought on the streets, not to mention in police stations, for thirty years for my crap. And I'm keeping it.'

I let go of the uniform. Clark walked slowly to the door. He turned around when Gooroo addressed him.

'What was it, Colonel? About 10,000 body bags you shipped over in the first week?'

The Colonel said nothing, but stood to hear more.

'You had contingency plans for at least 10,000 of your bodies to be brought back, dead. Which would mean contingency plans for four, five or more times that wounded.

And you lost fewer than a hundred.'

Mooney and Schmidt looked at each other to see if either knew what this history lesson was all about. I put my face between theirs.

'Don't you get it?' I said. 'Morphine.'

'Morphine,' the Gooroo repeated. 'Unrefined heroin.

'After every major war, since at least the American Civil War, morphine or heroin addiction have increased in particular parts of the world. In this century, Paris in the twenties, New York in the late forties. We were late starters in Australia. Sydney had to wait till the seventies for the aftermath of Vietnam. Now in the nineties, we're getting presents from the Gulf to supplement the gear coming from south-east Asia and Afghanistan.'

The Colonel maintained a professionally bored expression, untouched by any of what the Gooroo was saying. The military man straightened himself to his full height. 'Good evening, gentlemen.'

He moved through the steel door, and out into the twilight.

Putting my hands into my jeans pockets, I felt all the money jammed in there. I retrieved the wad and let it drop to the floor.

I took out my wallet, and emptied all the money in it at Mooney's feet. The sergeant looked down at the money before raising his head to snarl at me. Schmidt put a comforting hand on Mooney's shoulder and led his superior officer to the door.

The bloody five hundreds behind the wallet, I threw towards the opened door. I followed the money trail.

Stopping at the threshold to the sultry night, I stooped down to pick up eight bloody notes. I dropped the money inside my shirt and felt the warm bills fall past my heart to rest in front of my stomach. I bade the Gooroo goodnight.

Book Four

At the beginning

24

Brisbane, late spring in early November, 1986

I HAD SCAMMED Bub Applebee's school principal into stopping her being bullied by tricking him into believing I knew about the most embarrassing moment in his life. My most embarrassing moment was when I had to stare straight into the face of the chief steward of racing, with a bloody great copper standing off his right shoulder. The steward was asking the questions.

'You wouldn't know anything about this Brisbane Handicap fiasco, would you Hill?'

Would I ever? Kidnapping, deprivation of liberty, extortion, supplying illicit drugs . . . I was looking down the barrel of a minimum of fifteen large at the tender age of twenty-one. I would be lucky to be outside the nick for New Year's Eve 1999.

'No, Boss, I don't know anything about it,' I said meekly, staring into the face of the chief steward, Mr Joe Boss.

Mr Boss waved the copper out of the tiny office, saying he would call him when he was needed. As the copper shut the door, Boss stood up and leaned forward, spreading his fingers like two fans onto the table. He made a great effort to give me a look of utmost sincerity.

'I'm sorry about what happened to your mate, Clarence. Is it true he rang up the Canterbury stewards and abused them for ten minutes for moving the barrier stalls five metres after a sudden downpour?' Boss asked.

It didn't seem important any more, but I wanted to give Mick Clarence due credit.

'It's true, Boss.

'How old was Clarence when this happened?' Boss asked.

'I guess he was about seventeen at the time.'

'What, was he crazy or something?

'Mick wasn't crazy,' I said evenly. The chief steward let me go on. 'Well, maybe he was just a bit crazy, but he was a mathematical genius. After he gave the stewards a prolonged blast, he redid his sums with the barrier moved five metres, and it came out that his horse would get done by a nose rather than winning by a head.'

Boss looked at me in disbelief across his desk. 'You're only a baby, Hill. What the fuck are you mixing with these lunatics for? What do you think's going to happen to you?'

'I haven't done anything, Boss. Is this about that mad Russian?'

EVEN IF YOU have a history of punting, you won't know the Russian I'm taking about, because this horse trainer changed his name to sound as Pommy as you could get. I'll call him Bill Smith. Most of the racing crowd probably noticed that Smith talked funny, but your average gambler is neither an Einstein nor a Socrates, and the other trainers, owners and jockeys were never too curious about unusual speech patterns. Smith could not get rid of the last traces of his Russian accent, no matter how hard he practised in front of his children.

Bill Smith was a battling horse trainer, best known as the father-in-law of one of Brisbane's top jockeys. I was on nodding terms with him at early-morning track work, and struck up a conversation when I saw him down at the wharfies' club – properly known as the Waterside Workers' Club, though only its management and a few cabbies would recognise it by that moniker.

It turned out that Smith had worked on the wharves in the early fifties, having jumped a Russian cargo ship and successfully applied for political asylum. A short thin fellow, he had great strength beyond his size, and he knew his way around loading and unloading cargo. His smattering of English, gained from travelling around the world, along with his winning smile, landed him the wharfie job.

One night, we were sharing a bottle of vodka in his two-bedroom weatherboard house in the Brisbane trackside suburb of Hendra. He raised his two children here, after his wife scarpered. Bill did not hold a grudge against her. She had wisely predicted that he would not be a great provider, after throwing in his wharfie job to follow his love of training horses.

'Must be the Cossack in you,' I joked. He had recently confided in me his background story. He kept his Russian heritage private from most people. As soon he had the hang of the new lingo, he had changed his name to a very English moniker, which I have changed again to Bill Smith.

'I don't want you thinking I am ashamed of being Russian, Steele. Anyone who says I ran away from communism is a liar.'

'I'm not the KGB, Bill. I'm not judging you on why you chucked in the old country.'

'I didn't run from communism. I ran to communism. The Australian wharves where I worked were full of Bolsheviks. Most of them had turned that way after their experiences in the Australian or British defence forces during World War II.'

Bill told me he had jumped ship in Perth more on an impulse than anything else. He even had a notion that he might catch up with the ship in Melbourne. But he met the proverbial man in the proverbial pub, and this bloke was a public servant who said Bill might as well try his luck for asylum. I asked the Russian if he had had any State secrets to trade. He replied that he had devised a few before he applied, but the Foreign Affairs diplomats demanded nothing along those lines. 'They almost wet themselves, Steele, having a real-life defector standing in their office. You got to remember, this is Cold War time and anti-communism is like the flu spreading through Australia.'

Bill was glad he didn't have to divulge the secrets he had made up, written down and rehearsed. His false espionage concerned matters of which he knew little. He did know that the diplomats would catch him out with the simplest of questions. Instead, they just asked him about his childhood and where he grew up. They could not hear enough about post-war food shortages in Russia. Bill found that strange. 'After the war, you must have had shortages here. Later, my wharfie mates told me about the rationing, and women being made to work on farms and in factories during the war to try to keep up production. Australia, Britain, Russia, I don't know we were much different. But to the diplomats, Australia had to be better. That's when I decided anyone who wanted it enough could be rich in this country.'

He glanced around his tiny kitchen, with its old stove and small fridge, and the wooden table covered with discoloured and peeling linoleum. Bill smirked and I involuntarily repeated the gesture, as if I was catching a yawn. Then a laugh swelled into a roar as it erupted from his throat. We were both exploding in laughter, with him hitting the table and me slapping a knee to calm ourselves down.

When we finally got ourselves under control, I said: 'You're not a bad bloke, Comrade Zhivago.'

He returned the compliment. 'You are a top bloke, Magic Pudding.'

'Hang on – "Magic Pudding"?'

'Yes, Magic Pudding. What is wrong with that? It is an Aussie children's book I used to read to Felicity and Robert when they were toddlers.'

'Magic Pudding. Magic Pudding; I guess it's awlright as a nickname, Bill. In fact, it's growing on me all the time. Let's just keep it between ourselves, but.'

We managed to do that, to my everlasting gratitude. I don't think I could have handled that moniker from anyone else.

Bill's daughter Felicity, or "Flick" as most knew her, who grew up on the Magic Pudding yarn, was a pretty blonde. She married one of Brisbane's most successful hoops, a man who we will call Gregory Sailor. He was always near the top of the win tally for any given year, and won a couple of recent Brisbane jockeys' premierships. You cop that trophy for winning the most races in a season, running for twelve months from August 1.

Sailor's riding off the track was causing problems. There were rumours that he was making an impression on the hay with a teenage stable girl. The more outraged rumourmongers would tut-tut, 'He's supposed to be a Catholic.'

This surprised me. I always thought that Catholic men could do anything they felt the urge for, so long as they were riddled with guilt afterwards. The most outraged of all was a senior police officer who was on the take from SP bookies in a big way. This copper, one of the many Micks on the force, would shake his head in disgust: 'Bloody Howdy Sailor, and he calls himself a Catholic.'

The nickname "Howdy" for Sailor was inevitable, I suppose.

Felicity "Flick" Smith was twenty-three years old, eleven years younger than her husband. The consensus of the racetrack moral compass was that Howdy should be happy with his young wife at home, and not go seeking pleasure with even younger stable girls. When Flick Sailor fell pregnant, the crooked copper grew more indignant. Ironically, the copper was the head of a racing syndicate and Sailor rode all three of their horses. Indignation never reached the point where the police officer asked his trainer to replace the jockey. An observer can make of that, as we used to say, what they will.

Bill Smith was distraught when he came up to me in the Feed Bin early one morning. 'Is it true what they are saying about bloody Gregory and that young slut?'

I might have been sleep-deprived, but I was savvy enough not to buy into that one. 'No one tells me anything, Bill, and that's the way I like it.'

He had been around horses for too long, because he snorted in frustration.

'You keep your ears open, Steele, and you tell me everything. You know the slut I am talking about, don't you?'

I raised my out-turned palms in a gesture of complete ignorance.

Smith raged on. 'Gregory has always had a big head. This is a problem that comes with success. I would not have let Felicity marry him, except that he has money to provide for her and I haven't. If I could have trained ten more winners a season over the past few years, he would never have got past the front door.'

I hadn't been keeping records, but I doubted if Bill was

averaging ten winners a year, so training ten more would have been a Herculean feat. He was a good horseman, but he couldn't muster the gift of the gab when talking to owners. They didn't understand his corny jokes, and he refused to tell them they had another Phar Lap in their stable when he knew the pony was pretty ordinary. Both the trainer and owners knew any neddy that showed promise would be taken from Bill faster than you could say, 'Sydney, here we come.'

I saw Bill a few times over the next two months, and I was unable to provide him with any more information on his son-in-law's possible infidelity. He came up to me as I was leaving track work one Thursday morning, and seemed pretty hot under the collar.

'You get around a lot, Steele,' he said in a low voice. 'You should be able to find an untraceable drug for me.'

I told him that doping a horse was not my style, and the risks of being caught made it an extremely dicey proposition. I added that Bill should disdain that kind of caper too. But he had an excuse.

'I know you have only met Felicity a few times, but you are the only one who can help her, Steele. She has been kidnapped. I have to win the Brisbane Handicap with Who Loves Yer Baby for her to remain unharmed.'

This news, exciting as well as dangerous and sinister, had my full attention. I asked Bill if he knew who had kidnapped his daughter.

'Yes, I do,' he replied, looking earnestly at me. 'I did.'

I gave a half-hearted laugh, and told the Russian that his warped sense of humour still held surprises.

'I am not joking. I kidnapped Felicity, and I told Gregory if he wants to see her and his unborn child alive, he has to ride

Who Loves Yer Baby in the Brisbane Handicap on Saturday week.'

I looked into Bill Smith's eyes, and saw that he was actually telling the truth.

'Buddha, mate, you love Flick. Sailor must know you wouldn't harm her.'

Bill made no comment. He refused to expand on his tale, no matter how much I coaxed him. He looked tired and anxious, nervously rubbing the top of one hand with the bottom of the other. I wondered why he was telling me all this – surely, he didn't really want me to get drugs for him. He spoke slowly and appeared calm enough, though every so often his nerves would show through.

'There is nothing to worry about, Steele. Mecklam thinks that Gregory is going to ride his horse, All The Favours, in the Brisbane Handicap. I told Greg to let him go on thinking that, right up to the last moment when the jockeys have to be declared. A couple of weeks back, I heard Mecklam tell his trainer to set his horse for the race, and that's when I got this great idea. I think Mecklam will have a big go at the bookies, and we will have top odds about Baby.'

I was wishing I could swap places with Smith, so he could hear all this drivel he was spruiking. Jim Mecklam was a high-flying corporate lawyer and racehorse owner, who could do serious financial damage to Smith just for stealing Sailor off his horse. Anyway, Mecklam could obtain a more than competent replacement for Gregory Sailor if he planned to win the Brisbane Handicap and pull off the plunge, which is what we call an extravagant punting adventure.

Word around the traps was that the lawyer was spending a bundle on the dozen or so racehorses he had in work at any one time, with trainers in Brisbane, Toowoomba and the Gold Coast. Sure, Mecklam made a bundle from the legal game, but it was said, with enough authority to convince most, that he had fallen way behind in his weekly training bills. He obviously planned to give his debts a decent haircut by winning the Brisbane Handicap.

Bill Smith should have been asking me how we could obtain a packet of dough to put on Mecklam's All The Favours. That would piss the lawyer right off – snapping up the best odds before he hopped in with his cash. Instead, we were supposed to wreck Mecklam's party by doping another horse, without the stewards finding out, at the same time compounding Smith's crime of kidnapping Felicity with the continued deprivation of her liberty, and adding fraud, and extortion of jockey Gregory Sailor to the mix. This was the great idea that tin-pot trainer Bill Smith had considered so carefully. There was clearly nothing to worry about.

A racehorse with the stable name Baby was to set us on the path to riches. When Mecklam, Sailor and the stewards found out how they had all been duped, they would have a good laugh about it and wish Bill and me all the best for the future. Some people say I am easily led, but there was no way I was throwing my life away on this ridiculous scheme.

'I'M EASILY LED,' I told Mick Clarence, when he wanted to know why I was after undetectable drugs to dope a racehorse.

Mick didn't much fancy the idea. 'If you're that hard up, I can probably spot you five hundred, maybe more.'

You could spot me a lot more, I thought. Mick Clarence was only eighteen, but the mathematical genius was winning thousands every month on the horses. Trust me, most punters who think they can win big on the horses soon come down to earth, if they don't hit the water by taking a last dive from a tall bridge. But Clarence was different.

Mick was studying pure maths at university. His high school senior results had been good enough for him to do medicine or law, to perform operations on bodies and/or wallets. He had no interest in those lucrative professions as he already had a prosperous business, crunching racing statistics and coming up with long-priced winners. I found Clarence's short life story inspiring. What really made me warm to it was the fact that, as far as anyone knew, Mick had never been to a racetrack in his life. He did all of his analysis and punting from his one-bedroom Spring Hill unit which he had bought for cash after three months of success on the punt.

A friend of a friend of Mick's had taken me to see the maths genius, one Saturday morning on our way to the races. Mick and I hit it off straight away, as we shared similar sophisticated leisure activities. I would visit him to discuss gambling and rock music. Mick's place was like a clearing house for gossip, borne and refined by many visitors. You could meet some colourful characters in his little unit, always kept obsessively tidy, apart from bulging ashtrays. Two computers constantly hummed away.

When he had known me for a while, Mick told me that he had one of those tragic phobias that can nearly destroy people's lives. I forget the technical term, but his was the one where public places and crowds terrified you.

If Mick had to choose a phobia that would make life the most difficult for a punter and a student, he would have picked that one. But he was so brainy that he could get away with going to only a handful of maths lectures. At those, he would sit way up at the back, away from most of the other students. He had a medical certificate, signed by the eminent Doctor Hill, exempting him from the bulk of his classes. Yes, it was I who signed the certificates. I couldn't recommend Mick another reliable doctor, and a crowded medical waiting room was no place for someone with my patient's condition.

Stories of Mick Clarence's punting prowess were gold for impressing peers in my circle of young gamblers. I decided that if anyone could steer me towards some good dope, it was Mick.

He had other ideas though. 'Go-fast drugs are notoriously unreliable, Steele. They might not work. They might be detected in tests. Punters and stewards might notice the obvious effects on the horse. Why not arrange for a go-slow on Mecklam's horse? So much simpler and more elegant.'

Mick quickly warmed to the notion of using the antithesis of a go-fast: 'You don't need to take a test on Einstein to train greyhounds, but those trainers have delicious ways to get a dog beaten. Don't feed the greyhound for a couple of days, then fill it up with water before a race to keep its weight within the permitted range. That can't fail. Or put a rubber band around the testicles of a male dog, and swiftly remove it at the catching pens after the race. Now, that's gambling poetry-in-action to achieve a defeat. Let's not be obsessed with winning all the time, Steele. Losers can be winners.'

I saw his point, though I wasn't really interested in a career in go-fasts or go-slows. It would take the fun out of winning, when you could skite about how clever you were in predicting the future. Yet, for reasons still unclear to me, I was committed to helping Bill Smith. And Mick Clarence was the only person

I could think of who might be able to help me do it. I told him the whole story, and he summed it up before he would give an opinion.

'So, Bill Smith thinks his son-in-law Gregory Sailor did the dirty on his pregnant wife. To have revenge against the jockey for commonplace adultery, Smith kidnaps his daughter and is now threatening her life, as well as his unborn grandchild's. Added to this bizarre act, the trainer also seems to want to stuff the plans of hotshot lawyer Jim Mecklam, by having a doped-up nag ridden by Mecklam's regular hoop Sailor win the Brisbane Handicap.'

'That's about the size of it,' I agreed.

Mick Clarence declared correct weight: 'Bill Smith is as mad as a cut snake. It is our duty to help him with his demented plan, rescue the fair damsel, become moderately rich and take a holiday on Mexican beaches with the proceeds. I take that back – you have the Mexican holiday, Steele, and send me a postcard. The rest of it, we do together.'

This was quite a change from the Mick of ten minutes earlier, who hadn't wanted a bar of doping a horse. His enthusiasm made me slightly less uneasy, but I reckoned Mick just wanted to see if he could come out a winner backing the biggest roughie of his career.

Mick asked me what I planned to do if he couldn't help me.

'Not much idea at all, really,' I admitted. 'I have about a week until the race. I guess I would do what I intend doing anyway: find where Bill has hidden Flick, and release her. Smith's really flipping out at the moment. While you'd think he'd be the last person to hurt his own family, you'd just never know.'

If I did find and free Flick Smith, Mick asked, would that be the end to our doping scam?

'I doubt it, Mick. Bill would go totally apeshit if freeing Flick brought down the whole house of cards. I reckon there's more to this than Sailor spreading the loving around like stable manure. It's the final insult to Smith's whole life. He gives up a secure job on the wharves for the risky business of training. His missus leaves him with two kids to bring up on his own. He thinks he did right by marrying Flick off to a top jockey, and then the jock turns out to be full of himself, with no room for anyone else. To cap it off, Bill finds out about a wealthy lawyer scheming some dodgy deal to win the Brisbane Handicap because he can't live within his income of thousands of dollars a week.'

Mick shrugged his left shoulder and made a weird face. 'What can I say? Adults are fucked, eh?'

This pronouncement made me pause and look more closely at Clarence. People tended to forget that Mick was a teenager; this kid who made so much money, and was so self-controlled, you treated him as a sage. He didn't speak like a teenager. Rather, he spoke in racecourse slang, picked up from numerous visitors chasing race tips. Such visitors were only allowed to enter Mick's Spring Hill cave one at a time or in pairs.

Mick was skinny, of average height, and, despite his introverted medical condition, dressed in a colourful nouveau-hippie kind of way. A huge, framed poster of Jimi Hendrix covered a third of one wall of his small lounge room. Across two other walls were vertical shelves with hundreds of record albums standing on them. A round glass-topped table in the middle of the room held up stacks of racing and music magazines. It was semi-circled by electronic equipment: two telephones on a round table, a television and a hi-fi set, which included a turntable, radio and cassette recorder. On a rectangular table beside the hi-fi were what looked like two portable televisions sitting on oversized videocassette recorders.

These were Mick's personal computers, which he used to analyse the form of racehorses. I had always pictured computers as great big metal cabinets, housed in government departments, corporations and universities. I had never understood how they worked, or what you did with them. What made the computers in front of us 'personal' I had no idea, and I didn't ask, for fear Mick might try to show me what he did with them. They looked slightly menacing to me, the sort of complicated machine a stiff might spend his days labouring at.

The only other objects in the room were two ashtrays, brimming with cigarette butts, sitting on a round cane table beside Mick's armchair.

I was almost four years older than Mick, a lifetime at that age. Yet, his one-in-a-million ability to comprehend statistics gave him authority way beyond what I could ever muster. I sometimes wondered if his gift hid a curse. For all his nous, Mick could still state the bleeding obvious.

'Of course, our biggest problem is if we get caught.'

But he was just warming up for some more optimistic contemplation. 'You know, that might be our one and only problem. Our lawyer friend Mecklam doesn't need to know our part in the rort. When Flick Sailor is up and well, she and hubby Gregory will be keeping quiet about the sordid family secret of kidnapping and blackmail. That leaves the racing stewards. Unless they can trace the go-fast we administer, they'll be pissed off at us, but won't be able to prove a thing. Racing stewards are always pissed off at someone.

'You should have heard what they called me after I rang them to complain about moving the barrier stalls at Canterbury. Kept asking how I had their unlisted phone number, known to only a handful of people. I pointed out to them I was obviously in that handful, and that it could turn into a streetful if they kept playing around with the barrier stalls. I don't know if they spent any time or money trying to track me down. I do know from the sounds coming down the phone line, for ten minutes or more, I was their most hated man.

'The point is, Steele, the stewards will soon find another evildoer to take the pressure off us.'

So what magic drug did Mick have in store?

'I'll need a few days to think it through. I hate to admit it, but I don't have a contact to provide a list of drugs they test for. I'll see if I can find one, or else we'll need to think laterally on this one. If you can locate Felicity Smith over the weekend, well and good. Even so, I'll see you back here on Monday at 1.30. We'll have a late lunch of Chinese, followed by cogitation in prime thinking time.'

<u>25</u>

MICK RANG ME early two mornings later, saying we should go down to northern New South Wales for a Sunday drive. I should pick him up within the hour.

After finishing my shift as a bookie's clerk the previous day, I searched around the track for Bill Smith. I tried to convince him to let his daughter go. His son-in-law had already agreed to ride Who Loves Yer Baby, I argued. Sailor would keep his word, and not tell Mecklam about switching horses until the last moment. Smith was unconvinced.

'Like he kept his marriage vows? I might let Felicity go on the Friday before the race, if I see Gregory's name in the racing guide on my horse and someone else on All The Favours.'

I begged him to reconsider. Flick and her unborn child might not survive until Friday, I said. I asked if they were nearby, and whether I could check on them and take them food. Bill said they would be all right; he had everything taken care of. I needn't worry about the mother and child; I should concentrate on finding the right substance to make Who Loves Yer Baby win. I said I could concentrate better if I could just see for myself that Flick was okay. Bill assured me that everything was under control. I told him that I would phone him, and we could meet at the Feed Bin on either Monday or Tuesday morning.

Mick Clarence looked paler than usual when I drove up the next morning around eight o'clock. He wore a bandanna on his head, a tie-dyed T-shirt and faded jeans with frayed hems. I had a slight crack at his attire, and he told me cryptically that he was dressed for success.

Mick put one of his cassettes in my car player, and we said little until we passed Beenleigh. Then he turned the volume right down and asked me if I knew anything about drug testing. I confessed my ignorance and added, perhaps a tad self-righteously, that I'd never had an interest in the subject.

'Bad mistake, Steele,' Mick replied. 'You need to know every facet of the racing industry that might affect your livelihood. If there are trainers out there who have the good gear and it's untraceable, you wanna know about it.'

I had to disagree, on the grounds that the research was too hard and too uncertain. 'You'd go batty believing every racetrack rumour about top trainers going overseas for the latest big hits. And you're not going to ring them up to ask if they're putting their underachievers on the needle. Besides, I have suspicions that dopers are not nice people.'

'All probably true,' Mick conceded. 'But I should still follow my own advice about being mindful of doping. I might see patterns emerging, when certain horses run differently from how they statistically should. Anyway, Steele, you're the one who has me engrossed in drug research over the past couple of days.'

I asked Mick what he had come up with, running the stats on those weird personal computers of his. The teenager was upset about my characterisation of his cherished technology. 'You know how you were talking about rumours of trainers travelling overseas for drugs? I had to fly to America for my two personal computers. We won't have these beauties in Australia for months, maybe for a couple of years. This is me going to a crowded airport, to catch a crowded plane to a country with lots of people. It was serious stuff. Only a punter or a bookie with access to a mainframe computer, and the ability to talk to it, can generate more information than I can. It's all about playing the percentages and margins, and my two babies are giving me the edge. Hey, Yatala turn-off coming up; we gotta pull over for a couple of pies.'

Yatala, a seaside hamlet before Southport, had a reputation for the best meat pies in Australia, which aficionados figured made them the best pies in the world. When I was a child, a nun gave me a cold meat pie leaving me with me an antipathy to the humble delicacies, but I keep that to myself. You don't deride an Aussie icon until you work out the depth of the fervour of the worshipper you're with. Mick was pretty fervent.

He refused to say a word until he had applied the contents of his plastic sachet of tomato sauce to the hole he made in the mushy peas adorning the top of his pie. I watched his ritual closely, not wanting to munch into my lowly sausage roll before he savoured his first bite.

Mick finally rolled up the last crumbs of his pie into the greaseproof paper, put that inside his paper bag, and placed that in the rubbish bin beside the table in the park where we were dining. He drank his coffee-flavoured milk and lit a cigarette before resuming his conversation of ten minutes before about running the stats on his personal computers.

'People are always asking me for tips, yet no one ever asks me why I win at the horses. It's like asking me if I can give them a fish, when they should be asking me how to fish.'

'Why do you win at the horses, Mick?'

'Why do you win at poker, Steele?'

'That's different. No poker player has a mathematical

advantage over another, and no gambling house or bookie is taking a percentage of the winnings. That's why social poker playing is illegal and betting on horses is legal. Bookies and governments are copping a quid out of it.'

'Oh you cynic, Steele Hill. But you're right about the maths of social poker. In bookmaker's terms, the book is betting at 100 percent, with no outside party taking a cut and the money all staying among the players. But you win the most, because you are the only one consciously working out the odds of each hand and betting accordingly. I do the same at the horses. And I win.'

If Mick expected me to thank him profusely for his sage advice, he'd made an error in judgement. 'Hang on, Mick. We both know that bookies and totes take out between 8 percent and almost 20 percent on any particular race. The tote can never lose, because it adjusts the pool all the time before the horses jump. Bookies sometimes lose, because they adjust their markets as they go along, but punters will not put as much on particular horses as the prices say they might. But still, bookies have always got that 8 percent to 20 percent gross margin working in their favour.'

Mick shook his head. 'Which means no punter should ever win.'

'And in the long run they all lose,' I agreed.

'If that's true, it makes professional punters the biggest mugs of all, and we both know there are some pretty shrewd gamblers among them. Pro punters are human – sometimes they bet against the correct odds, and sometimes they have trouble working out the correct odds – but so do bookies. A bookie's odds are made up from statistics and subjective assessments. It is unscientific, unmathematical. So I redo the maths, solve the problem, and come up with reliable predictions which, in some races, overcome the percentage points' advantage a bookie has over me.'

I began the walk back to the car. 'That makes sense. By the way, Mick, how do you fish properly?'

Mick threw his flavoured milk in another bin. 'How the fuck would I know?'

We settled back into the ute, and were on the highway before Mick talked doping again. 'The number one conclusion I have drawn,' he began, 'is that dope detectors do not have it easy. You see, Steele, you can't just throw some chemicals in with a blood or urine sample, and get a computer printout saying this horse is full of caffeine, amphetamines, cordial, apple juice and, of course, horse-piss. The scientists have to make a specific test for a specific drug. Which puts someone with a new go-fast in a promising position.'

I wondered out loud if Mick was trying to snow me into feeling more confident about our dangerous endeavour. He swore he wasn't.

'Not at all, Steele. Think about it. What is most fascinating about all the rumours we hear of top trainers bringing in new drugs from overseas, or of drugging their horses in general? The rumour mill never says that the trainers are paying off the dope-testing officials, which is where you'd think a shrewd doper would start. Think about it, Steele. A list of the drugs and banned substances a race club tests for would be worth gold.'

I agreed it would. If the list was accurate, you could just give the horse a go-fast not on the list, and, if it worked as the chemists said it would, home free you would be, with a wad of cash in your pocket and a finger in the air to the racing authorities. I was much relieved that Mick Clarence had secured the precious list.

'I have not got that list,' Mick said.

If the lad in the front seat of the EH saw my disappointment, his only comeback was a big grin. 'It's good that we haven't got the list; it would make us too complacent. Now, we use our brains and our cunning to come up with the desired result.'

I asked Mick what our combined intellectual capacities had come up with, as I had zero to contribute.

'It's not some combination of heroin, speed and coke, which would be the obvious choice. I believe some greyhound trainers and owners use a combo of smack for the hit and speed for the stamina. Greyhound racing's a mug's game anyway, so I've never bothered to find out how much reward is in the cocktail.'

I wondered about the lad's contempt for greyhound racing. The sport's advocates say it's smarter to punt on than the ponies, because the dish lickers don't have the complications of a jockey aboard.

'You have no flattering words for the greyhound industry, Mick. Did you do a lot of dough on the puppies?'

'I don't bet on greyhounds,' he said sullenly.

'You have a lot of inside drum on greyhounds for someone without any interest in punting on them, Mick. Are you collecting info that might come in handy one day?'

'My Dad owned and trained greyhounds for years.'

'Have you talked him into giving it away, Mick, and getting a real job like punting on the ponies?'

'He sent Mum down to the tote one day to take a treble on the afternoon greyhounds, and she came home to see he'd shot his brains out all over the kitchen wall. He had the radio on, but the first leg of his treble hadn't even run. Mum said she could never understand why he did it.'

Mick Clarence turned up the music, then shouted across the blare, 'Adults are fucked.'

He had regained his usual happy demeanour by the time we had to decide whether to take the coast road to the New South Wales border, or to travel inland through Nerang. Mick said he wanted to see the tanned bodies and fried brains of the Gold Coasties. He switched off the music, wound down his window and pointed to the signpost heralding the coast road.

It was a warm day with a refreshing breeze, and we had a while to go before we crossed the border into northern New South Wales, which seemed to be our general objective. I was yet to ask my fellow traveller where we were heading. Mick would surely tell me when we were nearing our destination, which I guessed would be a happy hippie home with a cupboard full of exotic pharmaceuticals.

On the footpath to our left, half-naked men and women, children and geriatrics, carrying such religious totems as ice creams, soft drinks, towels, sun lotion, transistor radios and paperback novels, offered their bodies to the Sun God,

I had spent a lot of my youth hanging about the Gold Coast; not just at the racetrack, but on the beach, in nightclubs, bars and cafés. Yet I always felt a bit of a stranger there. When I see a thin, dark-brown adult body lying on a beach towel, to me it looks unfulfilled. I always feel that it should be weightlifting at the gym for hours each day, and pouring strange powders over its breakfast cornflakes, before strutting down streets, glancing at its own bod in department-store windows. Suntans sit most easily on bulging-muscled, thin-brained narcissists, or so I judge it.

They tell me the sun gives you vitamins and is good for you, unless, of course, it gives you cancer; then it's not so good for you. As a compromise, maybe we should take our doses of sunshine in less full-on conditions than beaches provide. Serial sunshine abusers could be locked up and shown bad American surf movies of the 1950s, 60s and 70s for hours at a stretch, to help free them from their habit. Lifesavers could announce regularly over the loudspeakers, reports have confirmed that it is almost the 1990s; the 1970s have indeed finished, and narcissism and exhibitionism are no longer compulsory. Anyone trying for a suntan should leave the beach immediately.

We passed through the Gold Coast beach hamlets, and crossed the border at Tweed Heads. I asked Mick whether the EH was pointing in the right direction. He said we should travel along the coast road for a while and then turn inland, looking for farmland. I asked whose farm and Mick replied, anybody's farm.

'We are gathering magic mushrooms of the golden-topped variety,' he said merrily.

'They better be to help you think, Mick,' I said. 'Because we can't go feeding gold tops to a racehorse.'

26

GOLD-TOP MUSHROOMS are hallucinogens. They contain the active ingredient psilocybin, or so amateur pharmacists investigating cheap thrills tell me. These shrooms grow very nicely in cow manure and, as the cattle farms near the cities were sold up for acreage residentials from the 1970s, their supply decreased in the 1980s.

As far as I know, urban hippies, grazing in the country, discovered magic mushrooms, of which gold tops were one variety. The popularity spread throughout the 1970s. The definitive Australian history of hallucinogens is yet to be written, so Buddha knows who was chomping on these mushies in the years before their colonisation by the hippies.

One amateur historian tells me adolescent country boys, never known for temperance, indulged in the mushrooms but they sparked what was considered bizarre behaviour. The lads reverted to strong rum, which prompted acceptable misbehaviour such as fist fights round midnight and verbal abuse of young women.

Mick pointed to a paddock after we had negotiated enough back roads that I only had a hazy notion of the direction towards the coast. Still, I was confident I could follow my nose home again, as long as I left the devouring of the mushies to my mate.

We had hardly seen a car in the fifteen minutes before we reached the paddock, so it felt safe enough, though I drove the

EH across a stretch of grass to park under a tree out of sight of the road.

Mick walked over to the paddock, enclosed by a wooden post-and-rail fence, and climbed between two rails. I leaned on the fence to look towards the road and the hilltop farmhouse, the best part of a kilometre away. Binoculars are almost as much loved in the bush as guns, so I was hoping that no one was enjoying a magnified view of our goings-on from the house on the hill. From deep in the paddock, Mick yelled to me. 'I need your help here, Steele.'

I walked over to him and saw he held about a dozen small to medium shrooms, with a gold ring around the top of each of their crowns.

'How many of them do you want?' I asked, thinking Clarence was looking greedy already, as one or two mushrooms was considered a standard dose.

Mick's eyes were still scouring the ground for the illegal fungi.

'We need as many as we can get,' Mick said, 'a hundred or 150, if we can.'

Only a lunatic would want that many – perhaps a loon who planned to feed most of them to a horse. We searched every centimetre of that paddock, without any hassles from the police or the farm owner. After a while, Mick had to take off his T-shirt to use as a bag for the mushrooms. Back at the EH, I found an old string shopping bag in the boot and we transferred the fungi there, counting 116 mushrooms. Now Mick could wear his cool T-shirt again, and not have to show off his thin, pale body for comparison with the tanned hides of the disciples of the Sun God.

'We going home?' I asked Mick. 'We're loaded up with what

we came for, so let's get out of here before our hair starts to turn blond and we develop an addiction to hamburgers and milkshakes.'

We made a concession to our surroundings by going for a swim in the ocean, near Burleigh. Mick wore his jeans into the sea, while I swam in my dress shorts. Judging from our swimwear, you might gather that neither of us brought a towel, and we sat on the bonnet of the EH to sun-dry ourselves. However, being Brissie boys with only a casual exposure to sunbathing, we quickly lost patience with that and were content to drip water on the seat of the EH ute. By the time we were on Brissie's outskirts, our clothes were pretty dry.

Back in Mick's unit, we spread the mushrooms out on a tea towel on the coffee table in the lounge. Mick discarded the three poisonous toadstools among the crop, lit a cigarette and lay back in his armchair to contemplate a large quantity of potential go-fast. I sat in the small kitchen chair across from the young man and stared at our haul.

'Them's a lot of mushies; do we need that many?' I asked.

Mick also stared at the bounty. 'I think so. I had a law student visit me one day and he was eating them like salted peanuts. He was still standing when he left, a few hours later. He was a big fella, but a fraction of the half-tonne a horse tips the scales at.'

'How are you going to feed them to Who Loves Yer Baby?' I was curious.

'I'll work that out with Bill Smith. Ask him to come over on Wednesday night. We may have to practise to get the dose right.'

'That's the tricky part awlright. How'll we know the right dose?'

'I really haven't a clue. In case something goes wrong, Steele, I hope you don't think this is science. You'll have to make sure to free Smith's daughter before Saturday's race.'

'You're right. I'll try, Mick. So, how did you come up with the idea of using mushies, anyway?'

He lit another cigarette, though there was hardly room for one more butt in the crammed ashtray. 'It was like I was trying to tell you on the way down in the car.'

That must have been when our conversation diverted to the subjects of greyhounds, and how his old man topped himself. Mick had clammed right up, but now he continued where he had left off.

'As I was saying, a few dodgy characters among the greyhound crowd use a mixture of heroin or coke and speed. That's mainly on suburban tracks, where they're racing for a betting plunge rather than for prize money.'

He digressed. 'If it made the papers, reporters would call that "a cocktail of drugs". Whenever some evildoer flirts with more than one drug, it's a cocktail. Reporters make drug addicts out to be swallowing half a chemist shop. I guess in the media's defence, a lot of cocktails only have a couple of . . .'

'Mick, will you get on with it?' I said, exasperated.

'Sorry, Steele. It's the way I think these unscientific cases through, bouncing one idea off another. As I said, we don't know what the drug detectors can or cannot test for. I'd suspect that heroin, coke and speed would be high up on their lists. Even if they weren't, we wouldn't have a clue what dose to give the horse. We would really be in it if our champion dropped dead from a heart attack before our eyes, and the eyes of thousands of other punters, not to mention the stewards.'

'Mick,' I said testily, to give him a hurry-along. So far, his

leisurely story was not letting through many rays of sunlight.

'All bloody right, Steele. You'd think you'd have a little sympathy for my medical condition. You realise I have limited social interaction, so I like to tell my tales slowly.'

I gave up. 'Awlright, Mick. I'll ignore the fact this place is like Central Station and agree about your limited social interaction. We're all counting on you, so I'll let you go on with it, any way you want.'

He took me at my word. Instead of continuing, he sat down cross-legged beside the mushrooms. He picked up a handful, sniffed them and rolled them around his palm with his fingers. Then he put them back, grabbed a second bunch with his left hand and repeated the ritual, finally stabbing his right index finger into the air in triumph.

'Sorry, Steele, I was distracted. I've just worked out how we're going to dope the horse. Let me and Bill worry over that. If you have a few pieces left out of your memory of what happened, it might help you justify yourself to the stewards or the coppers.'

He chewed half a mushroom, offering me the other half. I declined, so he ate it, then went to his fridge and returned with a litre carafe of water.

'I don't know what these mushies will do to a horse. I presume they only take them in the wild by accident when they're grazing. We're gambling that they won't ring the bells on a computer when they run a test on Who Loves Yer Baby. If they're testing for psilocybin, the racing authorities are a lot hipper than I give them credit for.'

Mick chewed half of another mushroom and swallowed it before he continued. 'We do know what shrooms do to people. They provide a great deal of stamina for work, play or prolonged contemplation of the universe. I've also seen people unable to sign their names after a few fungi, but Who Loves Yer Baby won't have to sign his scorecard even if he romps in and sets a track record. We just have to be sure that the human part of the equation, the jockey up top, does right by us.'

I had been thinking about that. When I finally found Flick Sailor, I would ask her to lie low until after the race, not to go running back to her husband. 'I told Mick Felicity being mad at her husband could work in our favour. 'I doubt she'll want to help her father but, if she's grateful to me for arranging her freedom, she might play along.'

'Offer her ten grand if the horse wins,' Mick said in an authoritative voice, which proclaimed that he had quickly solved that problem.

I told Mick I didn't have $10,000. I'd never seen such an amount in my life.

He took a hearty swig of water. 'If this horse wins, you'll see a lot more than ten grand. That I can guarantee.'

'You're going to have a go at the horse, even though you have no idea whether the mushies will work,' I said, shaking my head in disbelief.

'Why not?' he replied. 'If the stewards aren't going to find any trace of drugs, they can wonder as much as they like as to the reason for a successful plunge. They'll probably figure Bill Smith and Gregory Sailor have taken the horse to a private track, and it's been running sensational times. I'd really kick myself if, after all the hassle we're going through, it won without us backing it. I can only vaguely recall its recent form, but I know it's only been in open company for this campaign, and only has a couple of minor placings at best. It's got to start between twelve-to-one and twenty-to-one, so a few grand on its nose will not go astray.'

So Mick was going to the track? This would turn our spree into a life-changing adventure for him. On that score, I was wide of the mark.

'No, I will definitely be listening to our big one on my trusty radio. On Saturday morning, you swing by about ten. I'll give you a satchel. You probably won't want to put it all on at once, and create more suspicion than we need to. Every time Mecklam's boys have a go at their horse, you follow with a decent whack on ours. No need to put your own money on. You can have ten grand from any winnings, the same as Felicity.'

I rolled my eyes heavenward. 'Buddha, Mick, how much are you putting on?'

'At least twenty grand will be in the briefcase, Steele. And Bill Smith and Gregory Sailor receive not a cracker from any of our winnings.'

He nodded his head up and down to confirm his decree was fair. 'Those bastards have got themselves all in a sweat with their fighting and fucking, and they leave us to clean up the mess. Now, it's our turn to party.'

He popped some more mushrooms in his mouth, put Hendrix on the stereo and invited me to stay for tea. I asked him what he had to eat, and he pointed to the mushrooms drying on the tea towel.

I said I would grab some Chinese take-away. 'Don't eat all of our investment capital,' I told him. I left Mick Clarence laughing heartily as he slipped on a pair of headphones to indulge in a golden purple haze.

27

TUESDAY AND THURSDAY MORNINGS, most trainers give their horses serious track work hit outs before their big race on a Saturday. On other mornings, they might hack along at half pace – just a bit of fun for the horse, and it helps to maintain the relationship between animal and jockey. Some of the best jockeys only ride track work on the top-notch horses. The apprentices, and sometimes the stable hands or trainers, work the average neddies.

Before dawn on Monday morning, I stood in the shadows watching the car park. This was where the people who went by the misnomer of the 'racing fraternity' put their vehicles. The brotherhood was not an egalitarian one. BMWs and expensive four-wheel-drives sat close to, but not right beside, clapped-out V8s that could barely fulfil their purpose of towing horse floats. Nearby slumped twenty-year-old bangers, with a couple of cylinders on the blink, that would struggle to take the battling jockeys even short distances to work.

I recognised Bill Smith's ancient V8 as it entered the car park towing his battered float. Bill hopped out, followed by – and this would have shocked most on the track – Gregory Sailor. I couldn't see the expression on Howdy Sailor's face, but his head was bowed and, when he did raise it, he glanced from side to side as if worried about who might see him. Smith went behind the float to release a tall bay horse, and he handed the reins to Sailor. Son-in-law Gregory was about to have his first ride on Who Loves Yer Baby. I left the family enterprise to their preparations for Saturday's big race.

Bill Smith's place was less than ten minutes' drive from the track. His house had to be forty or fifty years old. The solid wooden construction could have done with a coat of paint for general aesthetic purposes. For my own purposes, it could have done with an open door or manageable window. The sun was about to peek over the horizon; I figured I had an hour at the most to uncover whatever clues I could.

No open window, but the back door had a huge old lock. A peek into the keyhole revealed a steel key resting inside. I shook the door gently, and the key's blade moved slightly more towards the vertical from its horizontal position. I found an old racing form guide in the EH's tray and, in my toolkit, a long thin round metal tool with a pointy end and a wooden handle. I'd no idea what the implement was supposed to be for, but it just might do the job for me.

I slid the newspaper under the bottom of the door, pushing it in until there was only just enough showing on my side of the door to retrieve it with my fingers. I poked the pointy round thing into the keyhole. I felt it get behind the key's blade, which I gently manoeuvred into a vertical position. Now I pulled the pointy thing back a little, and pushed at the round piece of steel above the blade. The key slid from the lock and onto the piece of paper. The key just fitted through the gap at the bottom of the door, as I gently slid the form guide back out to my side. I had backed a winner.

Walking into the house, I was about to turn on a light when I heard the sound of stone shattering glass. I turned to my right to see a leather-gloved hand brushing aside broken shards from the lounge room windowsill with a brick.

Sure, that was another way to get into Bill Smith's house. It was little less tidy than my effort, but it showed faith in Hendra humanity, at least when it came to sleeping through a little noise. I looked down at the pointy thing in my hand, thinking of my aversion to stabbing, either as the stabber or stabbee. I was glad to see the newcomer throw the brick into the room before turning the latch on the window.

I decided the element of surprise could not hurt. As a tiny man clambered through the window, I sprung on the light, revealing a familiar face – a retired jockey who I would see at every race meeting.

'Hi George,' I said.

I was gratified by the startled look on his face. He must have been similarly pleased at my expression when I saw the ex-jockey followed through the window by a huge man wearing a dark-brown polo shirt that could barely contain his chest and shoulder muscles. It was probably my imagination, but I felt the house shake when the big man squeezed sideways through the old wooden frame of the window.

The jock went on the offensive once his muscle was inside. 'What the fuck are you doing here?' He looked accusingly at what could easily be construed as a weapon in my hand.

I dropped the thin tool and apologised for carrying it. 'Just used it to break in,' I said.

'So what the fuck are you doing here, what's-your-name, Steve or some shit?'

I corrected him name wise, and told them I had left behind my diary. I kept all my calculations for backing winners in it, and I'd need it for Wednesday.

George considered my excuse for a fraction of a second. 'Bullshit,' he decided. 'You're supposed to be mates with this old bloke, but turds of a feather stick like shit, I guess.'

George was obviously a poet, in a charmingly repulsive sort of way. He could certainly mix his metaphors to create a noxious brew. But I'd heard small jockeys talking big before. I was keeping at least one eye on the giant most of the time. He just sat on the lounge and waited to be told what to do. I would have told him to go away, but my voice was not the one he was taking orders from. George put the big bloke into the picture.

'You keep an eye on Steve here, Phil, while I search this place.'

I'd already seen George's form with a brick, and his technique for searching was just as indelicate. He opened the freezer, produced a screwdriver from his pocket, opened a plastic ice-cream container and swirled the dessert around with the rusty tool. Yum. He went through the whole fridge and freezer, and any packet he could not see through was unsafe from the prods of the screwdriver. My plan to have a late breakfast was losing its attraction. I decided I'd help George, if only to stop the culinary atrocities.

'You know it's always in the last place you look, so why don't you try there next?'

George screwed his face up to consider my logic, and ultimately found it faulty. 'Smart-arse,' he concluded, without conviction, as if I might have suggested a breakthrough beyond his comprehension. 'You look too, Steve,' he added.

'Happy to help,' I replied, not bothering to correct George about my name, this time.

I walked towards a part of the kitchen where the retired jockey was not engaged in fruitless vandalism.

Big Phil was uncertain what to do, so he followed me. George turned from the freezer to follow him, making our section of the tiny kitchen crowded when the three of us reached it. I began to open and close a set of three kitchen drawers from the bottom, and in the top one, I saw an item of interest. I immediately closed the drawer and turned to George. 'Are we looking for anything in particular, or just having a perve because it's naughty?'

George had to think about that one too. I hoped whoever was hiring this comic duo received discount rates. George found the phone on a kitchen bench, and turned his back on me to dial a number. Phil looked up at his boss to see how he could be of assistance. I took the opportunity to put my hands behind my back and slide my fingers down, slightly opening the top drawer and feeling around inside for the business card I had seen there. I slipped what I hoped was the card into my trousers back pocket and shut the drawer. Unfortunately, I was concentrating so hard on this, I didn't pick up any of George's quick soft telephone conversation, which was now over.

'You're coming with us,' he said.

I told him I couldn't leave my EH ute parked outside, as I would end up being blamed for their wrecking work.

George turned to Phil. 'You go with him in his car. If he acts suspicious, you grab the steering wheel and turn it around as fast and as far as you can.'

Phil nodded earnestly, and I wondered where his threshold of suspiciousness was set. Just to be sure, I told them, unless they were going to put an anchor around me and throw me in the Brisbane River, I was happy to go anywhere with them, even if they refused to buy me flowers and chocolates.

'I'm not sure where we're going,' Phil told me as we hopped into the ute. 'I think it might be to Mr Mecklam's.'

I pretended to search my pockets for the car keys as I fished out the business card. It had attracted my attention because someone had scribbled 'loser' across the printed name on it. That name was Gregory Sailor, who had listed his occupation as 'professional horseman'. Buddha, jockeys with business cards! The conceit, bred of insecurity, of the new horse-riding professionals. Their job was remarkably similar to earlier generations of tiny farm boys, with riding skills, who used to call themselves jockeys. For the old school, the word 'professional' would be associated only with scantily-clad women who walked and worked the night away along Fortitude Valley streets.

I turned the professional horseman's card over to find an East Brisbane address scribbled in blue ink. I glanced across at Phil. He was pointing to George's old Mazda, turning into the street where we were parked. I threw the business card on the dash, found my keys in the pocket where I knew they were all along, and started the ute. We followed George to our breakfast meeting with a Prince within the Sport of Kings, the corporate lawyer Jim Mecklam.

The Prince of the Turf lived in a Hamilton mansion, worth about $2 million, in those days when that was a fair whack of dough. Mecklam lived with his wife Prue, who organised charity fundraisers and supported the Arts. The couple was childless, which Prue made up for by sponsoring Cambodian orphans. She fell short of actually importing one to add to the family, though she threatened to do so at every girls' lunch she attended. Rumour had it, rather than sponsor overseas waifs, her husband sought out young teenage runaways, of both sexes, closer, but not too close, to home.

Maybe the rumour mill was right about something else, that Jim Mecklam was having trouble with the upkeep of his racing stable, on top of an expensive wife, family support for international and Australian homeless children, and the domestics who looked after the Hamilton domicile and its master and mistress.

George drove his Mazda up to the imposing gates and spoke into an intercom. Perhaps he said 'open sesame', because the portals did just that. I followed the car down a long driveway, past the side of the house and around its back, past tennis courts and a guest house, to pull up outside the fence around the swimming pool. Another smaller gate opened magically as I alighted from the EH, to find big Phil moving to stand beside and above me.

George pushed me through the gate, which closed behind me. Unsure what to do, George and Phil stood outside the gate for a moment, before getting back into the Mazda. I waved goodbye as they reversed away.

The rising sun was fast removing the last shadows.

No one spoke to me through the intercom, so I strolled around the pool perimeter to find a glass door wide open. Inside a large room, Jim Mecklam sat in a deck chair beside, rather than behind, an imposing desk. This held only a steaming coffee pot, a glass pitcher of milk, another glass container of sugar, three teaspoons and two mugs. *Three mugs, if you count Mecklam*, I thought.

He was leafing through a racing magazine. Dozens of framed photographs of his racehorses in winning mode looked benignly down on him from three walls. A wooden library unit covered most of one wall. The library shelves were full of law books, catalogues from racehorse sales, breeding manuals and popular crime novels. Three folded deckchairs lay beside the library, while an unoccupied office chair behind the desk completed the potential seating.

I had plenty of time to take all of this in, as I stood just inside the room, awaiting a summons. The lawyer refused to look up from his magazine.

Finally, 'I suppose you've never been in a property like this before.'

'I've never been in a house where someone called it a property before.'

Mecklam sneered above the open pages of his racing magazine. My money was on his not having read a word since I entered the room.

'Come in. What's your name?' he asked. 'I've seen you around.'

I moved towards the desk. 'I've been around, and it's still Steele Hill.'

Mecklam produced a ballpoint from the pocket of his polo shirt with the moniker of a polo club stitched across it. He wanted everyone to know he was the real deal. He wrote my name in his magazine beside a picture of a grey racehorse.

'You forgot to ask why I had you brought here,' Mecklam said.

'The first morning cup of coffee activates my curiosity glands,' I replied.

I wondered whether he planned to offer me any of the heady-smelling coffee, or whether he had two mugs to prove some obscure point. He sipped on his mug and poured some more black liquid into it, before adding milk and two sugars. He was so enthralled in the ritual that he forgot to offer me the other mug.

'Do you know who I am?' Mecklam asked in a deep, proud voice, one that would command authority at company board meetings.

I nodded. 'John Mecklam. You own a couple of racehorses.'

He showed no offence at my deliberately getting his first name wrong and underestimating his contribution to the racing industry.

'And who usually rides these couple of horses of mine?'

'Gregory Sailor,' I replied.

'Exactly. And, of late, Sailor has been seen in the company of Bill Smith, who, I believe, intends to start a horse in the Brisbane Handicap against one of mine.'

I pointed out that Smith and Sailor were relatives, and that relos often hung out together. This made Mecklam angry. The only trainer a jockey should hang out with before a big race, he said, was his own trainer. Mecklam grew more indignant as he relayed to me how Sailor had said he might not be able to ride track work on the lawyer's horse, All The Favours, the next day.

'I want to know what is going on here,' Mecklam said.

'Beats me,' I replied. 'I haven't any horses with Smith, and Sailor has hardly said boo to me in the past three years.'

'Well, that may be so, but you're awfully chummy with Smith at the moment. If a dodge is going on, I feel sure you can find out about it.'

'What's the big deal, anyway?' I asked. 'You and your trainer have a horse in Saturday's Brisbane Handicap. Smith and his owner have a starter in the same race. It's far from the biggest event on the Brisbane racing calendar. Chances are both of you will lose. Bart Wood's gelding is going great guns.'

Mecklam's eyes narrowed and his mouth tightened. He looked most keen to win on Saturday, and my talk of possible defeat irritated him. 'You just find out what's going on. Phone me on this number.'

He hit a button on a device that looked like a portable pocket radio, only bigger. I figured it was one of those new mobile phones that business people had adopted as status symbols. A panel on the dog and bone lit up, and Mecklam wrote a funny-looking number down on a slip of paper and handed to me.

'Make sure you've got a few dollar coins with you. Phoning this mobile from a public phone is a lot dearer than a local call.'

The hide of the bloke, thinking I did not have one of those fancy mobile dog-and-bones myself. Of course, he was right – I'd heard they cost upwards of a grand. This gave me added incentive to dislike him.

Mecklam winked at me. 'There could be a sling in it for you on Saturday night. Have a cup of coffee.'

I poured the brew into the spare mug and added milk. Taking a hearty gulp, I found it was colder than lukewarm, just the way I hate it. I raised my mug in Mecklam's direction.

'Thanks,' I said, gulping the repulsive mixture in one go.

28

THINKING UP SCENARIOS in which Mecklam came a cropper from Saturday's race, I drove. The lawyer's bluster hid only panic, I decided. Hooking up with losers like George and Phil was evidence of that.

Night would be the best time to check out the East Brisbane address on the business card, but I decided to take a quick peek.

East Brisbane is an inner-city suburb, busy compared to what we denizens of remoter northside haunts are used to. North and south refer to banks of the Brisbane River which roughly runs east to west. To be more exact, I guess it runs west-east as Brisbane is on the east coast. East Brisbane is south of the river. If you can't follow all that, you had better come for a visit. I recommend it. It's pretty safe. Australians mainly kill and maim their own.

I steered the EH through the middle lane across the Story Bridge, a magnificent structure I would buy from a convincing hustler. I would set up walk-through cafés halfway across the pedestrian overpasses, to supplement the tollways I'd need to put at either end of the bridge to recoup my investment. I believe sentimentality about objects and people close to you can be a cover for doing the unspeakable to strangers. Still, I forgive anyone with a soft spot for the Story Bridge.

The East Brisbane address was an old, two-storey house. All its windows were shut and the two garage doors were apparently locked. I wound my driver's window down and could hear no sound from the house, though the ambient traffic noise meant I couldn't rely on that. I was tempted to park the car and knock on the front door. Instead I drove to the end of the street, did a U-turn, parked across the road from the house and pretended to look up my street directory.

Seeing no action for the next 10 minutes, I drove to the nearest TAB, where I whiled away a couple of hours, betting on gallopers, dogs and pacers. I went home broke, but with the names of certain future winners circled in my form guide.

I put a white rose against the door of My Cucumber, Natalie's flat. I always carry a pair of scissors in the glove box, in case I see a beautiful flower in the front garden of an apparently empty house. It shows, in the correct light, that I am a thoughtful boyfriend and, of course, it is a compliment to the gardener whose floral showpiece I select for snipping. Out of respect, I never snip the Iraqi Icicles at the front of our flats unless I am invited to do so. Except when I am sure the roses' owner, Amelia Barnes, is asleep and I can't offend her by taking a few Iraqi Icicles.

I retired to my own flat below Nat's and turned on the television to reassure myself that mind-numbing American soap operas could still educate and edify the Australian masses. That didn't work for me, so I settled for my much-preferred children's TV, in which adolescent hosts try so hard to be witty and clever that you could only forgive them for their perpetual failure. Every once in a while, a beautiful and sexy teenage hostess appears and becomes a regular on a children's TV show. This gives unemployed young men and jobless middle-aged male dopeheads incentive to set their alarms for 4 p.m. turning a program they would watch anyway into a cult experience. I settled down in my favourite and only armchair to enjoy the company of the sexy teenager with close-cropped blonde hair. She wore a tight-fitting T-shirt I had never seen her in before.

A knock at the door awoke me from my involuntary late-afternoon nap. Natalie held the white rose in her hand. A red drop on her thumb told how she had pricked herself. Her slight wound reminded me that I hadn't seen her since Saturday night, when I was too tired to go to the Beat nightclub as we had planned. She was almost forgiving, so the splendid pair of scissors had done its job again.

'Steele, I got the job,' she said excitedly. 'I'm trainee assistant manager in fruit and vegetables.'

'Go, Natalie,' I said, to let her know I shared her joy, though her new and daunting title had more work and same money reverberating through it.

'Let's celebrate, I'll get my wallet,' I said, without reaching for the empty leather container in my back pocket.

Nat, to her credit, declared that it was her shout. We would seek out the nearest pizza palace. Nat loved pizza, and the principle of the bill payer being the restaurant selector was well established in our relationship. Pizza was a culinary format I could take or leave, but my only rider was to try to find an Italian restaurant with snails.

I love snails. Not so much the sight of them as the taste. I reckon even vegetarians should eat snails. Buddha, they travel so slowly, it is their destiny to be caught for supper. Besides, they consume every fruit, every vegetable, they can put their mouths around. With vegetarians and snails, it is case of eat or be eaten by proxy, as the molluscs devour all sources of people's non-walking food.

Over dinner and a bottle of Chianti, Natalie asked what I'd been up to over the previous two days. I gave my stock answer, 'Very little.' She pressed me further, and I avoided a reprimand for my lack of communication with her. I gave an abbreviated account of my visits to Mick's place, leaving out minor details such as the mushrooms, the race fixing, the kidnapping and the threats from Mecklam. I talked about Mick, but I doubt she believed me when I explained how an eighteen-year-old mathematical genius could win reliably at the races. I couldn't blame her. I would never have credited it myself had I not met Mick Clarence.

Nat would have seen Mick's success as another of my excuses not to get out of the racing game to make a living in a decent job, whatever that is. She had worked at the supermarket for three years, since she was fifteen. She started full-time when she had finished senior the previous year. I decided that she was putting off going to uni by keeping her frightening job.

I was probably not the best judge, as the prospect of most regular jobs frightened the wits out of me. I was content to mix with the colourful, disparate and humorous characters among the racing crowd. The hours were good, and even the pay was all right, though I usually worked as a bookie's clerk only two days a week, on Wednesdays and Saturdays. I got other bits and pieces, which were usually legal, though, by some quirk of fate, quite a few quickly became illegal when the authorities woke up to what we were doing.

Work, I guess, is a big part of all our lives, though what most of us end up doing is beyond our control. For most of my adult life, many Australians who wanted a job were, for whatever reasons, unable to get one. That was pretty tough, especially considering that even more Australians were in jobs they hated. Those whose task it was to knead and prod, shape and raise the economy were doing a lousy job. So it was a bit rich to single out a happy little bookie's clerk as lacking direction in his career.

Over coffee, I told Nat that I had to go out later that night. To her credit, she didn't complain. When I awoke in her bed at 5 a.m. I wondered if she was psychic and had known that red wine and sex after a hectic weekend would induce a night's sleep rather than a trip to East Brisbane.

We had an early breakfast of scrambled eggs on that balmy Tuesday morning and Natalie asked how important the appointment I'd missed was. By the tone in her voice, I reckon she presumed it was a card game or going to a nightclub where she couldn't go because of work the next day. I became lost in pondering how serious the plight of Flick Sailor was.

Maybe I should go to the East Brisbane house as soon as possible. Perhaps I should give the police the address? No, that would be dumb, until I found out what was in the house.

Resolved to start thinking seriously about doing something pretty soon, I went down to collect the paper. I had it delivered daily for its form guide, as horse racing was evolving from a two-day-a-week sport to daily betting propositions. I went back up to Nat's flat to enjoy more coffee and the form guide. My Cucumber was bustling about, preparing for her first day with the auspicious title of Trainee Assistant Manager Fruit and Vegetables, which also involved looking after such exotic items as nuts and mueslis.

The main picture story on the racing page announced that trainer Bill Smith and jockey Gregory Sailor had linked up to try to win their first major race together in ten years. A cute picture featured a smiling trainer and a grimacing jockey holding on to either side of the bridle of a nodding Who Loves Yer Baby. The grimace on Sailor's face looked positively sublime compared with the one he would wear when he next met Jim Mecklam. I had to give Bill Smith credit. He must have given the story to the press so that the whole world would know why Sailor rode Smith's horse in track work.

Mecklam would have been suspicious when he learned yesterday about Gregory Sailor's potential track work aboard Who Loves Yer Baby. He had called me in to find out more details. Now on Tuesday morning, most of the racing world was laughing at Mecklam or scratching their heads wondering what was going on.

The first edition of the paper came out early, so Mecklam would have got the story in time to go down to the track and give Sailor a big serve for disloyalty. It would be the classic: 'You'll never work for a big stable in this town again.'

I was most disappointed to have missed such an altercation by sleeping in at Natalie's. But, somehow, I suspected Mecklam was too shrewd to go down to the track. His blood would be boiling at the insult, but he would not let it show in public. The racing crowd have a cynical and uncaring sense of humour: Mecklam ticking off Sailor in public would make them both the subjects of jests for weeks. Mecklam struck me as a particularly nasty piece of work. He would have a much more vindictive plan in mind for Sailor, and perhaps for Bill Smith too. I hoped Bill's crazy plan wouldn't wind up with anyone suffering serious physical harm.

The article carried the snappy headline "Baby love races into family affair". It told how Bill Smith had seen a dramatic improvement in his four-year-old gelding Who Loves Yer Baby over the past fortnight. His daughter Felicity was pregnant, and it would be fitting if his son-in-law, a top jockey, rode the horse to victory in a big race. Sailor said that he was surprised to be asked, but had accepted eagerly. Some people were expecting him to ride All The Favours in Saturday's race, he admitted, and he had not severed ties with that horse's stable. He would not be riding other mounts trained by Bill Smith, as taking such limited opportunities at the expense of much bigger stables would be unfair to their owners.

Waggish Bill Smith was quoted in the article as saying that, after the pair won on Saturday, some of those owners might be transferring their top gallopers to his stables. Smith had stuck the knife deeper into Sailor, even as the jockey was trying to downplay the significance of his new ride and stress his loyalty to his old owners and trainers. How this would play out in the long term was anyone's guess. Trainers like to sack jockeys every so often after what they see as one or more bad rides, but they detest a jockey sacking the stable without warning.

If Smith's horse won, most trainers and many owners would think the main loser was Mecklam, a martinet who didn't pay his way. As I said, the biggest worry would be Mecklam employing someone to hurt people who he saw as offending him. Whether I was one of these people, the lawyer would still be deciding.

I walked out to a public phone box, dropped two one-dollar coins into the slot and rang him on the mobile phone number he'd given me.

'Mecklam,' he answered.

'Mr Mecklam, it's Steele Hill here. I'm ringing to tell you that Sailor won't be riding your horse on Saturday. He's riding for another stable.'

'And where did you find that out?' Mecklam asked.

'You told me to sniff around, and I did.'

'Well, you're an idiot,' Mecklam yelled at me. 'It's all over the front bloody page of the newspaper, so there's no point in your ringing me late with the news.'

That was harsh. It wasn't all over the front page of the paper, just the front page of the sports section. And this was Tuesday's paper, so there were no big weekend sports stories to bump it off that prime spot. And he did ask me to ring, and I had.

'I haven't seen today's paper,' I lied to Mecklam, trying to convey how much his insensitive remarks had offended me. 'You don't want me to find out anything more, Mr Mecklam?'

'You just keep your ear to the ground, and report back to me with anything else you get. That horse of Smith's couldn't win the Brisbane Handicap if it started now. So what's he up to? If those bastards think they're going to get my horse beat, they are in for a rude awakening. And so are you, if I find out you are in bed with them, Hill.'

As a trader of non-specific threats, Mecklam was the best I had come across. He was the antithesis of the dog-owning police officer I had once annoyed. If I did it again, the cop said, he would hit me on the head with a lump of wood, ground me into mince, and feed me to his greyhounds. With that sort of clarity in a threat, I knew how to take the copper and that was seriously. With Mecklam, it could all be bluff and bullshit, or it could end up in my being maimed or murdered. I have noticed that people with undue reverence for money sometimes disrespect human life. I was beginning to hope I would discover Flick safe, and that Mecklam's horse would win on Saturday. We little people would have done our best to take the spoils, but the unscrupulous toffs would prevail again. That unhappy ending I could live with; my main emphasis was on living.

At 9 a.m. I drove back to the East Brisbane address. The house and surroundings were still lifeless. This time, I parked a hundred metres from the house, walked down the street fifty metres and had a good look around. The whole street was quiet; the workers and the students were at their various tasks in their workplaces and schools.

Taking a gamble, and knowing that few letterboxes were ever locked, I walked up to the front yard of the property which interested me, flipped up the lid with one hand and dived in for the mail with the other. I put the letters casually into my pocket and, at the same time, pushed down the top of the letterbox with my free hand. It all took a few seconds. When I looked up and down the street again, there was still no one in sight.

Three letters were addressed to people with the last name of Calder, a moniker that sounded familiar to me for some reason. I slipped the mail back into the letterbox without opening it. Mail can mean everything to the correct receiver, and yet nothing to someone like me who is not meant to see it.

Maybe my honesty in returning the mail gave me sufficient peace of mind to remember where I knew the name Calder from. Down at the Wharfies' Cub, there were lunchtime raffles, and winners' names were written on a blackboard. The name Calder was often written down and, after watching many raffle results, I knew it belonged to a firefighter who regularly downed a few lunchtime beers at the club.

I drove the EH ute through South Brisbane and across the William Jolly Bridge, towards Spring Hill, a suburb where single men's hostels had been ground into rubble to make way for expensive townhouses and motels, as the rich and anonymous discovered the joys of inner-city living. I knew somebody who would be home. I drove straight past the unit when I saw Bill Smith's V8 parked outside.

I headed towards a flash new coffee shop nearby. It was going to be one of those coffee days, where I'd end up with a jangling brain and a queasy stomach, unable to tolerate food. A headache would likely follow and, if I didn't ease back, a night of insomnia. A steaming espresso can be a really bad idea, especially when it is followed by two more in quick succession.

By the time I got back to Mick's unit, caffeine was short-circuiting the electricity in my brain. I had to search the Spring Hill street for a minute or two before I was confident that Bill Smith's station wagon was gone.

29

I KNOCKED on Mick Clarence's door even though it was ajar, all the invite I needed to enter.

Headphones gave Mick the look of a high-tech, and male, Princess Leia. He was reading a mathematics textbook. As you do for a bit of light entertainment.

Mick ground a new cigarette butt into one of his two ever-bulging ashtrays. I presume he emptied them sometimes. Perhaps the contents were simply composting under their own weight, constantly making room for more fag ends. Mick indicated the inferior chair with his elbow as he removed the headphones.

'What news?' he asked.

'Nothing much, apart from what's in the paper, which I imagine you've read.'

'Yes, our Russian friend is turning out to be one very cagey bee. You know he just left?'

I looked suitably surprised. 'No, I didn't. What did he want?'

'Have a look around,' Mick said. 'Our fungi have fled.'

'I hope you left a few to give to Bill.' My voice gave away a touch of annoyance, which Mick didn't respond to.

'He's got more than enough to get the job done. You didn't go to track work this morning, Steele?'

The problem with a conspiracy like the one we had going is that the conspirators will invariably begin to distrust one other.

'Did Bill mention it?'

'Only that you weren't there, and neither was Mecklam to see his horse work. It looks like he's putting Rowley up on Saturday. At least, he rode All The Favours in work this morning.'

You know the rules by now. Brett Rowley is not the real name of the senior jockey most likely to replace Sailor on Mecklam's horse.

Rowley and Sailor were bitter rivals, with no exaggeration in the adjective as there might be in a sports report. Both hoops copped substantial fines from a dust-up in the jockeys' room after they ran first and second in a race a few years back. In dishing out fairly stiff penalties, the stewards remarked that a protest against the winner was the appropriate reaction, rather than fisticuffs. I forget which jockey ran second, but he wanted a little more value for the fine he copped. He looked the chief steward fair in the eye.

'I was lodging my protest,' he said, and pointed towards another steward, 'when that bloke pulled me off the bastard before I could land a good one on him.'

I was told the chief steward could barely stop himself from laughing. He reprimanded the losing jockey for intemperate language, but did not increase his fine. The assailant had, in fact, wanted to lodge a protest against the winner, and his anger was exacerbated by the owners of his losing mount telling him not to. This prompted racecourse rumours that the owners had backed the opposition winner, and were quite happy to see its jockey indulge in roughhouse riding tactics. We racing enthusiasts get tremendous value from this sort of rumour. It adds a whole extra spice to the proceedings. Jockeys can be fiery; whether it's down to a Napoleon complex or to risking their lives each day at work, I don't know. A feud between Sailor and Rowley was born that afternoon.

'He's a good rider, Brett Rowley. Probably on a good sling, too,' I said. 'You were only kidding about putting twenty grand on Who Loves Yer Baby, weren't you, Mick?'

The young man stroked the stubble on his chin, and thought about it for a while. 'I'd forgotten about that. I'll have to go down to the bank. I've only got eight or nine grand lying around here.'

I looked around the lounge room and into the kitchen, glad not to see any cash, or indeed any signs of wealth at all, about the place. 'Don't tell me stuff like that, Mick. You're always leaving your front door open, and you tell me stuff like that.'

'I tell you because I can trust you. You're the only person who comes in here and doesn't give me the creeps with their obvious jealousy of my success,' Mick said.

'I suppose I am jealous, but I'm also totally ignorant of complex statistics. I've always presumed that you'd lose the lot one day, and your mates would drop off, and I'd be the only one left for you to bore with tales of past glory. But I don't want you to lose your dough by some desperado coming around here to bash you over the head for it. I think I'm going to have to take you to the track some time, so you can see that the phrase "gentlemen of the turf" is meant ironically.'

'I've never doubted it,' Mick said. 'Tell you what, I'll have a bet with you. If we win on Saturday, I'll lock my door from then on. If we lose, I won't have much cash left anyway. Sound fair?'

When you are eighteen, with thousands of dollars behind you, a unit you own outright, two of the world's latest model personal computers and an understanding of mathematics way beyond the ken of almost the entire world's population, you have the right to be confident.

When you are twenty-one, habitually penniless, own the car you drive as well as the clothes you stand up in, and are involved in a conspiracy you cannot, for the life of you, see working, you are entitled to be a little edgier. Mick set out to ease the pain.

'I meant it about the girl getting ten grand, and your ten grand, too if we win. I'll have the betting money in fifty-dollar notes on Saturday morning. Fifties are my favourite denomination. The name sounds nice, and they look great, especially when you have a hundred or more. Pile on as much as you can, and bring back an expensive bottle of Irish whiskey and some seafood with avocado, pepper, lemon wedges and fresh bread on Saturday night. And some mushrooms.'

Mick saw my face contort.

'Not those sort of mushrooms,' he said. 'Any other kind of mushrooms, just as a symbol of our success. Or failure.'

Mick asked if I had found Flick Sailor yet. I replied that I did have a lead, which I would follow up that night. I would ring him the next day with the news. He said not to bother; he was sure she would turn up safe. 'I reckon it's like that newspaper article fed to the reporters by Bill Smith, a bluff to keep Sailor's mind on the job of riding winners, not stable girls. It will have the jockey thinking twice about playing up on the missus, in future, whether she's preggers or not.'

Mick's talk of the captive Flick might have been what dragged my attention to the table on which lay an empty record sleeve of that year's Go-Betweens' album *Liberty Belle and the Black Diamond Express*.

Mick had hundreds of albums standing vertically and snugly beside each other on shelving a record-loving cabinet maker built for him. Mick even had air-conditioning installed but only for the records as he decided summer heat was good for people because it sweated out bodily toxins. Protecting the records was the main reason he kept the unit spotless, apart from the bulging ashtrays.

When I complimented Mick on his record care, he put his palms in the air in a gesture of resignation. 'They will probably be fucked in the end by the summer humidity and my smoking. I did the best I could.'

In October of 1986. John Farnham's *Whispering Jack* was the first album to be sold as a compact disc as well as on vinyl. Mick and I agreed those silly CDs would never take off.

Also in 1986, multi-instrumentalist Amanda Brown, who played violin, oboe, guitar and keyboards, joined The Go-Betweens. She also added backing vocals.

No one likes an over-achiever but Brown added variety to the guitar band. Many hardcore Gobees fans such as myself regard the 1986 line-up of McLennan, Forster, Morrison and Brown, complemented in 1987 by new bass player/ guitarist John Willsteed, as the sublime incarnation of The Go-Betweens.

I asked Mick if I could listen to the record on his turntable. He unplugged the headphones from the stereo. I expected Liberty Belle but Cliff Richard and the Young Ones were actually spinning. The Go-bees were eclipsed again.

With the help of a bunch of Pommy undergraduate geeks, Cliff Richard, pop's longest-surviving Godbothering musician, had returned to the top of the Devil's charts. Mick and I assisted the unlikely alliance belt out the chorus in which the old pop hand consorted with his socially alienated apprentices to cobble together their own walking talking living cash doll.

30

ONE OF MICK'S COMPUTERS buzzed and he went over to check it out. Shaking his head, he returned to his armchair and sat there thinking.

'What do you know about chemistry, Steele?'

'Chemistry?'

'Chemistry.'

'Well Mick, there might possibly be something I know less about than chemistry, but I wouldn't bet on it.'

Mick stroked his chin. 'It seems that psilocybin is an ester of phosphorous. They tried to talk me into doing chemistry on top of my physics in high school, but I resisted. What the fuck would an ester of phosphorous be?'

'Normally, Mick, I would ask why the hell you care. But I can see your interest. All I know about psilocybin is that it gets the druggie punters off their heads on mushies. Pardon me for wondering, but I thought you would know what it'd do to a racehorse before you prescribed it.'

Mick looked upset. 'Steady on, Steele, you were the one who came to me with your problem. I just had a hunch, and I've been researching on the Internet.'

'The Interwhat?'

'Nothing to worry about, it's just this system for academics to share data about their research. It's quite cool, actually, probably has a future.'

'Never heard of it.'

'I doubt if many Australians have. When I was over in the States buying my personal computers, I ran into a young maths tutor from San Diego State University. He told me six universities across the country had hooked up their computers in a network and academics could swap research over telephone lines. He asked me if I wanted to be in it.'

'Is that legal, tapping into American eggheads' expensive computers?'

'The Internet is so new that they haven't decided what's legal and what's illegal. Anyway, this tutor loaded all the protocols on to the hard drives of the computers I bought and put a back-up on floppies for me.'

'Computers have floppies?'

'Yair, a floppy disk. Here, I'll show you.'

'Whoa, Mick, I don't want to see your floppy disk! And I definitely don't want to see you put it in a computer.'

Muttering something about primary school humour, Mick moved over to the kitchen sink. On went the electric jug. He looked in my direction and pointed to a glass jar of instant coffee. I nodded acceptance of his offer and asked him how he could tap into this internet system as it was way over in America.

'I phone internationally and talk to these other computers using a device called a modem. I let Bradley – that's the tutor's name – know what time period I want to use the Internet. He's not sure yet whether we can both be on at the same time, so it's better to be safe than sorry. The American Defense Department developed the system, way back in the fifties I think, which eventually grew into the Internet. If the Internet system is built similarly to the military version, those computers would be programmed to be pretty paranoid about who is using them.'

'So how many Australians would be playing with this Internet thingo?'

'I could be the only one. Like I said, they've just hooked up the network.'

'But what about our Defence Department?'

'You kidding? Why would the Yanks share their most sophisticated intelligence-gathering tool with us?'

'But they're letting their universities have it?'

'Yair, a few of the warriors and eggheads must be buddies on some research projects, I guess. Anyway, I've been using the Internet for a while now, and no secret service agent has belted on my door yet.'

'That's good to know. So what has this Internet been telling you about what happens when you mix magic mushies and a racehorse?'

'Not much, to be honest. Psilocybin is a compound of carbon, nitrogen, oxygen, hydrogen, and phosphorous. In humans, it works on the brain and creates changes in mood and thinking patterns, as well as illusions and hallucinations.'

'We have both seen or listened to most of that, but what will it do to a horse?'

'That I don't know. It's not physically toxic, so my guess about the horse not dropping dead or throwing a huge fit on us is probably true. It might affect a horse's brain, too. I have some sympathy for the view that psilocybin makes you think more clearly. Maybe Who Loves Yer Baby will decide that winning the Brisbane Handicap is the right thing to do.'

The jug shrilled its boiling message and I waited for Mick to continue while he made the coffees, but he was done talking for a while.

'That's it?' I asked. 'It's not gunna physically make him run faster, but it might make him think he should run faster? Maybe Baby will start tacking self-improvement mantras to his stable door.'

Mick handed me a coffee as I shook my head at the hopelessness of our enterprise. He dismissed my concerns. 'Think about it, Steele. Even if the dope detectives know about psilocybin, they would scarcely bother testing for it.'

'Because only crazy people like us would risk jail by giving it to a horse.'

'Exactly. You should be happy I came up with an unorthodox experiment. I keep coming back to the fact that we're mainly risking only my money, though I'd feel a lot better if Felicity Smith was safe from her father. He could end up a most disappointed man if the drugs don't do the trick.'

'I'm still working on finding Flick. You didn't discover how psilocybin actually works on the brain? That might give us at least a little insight into what might happen to a horse.'

'I read a couple of medical papers on it, but it was totally beyond me. They might as well be written in a foreign language. I can call the papers up on the Internet if you want to have a look, Steele.'

I declined, telling Mick I had never used a computer before and was quite happy to remain a virgin in the field. To tell the truth, if maths whizz Mick couldn't understand the medical lingo, I doubted if I would fare any better.

Mick was not offended. 'Anyway, I want your opinion on the Salem witch trials.'

'How'd we get onto the Salem witch trials?'

'Through the Internet. You research one topic, and it leads you on to others. What do you know about Salem, Steele?'

'Isn't that the place in America where they tied young women to a dunking machine, and dunked them three times? If they drowned, they weren't witches. If they didn't drown, then they were witches and they were burnt to death instead.'

'Jesus, Steele, where did that all come from? They hung these witches, actually, and most of them weren't young women. Some were men; one poor bloke got pressed to death before they could extract a confession.'

'Buddha, Mick, don't tell me what those ancient coppers used to press him to death. I wonder if they were skiting about it in the pub later, after a coroner's verdict of accidental death.' I put on my best take of a deep-voiced copper: 'Pressed to death; they couldn't prove a thing. I never left a bookmark on him.'

Mick smiled and continued his history lesson. 'From most accounts, three young girls sparked the hanging spree. Less than thirty people were hung, but it went down as an important event in history. It spooked me when I read about it on the Internet.'

I was a little miffed that my understanding of Salem witchcraft was so wide of the mark, and I hoped to end the meandering discussion. 'What has this got to do with magic mushies?'

'It's like this. Some academics reckon the girls who started acting strangely and naming adults as witches had eaten ergot from contaminated bread. Ergot comes from a fungus; it acts much like LSD or psilocybin.'

Mick Clarence had my attention. It wasn't useful information, but it was certainly entertaining.

'So these girls flip out, Mick, and the stiffs start asking them questions, and they grass some adults they know. The stiffs try the adults and hang a motza of them. That's what went down?'

'Pretty much, Steele.'

'And some folks reckon the girls were tripping, and that's what started the whole unfortunate train of events.'

'Pretty much. What do you think, Steele?'

'I hope I think a lot better than some of the professional thinkers running around the place. If the kids were tripping, then their parents must have been tripping on the bad bread too. I'd say the kids were busted for having a good time. The boss stiffs were having bummer trips themselves, and decided to hang some of their neighbours. I don't know what happened in the middle, but the kids probably just told their elders what they thought they wanted to hear.'

'Brilliant, Steele. What poetry! The authorities are having bad trips, so they get their tripping kids to rat out some harmless adults. I did read a theory that adult accusers of other witches could have been eating the ergot. It seems most of the accusers lived on the western side of the river. It rained more there, which could have nourished the fungus that produced ergot.'

'I never did quite trust those Westies, Mick, at least the lot that run around on the loose in Brisbane.'

Mick rolled his eyes upwards to indicate that I was stretching a comparison, but he turned the conversation back a few centuries to pay me a compliment. 'I've read about the possibility of the accusers freaking out, but you're the first I've found to suggest that the judges could have been out of it, too, Steele.'

I gave a theory. 'Well, maybe the judges lived west of the river too. Also they risked their corn and rye futures dropping through the floor if it got out that heathen witches were running riot up and down and round and round their town. Compound that with some bad acid, and the judges' brains could have been short-circuiting something fierce. I'd bet that the judges who called the shots in court 400 years ago were just like ours today.'

'It's a good theory, Steele.'

'So that's what you think happened, Mick?'

'Nah,' he said. 'I think some authoritarian pricks spoofed themselves when they saw peasants being hung. Your version's much better, Steele, but life is rarely so poetic, even in a perverse way. Adults are just fucked, Steele.'

He picked up the empty mugs and went to the kitchen to boil the jug again.

31

MICK RETURNED with more coffee. He put down a slim book, placed my coffee mug on top and pushed the book towards me. I read the title: *The Crucible*.

'What's this?' I asked.

'It's a play, by Arthur Miller. You might like to read it.'

'And why would I want to do that?'

'You look like the sort of bloke who's seen plays.'

'I've never been to a play in my life. No one goes to plays. I doubt if I'll ever see a play.'

'It's about the Salem witch trials.'

I was vaguely interested. 'Oh yair? It looks brand new. Where'd you get it??'

'I got a bloke to get it for me yesterday, after I read about it on the Internet.'

'What the bloody hell is this Internet all about? First, you're looking up magic mushies, then you're on about psilocybin, then it's witch trials and now it's a play.'

'That's just what happens on the Internet. One topic leads to another, and you're switching from page to page trying to put it all together.'

'Sounds like way too much hassle,' I said. 'It'll never take off.'

I had a sip of coffee and put the mug back on the play. 'So what does this bloke reckon about the trials?'

'I haven't gotten too far yet. But it's supposed to be about some pisspot American Senator with a name like Paul McCartney.'

'The Beatle? But he's a Pom. Did I ever tell you there is some evidence that I am John Lennon's lovechild?'

Mick ignored the last and corrected the first. 'No, not Paul McCartney. A name like that. It's about both the witch trials and this American Senator. I'm into maths; in maths, you don't have two problems entwining around each other. You solve one and then progress on to another. That's the way maths works. Anyhows, Steele, this Senator from the 1950s set up an un-American committee to smoke out communists in the arts, entertainment and the public service.'

'How did we get onto this?'

'They reckon it's what the play, *The Crucible*, is all about. That these Salem witch hunts in the 1600s were like what this Senator did in the 1950s. But I don't get it; what has politics got to do with an outbreak of drug use?'

I considered the question and looked at the book cover for inspiration. 'Maybe not a lot. I can't help you, Mick. You're talking writers here; they're not normal people. I figure you'd know more about that sort of thing.'

'Fuck, Steele, English was my worst subject at high school.

'I meant to ask you about that, Mick? How'd your Mum afford to send you on with your Dad gone?'

'Insurance money.'

'But you said he blew his head off. How'd they work that?'

'Never asked. I guess Mum knew someone who worked the angle. Maybe she paid someone. Adults are fucked. They'll do anything for money. No, that's wrong. Adults will do anything for anything, they're so fucked.'

32

WHEN SHE CAME into my flat after work, Nat straight away started complaining to me about the other Assistant Manager Fruit and Veg. The bloke was twenty-two, and Nat felt that he saw her as a threat. The overall Manager Fruit and Veg had a few more years' experience behind him. He noticed the tension, but refused to buy into it.

'Ah, the cut and thrust among the cucumbers and the tomatoes,' I consoled. 'The treachery amid the turnips.'

I would have continued, but I could see that My Cucumber was unimpressed. I should not have been making light of her work hassles.

'Sorry,' I said. 'Why not just tell the jerk to back off? See what he says. If he doesn't, go see the big boss of the supermarket.'

Natalie looked at me in disbelief at my advice. 'As if you'd do that,' she said, while I poured a glass of white wine to calm her nerves.

I conceded Nat's point. 'I never said that's the way I'd approach it. But that's because of my – how do you usually put it? – stupid code of not dobbing, even if I was lying in a pool of blood and a policeman asked me who did it.'

We'd be a boring lot, I reckoned, if we all lived by the same code. The bloke giving her a hard time sounded like a loser, I told her. He was right to think that Nat, with her obvious talents, was a threat to him. If he wasn't made to pull his head in, he might end up running the joint, and giving a lot more people than Nat a hard time.

She surprised me by saying I was right. He could end up being promoted, because the obnoxious little prick was ambitious and crawled up to management. For days after a staff meeting, he would repeat the same catchphrases the bosses used. Nat had noticed that, though women well outnumbered men at the supermarket, most of the managers and supervisors were men. She would remember any snide put-downs her rival made, she decided, and record them when she had the chance. And she would go to the supermarket manager, if he kept it up.

'Good for you,' I agreed. 'Just promise me one thing, Nat.'

She looked at me to say what I was asking before she agreed.

'If you ever do dob him in, please don't tell me about it.'

She hit me on the arm. Ouch, she had a pretty tidy jab there.

THE EAST BRISBANE HOUSE looked different at nine o'clock at night, but the letterbox was still the same. The mail I had pilfered and returned poked up through the slit. There were no lights on. Flick could be tied up inside. I walked up the concrete path to knock on the front door. I pressed the doorbell, knocked again and waited. I was about to leave when I heard a sound.

It was a voice, varying in intensity, though never loud. It came from the garage. It could have been from a mouth bound by a gag.

I'm not sure whether it was tradition or television, but I felt I should have a baseball bat in the ute for moments like these.

Any sporting weapon would have done: a cricket bat or a hockey stick; perhaps not a football, but a football boot might do, at a pinch.

All I had was a large bookie's satchel, which is usually crammed down under the glove box on the passenger side in the ute. I could swing it by its handles, but it would weigh me down if I had to grapple or run, which would be my first instinct in a confrontation. Well, it was all I had. Satchel handles on shoulder, I went quietly around the back of the garage to have a peek.

There was a small window at the back, just above head-high and with bars on the outside. I stood on tiptoes and gained a partial view of the inside. The noise was coming from a small television set and I saw, above a high-backed chair, someone's head watching the TV. This could be Felicity's captor, but I could not see her anywhere in the part of the garage available to my view. I saw another light squeeze through the door of a small portable fridge, its open door only a few centimetres from the brick wall it faced. Satisfied I had seen all I could, I edged around the wall in the dark, feeling along with my fingers, until I came to a wooden door.

I turned the metal knob and pushed gently. It was unlocked. With an unlocked door, George and Phil might be inside. Mecklam's hapless heavies were just the sort to leave their jail open. The door made only the slightest noise as I eased it inwards, just enough to put my hand inside. I felt around for a light switch, and found it above my head on the wall to my right. I gently closed the door again.

The plan was simple. I would open the door and turn on the light. That was it. What happened after that was out of my hands; I just hoped the person in the chair played fair and did not produce a gun. I was pretty sure Bill Smith had no guns, and I couldn't think of anyone we both knew who had a gun. Still, quite a few in the racing crowd grew up in the country, and they sure do love their firearms west of the Great Divide.

Enough speculation. I wound the satchel's handles around my left hand, pushed slowly on the door with my right hand, then clicked on the light and pushed the bottom of the door with my right foot.

'Jesus!' a woman's voice said.

A plastic container hit the floor as I barged in, swinging the satchel over my shoulder and striking myself soundly on the back of the head and right shoulder.

As I fell forward I spotted a set of handcuffs, with one half locked around a large metal hook embedded in a wooden support. A key was in the opened other half of the cuffs. I braced myself to stop my forward momentum as up from the chair leapt a heavily pregnant Felicity Sailor, clutching a wooden dessertspoon in her hand. She looked down at a half-empty litre container of ice-cream on the floor and up at me.

'Jesus,' she repeated. 'Dad's gunna kill me.'

<u>33</u>

LOOKING AROUND FELICITY'S CELL, I saw the amenities were fair to good. Sure, she had the traditional bunk set in one corner, but I could see that no one had forced her to make the bed, as the coverings were pushed back against a wall. The floral sheet and matching light doona were colourful for prison issue. She also had her own shower and toilet block; its door was ajar, revealing a towel and nightgown hanging over a Perspex sliding door. The handcuffs I was not too sure about. In these surroundings, they looked more kinky than threatening.

'It's true what they say,' I said to the embarrassed Felicity. 'They are mollycoddling prisoners these days.'

She waved the spoon in her hand. 'Hello, Steele,' she said. 'How are you?'

'Fine, Flick,' I replied. 'Though, as your official rescuer, we might have to embellish our account at the bravery awards.'

'I'm not really a prisoner,' she said.

'You're joking,' I replied, with a huge dollop of sarcasm.

'It wasn't my idea,' she continued. 'Well, I suppose it sort of was. I wanted to get back at Greg. It was bad enough I had to pretend I didn't know what was going on, but when I heard people on the racetrack were laughing behind my back . . .' She stopped there.

'Awlright, Felicity, you wanted to get back at your cheating pig of a husband. That's fair enough. But where did you come up with this kidnapping scheme?'

She began to smile, and put her lips together to cover it. 'That was Dad,' she said, in a voice half ashamed and half proud.

As it turned out, Felicity was privy only to her part in the hoax. Her Dad had found her crying one night, shortly before he came to me looking for confirmation of her husband's infidelity. In the end, father and daughter decided that enough circumstantial evidence against Sailor warranted retribution. Smith would tell the jockey he had kidnapped Felicity. If Sailor could convince him he had ended his affair, and would transgress the marital vows no more, Bill would let his daughter go.

His friends the Calders were on an overseas holiday, and had asked Bill to look after the place, and this presented an opportunity not to be wasted.

I asked Felicity twice whether there was any more to the story. She seemed to know nothing about the race fix and how her husband was blackmailed into swapping mounts on Saturday. As Mick said, Bill was a cagey bee. He knew Flick might see the potential dangers of the full plot, which only three of us were aware of. I suspected, given Bill's form, that he still had an ace up his sleeve, to reveal to Mick and me when he felt the time was right.

Felicity explained that her errant husband had souvenired the authentic police handcuffs from a buck's party, and had long forgotten them in the bottom of a drawer. She had found them and shown them to her father as a joke, only, months later, to have him suggest the prisoner idea.

Bill had allowed her to pack enough clothes, linen and toiletries for a fortnight, and driven her to the Calders'. He took a photo of her, feigning misery shackled in the cuffs. He said she should put herself back in them whenever she heard a noise, in case one of Gregory Sailor's few mates managed to track her down.

Three days into the caper, Flick had tired of it. She bought herself a small television and some junk food, to provide a change from the set of classic Russian novels Bill had provided for her. Her father suggested she should 'start with an easy one', Dostoevsky's *Crime and Punishment*, before progressing to Tolstoy's *War and Peace.*

'I grew up on *Rage* and Summer Bay. What do I know about classic Russian literature, Steele? Give me a good soapie or a few hours of music clips, any day,' Flick said. 'Anyway, it doesn't matter anymore. Greg should have learned his lesson by now. If you or Dad can pick me up tomorrow morning, I'll go home.'

'That's not a good idea, Felicity,' I said, straining to think of a plausible reason why going home before Sunday was not an option.

I came up with: 'I saw your father today and he said he thinks Greg hasn't told his girlfriend it's over yet.'

I needed a better reason than that. If Felicity was really sick of being cooped up here, she might storm back home and tell Sailor their marriage was finished, and that she would take him for half his accumulated worth plus a healthy weekly sum for their child when it was born.

'I am really pissed off at your Dad, you know,' I added. 'He could have told me this was all a put-up, so I wouldn't have been racing around all over Brisbane looking for you. I want to teach both him and your husband a lesson neither of them will forget.'

That cheered her up.

I continued. 'Why don't you use your credit card to book into a four-star hotel until Sunday, Flick? I promise I will pay the full bill on Sunday morning. You'll still have to stay out of sight, but that's pretty easy in a good hotel. You won't run into anyone Gregory knows and, even if you do, just duck out of sight.'

'You sure you can afford that, Steele?' was Felicity's astute question.

To show good faith, I emptied my wallet of its thirty bucks, for Felicity's incidental spending money until the next morning when she could start running up her credit card.

'By the way as part of your Dad's discussion with your husband, Gregory has to ride Who Loves Yer Baby on Saturday,' I told Flick.

'Aw, isn't that nice. I'll have to listen to the race.'

Driving us to Brisbane's inner city and the Sheraton Hotel, I explained I was due a big bonus on Saturday. It was worth it for me to spend the money, to get back at her father with a practical joke he would remember forever. The bonus I was thinking of was clearing it with Mick for me to take $500 out of the twenty grand for expenses after I explained the latest unplanned twist in our carefully laid and gently unravelling plans.

It was around midnight when I went to bed. Before I fell asleep, I promised myself, after all this was over, six nights straight of live entertainment with Nat and whoever else could tolerate my barely adequate company.

I would contact Mick Clarence in the morning. Bill Smith I would let stew for at least a couple of days, wondering where his daughter was. I suspected Felicity would ring her dad before I let him off the hook, though I asked her not to. I would be quite happy if Bill called off the fix, now I had wrestled a few of the puppet-master's strings from his fingers.

As a student of form, I was picking crazed mathematician Mick Clarence to be putting twenty grand on a premonition rather than cold science. I figured a human emotion deeper than solving a complicated equation lay at his desire to roll for such big stakes. As he was young, at race's end with a bad result, Mick could shrug and calculate how many weeks it would take to get his money back.

Bill Smith, on the other hand, was betting the lot on Saturday. I heard Mecklam was threatening to drum Bill out of Australian racing, which, at the Russian's age, would destroy him financially. That might urge him to keep going with the plan, which had a big, if unlikely, reward. As it was, he stood to lose his life's savings, his career, his family and his liberty. He would not be recovering from that. The Russian who had jumped ship on a whim had one life raft left, an unlikely win on Saturday. This made him a most dangerous man.

Me, I was along for the ride. I might have been in it even if I wasn't playing the noble knight on a mission to rescue the soon-to-be fair matron Felicity.

Ignoring much evidence to the contrary, I saw myself as a survivor. Whether I was or not, I believed I had that air about me, and that was why someone like Bill Smith, riding a million-to-one shot, wanted me around. For a survivor, I was light on back-up strategies for covering my arse as I followed Smith into the unknown.

Happily, such worries would be cast aside the next day as I headed to honest toil in the Ipswich suburb of Bundamba, an Aboriginal word for 'place of the stone axe.' I hope that's what it means because I read Aboriginals sometimes, for a bit of fun, fibbed when asked what a word meant. Maybe Bundamba means 'place of the stoned white fella, leaving the Racecourse Hotel'.

I HEADED SOUTHWEST along the Ipswich Motorway to, you guessed it, Ipswich, where Bundamba racetrack hosts regular mid-week races. The crowds are rarely big and my bookie fielded mainly to cover expenses and give us all a day out. I tuned in the car radio to a romantic duet.

It was about the next time I fall in love, repeated a few times, with a verse full of ooo ooo ooo and that it was you I would love.

Believe it or not, this was smash hit of the day. I put it down to the verse consisting entirely of ooos. I imagine the first pop songwriters stuck ooos, aahs or lalas in their work, intending to come back later to fill in the words, only to find that those meaningless fillers were paving stones on the road to gold records.

Switching channels on the radio, I found British actor-come-singer Nick Berry trying to convince us that *Every Loser Wins*. I could not quite follow his reasoning, how losers were actually winning just because we poor sods had a go. Sounded like young Nick got beaten by a few lengths in the Love Handicap, but was being quite the British stoic about it all.

Trying for third-time-lucky on another station, Aussie pop veteran John Farnham had returned from the dead, or at least from the club circuit, to front aging pop rockers The Little River Band. His enormous solo hit *You're The Voice* had some pretty left-of-centre lyrics for a pop anthem, disguised by the trademark cheery Farnham delivery. The ditty declared we should stop staring at each other down the barrel of a gun, and give up living in fear.

The words might have been a rallying cry for the suburban punter to pacifism, but if you took the hostility out of the burbs, they just would not be the same, would they? Buddha, I dislike pop music, but at least its Aussie exponents were having a go at making it mean something. Besides, how could our John-oh go wrong-oh, with a couple of interjections in his song-oh?

I parked the ute, flashed my pass into the race course and found my bookie having a soft drink and checking the odds he was likely to put up for the first couple of races.

We enjoyed a fairly peaceful afternoon on the track. The few professional punters who showed weren't too keen to lash out on second-string horses.

We had a fright in Ipswich race four, when a group of punters came for a horse called *Mum's Darling*. I did not recognise any of the blokes betting in hundreds, when other gamblers on the race were hitting us with tens, twenties and the occasional fifty. In between the bets, I heard our bookie tell our payout man that the horse came from northern New South Wales. It hadn't raced for three months, and had won only one race.

It is funny how the mind works, but I immediately associated northern New South Wales with our outing, picking magic mushies. It was ridiculous, but I started thinking that these southerners knew about doping with gold tops.

We won on two of the first three races, and did little damage on the one we lost. So we laid the southern horse I supposed was doped to the eyeballs on shrooms. It ran second last. They must have fed it toadstools by mistake.

34

I GAVE THURSDAY MORNING track work a swerve, even though my body clock woke me at 4am. It would be best, I decided, if the early-morning crowd watching Bill Smith's horse work did not see me near the trainer. Who Loves Yer Baby was always a pretty ordinary worker on the training track. Smith might have a little trouble convincing onlookers that his horse was going so well that he came up with the idea of playing Happy Families and winning the Brisbane Handicap with his son-in-law. He could cop the suspicious glances on his own.

Bill might have asked me some awkward questions about his daughter's whereabouts too. Best I plodded about the flat for the morning, before tidying up some loose ends later in the day.

I was having coffee and toast when a noise outside made me wonder if Nat had pulled an all-nighter. *Atagirl*, I thought. It's a long way to the top of fruit and veg, so you might as well rock 'n' roll. I opened my door slightly to see retired jockey George huddling over the lock with a credit card in his hand. Leaning in and watching attentively over the little man's shoulder was Big Phil. I pulled the door wide open, and their expressions slowly changed from concentration to embarrassment.

'We didn't think you'd be home.' Big Phil surprised me by talking on behalf of the partnership.

'That's a reasonable presumption,' I conceded. 'However, I've seen what you fellows do to a place during a visit, and leaving a credit card to cover damages is no good. I'm strictly a cash man.'

George explained that he was going to use the card to force the lock. This impressed me no end. I asked if he was tired of his effective strategy of a brick through the window. I also wanted to know about his success rate with credit cards. As I suspected, it was zero. So far.

'I've only started practising,' George said defensively. 'The credit cards keep getting bent or the edges snap off, and the bank is starting to charge me $5 for replacement cards.'

I nodded sympathetically towards the new international spy, Ratbag of Brisbane, who, like his historical Singapore counterpart Raffles, might soon be working alone.

'You didn't tell me that,' Phil said to his partner. 'That's my credit card you borrowed.'

The way these two worked together could only be described as a crime. I invited them in. Their company was entertaining and, while big Phil looked like he could inflict a deal of physical hurt, he was docile enough. George was the surly one, but his instructions from Mecklam probably forbade bodily harm except as a last resort. I promised myself I would not bait this small but easy target beyond his boiling point.

I made the coffees and put out some savoury biscuits for our morning tea, served at the untraditional time of dawn, and asked them how long they had been working for Mecklam. Their contract had been running for three months, but they were becoming jack of the terms, as Mecklam only slung them a few dollars on an irregular basis. He had told them little about Saturday's race, but they figured he was going to have a big go at All The Favours. At least, George figured that and passed on his hunch to Phil. If Mecklam failed to come good with a decent salary, they were going to ditch him. They might even threaten to reveal to the relevant authorities the illegal jobs he made them do. Phil nodded as George talked.

Of course, they would not do any of that. George was a bitter middle-aged man, but he was too smart to implicate himself in such capers. If he did, chances were Mecklam would end up walking away from it all, while the ex-jockey took the brunt of the blame.

George's depressing tale was a recurring one in the racing industry. It was a merciless world which often left the prospects of the unlucky trailing in the dust. George had survived as a journeyman jockey for twenty years in Perth. Then a race fall laid him low for six months, and his weight rose. The bachelor had always liked a celebratory drink, and he hit the piss during his recovery. When he was ready to go back in the saddle, he had few rides because of his weight. For a while, he sat in jockeys' rooms in the forlorn hope that he might pick up a replacement ride on a top weight with good form.

His weight did drop, but this was due to the success of a rum-based diet. On some race days, he did not even try for rides. He went to the pub instead, where he told his life story and gave out tips to strangers, often getting beer and sometimes a few dollars if they won. At the end of one particularly miserable year, George surrendered his jockey's licence.

Reasonably smart and flat broke in a cockroach-infested boarding house on his forty-second birthday, George decided he wanted to be as far from Perth as he could get. He continued urging in pubs, but cut back on the grog and saved whatever money grateful punters gave him. That was how he had ended up in Brisbane, and he was soon working happily enough in a factory job. This was where he met Phil, who was in his late twenties.

The manufacturing company where they worked went bust and they were forced onto the dole. George knew this was not serious enough money for a man staring at the world from beyond the second half of his working life. He went back to the only industry he really knew, and he invited Phil along to race meetings. They bet a few dollars, but mainly hung around the stables, hoping to put faces to some of the names in the racing form.

They were sure they had scored an in when they met Mecklam, and he told them his gardener needed some help around the Hamilton mansion. George assured Phil that Easy Street was just around the corner after Mecklam paid them well and gave them a six-pack of beer to take home, to boot. They figured the corporate lawyer had any number of contacts to give them decent well-paid jobs.

The pair came to realise that Mecklam liked them having plenty of free time on their hands. He developed ever-increasing stinginess in paying them for occasional work, some of which could have them in a lot of legal trouble if they were caught.

I had caught them, but I would not be giving them trouble, even if they refused to tell me why they tried to break in to my flat. They were happy to trade information for trophies to take back to Mecklam. They were supposed to steal small items from my place, but what they were really after was my telephone answering machine, a gadget I did not have. They were to take the answering machine, among other household items, and to look for any letters or a diary I might have lying around. Anything with the name Gregory Sailor on it was to be seized. Mecklam had gone to track work, and they felt he was going to confront Sailor, but for what, they didn't know.

I went to a cupboard to retrieve a broken old portable radio that I kept forgetting to throw out, and handed it to George. Looking around some more, I found a writing pad I used for shopping lists. I put my name and address at the top left and carefully composed a letter, beginning, 'Dear Greg'.

I'm posting this today so I hope you get it before Saturday.
Think he might be on to us.
But there is no need to change our plans, as we both know every loser wins once the race begins.
When you hit the straight on Saturday, make a noise and make it clear. Oh, and I didn't really mean that crack about the next time I fall in love, it will be with your wife.
Let's hope all the favours go our way.

Cheers,
Steele

I showed the note to George, who screwed up his face at the doggerel. I said it was better to keep it cryptic. Mecklam could read whatever he wanted into it. I gave George a couple of outstanding household bills I was waiting to pay when I received final notices, and added form guides, circling the recent runs of All The Favours with a biro. Mecklam would have plenty to think about, though I suspected only the Marx Brothers enjoying a day at the races could come up with answers to my riddles.

George appreciated my being so understanding of their needs. He said maybe the three of us should team up. We should surely be able to come up with some good money-making ideas. I said I would think about it, but, to be honest, these two blokes had desperate losers written all over them. With respect to Nick Berry, there are exceptions to his rule of 'every loser wins'.

THE SHERATON HOTEL was beside Central railway station; a strange location to my mind, as I had a notion that rich people disliked public transport, fearing that they might catch something besides a train or a bus. I paged Flick's room and caught the lift to her floor. She opened the door to my knock and dragged me inside.

'This is heaven, Steele,' she said. 'I've got all I need and they have a restaurant, too.'

She had given her credit card a solid workout, and I again promised to reimburse her. Flick was the very picture of the glowing pregnant woman. She admitted breaking her promise and ringing her father. 'I had to, Steele,' she said. 'He would have been worried sick. I only told him I was safe and well, and I didn't mention your name and didn't tell him where I am.'

I forgave her, but insisted that she had to do everything else we had agreed on, including hiding from anyone she recognised and not leaving the hotel unless she really had to. She could use her credit card to shout a couple of girlfriends lunch on Saturday afternoon as long as it was after 12.30 when everybody we knew would be at the track. Flick was happy with these terms.

We watched a movie after raiding the mini bar for expensive peanuts, soda water and a wee drop of rum for me.

After our pleasant smoko, I headed up the road to Spring Hill to make sure I could meet the ballooning hotel bill.

Mick Clarence's front door was wide open again, and a tall man walked out without closing it.

He nodded at me and headed towards a 1960s British MG sports car. I had seen the man a few times. We were never introduced, and I picked him for a bit of a mug lair. His name was Marcus Georgio.

35

MICK CLARENCE WAS AT HIS COMPUTER when I entered to tell him how I had found Felicity Sailor. I gave him the full story after I made him promise he would not tell Bill Smith where his daughter was or who had delivered her there.

'I doubt I'll see Bill until well after the race, but I might work with him again,' Mick said. 'I like his style. None of this would have happened had any of us realised he hadn't really kidnapped his daughter. We were so busy concentrating on steps B, C, and D we forgot to question Step A, the kidnapping. I must remember that for the future.'

'So it doesn't piss you off that we were played for mugs?'

'No, not at all. People with far worse intentions than Bill Smith play me for a mug every week, Steele. I like Bill. You can't complain about the outcome either, because you're enjoying your revenge by kidnapping Flick a second time.'

I nodded, though the reason I had asked Flick to stay at the Sheraton was it seemed like a good idea for me to know her whereabouts when others, such as her father and her husband, did not. To tell the truth, I did not mind Bill running the show. He had a plan of sorts. He had achieved everything he wanted so far, with Gregory riding his horse, Mecklam showing signs of worry, and me supplying him with a drug connection. Now I needed more help from that connection.

'You know that money you want me to put on Who Loves Yer Baby? Can I use some of it to pay Flick's hotel bill?' I asked.

'I'd rather you didn't, because twenty grand is such a nice round figure, but I'll put another grand in for expenses. You may not be able to get the full twenty large on, anyway, without taking ridiculous odds and raising more suspicion. It's your call. I'll be happy if you get five or ten grand on at an average price of ten-to-one to win. With ten grand for you and ten for Felicity, that should still leave thirty or more for me.'

He saw my sceptical look.

'Even if it loses, there's no great harm done,' Mick said.

That attitude was a relief for me.

'At least we won't be fronting the stewards, unless it jumps the fence. You'll have to excuse me now, Steele. I'm working, and I just might win that $20,000 stake money this afternoon.

I looked at the indecipherable figures and squiggles on the computer screen. As I walked through the door, I gave Mick a warning: 'You'll definitely have to lock the door now. Anybody could walk in off the street and steal that betting system from under your nose.'

Mick laughed and waved me away.

WAKING AT 9 a.m. I mentally noted that this was the latest I could remember greeting a Friday morning. I was sweating and it was shaping up to be one of those sweltering November days that make you wonder how Australian meteorologists can say with a straight face that it is still spring. I am sure the European lunatic who invented the four seasons had the best of intentions in interpreting the natural world, but I pity our convict ancestors, toiling at road building under the lash and being reprimanded for not having sufficient refinement to enjoy our balmy spring weather.

Under the shower – hot, of course, to appease those European genes – I predicted the likely track conditions at Eagle Farm the next day. It would almost certainly be a fast track, as the weather could well provide a stinker like today.

This was promising weather for my anticipated date with the stewards. It would be a barbecue, with me being grilled. In my head, I could hear the stewards asking me if I had any explanation for Who Loves Yer Baby running in a zigzag pattern down the straight, and the jockey not being able to pull it up for 200 metres after the winning post.

'The heat,' I practised saying in the shower.

It sounded better when I said it a second time, as I rubbed the hot water through my hair. When I turned the shower off, I heard a pounding at my front door.

'Keep your shirt on,' I yelled to my visitor as I donned mine.

Bill Smith was at the door, and he was an unhappy camper.

'Where have you been all week?' he asked. 'It took me ages to find out where you live. We need to discuss what's happening tomorrow, and you haven't been at track work. You haven't rung, and you haven't dropped by my place. Unless you were the one who messed up my fridge earlier in the week.'

I let Bill unleash a few less important objections before I set him straight. 'It's best if we aren't seen together,' I said calmly. 'And I don't know what you're on about, messing up your fridge,' I lied, not to protect wee George, but to deny any association with the man who had lustily ravaged the contents of Bill's refrigerator.

'I have everything under control for tomorrow,' I went on. 'I told my bookie I wanted a relaxing day out at the races. He wasn't too keen, but he's found a replacement. Mick Clarence said you and he had worked out how to give the horse the good gear, so there isn't much more to it, unless I'm missing something.'

Bill calmed down a fraction. 'Sheesh,' he said. 'It's just that I want you to put a bet on for me. I can't be seen betting. Also, I want to find out what you know about Felicity.'

'Why, is Flick awlright?' I asked, crossing my brows to appear anxious. 'I said you could let her go without it changing the score one iota,' I reminded him for good measure.

A touch of shame crossed the trainer's face, but my money was on him reciprocating my lie. I was right.

'I saw her earlier this morning and she's fine,' he said. 'She just said she had run into you, that's all.'

I had the advantage in the fibbing department, because I knew all he did about Flick and then some. Flick had not dobbed on me, or else Bill would be calling me all sorts of names for re-kidnapping her without telling him.

'When did you say you looked in on her, again?' I asked.

'She rang early today,' he said, which I would wager was the truth.

'I mean, I went to see her early this morning,' he corrected, steering back to the lying course that he had resolutely followed for more than a week.

Bill now produced four wads of notes, each with a rubber band around it.

'Where'd you get that?' I asked, fearing he might tell me he had robbed a pub in the early hours.

'I took out a bank loan,' he said. 'The bastards made me take out a second mortgage on my home for a lousy five grand. Put it on each way, Steele. There is 1250 dollars in each bundle. I'll look after you when Who Loves Yer Baby wins.'

The whole world would be looking after me, following the win of a horse racing above its class and doped on a substance that might make it do anything with the probable exception of running faster.

'This is mad, Bill,' I said. 'You could finish up doing your house, because I doubt you can afford to pay back five grand on top of your other commitments. Just put the money back. If the horse wins, you can pay back whatever interest and fees the banks saddled you with from your trainer's percentage.'

I was wasting my breath. Smith put the four bundles down on my kitchen table and pushed the cash towards me. Sighing, I gathered them up in my hands. I drew open a kitchen drawer full of cutlery and tossed the money in.

'I wish I had a lock on this cabinet,' I said.

'Have you ever been robbed?' he asked, more out of curiosity than concern for his thousands of dollars.

I realised that I had never been robbed in my life, though I often kept the doors to my flat unlocked and usually kept windows open when I went out in summer.

'Being involved in your silly scheme will probably take a few years off my life, one way or another, Bill, so I guess this will be the first time I've been turned over in my life,' I said.

'You should have more confidence in your mate, Mick Clarence,' Bill said. 'He knows it'll work out well with those mushrooms. We have a really good plan for getting them into the horse. We're gunna . . .'

'I don't need to know,' I interrupted. 'I am sure you two madmen have it all worked out, but you're kidding yourselves if you think Who Loves Yer Baby is going to race like Phar Lap with that stuff in it. Even if it does, the stewards will hound you until Doomsday.'

'I doubt it, Steele. I've been feeding the journos with all sorts of stuff about how much it has improved on the track.'

Yes, we all read the papers. The trouble is, a lot of us, including the naturally suspicious stewards, do not believe all we read. I asked the trainer how the horse had worked on the previous morning. Thursday morning track work was often a reliable predictor of Saturday afternoon performance. The trainer tried to exude confidence in his voice, though I noticed he quickly cast his eyes down before lifting them again for his report.

'I asked Sailor to give him an easy time, and he ran four furlongs in fifty-five,' Bill said.

Buddha, 800 metres in fifty-five seconds. On the strength of that, I wouldn't be confident backing the horse to win a bush maiden. The bad news continued when I asked what Mecklam's horse had run. Smith told me it also worked over the same distance, but it had covered the ground in forty-nine seconds. I was definitely putting $100 on All The Favours to win the Brisbane Handicap.

'That's good isn't it?' he asked.

'That's very good – forty-nine seconds, when it's been set for 1600 metres,' I agreed.

'No, not its time; our slow time. It'll make the smarties and Mecklam think his horse is a good thing. We'll get our price tomorrow.'

I gave up trying to bring any reality to the conversation, and considered the logistics of trying to punt $25,000 on Who Loves Yer Baby. The exercise would be throwing money down the drain, but I owed it to myself as a professional to get as much on at the best prices I could.

'I have a fair whack of Mick's dough to put on,' I told Bill.

'You'll work it out. You put mine on first, and then yours and then his,' he said, still trying to call the shots.

'I think not,' I replied. Smith looked petulant as he waited for further explanation. 'You see, Bill, you have kept me in the dark over a few details. If your horse wins, it will be down to Mick's theory about the mushies – which, by the way, involved only him and me, keeping it nice and simple. You, on the other hand, have come up with the most complicated plan, involving a cast of thousands like Mecklam, Sailor, Felicity, the journalists you've been lying to and Buddha knows who else. I'm surprised it has come this far without falling apart, and, as I said, I probably still don't know the half of it.'

'I can't keep you in the picture if you're never around,' the miffed trainer replied.

'I've been around,' I told him, 'tidying up loose ends, and tomorrow I'll be the one drawing all the attention, when I go splashing a lot of dough around the betting ring. I think that entitles me to play the game the way I see it. Half of Mick's bugs bunny goes on first, at the best prices around. Your five grand is on next, and then as much as I can get on of the rest of Mick's.'

Smith pondered my betting strategy, and decided to back down. 'Fine,' he said. 'And I tell you plenty. Yesterday morning, we gave the horse a few of the mushrooms before his gallop, and he ran just normal. You wouldn't know he'd had anything.'

Well, that was promising news. Bill Smith imagined the next day's race meeting would gain him fame and fortune. All I wanted was to be able to go home from the track without the expectation of being locked up.

36

I BUMMED A LIFT WITH BILL to the nearest newsagent to buy a copy of *The Sportsman*, the punter's Bible, carrying Australia's most comprehensive form coverage.

Seventeen starters had put up their hoofs to play in the Brisbane Handicap the next afternoon. In the early market, Purple Haze was the two-to-one favourite. Mick Clarence had to have some measure of confidence to even consider backing against Purple Haze. Hendrix would be looking down and shaking his head. Mecklam's All The Favours was at five-to-one and Who Loves Yer Baby a distant twenty-to-one.

Purple Haze was a five-year-old gelding, trained by the experienced Bart Wood. It had won six races in open company, including two out of its past three starts. The favourite would have been at an even shorter price, but it had only once raced over 1600 metres, and that was fourteen months earlier. An on-pace runner, drawn well in barrier 5, it was likely to run in the first four or five until they entered the straight. Then it would make a quick sprint to catch the staying types, back in the field, flat-footed.

Mecklam's horse did not live up to its name, as it received no favours in the draw. It would start from barrier 15, and this accounted for its price being about a point longer than most punters would have expected. All The Favours liked to sit mid-field in his races, and preferred the pace to be on all the way. I fancied Mecklam's horse had every chance of an easy run, and

I doubted the wide barrier would stop the lawyer from having a real go, just as he had been planning.

Who Loves Yer Baby drew barrier 8.

I did the form on every runner in the Brisbane Handicap, and then repeated the exercise. I was sure Purple Haze was a false favourite. All The Favours would win unless it was caught wide or found trouble during the run. I planned to put $150 of my own hard-earned on Mecklam's horse to win. This should not only return me plenty of bugs bunny, but also make the stewards ponder if I got caught. I was just putting other bets on for someone else, on commission, as we call it, without a clue as to why my employers wanted to back Who Loves Yer Baby.

For luck, I went through the form again, and came up with the same result. It was 11:30 a.m. and I rang the mobile phone number Mecklam had given me. The lawyer was pissed off at me for ringing him at work, which must have had good conditions as I heard laughter, clinking glasses and talk of meal orders in the background. Mecklam was celebrating early his horse's win tomorrow, and was ill-pleased at being interrupted, which made me feel good. I said I had important news about the big race, and I would need to see him in person to talk about it. Now he was interested. He said to meet him in the public bar of the Hamilton Hotel at 3:30 p.m. That was a disappointment. I would have liked to go to his mansion so that one of the domestics could tell his wife I was there again or, even better, for Prue Mecklam herself to see me haunting the family domicile.

I still had to work out what important news I was going to share with Mecklam. My real reasons for our meeting were to embarrass him and to try to find out how confident he was of his horse winning.

At 3:25 p.m. I eased the EH into a vacant space in the pub car park. The Hamilton, which goes by the obvious nickname of the Hamo, has the distinction of being the closest pub to the Eagle Farm and Doomben racetracks. I was never a regular, but I knew my way to its public bar, where a suited Jim Mecklam sat at a table by himself, unless you counted the scotch he cradled in his left hand.

I sat down opposite him and nodded a silent greeting, which he returned with a nod of his own. Mecklam looked like he had indulged himself at lunch, and this was confirmed by the trace of a slur in his voice. You meet all sorts on a racetrack, so I know the ways many of the other halves live, if you get what I mean. Heavy social drinkers, in business like Mecklam, are adept at feigning sobriety after a session, so he must have had more than usual to slightly give away his condition. Or maybe I didn't rate enough on his radar to have him don his verbal disguise.

'You better have something good, to get me out here before the close of business at work,' he said.

'I'm putting a packet on Who Loves Yer Baby,' I said, before walking to the bar to buy a schooner of beer.

I placed the large beer on the table opposite Mecklam. He looked at me with interest, but if he was after more information, he was to be disappointed. I remained silent, and the lawyer tried with little success to hide his annoyance.

'So?' he asked, trying to make me keep the ball in play.

'So, someone in the Smith stable thinks it's a winner,' I said, and took a gulp of beer.

'And who might think that?' Mecklam asked.

'All I know is, Smith asked me to put a bundle on it at the track tomorrow. We both know Smith hasn't got a cracker to his name, so someone's gotta be putting up the dough.'

'Why?' Mecklam asked.

I was thinking it was lucky this bloke was a corporate lawyer. These monosyllabic questions wouldn't win too many court cases.

'Well, obviously someone thinks the horse will win.'

'Why?' Mecklam repeated, beginning to sound like a three-year-old pestering his mum on a bus.

'I guess he or she thinks the favourite's a dog, and your horse can't win from its wide barrier,' I said.

'They're probably right about my horse and the barrier, while the favourite could be a risk. But eight other horses should still finish in front of Who Loves Yer Baby.'

'You don't think your horse can win?' I asked, but Mecklam just shrugged his shoulders.

'I was thinking of backing All The Favours, myself,' I said, trying to bait him into giving me a hint. Which he did.

'Has someone been feeding you info, Hill? Who is it?'

I was pleased to see his agitation, but I denied receiving any inside information. 'I never listen to tips,' I said, wishing it were true, as I would have sat there a wealthier man. 'I've just studied the form and come up with your horse.'

Mecklam thought that over. 'I might take a few quinellas and trifectas around my horse, just for an interest,' he said, before delivering the crucial rider. 'But, if we were to have a go at one of my horses in the future, I would be most annoyed with anyone who backed it before us and knocked off the good price. Anybody would be annoyed at that, and start seeking justice,' Mecklam warned.

'But that won't worry you tomorrow, Mr Mecklam, because you're not going to have a go at All The Favours.'

'It could happen on any race day,' he said.

It was as close to an admission as Mecklam was going to make that he intended to have a big lash on the Brisbane Handicap. My $150 bet would be peanuts compared to what he put on, but, if I could put on my stake before his crew unloaded, it might give the bookies a bit of a leg-up as to what was about to go down. It would not make me any more money, but I would be satisfied if Mecklam won a little less than he expected.

'You still haven't told me why these knuckleheads think Who Loves Yer Baby can win the race,' he said.

'I don't know,' I lied, or admitted – take your pick. 'They asked me to put the money on, because the bookies will take the bets less seriously coming from me. They might get more on at a decent price that way.'

'What's in it for you?' Mecklam wanted to know.

'I'm doing Bill Smith a favour, that's all,' I said. 'Of course, they reckon I'm in for a good sling if it wins, but I'm not holding my breath.'

Mecklam wanted to know where my calculations placed Who Loves Yer Baby. I said I doubted if it would run in the first six.

'That's good,' Mecklam said. 'I'm holding you to that.'

I laughed but he didn't.

'You can't hold me to that,' I said. 'I'm not Nostra-bloody-damus; it's an opinion, that's all.'

'And it's my opinion that Who Loves Yer Baby better not come in the first six.'

'What do I get if it doesn't?' I asked, pretending to be as greedy as the man opposite me.

'Continued good health,' Mecklam said in a sinister tone.

I gulped the last of my drink and stood up. 'Thanks for the beer and for the hints on punting,' I said. 'Good luck tomorrow. I'll let you get home now, Mr Mecklam. If you ask me though, I think you should seriously consider backing your horse for heaps. I know you'll hate paying out the winning jockey's and trainer's percentages, but it'll still be worth it.'

He picked up on my sarcasm and scowled, only to find me keen to have another go at him.

'Don't work too hard,' I advised. 'Those four-hour lunches and unpaid training fees are such bastards to have hanging over your head.'

Mecklam drew my face down towards his by crooking a finger back and forth. 'The best you can do for yourself is to call in sick tomorrow. Tell Smith you can't make it to the track,' he said.

'And lose the chance to watch you in action, Mr Mecklam? I wouldn't miss that for quids.'

'Stay out of my way, Hill, that's all I ask. Is that too much to ask?'

In normal circumstances, I would run a hundred metres to stay out of Mecklam's way, and it would not be much to ask at all. But whether our paths would cross at Eagle Farm the next day was anybody's guess.

Mecklam was on his mobile blower before I could push my chair back in. I heard him tell someone where he was, listen to the reply and say he did not want to take a taxi. He told the person on the other end to bring the four-wheel-drive if they did not want to take the BMW to the pub. He was halfway through another sentence when he stopped and swore. Looked like he was in the poo with Prue after all. I congratulated myself on my good deed for the day, and whistled on my way out.

<u>37</u>

FEELING TIRED after an eventful week, I needed a blast of harder, faster music to refresh my mind. Nat had taken a recent liking to the Beat, a Fortitude Valley gay nightclub, after it had bunged on a Madonna night. Half of us being a big Madonna fan, of course we had had to go. Some hipper straights also embraced the Beat to exorcise their homophobia, and some perhaps to exercise it. The music was too 'dancey' for my liking, too much synth-and-drum-machine sounds. I mentioned this to Nat one night, and was unkindly labelled a rock pig.

I have no objections to musos mucking about any way they like when they make it big, as long as they remember the basic equation: two guitarists plus one drummer equals one rock band.

As it turned out, I had wasted my time practising my part in our Friday evening pre-gig squabble. We had tickets to the Go-Betweens' return-to-Brissie concert at Queensland Uni. I had bought the tickets weeks earlier, and luckily My Cucumber remembered this, as well as which drawer I had put them in.

The Go-Betweens were Brisbane's fave indie band, who had left for London as their first port of pillage on the way to world domination. As Those Who Must Wear Black could tell you, by 1986, the Go-Bees were possibly the best alternative pop-rock band in the world, and definitely Australia's answer to American band R.E.M.

It turned out in the end that R.E.M. were Australia's answer to R.E.M., but the vanquished Go-Betweens, after a warm-up gig playing to Queensland's future potato farmers at Gatton Agricultural College, were now returning to the uni where they had started.

I first saw the Go-Betweens at the Cloudland ballroom in Bowen Hills in 1981, a couple of months after I left the orphanage. Cloudland was an interesting place as it had opened in 1940 so it could claim to be a venue that provoked there generations of romance.

I caught the train to Bowen Hills and climbed the steep rise to bluff my way in.

Quirky Pommy ska band Madness headlined, supported by Melbourne outfit the Sports and the Brissie three-piece, the Go-Betweens.

The previous year, duo Grant McLennan and Robert Forster had returned to Brisbane and formed a three-piece with drummer Lindy Morrison. The Go-Betweens had most of their engaging mix of clever lyrics, catchy melodies and edgy sounds ahead of them.

In the taxi home, I had to admit I was a little disappointed in my first live rock concert, but it was a good adventure with skin-heads rubbing shoulders with the grungy, the cool and the unclassified, such as me.

In the summer of '82, Cloudland's owner decided that he had pandered enough to the rock crowd, and tore down the ballroom to make way for yuppie apartments. As a teenage rock punter, living happily in a cheap flat, I was pissed off to the max. But I did little, short of screaming 'bloody yuppies' when I walked past the building site, where virginal-white hilltop apartments were reaching skyward to kiss God's down-stretched hand. The Go-Betweens wrote a song about it.

Four years later, clever lyrics, experimental musical structures, and the addition of pretty fiddler Amanda Brown could not push the Go-Betweens to the top of the alternative credibility pole. R.E.M. still teetered at the top, despite the usual sell-out jibes from hip punters as well as competition from a group of British social misfits calling themselves the Smiths.

This poppy Britband's outrageous lead singer and lyricist, Morrissey, voiced his poetic angst and depression at the world and his place in it, abetted by music writer Johnny Marr, who came up with some nifty arrangements. The band had a following among gays which was often a positive for an alternative pop-rock band. But I figured the core record-buying constituency for the Smiths were males in their late teens and early twenties, largely students and the unemployed, with bleak views on personal relationships, masking fears of betrayal by any inhabitants of the social world they got close to.

I didn't mind the Smiths myself.

I even started to pen a tribute song to the band in that summer of 1986. I didn't get much past the chorus, but I was pleased with that effort. It went:

Never been laid
Never been paid
Morrissey save me

It was my most productive summer of song-writing, as a warning letter from a collection company set me to writing another chorus.

Who you gunna sue now?
Sue now, sue now?
Who you gunna fuckin' sue now?
Sue now, sue now.

A callous disregard for writing verses stymied my burgeoning career as a lyricist. Still, My Cucumber and I knew decent street poetry when we heard it. Whatever was happening among the cool crowd, where life started with sex and ended with death and in-between consisted of a loop of the two, Nat and I still liked the Go-Betweens, circa '86. Not because they made it big, as Those Who Knew Them Before might have hoped, and not because they failed to make it big, and in that failure evaded abuse as sell-outs from Those Who Crave the Failure of Others. We liked the Brisbane band just because.

The Go-Bees as a duo released their first single, *Lee Remick*, in 1978. At this time, I was in the orphanage, receiving no exposure either to the Queensland band or to the American actress in whose honour they penned the song. *Lee Remick*, the song, not the actress, was a quirky, funny expression of the anxiety of the adolescent male in socialising with young women. Robert Forster wrote the song and both he and bandmate Grant McLennan had attended private boys' schools.

Beyond gigs like the 1981 evening at Cloudland, the band made its first significant impression on me and a lot of other punters in 1984. Their album of that year, *Spring Hill Fair*, was a kinda cheesy and kinda cool tribute to a big annual flea market held in an inner-city Brisbane suburb.

By 1986, the band's fifth album *Liberty Belle and the Black*

Diamond Express was spinning on my deck. I guessed most of us got the pun Liberty Belle, and it was only a matter of listening to the record to see whether it was a pisstake or not. Fellow Go-Bees fan Mick Clarence learned from his fledgling Internet connections that the Black Diamond Express was contemporary American slang for taking a walk on the wild side. I did not know if the translation was correct and, if it was, whether the Go-Bees were aiming to make it big on the lucrative American college radio and performance circuit where the reference might resonate. I guessed they were the sort of band which kept you guessing and that sharpened your mind and was all right with me.

We drove along Coronation Drive and turned into Sir Fred Schonell Drive. I pondered aloud why the rich Westies had drives, when we poor northern-suburbs folk had to make do with streets and roads. Natalie warned me not to start with that class number of mine, so I switched to geography, inquiring why the Westies in Brisbane were rich and the Westies in Sydney were poor. The sun sets in the west in both Sydney and Brisbane. Why was it fashionable to be driving home into the setting sun in the Queensland capital, and unfashionable in the New South Wales capital?

Natalie smiled thinly. 'I know it is an imposition to ask you to travel from the northern suburbs, Steele. I know you are uncomfortable among university students. But let's just enjoy the Go-Betweens, and forget the sarcasm that we both know masks your inferiority complex.'

Bloody hell, that put me in my place.

We found a spot in one of the student car parks, a bleak area of dust, gravel, and tufts of grass that told the kids they might be tomorrow's leaders but they were today's plebs. We went up to the large building, the "refectory", which is a fancy word for canteen. All the tables and chairs had been moved out, and the imported stage did not take up much space, so hundreds were able to stand to listen to the band.

The Go-Betweens hit the right chord with the students, who, for the most part, were seven or so years younger than the band members – a lifetime for anyone between the ages of seventeen and twenty-one. The youngsters showed respect verging on awe for the quartet, returning to the Alma Mater where it all began. The staid and ancient University of Queensland had produced international rock stars, so cool they had survived a decade without a hit album. Maybe the freedom-loving American beauty Liberty Belle was about to change all that.

God was on their side, as lightning flashed outside to cue the band for *Twin Layers of Lightning*, a song we faithful loved, soaring and plunging through the glorious, bleak and in-between styles of Go-Bees humour. Robert Forster took the piss, bluntly announcing that the band had made it, despite being thrown out of a club.

Listen Jack, don't you know, I'm a star.

We punters adored it: ridiculing world domination, while keeping the possibility alive in the corner of our minds: Go Go-Betweens. The set flew by, and we enticed them back for three encores, one of which was a surprise cover of reggae man Jimmy Cliff's *You Can Get It If You Really Want*. Again that hint of ambivalence to fame appeared, and didn't we all have that? Even us occasional visitors to the halls of learning how to enter exclusive societies and clubs that you never get kicked out of, no matter how obnoxious you are.

Spilling out of the hall at the end, satiated and smiling punters were nodding in rhythm, telling one another what a great concert it had been, and how glad they were that they had taken a break from studying for the last of the end-of-year exams. Nat and I congratulated ourselves too on our choice of outing, but the happy times grew a little bleak when Nat returned to her increasingly common theme of saving money to spend six months or more in London.

I had absolutely zero interest in going to London for six days, let alone six months. If it were a decade earlier, sure … The next day, though, Who Loves Yer Baby could provide us with enough cash for the trip. I had a strange feeling I would end up in London with Natalie in the unlikely event of the horse prevailing. I am easily led.

After the necessary chatting to strangers at the uni, we drove on to Fortitude Valley. Natalie talked me into taking in the Beat nightclub where we sipped two stubbies each of overpriced foreign beer, watched a low-key floor show and listened to some composite audio tapes.

A lot of it was dance-type product, some top forty along with some alt pop such as R.E.M. and U2. They even played the Smiths for the young hipsters. There were Talking Heads and Headless Chickens from New Zealand. But nothing from the Go-Betweens' new album.

We got home from the Beat about 3am, both knackered, but up for a couple of rum and cokes for nightcaps.

We were happy to crash out in Natalie's double bed without screwing.

38

I NUDGED MY CUCUMBER awake at 7 a.m. only to cop an earful of curses for my trouble. I had presumed, for no particularly good reason and incorrectly, that Nat would be working that morning. Unlike myself, Natalie has the ability to sleep in until noon when the occasion allows it, and I had destroyed her opportunity for slumber.

Good did come of my mistake though. The lingering effects of a great gig, boutique beers and rums made us in the mood for early morning sex, after which I did the manly thing. I fell asleep, waking to slink back to my flat for breakfast.

I grilled a few snags and fried onions, zucchinis and cabbage for a hearty breakfast, complemented by bread too fresh to toast and white filter coffee not defiled by sugar. I opened the daily paper to the sports page and was greeted by a photo of Mecklam standing beside All The Favours as the horse was being blessed by a Catholic priest.

The story underneath told of the lawyer's plan to donate part of any prize money won to the Church's missionary work in Africa. Mecklam was quoted at length. He hoped some of his corporate clients would top up his contribution. We in Australia, he said, did have All The Favours, with democracy, and wealth for toil, and other yummy gifts. This made it our duty to assist the less fortunate in other parts of the world.

Well, that was news. Mecklam was a saint, and not the selfish, conniving bastard I had thought he was. Who would have conceived that his winning thousands, and my winning hundreds, on his horse would benefit the third world?

Given normal circumstances, the bookies might have chipped in for the African kiddies, but they would not be cheering Mecklam's divine plan this time. Helping orphans is one thing, but getting fleeced by Mecklam was another. Charity begins at home, and bookies had private schools to support for their own children, as well as assisting the kids of luxury car dealers where the successful ones shopped every three years.

Religion had never come up in discussions with the mad Russian Bill Smith, but I imagined his heritage allowed him few spiritual ties with the Catholic Church. If his Mick son-in-law Gregory Sailor was an example, Smith probably associated the Church more with hypocrisy than honourable works.

The Russian would really have been ticked off with the way Mecklam was upstaging him in the press war. Smith had come up with a ripping yarn. Noted track-work duffer Who Loves Yer Baby, with the prodigal son-in-law and father-to-be on top, scorched up the grass in preparation for today's race. His rival had trumped him all ends up with a prediction of divine intervention, which Smith would try to thwart with only a handful of magic beans or, hopefully unknown to most of the general public, several handfuls of magic mushrooms.

I tried to work out a few trebles and doubles to put on at the tote before I went to the races, but I had trouble concentrating. I scribbled out the unlikely combinations of eight and eight in the double, and eight, eight and eight in the treble for the Brisbane, Sydney and Melbourne races. I lay there on the couch listening to the radio racing previews and surprised myself by falling asleep for more than an hour.

I woke and did my ablutions, a wonderful expression,

unfortunately slipping from our language. My future Melbourne Cup winner will be called Doing My Ablutions, even if the stewards refuse my request for a cake of soap rather than a boring shamrock at the centre of my racing colours. I am sure they will let me play the song *Doing My Ablutions*, a parody of *Losing My Religion*, at the winner's ceremony.

It was 11 a.m. four hours before the big race when I parked the EH ute down the road from Mick Clarence's flat. I had become used to parking a short distance from my destinations over the past week, and decided that it was a practice that I would follow in life from now on.

Mick's door was slightly ajar and the stereo was up loud. I knocked and received no acknowledgment, so I walked on in, almost tripping over a vinyl briefcase lying horizontal next to Mick's beloved armchair. I called out and received no reply. The door to the toilet and bathroom was wide open, but no Mick inside.

That probably placed him in his bedroom, the door to which was slightly ajar. I would go back to the lounge, to listen to the music and wait for the young punter. I gave the bedroom door a slight nudge and, as I turned to go to the other room, I saw a leg on the floor.

Mick Clarence lay on his back on the floor of his bedroom, with a piece of rubber tied around his upper arm and a hypodermic needle in front of his outstretched fingers. My first strange notion was that he was playing a practical joke, but that idea was washed away by a wave of nausea that rose from my stomach, up through my chest and caught in my throat. I felt for a pulse, mostly so I could look away to pretend to concentrate on feeling the vibration that was not there. Mick Clarence, maths whiz, professional punter, eighteen-years-old, someone I never ever suspected of being a junkie, was dead.

Impressions rushed in on me as I staggered back to the lounge. I had a crazy notion of hopping in my car, driving around Spring Hill, coming back and finding Mick alive. I conjured a scenario in which I would track his murderer down. It would turn out to be Mecklam.

I told myself out loud to switch off the music and calm down. If the coppers or anyone else found me here, they might declare me as a cert for bringing about Mick's death.

I would sit down, think the situation over, leave quietly and contact an ambulance. That's what I would do. Sitting in the humble guest chair, I again noticed the briefcase next to Mick's armchair. I could see it was not locked, so it could not contain much of value.

It contained wads of $50 bills, rolled over one another and bound with thick rubber bands. Twenty bills I counted in one wad, and there were twenty-two wads. Mick the mathematician would have put the same number of notes in each wad. I was staring down at $22,000, enough motive in the mind of any ambitious copper for me to have slipped my friend an overdose.

I snapped shut the latches on the briefcase, grabbed it by the handle and stood up, to find that my hand holding the case was shaking beyond my control. I slipped the case under my arm, and nudged through the front door with my hip.

I'd had minor run-ins with the coppers, but they were yet to take my prints. I felt safe about leaving my dabs behind. Knowing some of the company he kept, Mick's place would be full of prints, some of them among the cops' records, some of them from coppers. I hoped one set belonged to his heroin dealer, and the coppers would look closely at those prints.

39

I DROVE HOME, using my key to let myself into Nat's flat. I had a great desire to tell her what had happened. I usually manage to keep the dangerous aspects of my career hidden from her, but I felt the need to offload this terrible news. Nat was still sound asleep, so I left a note saying I was off to the races and would be back at 6 p.m. or later.

I picked up Bill Smith's five grand from my kitchen drawer, pushing it into the briefcase on top of Mick's punting money. Then I got back into the ute, dropping the briefcase onto the passenger's side of the one-piece seat. I was operating on instinct and drove past Eagle Farm racetrack without even knowing why.

I headed to the city, but swung a left into Kingsford Smith Drive towards the sea, before dropping a U-turn and parking in front of a small jetty beside the Brisbane River. I opened the briefcase and took out Bill Smith's five grand and four bundles of Mick's bills. I stuffed some of the money in my wallet and some in the two front pockets of my trousers, putting one grand of the nine in my back pocket for Flick. That left $8000 for betting. I took the bands from the remaining wads and roughly spread the money across the floor of the briefcase.

Locking the driver's door of the ute, I went to the passenger side and wound down the window. I looked at the open briefcase, and the faces on the fifty-dollar bills stared back at me. I reached in and flipped the top of the case over to meet the bottom, without bothering to secure the latches. I grabbed the case between the thumb and fingers of my right hand.

A wind blew up around me as I walked to the end of the jetty, swinging the briefcase across my chest, opening my outstretched hand, allowing the case to open wide. Some of the bills flew into the air as the case hit the river, displaying its contents to the sky. It floated for a few moments, slowly taking on water until it slid away under the surface, leaving the fifties to float gently down the river to the sea.

The money looked peaceful and at home on the tidal river, and I waved it farewell on its journey to the Pacific.

'Goodbye, Mick,' I said.

I turned to see three teenagers, two boys and a girl, standing on the footpath and staring at me. They all wore jeans and flannelette shirts though it was the dead of summer, and the girl had a jumper tied around her waist. For some reason, I thought they were homeless, so I reached into my pocket and eased off three fifty-dollar bills. It was only November, but I wished them Merry Christmas anyway as I handed each a fifty. None of them said anything in reply. They just looked at me as if I was deranged and, at that moment in time, they were probably right. I quickly unlocked the door, climbed into the ute and headed to the racetrack.

40

IT WAS A LITTLE PAST NOON when I entered the track. The Brisbane Handicap was on after 3 p.m. so I bought a race book and sat reading in a far high corner of the public grandstand. My head was muddled as I read all the details on the horses' breeding, trainers, owners and form. Usually, I would sift through and collate this information in my mind to pick a winner, but I couldn't hang on to the bits and pieces as they rose to the front of my brain and receded. I heard two indistinct calls of southern races from a loudspeaker and I could not make out the winner of either race. I watched the first race in Brisbane, then went down to see if any bookies were betting early on the main event.

Fifty metres ahead of me, ex-jockey George and his big mate Phil were prowling around the bookies' ring. George had a handful of notes – it looked a lot more than he would normally have at the races – while Phil had his hand over his shirt pocket as though protecting something valuable. George claimed a bookie for a bet, but I was too far away to see what he was backing and how much he put on. He was gone before I was close enough to see that the bookie was betting early on the Brisbane Handicap. He had Mecklam's All The Favours at nine-to-two.

Walking up to put $100 each way on the horse, I noticed Mecklam stride in through the gate. He was with a wealthy Brisbane businessman who sometimes bet with the bookie I worked for. Mecklam grinned as he told the businessman an obviously funny story, well out of range of my hearing. The bookie I was standing in front of was annoyed at my silence and he barked at me. 'What'll it be?'

'A thousand dollars each way Who Loves Yer Baby,' I demanded.

'You're joking, right? You work for Brownie. But Brownie's not laying off this early, is he? What do you really want?'

I ignored his insinuation about only having that sort of cash if I was fronting for Brownie, the bookie I worked for.

'Well, can I have $400 each way on Who Loves Yer Baby?'

'I suppose, but it is cash on the knocker and you are holding me up.'

I pulled out a wad, counted it and gave the bookie $800.

'Ten thousand to 400 and twenty-five hundred to 400,' the bookie said suspiciously, writing out the ticket. As he handed me the stub, he leaned down to ask me if there was something he should know. We were on the same side, he suggested. I shrugged, folded the betting slip in half and put it in my shirt pocket, while the bookie lowered the horse's price to fourteen-to-one. I claimed another bookie for $200 each way at twenty-to-one, and another for $100 each way at sixteen-to-one. These were the only three bookies betting early on the race, so I went to the tote. I put $400 each way on Who Loves Yer Baby, knowing, if it came up short on the tote because of my bet, other punters would leave it alone instead of backing it, giving me the opportunity to get a good price later. I also took a trifecta with Who Loves Yer Baby to win and all other possible combinations to run second or third. That cost me another $240. All up, I had spent about $2600 counting the $150 I had given away. I still had more than $5500 left, including my own money. After seeing Mecklam giggling like a fun human being, his horse would not get one dollar of my funds. If Who Loves Yer Baby went down, it was taking Bill and me with it.

Father Reilly, the priest who had blessed Mecklam's horse, was eating a plate of fish and salad at the cafeteria on my way back to the grandstand. I reached into my pocket and pulled out one of my betting slips, which I unfolded and saw it was my $200 each-way bet. I walked over to the priest and put the ticket on his plate next to a pile of mayonnaise.

'I read your story in the paper, Father. Here is a bet on Who Loves Yer Baby. It's an insurance policy in case Mr Mecklam's horse loses. I know how bad he'll feel about the African orphans, so you can console him if this one wins instead. By the way, my name's Steele Hill, if Mr Mecklam asks.'

The priest was surprised, but managed to mumble a blessing with his mouth full of chips. He put the ticket in his wallet and carried on eating his lunch, while I made my way to the top of the grandstand.

The bookies were having a good day, with only one favourite winning in five races. Two of the winners were twenty-to-one shots, so they were in a good mood for race six, the Brisbane Handicap.

After I had watched all of the action from my lonely seat way up in the grandstand, I went down to the crowded betting ring. Mecklam's horse was four-to-one with most bookies. The favourite, Purple Haze, was at five-to-two, with Who Loves Yer Baby mostly under the odds at eight-to-one, with ten-to-one the best price available.

Mecklam's crew came for All The Favours with some commission agents I recognised. George, Phil and an attractive leggy blonde I heard someone call Crystal also worked the ring to back the horse. All The Favours came into a general price of two-to-one, with nine-to-four the best bet, despite some healthy bets on other runners.

I had $500 each way on Who Loves Yer Baby when one bookie blew it out to sixteen-to-one.

I put $2250 on each way, at prices ranging between fourteen-to-one and ten-to-one.

With my bets on the bookies and the tote, I stood to collect between sixty-five and seventy-five grand if Bill Smith's horse won. I did the rough maths in my head, giving myself a healthy collect on the trifecta and subtracting the ticket, potentially worth more than four grand, I had given to the priest to rub it in to Mecklam if his horse lost. All my tickets were in my left shirt pocket, where I always kept my betting slips.

I decided to watch the race from the grassy incline near the winning post, and that was where I met Bill Smith for the first time that day.

'How you going?' he asked.

'Good.'

'That's good.'

Smith was sweating profusely from his top lip and his temples, and his voice was shaky. I was wondering why I was oddly calm. I had left the unit of a dead teenager that morning and, in the afternoon, had put seven grand on a doped horse in a race that Mecklam's neddy was supposed to win.

'The horse is behaving well,' said Bill. 'I left him with his strapper to saddle up Sailor. Everything's good.'

'That's good,' I said.

I had to get away from this conversation, so I told Bill I had another bet to put on. I walked around to the up escalator, which would take me to a part of the grandstand far away from

Smith. I hopped on the escalator and looking up, saw Mecklam, still with the businessman, four steps ahead above me. I figured the owner of All The Favours had urged the other bloke to back the horse, trying to build a bank of favours. Relying on the result of a horse race was a high-risk strategy for making friends.

The pair stepped off the escalator and took up a position to watch the race. I deliberately walked to stand a metre in front of them, and imagined Mecklam's glare trying to burn a hole in the back of my head.

The horses came onto the track. All The Favours and Who Loves Yer Baby were both fractious, turning their heads to the side and fighting the reins, as their jockeys persuaded them to canter down the straight before heading to the starting stalls. Early favourite Purple Haze sweetly did all its jockey asked, including easing into the barrier stalls without a fuss.

The barrier attendants finally got the two skittish horses into their stalls and the starter let them go.

Who Loves Yer Baby, which had not led in a race since its two-year-old days, zoomed from the starting stalls and led the field by three lengths by the time they had gone 100 metres. I silently begged the horse not to go further in front, as this would ensure that the stewards came knocking on my door with a folderful of questions.

All The Favours was running second, also a more forward position than it usually took. Purple Haze was fourth, one horse off the fence, which would have made its backers happy if the front runner wasn't going quite so quickly. That might test the early favourite's ability to get the distance.

Who Loves Yer Baby appeared to be running a very fast time, and the horses in fifth and sixth spots were being niggled at by their jockeys to keep up. The stayers at the back of the field were twenty lengths from the leader, which showed its first signs of distress near the home turn.

I could have sworn I saw Gregory Sailor pull on the left rein. He would never normally do this on a right-handed track like Eagle Farm, as it would cause a horse to veer out.

Who Loves Yer Baby, more than three lengths clear, resented the unexpected tug and shook its head from side to side, losing the fluency in its galloping action at the same time. The margin to All The Favours was reduced to little more than a length, and the jockey of the second horse waited to see whether the leader was going to run out on the home turn.

Who Loves Yer Baby did run out, about seven horses wide, and All The Favours and Purple Haze, both near the inside fence, ran to a joint lead.

You crooked bastard, Sailor, I thought. You can't even be trusted in a race fix.

Knowing his unsettled mount had run its race, Sailor relaxed the reins. With its new freedom, Who Loves Yer Baby took off. It still refused to run a straight line but, at high speed, it wobbled past All The Favours and the tiring Purple Haze on its inside. With fifty metres to go, the only way Gregory Sailor could lose the race was to jump off his mount, and he did not have the courage for that. Who Loves Yer Baby won by two lengths from All The Favours, with the fifty-to-one stayer White Knuckles third. The time on the semaphore board declared a new race record.

I turned to go down the escalator. Mecklam was standing, hands clenched into fists, white with rage. His business mate had turned red with anger, and tore up his tickets even before weight was declared.

'I'll see you later, Jim,' the businessman said testily, storming off to the escalator.

'It's not correct weight,' Mecklam called down, but he knew no protest could eventuate, as the first and second horses never got near one another in running. The best he could hope for was for the winner to return a positive swab, days later, giving him first prizemoney. But he would not get back the money he had lost on the punt. Nor would he get back the time off his life he lost with that look of sheer hatred he gave me, as I tapped my shirt pocket, produced my winning tickets, looked at each one and smiled breezily at Mecklam. I walked very close to him so he could talk to me in a whispering snarl.

'You're dead, Hill, and so's Smith.'

Smiling warmly, I wished him a most happy day, and asked if he wanted the contact number of a reliable Sydney hitman. I had good referrals on a Nordic bloke they called the Nutcracker Swede.

At the bottom of the escalator, I heard the course announcer advise punters to hold all tickets, which meant that the stewards had discovered a discrepancy. I grabbed the rail of the escalator and felt my hand drag me downwards. The announcer said the inquiry was into the second last race in Melbourne.

41

BY THE TIME I had lined up at the tote window, they had announced the 'all clear to pay' on the Brisbane Handicap. The totalisator declared a dividend of $4376.85 for the trifecta, which made my total collect from the tote just shy of twenty grand. They paid $18,000 of this with a cheque.

As I expected, the bookies asked me to come back after the last race, and they too wanted to pay me most of my winnings by cheque. After some hostile negotiations, I was ready to leave the course with about twenty grand in cash and another fifty in cheques. I asked two bookies if they could tee up a security guard to escort me to the car. They both told me to fuck off.

The leggy blonde, in her mid-twenties, who I had heard someone call Crystal, came up beside me. 'Looks like you've had a good day. Need someone to help you celebrate?'

'Shouldn't you be out commiserating with Jim Mecklam?'

'Who?'

'How quickly they forget.'

'Life's too short to hang about with losers,' she said.

'Life's too short for winners, too.' I was thinking of Mick Clarence. 'I'll give your kind invitation a swerve, Crystal, because My Cucumber awaits at home, and a pregnant friend is holed up in a hotel room.'

Only one part of my info got through. 'You know my name?'

'Only your first, but I would imagine your second is "Trouble".'

'Only for the slow coaches who can't keep up with me. See you around, Winner.'

Crystal slinked across the racecourse. She called out to a fifty-something man by name and told him to wait up. I looked around at the faces of the other stragglers leaving the course, but I couldn't see Bill Smith or anyone else I knew.

Shoving notes from my pockets into the glove box, I started the EH's engine, turned on the radio and headed to the city. I stopped in a quiet corner of King George Square car park and counted out $10,000. I put this into a plastic bag and shoved the bag down my shirt.

The woman at the front desk of the Sheraton paged Flick Sailor's room. The pregnant woman must have been near the door, for she flung it open as soon as I knocked and before I could announce myself.

'I'm bored, Steele. Can I go home now?'

'Not just yet, Felicity.'

I looked up and down, round and round the corridor before I closed the door and locked it.

'Did you listen to the radio?'

'Yes, I did, but you have to dial 'o' before the number from this stupid room phone, and I was always too late. I knew almost every song, too.'

She had been playing contests on FM radio rather than listening to the exploits of her father and husband on the racing channel.

I took the plastic bag from my shirt.

'Those Fun Guys from 1SquillionFM Radio told me to give you all this, as they reckon you were deadest robbed.'

Flick looked inside the bag, and asked me where I had got all the money. I told her that her Dad's horse had won.

'Don't tell me that, Steele. I wanted to watch the race on the six o'clock news. That looks like a lot of money; what are you going to do with it all?'

'It's all yours. It's a long story, but some bloke you don't know gave me some money to put on Who Loves Yer Baby, and he said to give you $10,000 if it won. It's all yours, and your husband knows nothing about it. But just stay here a couple of days more. Then I'll tell Bill where you are, and you and he can work out what you're doing.'

She threw her arms around my neck and kissed me on the cheek. 'I've never had so much money of my own in my life, not even after Greg won the Stradbroke.'

Flick took the bag to the double bed, and emptied all the money onto the quilt. 'But why do I need to stay here? I'll go home to Greg now that he's promised to mend his ways. Our baby needs a mum and a dad. Not like our family was.'

'That's fine, but Greg will be in a foul mood for a couple of days. He could be a more popular bloke right now with a certain owner after he won on your Dad's horse.'

Flick started into a speech about sharing her husband's happiness and his disappointments, and about how Sailor would be starting to really worry. I cut her short.

'It could be dangerous, awlright? It'll blow over in a few days, but right now, it could be dangerous. Stay in the hotel, have a bit of a splurge, and wait until your Dad or I, or even Greg, say it's awlright to leave.'

'Does Greg know where I am?'

'Not at the moment, but when he does, it'll mean it's awlright to go home.'

She promised to do as I asked, telling me I was the best and I knew what was what. I agreed with her, to keep up her confidence. The truth be known, all I knew was that you could get an honest but not brilliant racehorse to run a race record under the effects of psilocybin. For the rest of it, I had no idea what demons you let loose when you did it.

Why I felt an obligation to Flick's father, I will never know. But I rang Nat to tell her I was going to be a little late home, and went searching for Bill Smith to reassure him I had his winnings. As luck would have it, he was at the third place I went to, the bowls club just down the road from the racecourse.

He was sitting next to Who Loves Yer Baby's owner, a schoolteacher on the verge of a retirement, which would be enriched with her ability to tell the saga of winning the 1986 Brisbane Handicap. The trainer and the owner had their backs to me. They were speaking loudly above the din of the punters swapping post mortems on the day's races.

'I don't know what happened to the price, Bill,' owner Claire Levy was saying. 'I know you said it had a chance and you did get Sailor to ride, but it still should have been twenty-to-one and the best I got was twelves.'

'Who knows how it happens, Claire?' said the ever-honest Bill Smith. 'Someone might have read about it in the paper. Someone having a big win decides to put a few hundred on as an omen bet and it snowballs from there. I'm sorry you missed your price.'

'I'm not, because I saw the price and put on three times as much as I planned. To tell you the truth, Bill, I thought you were pulling a swiftie.'

'Would I do that?' said Bill, feigning innocence.

I interrupted, tapping Bill on the shoulder and nodding to Ms Levy. Bill smiled at me, slapped me on the back and introduced me to his companion. She was the best owner any

Brisbane trainer ever had, apparently. He offered to shout me a wine, but Ms Levy swore she was buying while any of us were drinking. She pressed a $10 note in my hand and requested a gin squash for herself and a vodka and ice for Smith. Bill said he had to go to the loo, and followed me to the bar.

'How'd you go, Steele?' he asked.

I replied in a flat voice. 'I owe you about forty-two-and-a-half grand, but most of it's in cheques.'

'I'm sweet about my share, Steele. I was hoping you had a good go at it, but I can always give you some of mine.'

'I'm awlright, Bill. If you want to look after anyone, give Flick a bit of a sling. You were out of line with what you put her through. By the way, I hear she's fine and she'll ring you soon. As for that husband of hers – was it my imagination, or did he try to throw the race on the home turn?'

'You saw it, too, Steele? That cheating bastard will never put his leg over one of mine again.'

I had to smile, because Sailor would be the most relieved man in Australia had he heard the trainer's threat. I reached into a pocket to grab a wad of money, which I passed to Bill.

'We'll settle up for the rest towards the end of the week,' I said.

'Sure, but we should both go around to see Mick Clarence tomorrow. I half expected to see him with you today, but he told me about his medical condition. I bet he's as happy as a pig in mud right now.'

I was not up to telling Bill that Mick was as dead as a pig in a pork pie, and I refused to answer his questions about who had told me Felicity was all right. All I said was I would pick the trainer up on Tuesday morning and we would go around to Mick's Spring Hill unit. Tuesday seemed a long way away, and

I expected any number of humourless authorities would be grilling us both before then. I toasted the victory of Who Loves Yer Baby with two glasses of red, left the winning connections to party into the night and drove home to Hendra.

When I put $5000 in Natalie's hand, she asked me what I had done, and I told her I backed a winner. I could have looked more excited, she said, but I declined to offer any more details. It had been a long day.

The truth is that I didn't feel any satisfaction from winning a big bundle. A gambler can never win enough, but they can lose the lot, as Mick Clarence did. Gambling is a beautiful tragedy, which is why it attracts the glamorous and the self-destructive. I think that's why I threw all that money in the river. I was not making an audacious gesture, or shaking my fist at the gods; I was just admitting to myself that money is a lousy way to keep score.

42

ONCE I HAVE A NOTION firmly planted in my brain, it stays fixed. A quick calculation told me I would have more than twenty grand left after I gave Bill Smith his forty-two and change. Because Mick Clarence had said he would give me ten grand if our horse won, I decided that was what I was entitled to. I had five grand to spend quickly. A romantic might have given more to Natalie, but I never entertained that notion. A smart man would have bought her a ten-grand diamond ring, something to wheedle from her to pawn when I was down on my luck. I was not doing that, either

THE CHIEF STEWARD RANG me at seven on Monday morning.

'You woke me,' I said, sipping coffee in my lounge room and peering down at the racing page of the morning paper. 'How'd you get my number?'

'You're a licensed bookmaker's clerk; we have your details.'

'Sure, that's right,' I said, and waited for him to get to the point.

Joe Boss, which is still the name we are using for the chief steward, reminded me of the $60,000 in bookies' and totalisator cheques I had in my possession.

I didn't ask how he knew about the money, but let him

move on instead.

'I'd like you to promise not to deposit those cheques until after you come to my office on Thursday morning,' Joe Boss said.

I asked why, but he simply repeated his request. I asked whether he had instructed people to stop any of the cheques.

'I would need authorisation from a court to do that, Steele. I am just asking you not to deposit the cheques until Thursday afternoon. I can only add that it might prove beneficial to you, if certain circumstances prevail.'

'Awlright, you have totally confused me now, Boss. You want to see me on Thursday morning about something or other, and you want me to hold on to the paper I could turn into cash today. But it's still my choice. So, it's also my choice to give our Thursday appointment a miss.'

'That's a different kettle of fish, entirely. You have to attend the inquiry I am calling.'

'An inquiry into what?'

'That you already know, so I believe I am safe legally to withhold further details. But I would like you to reassure me you will do what I ask, and refrain from depositing those cheques until Thursday afternoon.'

'Sure, Boss, I'll do that, because, if you know about the cheques, you also know I collected thousands in cash. I can hold off until Thursday afternoon. Will I need a lawyer for this inquiry?'

'That's up to you, Steele. My advice would be to keep the lawyers out of it until we are clearer on a few details. As I said, that's up to you.'

'Yair well, I might bring a lawyer, because I know a good one. His name is Jim Mecklam.'

I heard Boss snort a laugh down the phone. 'They tell me you're something of a comedian,' he said. 'Leave the jokes at home on Thursday and, for now, let's have the record clear. You will cash those cheques in your possession on Thursday afternoon at the earliest.'

'I've agreed to that twice already,' I said, offended by his distrust.

I was the first person through the door of my bank when it opened later that morning, and I paid for six-hour clearances on all the cheques. I didn't like the way Boss described my cheques as cheques in my possession. I would turn up for the Thursday morning showdown, but I was determined that Bill Smith and I had the flexibility of stacks of cash in case we were unhappy with what we heard.

At Bill's place, he told me Boss was not seeing him until Friday morning, which set us both thinking. You had to figure Smith for a badder guy than I was in a race fix, when all they had me for was being the moneyman. Unless Boss knew more than we gave him credit for.

Bill's daughter Flick had contacted him and told him that their stupid kidnapping prank was their last together. He said she was quite cheerful, but she gave him a good dressing-down. She was returning home to Sailor that day.

With Flick safe, our main worry was the chief steward and what information he had. As far as Bill and I could figure, only three people knew the full details of the scam. Mick Clarence was dead, leaving Smith and me.

Bill had read about Mick's death in the morning paper, but I could see he did not want to talk about it. He asked me if I knew anything, and I said that the last time I had seen Mick was on Friday night. Smith muttered 'sad' and 'good young bloke', and the topic returned to our meetings with the chief steward.

Of course, Bill thought he had hidden the full story about his daughter's role in the hustle from everybody. I guess that put me at the top of the tree for seeing the whole scene, not that it gave me extra protection. It did make me wonder if Bill had been too clever by half in other matters, and allowed someone else to work out parts of the hustle. Bill and I decided that Boss wanted to get as much from me and from other unknown parties as he could, to be able to throw some scares into the trainer on Friday.

I rang the bookie I worked for, saying I was crook and would be unable to field until Saturday at the earliest. He sounded pissed off, though plenty of casual clerks were available. I realised word of my big collects would have been all over the bookies' ring. He would have felt a dill, being no wiser than anyone who I was fronting for when I pulled off the big plunge on Who Loves Yer Baby. My bookie never went so far as to fire me, so he could tell the other bookies whatever he liked as far as I was concerned.

JOE BOSS DISMISSED the copper to outside the tiny office. He looked at me after the copper shut the door on us.

'I'm sorry about the death of your mate, Clarence. Is it true he rang up the Canterbury stewards and abused them for ten minutes for moving the barrier stalls five metres after sudden rain?' Boss asked.

I said it was, and we discussed the details that Mick had shared with me. Boss looked at me across his desk.

'You're only a baby, Hill. What the fuck are you mixing with these lunatics for?'

It was funny, the impression Mick Clarence made, even on people who only knew of him second or third-hand. Boss was calling him a lunatic for leading me astray, though Clarence was almost four years younger than me and the only favour he had ever asked of me was to put his twenty grand on Who Loves Yer Baby. One of the other lunatics he was referring to had to be Bill Smith, and I played along.

'I haven't done anything, Boss. Is this about that mad Russian?'

Boss shook his head, not in answer to my question but in general disbelief at my audacity.

'I don't know how you blokes reckoned you could possibly get away with it. When I looked at the time, a new race record, almost a course record, and with what I had seen of the race with my own eyes, I couldn't believe it.'

I looked blankly at the chief steward, knowing he had more to say.

'I took all the reports from the other stewards. Together, we watched the patrol film over and over. Of course, we declared correct weight, as no interference to other runners occurred. But we knew we would be taking the race from you. So we ordered a routine swab of the second placegetter, which we intended to promote to first, once we found out what Smith gave your horse. We asked for a quick process of the analysis, and we had the results yesterday afternoon.'

'That was quick,' I said.

'Oh, they've been checked half a dozen times. So, what would you like to say at this point?'

I could see through the blinds of the solitary window that it was a fine day outside, but apart from chitchat about the weather, I had nothing to add.

'Okay,' Boss said. He sat upright in his chair and stared hard into my face. 'If anything remotely like what I am about to tell you comes back to me, you will never enter any racetrack anywhere in the world ever again. You understand me?'

Boss had my full attention as I nodded agreement.

'The second placegetter, All The Favours, came back positive for a go-fast they discovered in Italy three months ago.'

'Mecklam's horse was doped,' I said.

I was trying to control my smile as Boss gave me a filthy look.

With my best serious expression, I said, 'You wouldn't expect that sort of thing from a member of the legal profession.'

It was Mr Boss's turn to suppress a smile. I began to ponder why we were discussing Mecklam's results rather than ours.

The chief steward opened and closed his mouth twice before he spoke, as if unsure whether he should offer the next piece of information.

'Who Loves Yer Baby came back clean,' he said finally and with little enthusiasm.

I stared hard at the other man, and his dejected expression confirmed the good news. Who Loves Yer Baby clean. Clean as the whistle that legend has top jockeys using to tell their peers they need an uninterrupted run through the field.

Mick Clarence had been spot on with every prediction. Psilocybin was an effective undetectable go-fast. I wished I could meet Mick back in his tiny Spring Hill flat to congratulate him. I rose from my chair as if our session was over.

'I guess I can cash those cheques now,' I said, and turned towards the door. 'You know, you only had to ask on Monday, and I could have told you that Bill Smith had trained the horse to perfection because he wanted to win the race with a passion.'

Mr Boss ignored my regrets at the misunderstandings between us. He rose quickly and took a few large strides to place his hand on the doorknob before I could reach it.

'Sit down, Hill, I am not finished with you yet. What if I tell you all the money you defrauded and your job as a bookie's clerk are both still yours, if you tell me what you used to dope the horse?'

'Fresh air and good feed, that's all Smith used.'

'You know I can pull your licence before you get to your car.'

'That would be corruption.'

'That would be justice. You're lucky half of Brisbane hates Mecklam's guts. I'm sick of trainers asking me to make him pay his bills. Maybe this will force him out of the game.'

'I doubt it.'

The chief steward agreed. 'I do, too, but we won't have you around much longer, Hill, unless you pull your socks up and stay away from the wrong crowd.'

'You know, Boss, I'd love to do that. The trouble is, these days, you never know who the wrong crowd are.

Book Five

At church

43

I SEARCHED THE DEATH NOTICES and found that Mick's funeral was on Friday at Nudgee cemetery, not far from the orphanage where I grew up. I told Bill Smith about it but he said he had to go to the race inquiry. I am sure he could have had the inquiry postponed but he chose not to. For some reason I did not press him on, Bill thought Mick's death had a connection with our race fix. The racing mob are a superstitious bunch and Bill Smith wanted to erase Mick Clarence from his memory.

I was tossing up whether I should go, and spun Natalie a yarn about a bloke I knew from the track who been killed in a tragic accident and I did not think he had much of a family. Nat asked if she had ever met him, and when I said no she still insisted I should go to the funeral.

I didn't make the funeral mass because I had a bet going in the third at Hawkesbury, which I listened to on the car radio on the way to the cemetery. I backed Bright Side each way or to run in the first three, and it ran fourth.

I parked the ute outside the grounds and waited for the funeral procession of eleven cars, including the hearse. I followed the group to the graveside and looked around, to discover I was about the only mourner under thirty-five years-old. You would have thought Mick's smack dealer could have turned up to pay his last respects. And where was that parade of punters who frequented his Spring Hill flat, eager for a tip on a twenty-to-one shot?

People waiting for the ceremony talked quietly among themselves. A short, middle-aged woman came up to me and asked if I knew Mick well. The other mourners had taken turns to cry on her shoulder, so I figured it was Mrs Clarence.

'Did you know my son Mick well?' she repeated.

'Reasonably well,' I answered with due solemnity.

'You know they're saying he killed himself, and they never found the man who helped him do it, the man who rang the police,' she said.

'I don't think he killed himself,' I said. 'It was a mistake.'

'I do not think my Mick would do anything like that; it just wasn't him,' Mrs Clarence said.

'No, you're right,' I said. 'It was a mistake.'

She was reassured, or, at least, I hoped she was.

'You don't take drugs?' she asked.

'No I don't, Mrs Clarence,' I lied. 'Are you awlright? Did your doctor give you something?'

She said her GP had fixed her up with some Valium. She had never heard of it before, but he told her that other patients took it all the time; it settled their nerves and was safe as houses.

'You know, he was never the same after his Dad died.'

'It must have been hard on you, too, Mrs Clarence,' I consoled.

'You know, the driver of the other car was drunk, but they could never prove it.'

'The other driver?' I asked.

'Yes, Mick begged his Dad to let him go with him to the greyhounds that day. He'd done it lots of times, though they both knew I didn't like it. But his Dad would not let Mick go that day.'

This was Dad who Mick told me shot his brains out across the kitchen wall. And Mick that we all thought had never been to a racetrack in his life.

'You know, the other driver was drunk and they couldn't prove it,' Mrs Clarence repeated.

'This was when your husband died?' I said softly.

'Yes, killed in a head-on, with two of our greyhounds in the back of the station wagon. Mick was twelve at the time and he never really got over it. Did you know him well?'

I nodded in answer and realised I didn't know him at all.

The priest said Mick was free now, safe in the shadow of God. Mick was in pain but had not resorted to the coward's way out, said the priest, betraying his Catholic fear of suicide.

'Bloody right,' I echoed out loud, though I did not mean to. 'It was a mistake.'

Some of the middle-aged mourners turned to admonish me with their glares, but I was happy to have paid the tribute I involuntarily blurted out.

A GREY-HAIRED MAN approached me after the ceremony.

'That was quite a hustle you and Clarence pulled,' he said.

I looked up at the kindly, knowing face.

'What are you, a fucking Guru?' I said.

'No, I'm no Guru. Mick Clarence took about $120 grand from us in eighteen months. We knew he was under the legal betting age, but who were we going to tell?'

'You a bookie?' I asked.

'SP. My boss Cheerful took to eating anti-acid pills like they were potato chips every time Mick rang us for a bet. You know, you can't blame yourself or the fix for Mick's death.'

'There goes the Guru again,' I replied.

The man, who looked to be in his late fifties, put his hand around my shoulder and guided me to the exit. 'Mick's time had come,' he said. 'Let me buy you a drink. My name's Con Vitalis. And can you stop that Guru shit? By the way, there's a copper named Mooney standing over on that hill. I'd say he is checking you out, because you're the only young person here. He probably thinks you work for me now.'

We walked through the gates and Vitalis told me to follow him in my ute before he went to his white Holden Commodore. The SP bookie began to hop into his driver's seat, but he stopped in mid-crouch to stand up and turn towards me.

'Is it true Mick abused the stewards for twenty minutes because they moved the starting barriers five metres at Canterbury?' Vitalis asked.

I assured him it was indeed true, but it was only ten minutes. He shook his head in wonder, then eased himself behind the steering wheel. I told him to wait up, and fetched a large envelope from the ute's glove box. I handed it to Vitalis.

'Can you give this to Mrs Clarence?' I asked.

'What's in it?'

'Money.'

'Much?'

'Ten grand.'

'You trust me?' Vitalis asked.

'Doesn't matter. It's only money.'

I followed his car to a pub in Fortitude Valley.

44

Spring, October, 1992

THE CREAKY WHEELS OF JUSTICE move pretty slowly. It took the coppers eight months to reconstruct the plot of what had happened to the Federal copper in Cheerful Charlie's SP betting shop in late 1991. I hadn't thought about Mick Clarence for a couple of years until the coppers repeatedly appeared on my doorstep dispensing new and improved versions of what had happened on that Saturday evening in the back of the butcher's shop. I told Senior Constable Schmidt I would continue with our historical rewrites only if he found out the details about the death of Mick's Dad.

From 1986, waves of sadness overwhelmed me from time to time, as I thought of Clarence's death. It was a tragic passing of a unique person, with an unusual mathematical gift that might have dragged him up a nobler path than picking winning racehorses. I felt I could put the jigsaw puzzle away in the cupboard if I just had all the pieces of his Dad's death.

Mooney threatened to kick my teeth in and have me charged with murder, but I stood on my digs until Schmidt said he would look into it.

____ooo____

HALF A WORLD away, another man received a resolution of sorts. On October 24, 1992, in a baptism provided by American

Rehabilitation Ministries, General Manuel Noriega was immersed in the name of the Father, Son and Holy Spirit at the Federal Court House, Miami, Florida, in the chambers of United States District Judge Honourable William M Hoeveler. Born again Manny applied for a pardon soon after, but the earthly U.S. authorities were in no mood for forgiveness.

AN UNHAPPY Mrs Applebee answered after I fingered the correct buttons, in my third attempt at using another of Cheerful's mobiles that I inherited. Gooroo made me promise not to pawn this one, and guaranteed he would pay the bills. I felt honour-bound to fulfil the oath I gave my mentor. Mrs Applebee let me speak to Natalie after I promised I would not ring again. I was missing My Cucumber, but I was unsure she reciprocated.

I started by apologising to Natalie for her not finding me at home. It's okay, she said, she had not rung. I said I had wanted to tell her about the danger I was in, but she might have worried. Worse, she might not have cared.

'I need to see you soon, Nat.'

'I still haven't made up my mind, Steele. I'm coming down to see Bub's play at the Avalon Theatre, and Jane's probably expecting you to come along anyway. It's best we meet in public, but it's not a date.'

Nat told me the theatre for Bub's graduation play was in Sir Fred Schonell Drive, St Lucia. Queensland Uni owned the premises, and used them for drama lessons and occasional student productions.

I supposed that naming a theatre after fifties pop heart-throb Frankie Avalon was an example of that new trend, postmodernism, which a bunch of newspaper arts columnists loved to embed in their Saturday morning pieces. Yair, since that murder at La Boite, I had taken to reading the arts pages sometimes, though I rarely understood much of it below the headline or picture caption.

The play was called *Six Characters in Search of an Author*, and some dead Italian fella named Pirandello did the show business. Mr P. was another one of those famous playwrights no one ever heard of. I guess university professors get the big money for discovering a play's genius, missed by most of the other forty-nine punters who take in an obscure piece on opening night. I imagined – to myself, of course – these high-minded judges of literary genius patting themselves on the back for their discovery of the depths of the author's genius: *Listen Jack, don't you know, he's a star.* Just like me, for finding it out. I put my foot into it with Natalie by jokingly asking if this playwright won a Nobel Prize, because it turned out he did.

I joined the crowd of about fifty mingling in the Avalon's foyer, and spotted Natalie by herself in a corner. I caught her eye, waved and pointed to a makeshift bar where I bought a glass of red and another of white at the attractive price of a dollar apiece. I handed Natalie the white and asked if I needed to buy a ticket. Nat rolled her eyes just a wee bit, before producing two entry slips from the glossy pages of a program.

'Pirandello – it sounds a bit like a ballet move,' I said to relieve the tension.

'Don't start, Steele,' My estranged Cucumber reprimanded.

'I'm not starting. We're quite the arty couple, you and I: electric violin music, movies with subtitles, theatre and ballet.'

'When have you ever been to the ballet with me?'

'We went to that play by the Chinese herbal cold remedy fella.'

'Tchaikovsky,' Natalie scoffed. 'Only because you read the title in the paper and it sounded like that Sydney mate of yours.'

'He was hardly a mate; I only met the big blond Viking a couple of times. I just wanted to see the ballet the Nutcracker Swede got his name from.'

Natalie's shoulders shook in revulsion at the implications of the nickname, but I merrily continued.

'You know street slang is my thing. I wanted to see if the moniker was more than just a play on words.'

'Yair, right, Steele, among those lowlife mates of yours lurks a twentieth-century Shakespeare, just itching to erupt on the world stage.'

'A lot of good it did me anyway, Nat. Talk about subtitles; that ballet needed babies crawling around the dancers' ankles and holding cue cards to tell us punters what was going on.'

I saw Natalie wanted to laugh at that image, as she put her tongue onto her top lip to suppress any mirth. She demanded I just stop it, but I was having fun and was determined to raise at least a smile.

'You know, Nat, I happily tagged along to all your arty occasions, though you hardly ever went to the races or the trots or the dogs with me in the days I was allowed in.'

'I wonder why, when you'd race off to the betting ring or chase red hot tips all day, and leave me with one of your sleazy mates either trying to look down my dress or borrow $5.'

'Most of them weren't mates, Nat. They were gambling acquaintances, and you can't choose them – they just luck upon you in the course of your work.'

That last observation could best have been left unsaid, because it was our differences over the definition of gainful employment that prompted our rift. As luck would have it, I was saved by the bell announcing the imminent raising of the curtain on the play.

We settled into our seats in blocks of aluminium chairs welded together into rows that were movable by hand. They could have been more comfortable and, as it turned out, bigger seats, as a lot were empty. Most of the audience appeared to be students, who didn't seem to mind the discomfit. From my limited experience of higher learning, uni students did not expect much, and those who did were quickly brought down to earth. The highs and lows were accepted equally when you learned Plato during the day and cleaned plates at night.

The play was a minute old when the smell of a familiar perfume prompted me to look to my right. Crystal Speares had settled into the seat beside mine.

She wore a strapless black cocktail dress, which declared she had forgotten her bra again. While I tried to work out the odds of seeing her at the play, Crystal stared ahead at the stage and gave no hint of knowing I was beside her.

Unlike any poor student writing a review of the play, I had a top excuse for not understanding what the first act of *Six Characters in Search of an Author* was about. I remember getting the impression that bits of it were funny as I followed the lead of others and laughed. I suppose it is a good idea to have funny stuff in a work that people have little hope of understanding.

Despite my outbursts of mirth and my need to stare straight ahead at the stage, most of the action and dialogue blurred into a sense of dread. When I did glance to my left, Natalie was clearly captivated by the plot. When I could not help myself looking to the right, Crystal was watching blankly ahead, only allowing herself a trifling smirk as she sensed I was sneaking glances at her. Act one seemed endless.

Crystal Speares followed us into the foyer and I felt the sweat on my face when she touched Nat on the shoulder. The blonde beauty shook her head when Natalie turned her face.

'Oh, I'm so sorry, I thought you were someone else,' Crystal said sweetly.

Natalie said it was all right – she did it all the time herself. She excused herself to me to go to the toilet.

'What the hell are you doing here, Crystal?' I asked, softly and vehemently.

'A night out at the theatre, Steele. You're not the only one who knows how to find people. But you did not seem to enjoy the first part of the play much. You should identify with it. There are about six of us characters still living in our little drama and, as our author has abandoned us, nobody knows who is writing the rest of the script.'

'I hope it's not you, Crystal, because you lack a little in subtlety.'

'It's like this, Steele. The script I'm writing has me living to a rich, ripe and mildly decadent old age. The way you're acting, you will get me bumped off early in the second act. Your pretty girlfriend will be back soon and I'm seriously thinking of telling her we're sleeping together.'

'That is flattering, Crystal, but I'm not sure Natalie will believe it. I would have thought you might prefer death before the dishonour of having me as a trophy.'

'Well, that just shows you how desperate I am getting. Shush, here she comes. Ask yourself, Steele, how did I find you here? You are blundering around like a baby feral pig when it's open season on them. You don't seem to want to help the state police bury this to everybody's satisfaction, including dead Fed Bradshaw's vicious business partners.'

She tinkled a laugh as Natalie came nearer.

'Oh yes, it is quite a clever little drama, isn't it? Seems to be about trying to distinguish between fantasy and reality. Can't wait to see how it ends. See you round.'

Crystal walked away. I noticed some teenage students, male and female, eye off her sleek figure as she approached the bar.

Natalie wanted to know what our conversation was about. I told her some bloke had stood Crystal up, and I guess she had nobody to discuss the first act with at interval.

'And what great insight did you come up with, Steele? That any bloke who stood her up had to be mad?'

Crystal left the bar and I edged Natalie towards it. 'Now, Nat, I'm no longer the yobbo you fell head over heels in love with. When we first met – what, almost seven years ago? – if someone had stood you up, I would have made such a remark. Tonight, with that blonde, I only thought it. You have to agree it's progress on my personal journey. Apart from that, the two of you have a lot in common.'

'Like what?'

'When I said Pirandello sounded like a ballet move, she didn't find it funny either.'

At play's end, Natalie couldn't wait to congratulate Bub. I said I needed a piss. She handed me a ticket to get backstage, and headed off that way as I made towards the toilet.

Through the open doors, I noticed Crystal Speares smoking a cigarette on the footpath outside the theatre. She was also talking down a mobile phone and raising a finger to hail me.

Not only could she do lots at once, Crystal knew where I would be before I got there.

The battered dark green Holden V8 squealed rubber as it veered from the middle of Sir Fred Schonell Drive and sped towards Crystal. The car bounced off the kerb as its hooded driver over-corrected and narrowly missed two cars coming the other way from the university.

Crystal lunged towards me and I instinctively opened my arms. She brushed her blonde hair against my cheek and whispered in my ear. 'I told you, Steele, you'll have us both killed.'

Protectively, I put my hands on her shoulders and asked if she recognised the driver. She did not have a good look, but it was definitely a man wearing a balaclava. She couldn't see anything else.

I could. 'You know Crystal, if that was a professional killer, he needs to get a day job. He couldn't even make the car jump the kerb. And I don't want to be size-ist about this, but a bloke built like a jockey hardly cuts the terrifying mustard at the wheel of a V8.'

She looked into my smiling face as I continued. 'You've been known to have a bet in your life, so what're the odds on me going down to the Feed Bin café next week to find Billy Scharfe or one of his mates parking that car?'

She gently pushed my chest to free herself from my gallantry. 'Fuck you, Steele. I'm trying to be nice about making you get lost. The people who want you dead aren't amateurish worrywarts like Billy.'

She saw the cab she had rung pull up beside the kerb and walked over, turning towards me before she got in. 'I take care of myself because I know there won't be anyone crying over my coffin. My admirers like me alive. I'm sure your girlfriend is less fickle than that. She'll throw flowers into your grave.'

I turned to go back inside and saw three rose bushes struggling in a bed in front of the theatre. 'Wait up, Crystal,' I called out.

I recognised one of the bushes as an Iraqi Icicle, nowhere near as well-nourished as my neighbour Amelia Barnes kept hers. Even her Iraqi Icicles had battled in the past week, though I watered them twice.

SEVEN DAYS EARLIER, an ambulance had arrived at our block of flats and a squat man about a generation younger than Mrs Barnes let the ambos, pushing a trolley, into her flat.

They returned through the front door, pushing the trolley, with a sheet covering a body about the size of Mrs Barnes. I thought about asking what was going on. I decided against it.

I HAD MY FLOWER-SNIPPING SCISSORS in the glove box of the EH, but Crystal Speares would be too impatient to wait for me. I tried to snap an Iraqi Icicle branch with a cluster of small white flowers on top. The branch was not firm enough and I twisted it off, pricking myself in the process. I looked to see Crystal tapping her foot while she held the cab's front door open.

'Here,' I said presenting the rose. 'I'll bet you don't know what this is called.'

'It's called a rose,' she said sarcastically.

I let the jibe pass. 'We first met at the races six years ago, Crystal, and I said your middle name had to be Trouble.'

She raised her eyes and shook her head slightly, to indicate so many men, so many race days.

I gave her the Iraqi Icicle. 'The name of this rose is White Trouble,' I said.

She sniffed the cluster of blooms. 'How sweet, I will keep it under my pillow.'

She hopped in the cab and turned up the window to maximise the value of the air conditioning against the hot night. The cab did a U-turn to head back through the city to Ascot. I thought I saw Crystal's window turn down, and wondered if she was sick from too much wine.

A few seconds later a car came from the university. In its headlights I saw the cluster of Iraqi Icicle flowers lying in the gutter.

Back inside the theatre, a young student breathed alcohol into my face. 'Way to go, man. I seen you with both those hot chicks. What deodorant you wearing?'

I took a step backwards away from the alcohol fumes before I replied. 'It's called Morbidity.'

I could see him trying to log the brand name in his soggy brain.

Backstage, Bub asked me if I liked the play. I told her I couldn't get my head around it, but that she was terrific.

'And no dead bodies among the cast this time, Steele,' Jane said, recalling our evening with Godot.

I replied that it was a pleasant change. Maybe these Queensland Uni students were not as emotional as their Kelvin Grove counterparts? Bub declared that her new Alma Mater was as close to the edge as her previous campus. They just channelled their raw passions more effectively, she said.

'Bub, you are full of shit,' I answered. 'And I love you for it.'

Bub replied that she loved me too, though she was the only one of the three Applebee women who would make such a claim at that moment. She would have a word with sister Nat on my behalf.

As a notion, it had no merits I could see. 'Before you do that, Bub, just plunge a dagger into my heart, right now, and be done with it.'

Bub said proudly I had the instincts of a true ham, and should enrol in drama classes. She was serious; she would help me fill in the forms for the next semester. With Bub in my corner, my prospects for a happy life were sinking fast.

45

NATALIE AND I HAD SEX that night, or the next morning to be pedantic about it, but she refused to promise to transfer her job back to Brisbane and come home to Hendra. The best she gave was an unconvincing agreement to think about it. She went back to the Sunshine Coast later that day.

____ooo____

A WEEK LATER, about eleven on Saturday morning, Senior Constable Schmidt thumped on my door. Mooney wasn't with him and I surprised myself by offering him a mug of coffee. He surprised me by accepting. Schmidt eased his bulk into a kitchen chair.

'Tracking down Clarence's death was harder than studying for Sergeant's exams. Our records were not much chop in those days.'

'They're making you a Sergeant?'

'No, I am helping out another bloke, though I reckon I deserve the promotion for sorting this Tweed Heads mess. Mooney's no help at all. He wants you charged with manslaughter, and that Fed bastard Bradshaw disgraced and his widow's service pension pulled. He knows it can't go down like that, but he hates the way you showed him up for backing down to that American Colonel.'

Schmidt climbed out of his chair and roamed around the

kitchen and lounge, looking at the pictures of racehorses and rock bands on the walls until he got on my nerves.

'Do you mind?'

'Sorry.'

'Yair, I know, force of habit.'

'Your trouble is, Hill . . .

'Yair, I know, I'm a clown."

'Your trouble is you've got a problem with authority.'

'I doubt it. I don't go about banging on business boardroom doors screaming at them to stop ripping off the stiffs. I don't go around rattling the bars of prison cells, demanding to be let in. For some reason, authority has a problem with me.'

'We can fix that problem and put you away for five years. You won't be such a smart-arse clown when you come home from that little holiday.'

Schmidt sat down again and I refilled our coffee mugs. I had long grown bored with the Tweed Heads song and dance, having quickly realised that their charging me with anything could lead to reality rupturing the fiction they were carefully concocting. I waited patiently for Schmidt to get back to the death of Mick's father.

'Single-person motor vehicle accident on Beaudesert Road on a Monday afternoon.'

'That can't be right. Mick said his father . . . and Mrs Clarence said . . .'

'Oh, it's right enough. I tracked down the officer who made the report. The incident was strange enough for him to remember it as clear as day.'

'He remembered his report as clear as day.'

'I didn't say that, Hill. You know, you really need to start listening better. I said he remembered what he figured happened as clear as day. Not what he wrote in his report.'

I was becoming a little uncomfortable. I couldn't understand why Mick had lied to me, when his fiction had to be uglier than the truth. I rose and paced about, and Schmidt waited for me to sit down before he continued his tale.

'His station wagon hit a tree and, without a seat belt, he was killed instantly. There were no skid marks before he left the road and no sign of his braking.'

Mick had been right about the suicide, but I wondered how he worked it out.

'It was obviously a suicide. Any accident investigation team should have twigged to that pretty quickly. Once the officer saw the pictures of a wife and son in the wallet, he wrote it up as a traffic accident, where the driver had swerved to miss an oncoming car and hit the tree.'

I asked Schmidt if that was the final verdict, and he said it was. 'I don't know why the accident investigators agreed with a report contrary to the physical evidence but it seems they did.

'But that wasn't the end of it,' he continued. 'The copper who wrote it up said he wanted to tell the wife. The stupid bastard could have gotten into a lot of trouble, because he tells the missus they suspect a drunk driver caused the accident and left the scene.'

'Why would the copper want to make that up?'

'Who knows? He had already gone out on a limb for this family he'd never met, so I guess he decided to go for the jackpot. He said he just wanted to meet them and then felt sorry when he found the twelve-year-old son was home sick from school the day his dad died. Only later did he discover the kid was home on a forged medical certificate.'

That would have been Mick all right, having at least one

fictitious GP before Doctor Steele Hill came along.

The police officer dropped in to see Mick and his mum from time to time over the next few months, to check if they were paid out on the insurance policy.

Schmidt refuted the conclusions a cynic might reach. 'He was not trying to blackmail the family or get into the widow's knickers; he just wanted to make sure his historical rewrite achieved a good result. You gotta remember he could have lost his job over this.'

But the rewrite of history stuck. The insurance money allowed Mick to finish his high school years at a private school and go on to uni.

Mick showed little gratitude for his improved social prospects and the police officer remembered him as being surly every time he saw him. Eventually the copper didn't need the ingratitude and stopped visiting. But not before he found more puzzling aspects to the death.

Mick often used his forged medical certificates on a Monday afternoon when the Beenleigh dogs were on. His schoolmates said he sometimes went one better. He had the hide to feign sickness before lunch, go down the local café for an ice cream, return to school with a med cert he had forged that morning and go home to meet his Dad for their day at the dog races.

Mr Clarence tolerated his son's ruses because Mick had an uncanny knack of going through the race book, scribbling numbers in the margins and picking dogs which went on to win, often at good prices. Mick's Dad loved it when, on rare occasions, his son declared for one of their own dogs, which invariably won.

The day he died, Mr Clarence promised to take Mick to the track, but changed his mind at the last moment. Mick's last words to his father were to call him a liar and a welcher for not taking him to the Beenleigh dogs.

No one ever found out what happened to the two dogs Clarence took to the track that day, because they were not in the back of the station wagon. The investigating police officer figured Mick's Dad, their owner-trainer, had given them away, and they probably wound up racing under new names and false registrations. The copper's reports were not complicated by any mention of missing dogs.

I thanked Schmidt for the information and gave him some parting words of wisdom. 'Greyhound racing is a mug's game.'

He nodded in silent agreement as he walked across the yard. Then he turned around. 'What's that?' he asked.

'Nothing,' I said. I refrained from repeating Mick's other favourite saying, which I had delivered under my breath.

Adults are fucked.

46

A BATTERED DARK GREEN HOLDEN V8 was parked along Nudgee Road, 200 metres from the Feed Bin café, and I pulled in behind it.

The previous day I had put in my annual application to be reinstated to all racecourses across Australia. I had woken in the middle of the night with an inspiration. As keen as anything to start a new year fresh, I always put in my application to re-join the racing fraternity in January. In 1992, I realised I was playing a mug's game. If I put the application in during November, by the time the final verdict came down, it would be near Christmas, the season of goodwill and Christmas parties, the time for all good prodigal sons and true to come to the aid of horse racing's just cause. With my new strategy, I had to be a shoo-in, and I whistled on my way to the Feed Bin.

Billy Scharfe was hunched over a cup of coffee in the corner. His eyes darted from side to side, but never beyond his table, as if he feared to look up. For a jockey in his early twenties, his face was thin and lined like a hoop twenty years older, who had seen the inside of too many saunas. I was thinking of sitting beside him, but decided the table was already crowded with his personal demons. Instead I walked past on my way to order coffee, toast and a newspaper, and whispered in his direction.

'Nice driving last month along Sir Fred Schonell Drive. You'd get beaten on Phar Lap if you rode like that, Billy.'

To his credit, Scharfe pretended he didn't hear me and

focussed his vision into his half-empty coffee cup. I had no follow-up line, so I let him be. Billy's riding career was all but over. The word was about that he was "bad news", though no one could agree why it was so.

Billy was never very bright, but he tried to please, putting all the contradictory advice he received into practice as best he could. He was never supposed to run me down outside the Avalon Theatre, but he was supposed to make me think his intentions were bad. Like most projects he touched, he stuffed the whole thing up good and proper. The Billy Scharfes of this world will always end up doing the bidding of the unscrupulous. The Billy Scharfes need a truckload of luck to survive with their dignity. That much luck is not out there.

The daily paper had some good news on page seven. Brisbane lawyer Jim Mecklam, who had gone back into private practice after years in the corporate sector, was caught diddling his clients' trust accounts to the tune of a quarter of a mill. Former prominent racehorse owner Mecklam was suspended from practising law, but strenuously denied any impropriety. He engaged a leading Queen's Counsel to process his defence, as well as his bankruptcy and divorce proceedings.

My money was on Mecklam to come out of it with a wad of cash, but I wouldn't want to be waiting in line with his wife Prue, the trainers he owed or even his Queen's Counsel, looking for a share of it.

I flicked aimlessly through the sports pages, declined a second cuppa and left.

As I took in the pleasant but heavy morning air outside the café, I couldn't fail to notice Crystal Speares in white jeans and a tight white T-shirt, as she smoked a fag beside her red Mercedes Sports. She pretended she was waiting for someone and ignored me when I walked alongside. As you did, I wondered if she and Billy Scharfe were fucking. It would be a stranger-than-fiction reality. They do happen.

I played it cool and nudged Crystal gently with my elbow as I passed.

'Oh, it's you,' she said as she stubbed out the cigarette under the edge of one of her expensive running shoes.

I kept walking and the blonde beauty told me to wait.

'Hold up, Steele,' she said. 'I admit I've been waiting for you.'

She slid into the driver's seat of the red Mercedes and invited me to sit beside her.

'You gotta hear this, Steele. I've hooked up with this preacher,' Crystal said, as she hopped out of the car and caught up with me. 'There's squillions in it.'

I stopped and faced the blonde. She had my attention now.

'They fleece fucking hundreds of these rich dumb marks at their weekly prayer meets. I didn't believe it myself until this preacher Ralph dragged me along to one of his gigs.'

'His name's Ralph?'

'That's his real name, not his stage name. I met him at an Ascot dinner party and we got chatting. Dead set, this bloke owns three Rolls-Royces. They're all over ten years old, but they're still fucking Rollers. After the dinner that night, we ended up banging in the back seat of the Roller he'd brought to the do. Dead set, just as he was about to come, he screamed, 'Praise the Lord.'

I had lost interest and kept walking, but Crystal ran after me to tug the sleeve of my T-shirt. 'Shit, Steele, these bastards are deadset babies. We can take them for everything. I know you like me, Steele. We can do this together. Whaddya say?'

Looking into the pale, infantine and slowly lining face of the most beautiful woman I had seen in my life, I gave way at the knees.

Here was something I didn't want to tangle with, something that could bring my whole world crashing down.

I ran.

Glossary of Australian slang

THIS GLOSSARY of Australian slang is necessarily partial as it comprises words and phrases used in the novel.

Many good slang dictionaries use a similar methodology by tracing the oral slang term to its early uses in fiction. Doubtless some slang has written sources conquered by the oral idiom. When you Google 'not the brightest light on the Ferris wheel of life' you will see I have created a new slang expression in *Iraqi Icicle*. It combines the notions of the merry-go-round of life and 'not the brightest bulb on the Christmas tree/ in the shed.'

You may note that 'brightest bulb in the shed' and 'sharpest tool in the shed' are interchangeable' while 'the lights are on but nobody's home' means roughly' the same thing. Slang, a living language is constantly borrowing from itself and external sources to remain fresh and attractive.

In these days of globalisation, a decreasing number of the words are uniquely Australian. International trade in slang replenishes idioms around the world.

Akay: the Australian version of okay. See awlright.

Al capone: phone (rhyming slang**)**.

All over bar the shouting: The outcome of an event is obvious before the finish.

Ambo: ambulance officer, paramedic.

Arse: the Australian version of ass as in posterior, not donkey. A smart-arse is the neo-noir equivalent to the classical wise-cracking PI. Other uses are arsey as in lucky (hence 'more arse than class') get your arse into gear, and ugly as a hatful of arseholes.

Awlright: how many Australians pronounce all right as one word. Awlright has the same versatility as the American okay which, when Australians use it, invariably comes out as akay.

Bag of fruit: suit (rhyming slang). My Irish editor (G'day Eoin) tells me the expression is 'tin of fruit' in his homeland. One of the benefits of life in Australia is year-round access to reasonably priced fresh fruit which you put into bags rather than take from tins. I should say, at this stage, that, whether by good intent or good luck, some of the best slang is mellifluous and image provoking. A bag of fruit has lumps and protrusions like the human body. Lumps and protrusions in the human body – doesn't that sound sexy?

Bar of soap, not know from: The incongruous expression 'not know her/him from a bar of soap' appeals because of that very incongruity.

Batty: crazy.

Belly-up: kaput, bankrupt or dead. The image I have is of a dead fish floating.

Bikies: Australian for bikers

Billy-o: the max, completely. Steele says, at one stage, his confidence is shot to billy-o.

Blower: phone. I have yet to find a convincing explanation of the origin of the word blower.

Blue: an argument. Capitalised it is the perverse nickname for a person, usually a man, with red hair.

Bodgie: false, dishonest. Male and female bikies of the 1950s were called bodgies and widgies so there is probably a connection there. The word also rhymes with dodgy.

Bookie: a bookmaker who takes bets and records them on a large ledger (his book).

Brought down to earth: disabused of notions of privilege.

Brown bread: dead (rhyming slang).

Brumby: wild horse, bronco.

Bugs Bunny: money (rhyming slang**).**

Bum a lift: Ask to ride in someone else's car.

Bush, the: rural Australia most of which is not over-endowed with the vegetation that gives it its nickname.

Butcher's hook: look (rhyming slang**).**

Cheap thrills: hallucinogenic mushrooms.

Chief Steward: the head of the horse-racing 'police'.

Come good: to fulfil a promise.

Crim: criminal.

Cut each other's throats: What two jockeys metaphorically do when they allow their horses to engage in a speed battle which ruins both their chances.

Dead cert: a curious expression for predicting a certainty, a horse which will win for sure. As it is a prediction, a dead cert sometimes comes last.

Deadset: utterly, completely.

Dee: detective. As detectives usually travel in pairs, it is most commonly used in the plural. The derivation of the slang word is obvious enough.

Dirty (filthy) on someone: mad at or annoyed with someone, hence a dirty look. Filthy became a positive by 1990 among the grunge and hardcore sets.

Dish-licker: a racing greyhound, for obvious reasons.

Dob someone in: Report someone to authority. See 'give someone up'.

Dog and bone: phone (rhyming slang**).**

Dole: unemployment benefits, social-security payments. English reggae band UB 40 derived their band name from an unemployment benefit form.

Dough: money.

Dud someone: cheat.

Duffer: a racehorse incompetent in some circumstances, hence a wet-track duffer, a track-work duffer. A duffer is also a cattle rustler.

Fair enough: This expression, often a question, and 'can't be any fairer than that' imply that utter fairness is unobtainable.

Farfetched: implausible.

Filthy: extremely, as in filthy rich. See 'dirty' for other meaning.

Fleeced: relieved of money. The story goes Australia rode to prosperity on a sheep's back but the metaphor fleeced seems to look at it from the sheep's POV.

Flicks: movies, perhaps named after the flickering at the beginning and end of motion picture reels which made the magic happen in the old days.

Fluke: be lucky in achieving a goal (verb and noun). That shot was a fluke. She fluked it.

Form guide: a newspaper lift-out, detailing the form of racehorses competing at a meeting which is held not in a boardroom but on a track where the equines race, usually on turf in Australia.

Gallopers: thoroughbred racehorses.

Geezer: English bloke.

Give it a swerve: Decide not to go somewhere.

Give someone up: Report someone to authority or dob them in.

Glitterati: the party crowd.

Godbotherer: Someone who is ostentatiously religious as opposed to a person who keeps their faith to themselves.

Good oil: reliable information not in general circulation, hence a racehorse tip.

Grasshoppers: Rhyming slang for coppers. I somewhat recently heard a young man refer to police as grassies. I would bet the house the modern word derives from grasshoppers and I wonder if contemporary users are aware of that.

Grub: despicable person, criminal (police slang).

Hammer: heroin, an international rather than Australian slang word. As discussed in the novel, Grant McLennan swore the song *Hammer the Hammer* was not about heroin. Not many among the in-crowd believed him.

Hang on: that doesn't sound right (interjection).

Hardly say boo: To be quiet in a social situation or to ignore someone.

Have a go: gamble heavily.

Have a lash: gamble heavily.

Heavies: enforcers employed by criminals. Heavies, invariably used in the plural, are not nice.

Horny, horniness: sexually aroused.

Hot under the collar: Furious. The expression reminds me of a cartoon character steaming.

How you doing? Hullo.

Hustle: con.

Info: information.

In the know: The professional gamblers who get the 'good oil' are in the know.

Jack of: tired of.

Kettle of fish, different: The phrase different kettle of fish originated in Britain. As it means 'a different matter', Australians are breaking tradition to use a longer expression because it is amusing or attention-getting. You will notice some other examples such as 'not half bad' for good.

Knock off the price: Place a bet before someone else and take the good price which the bookmaker then winds down.

Kybosh on, put the: veto.

Live on Easy Street: Win enough money to never have to work again.

Long shot: a racehorse not expected to win, also called an outsider. A long shot is also a gamble unlikely to result in a collect.

Long walk off a short pier: suicide, not necessarily by drowning oneself.

Mark: victim of a con game.

Med cert: medical certificate.

Mend one's ways: to give up bad behavior.

Mental: hostile.

Micks: Catholics, probably because Michael is a common Irish Catholic name.

Mobile (phone): cell (phone).

Mug: a gullible person waiting to be swindled.

Mug lair: A person who fancies themselves but comes across as a creep.

Mug's game: an activity which is meant to be rewarding but is not.

Mushies: hallucinogenic mushrooms.

Muso: a rock performer, probably because musician sounds too staid.

Nag: a racehorse, the term for an unattractive horse goes way back to Middle English.

Neddy: a racehorse.

Nick: prison.

Nose: smallest winning margin in horse-racing. Other bodily margins are half-head, head and neck.

Not half bad: good.

Odds on: A bet where you win less than your stake so you do not even double your money.

Old dogs for a hard road: in some instances, age has an advantage over youth. The metaphor could refer to old dogs having callouses protecting their sensitive paws.

One iota: one little bit.

Packet: a lot of money.

Pack it in: stop working as in a car or a heart.

Pants man: womaniser.

Pea, the: the best person for a task.

Photo finish: when a horse-racing judge cannot decide which horse has won, he looks at a photo or nowadays a video of the result.

Pissed off: very upset.

Pisstake: Making fun of someone.

Plebs: poor people.

Plunge: Putting a lot of money on a horse.

Poke around: look over.

Pony: a racehorse, could be an example of perversion in Australian slang as most thoroughbreds are big and muscular.

Present: evidence such as drugs or a firearm planted by police.

Pretty: relatively. Pretty as an adverb did not originate in Australia but Aussies like to use it pretty often. Pretty seems always to carry a vestige of the sardonic. In Chandler's *The Big Sleep*, Marlowe nails its use like an Aussie when describing his manners. 'They're pretty bad. I grieve over them during the long winter nights.'

Punting: betting, gambling; usually on race horses; hence have a punt and on the punt. Interestingly, a punter is also an alternative-music fan, especially one willing to try a new band or musician.

Quid: Dollars have been the currency in Australia since 1966 but the slang for the superseded pound, quid, is still used. 'I wouldn't be dead for quids' is popular though it makes little sense. Slang is passed down the generations and, as such, outmoded words survive.

Randy, randiness: sexually aroused.

Ratbag: a person who does or says stupid things.

Rock 'n roll: the dole (rhyming slang**)**.

Roller: Rolls-Royce car.

Roughie: an unfancied racehorse which is at big odds.

Rumour mill: grapevine, as in I heard it on the grapevine.

Scarper: go. This word is in the half-way house where slang lives awaiting admittance into conventional usage. While it means to 'go' there is a hint of impropriety such as not paying the rent or in the novel when Bill Smith's wife leaves him. A suggested origin of the word (probably incorrect) is that it comes from the Cockney rhyming slang of Scapa Flow (go). Scapa Flow is a large natural harbour off Scotland.

Sheila: woman.

Shout: pay for someone else.

Shrooms: hallucinogenic mushrooms.

Slow coach: Someone who cannot keep up with a fast lifestyle.

Smack: heroin.

Smackies heroin addicts.

Smoko: a break from work.

Song and dance: hullabaloo.

Sook: a weak-willed person.

Sorta: sort of, again showing the Aussie penchant for truncation. Australians were lingual minimalists before the word was invented.

Spiel: a speech, often misleading

Spoof: (rhymes with woof) semen.

Spoof himself: ejaculate.

Spruik: to speak, especially like a carnival barker.

Stand on your dig(s) to be inflexible on a point of negotiation.

Sticks, the: areas away from the capital city. The sticks are not usually a synonym for the (rural) bush as the phrase is invariably used ironically. People in a provincial town or even an outer suburb of a city are likely to refer to themselves as being in the sticks. The cute rhyme, flicks in the sticks, refers to the practice of someone bringing a projector and film reels to a place without a cinema or drive-in. A 1977 Australian film was called *The Picture Show Man*. More than half the film's $600,000 budget was met by the Australian government ($250,000) and the New South Wales state government ($120,000.) Those were the good old days when Australia was exercising its cultural cringe by trying to shake it off.

Stiff: unlucky.

Stiffed: cheated.

Stiffs: Steele describes stiffs as 'clock-watching, bored and boring sods who do what they do because that's what they did yesterday'.

Sweet: good.

Swiftie: a trick or con.

Thesp: thespian, actor.

Tin-pot: insignificant.

Toff: a snob

Top yourself: Commit suicide.

Tout, touting: tipping racehorses

Turn-up for the books: surprise result in a horse race. The books refers to bookmakers.

Twig: to understand.

Urgers: People at the racetrack who try to convince you to back a certain horse. Some urgers do it hoping to get a financial reward if you win. Others are actually trying to get a better price for a different horse than the one they are tipping you.

Ute, utility: the Australian version of the pickup truck. It sometimes goes by the name of coupe utility, though 99.9 percent of Australians refer to it as a ute. Steele's ute is a Holden EH, made by the General Motors' Australian division between 1963 and 1965. The EH is a true work of art (and science).

Welcher: Someone who reneges on a bet or a promise.

Wharfie: waterside worker, longshoreman. Before it was sold in the 1990s, the Brisbane Wharfies' Club attracted a diverse clientele including gamblers, trainers, jockeys, firefighters and other public servants as well as wharfies and their relatives and friends.

Winning post: the finish line of a horse race. In some ways, winning post is an odd expression as most horses and gamblers lose when that point is reached.

Worrywart: This word for a person is self-explanatory.

Worse for wear: drunk.

Yobbo: uncultured uncouth (usually) man.

You got me? Australian for Capisce?

Acknowledgements

THE Go-Betweens' concert at Queensland University in 1986 happened in the first half of the year, not in November. I moved it to place most dramatic events in summer. November in Brisbane is summer, despite the seasonal theory it is spring.

NO gambling boat The African Queen conducted business on the Tweed River in 1991.

AN SP bookie did work from the back of a butcher's shop, a decade earlier, and in Brisbane not Tweed Heads.

THANKS for permission to include Go-Betweens' lyrics:
From *Streets of Your Town*, and
From *Twin Layers of Lightning,* both written by Robert Forster and Grant McLennan, publisher Complete Music Ltd.

THANKS to my editor Eoin O'Brien. I backed a winner with Eoin, who is not only an astute and clever wordsmith, but also a multi-instrumentalist and a member of a rock band.

THANKS to photographer Russell Brown for his cover photo on first and second editions.

THANKS to Ian Curr for typesetting and layout help.

THANKS to designer Dhrupod for working with me to create the third-edition covers. We shared the ideas. The artistry and science belong to Dhrupod.

Lightning Source UK Ltd.
Milton Keynes UK
UKOW01f2332130717
305285UK00001B/174/P